Outstanding praise for Nancy Bush and her Jane Kelly mysteries!

ULTRAVIOLET

"Fun to read"
—*Pasadena Star News*

ELECTRIC BLUE

"With her clever ability to handle the zaniest of life's circumstances, Jane won't disappoint readers."
—*Publishers Weekly*

"Bush has a winner with this wacky, sexy second book featuring an insanely dysfunctional family and a zany wannabe P.I. with a gorgeous and intelligent partner."
—*Library Journal*

CANDY APPLE RED

"Funny, sex scenes, good drinks, and a likable dog lift Bush's first Jane Kelly mystery."
—*Publishers Weekly*

"Jane Kelly is a new and worthy addition to the private investigator scene. Unique and extremely likable, she has a quick wit."
—*Romantic Times*

"As long as Bush sticks to writing compelling mysteries, she'll have a franchise that could soon rise to the level of Sara Paretsky's great V.I. Warshawski books."
—*Chicago Sun Times*

"A fun, frantic, sexy murder mystery . . . I was hooked from the first page. *Candy Apple Red* is an intriguing mystery that kept me guessing all night!"
—Lisa Jackson, *New York Times* bestselling author

Books by Nancy Bush

CANDY APPLE RED

ELECTRIC BLUE

ULTRAVIOLET

Published by Kensington Publishing Corporation

ULTRA
VIOLET

NANCY BUSH

Kensington Publishing Corp.
http://www.kensingtonbooks.com

KENSINGTON BOOKS are published by

Kensington Publishing Corp.
850 Third Avenue
New York, NY 10022

All Kensington Titles, Imprints, and Distributed Lines are available at special quantity discounts for bulk purchases for sales promotions, premiums, fund-raising, and educational or institutional use. Special book excerpts or customized printings can also be created to fit specific needs. For details, write or phone the office of the Kensington special sales manager: Kensington Publishing Corp., 850 Third Avenue, New York, NY 10022, attn: Special Sales Department, Phone: 1-800-221-2647.

Kensington and the K logo Reg. U.S. Pat. & TM Off.

ISBN-13: 978-0-7582-0910-8
ISBN-10: 0-7582-0910-X

First hardcover printing: October 2007
First mass market printing: September 2008

10 9 8 7 6 5 4 3 2 1

Printed in the United States of America

CHAPTER ONE

I had mere seconds to get out of the bedroom. There was no bolt for the door and escape back the way I'd entered. I stood frozen, my hands useless appendages in front of me, my frantic heartbeats a roaring surf in my ears.

Three strong strides and I was at the sliding glass door that led to the bedroom balcony. The door opened soundlessly to an itsy-bitsy, terra-cotta-tiled area wrapped by a wrought-iron rail. I looked down two floors. For a dizzying moment I considered jumping, but the patio below was cold, unforgiving stone.

I whirled back to stare across the room. Twelve feet of carpet led toward the bedroom door, the only other exit. My pursuer was not far behind. From my peripheral vision I caught sight of the maple tree. I glanced over. Too far from the balcony, but just outside the bathroom window.

I could hear his approaching footsteps from the exterior hall. Quickly, I scurried into the bathroom and threw open the window. One branch was close enough to reach. For an instant I considered climbing down as I was: gowned, bejeweled, wearing the most expensive sandals I ever planned to purchase.

Kicking off the shoes, I threw them out the window. I ripped the zipper of the dress downward, yanked the slinky lavender dress over my head, sent it flying after the sandals. As I pulled myself through the window, cursing the space that was scarcely large enough for me to wriggle my shoulders through, I heard the door open. A mewling sound entered my throat but I held it back. I reached for the branch, missed, reached again, arms shaking, fingers splayed.

I heard his breathing.

My fingers connected and I hauled myself out with adrenaline-laced strength. I swung my legs upward to catch the limb with my ankles and hung like a lemur. Then I shimmied toward the tree trunk and carefully eased myself down the bole. I lost swatches of skin. My pulse hammered in my ears. My face was wet with tears.

When my toe hit the ground I drew a breath and glanced upward. He was on the balcony looking down at me. In that strange, heightened moment between quarry and prey, I was very, very glad I stood where I was.

"Ms. Kellogg?"

The voice came from somewhere to my right, near the front of the house. I stooped to pick up the gown Violet Purcell had given me, shivering, glad Violet had talked me into the padded lacy bra, equally glad I'd held out for bikini underwear rather than a thong.

The newcomer was my other admirer, Martin.

I smiled at him as he approached, hoping my lips didn't quiver. I could feel the gaze from the man on the balcony boring into the back of my head. I shook out the gown. Stepping into it, I said with forced nonchalance, "Would you mind helping me zip up?"

I thanked the Fates Martin liked me enough to obey without question.

Earlier

There's a weirdo in every neighborhood.

The old lady with forty-nine cats. The man who's formed art pieces out of painted car parts and littered them across his front yard. The couple who've carved mysterious symbols in the bark of a tree and hung a plaque on the limbs declaring themselves lovers of evergreens, while fir needles blanket their dilapidated roof and hang in a shroud of spiderwebs from the sagging eaves.

I fear that Dwayne Durbin is becoming the latest neighborhood weirdo.

Ever since the accident that broke his leg and temporarily incapacitated him, he's taken to spying on the properties across Lakewood Bay, his leg wrapped in a cast from ankle to thigh, his eyes glued to a pair of binoculars. A strange chortling sound issues from his throat. He can tell you more about the Pilarmos' dog and the Wilsons' new alarm system than you should ever want to know.

I've sort of avoided him these last few weeks. He's drawn me into watching the sexcapades of a nameless couple whose energetic and inventive forms of copulation both impress and shock me, which is saying a lot. Dwayne has named all the houses/families he spies on; these two he calls Tab A and Slot B. Their stamina and vitality while inserting said Tab A into Slot B makes me wonder about my own tepid sex life. Lately, a few random kisses are all I can measure in the plus column.

Which is the main reason I've been avoiding Dwayne: my newly refined awareness of him. Yes, he's an attractive member of the male gender, but so what? Dwayne is still my boss/business partner and that is *it*. Thinking about him in any romantic context is just plain trouble.

I reminded myself of this as I parked my Volvo wagon next to his truck, which sat on the concrete pad outside his cabana. I'd told him I would bring lunch and so I had. The white bag containing a stack of plastic containers lay on the passenger seat.

Before I climbed out of the car I took a deep breath. I'd been using the excuse that, as temporary lead investigator for Dwayne Durbin Investigations (of which only Dwayne and I count as company employees), I was too busy digging into the death of one Roland Hatchmere, the third and most beloved ex-husband of our client, Violet Purcell, to hang around much. I'd gone so far as to call from my cell phone near heavy freeway interchanges and scream over the roar of the traffic that I would report in when I was closer to Lake Chinook, the town in which we both reside. It's a testament to Dwayne's interest in his friends across the bay that he hasn't been calling me on my bullshit. He knows me too well to seriously believe me. Honestly, I don't think he notices that I'm having such a hard time with the current form of our relationship, which should piss me off but worries me more than anything else.

When Dwayne asked me to bring him a burger from Standish's I finally broke down and agreed. What can I say? I want to see him. Still, I couldn't make myself be Little Miss Fetch-all so, in a moment of pure orneriness, I drove to a nearby deli neither of us had tried before and bought an array of items in little clear boxes that looked great but might be more healthy than either of us can stand. Why did I do this? I don't want to even speculate.

As I let myself inside his cabana I put my feelings for Dwayne aside as best I could and instead scolded myself for not being further along on the Violet Purcell matter. The problem for me is Violet herself. Before Dwayne's accident, she'd made a strong play for him and they looked to be heading into that "you woman, me man" thing with the speed of a locomotive.

I hadn't liked it one bit. And so I was having trouble treating Violet as a paying client who needed rescuing. To be fair,

Violet is currently so distracted by her own problems that she appears to have no interest in Dwayne whatsoever. I'm not going to be fooled, however, because these things have a habit of resurfacing just when you're sure it's safe to go back in the water.

Not that Dwayne's for me. I'm just saying . . .

I was juggling my laptop in its smart, gray wool case, a cup of black coffee from the Coffee Nook, the white bag containing our lunch and a copy of the *Lake Chinook Review,* and I dropped everything in a heap on Dwayne's kitchen counter. Dwayne, as ever, was on his back dock. He heard me arrive and from where he was stretched out on his lounge, he half turned his head in greeting. I could see his profile in front of the green waters of Lakewood Bay. It arrested me for a moment, as the sky had darkened in that eerie way that foretells of a thunderstorm, something that rarely happens in Oregon. I looked through the window at that gray-green backdrop just as a shot of lightning sizzled across it, leaving a bright afterimage against my retina. Dwayne picked up his binoculars and scanned the heavens. It was nearly November and unseasonably warm. As I off-loaded my items, thunder rumbled and then a horrendous blast of rain poured down. Loud rain. I looked up sharply. Hail, actually.

I squeezed through the twelve-inch opening that leads to Dwayne's dock—which is all the sliding glass door allows as Dwayne's desk is shoved up against it—and rushed outside. Dwayne was struggling up from his chair. I grabbed his arm and together we managed to knock over his small side table as we bumbled around, then squeezed back through the door to safety. In those few seconds we both got soaked to the skin. After that we stood just inside and stared at the blackening sky and silvery, bouncing hail.

I felt the warmth of Dwayne's skin through the damp. I could smell him. Something faintly citrusy today that spoke of last summer. I've never been one of those women who wants to "drink in a man" but I felt that desire now so strongly I could scarcely think. It took serious willpower to move away from him.

Abruptly the hail stopped.

"Cool," Dwayne said thoughtfully, brushing at his shoulders. Bright drops of water melted into the light blue denim before my eyes.

I said, "Lunch is on the counter."

"Standish's?"

"This is from that new gourmet catering shop on B Street."

Hope died in his face. "Tell me there's nothing with raisins."

"There's nothing with raisins."

Beets, though. I knew better than to mention them as I opened the white bags and pulled out clear, plastic containers of dishes that had made my mouth water as I stood in front of the counter. Dwayne eyed the Szechuan noodles suspiciously and actually sniffed the container of chicken, arugula, corn and rice. The purple red beets swimming in their own juice he studiously avoided. I didn't blame him. I'd thrown them in mainly for the shock value. I don't mind a beet, but their tendency to dye clothing with one ill-placed drop kind of puts me off.

"I suffered a moment of worry about my health."

Dwayne grunted as he swept some plates and silverware from his drawers. He moved with surprising grace on his crutches, dishing up heaping helpings onto two plates. He stuck a serving spoon in the beets but didn't partake. I felt duty-bound to have some and left a spray of magenta juice in a semicircle on Dwayne's counter. I found a paper towel and swiped it up. I didn't tell him about the drops that landed on his dish towel. I was pretty sure no amount of washing was going to get those suckers out. He gestured at me to ask if I wanted something to drink, but I lifted my Coffee Nook cup in response.

I sank onto his couch, which doubles as my workstation,

and Dwayne perched on one of his kitchen stools. He's trans-
formed his jeans to accommodate his cast, in effect making
one pant leg only about twelve inches long. His cast takes
over from there and it has various writings on it. I wondered
about the sweet little red heart with initials.

"Anything new?" he asked, scooping up the Szechuan
noodles and eyeing me.

"Roland Hatchmere's family doesn't think much of Violet. They'd like to see her go down for this."

"She didn't kill him."

"So you say. And so says Violet. But somebody hit him
with the tray she gave as a wedding gift." I forked in some
rice and pea mixture that had a hint of saffron.

Dwayne swept an arm toward my laptop case. "You got a
report for me?"

"There's nothing to report."

"Give me a list of the players. Hatchmere's family members, the wedding guests, people from work. There's a reason
somebody killed him."

I fought back a natural obstinance, finished my salads,
then switched on my laptop. Dwayne loves hard copy. He's
always yammering about how I should spend more time log-
ging data and generating pages and pages of information to
impress the client, and he likes to look at information on
paper himself. It helps him think. Unfortunately I wasn't
kidding: I had nothing to report. Since Violet had announced
to me and Dwayne that she was suspected in Roland Hatchmere's death, I'd barely learned anything of note. Certainly
nothing worth writing up and printing off.

Most of what I had pertaining to this case was from
Dwayne's own hard copy on the Wedding Bandits, a group
of robbers who'd been systematically ripping off the families
of brides and grooms, stealing both personal belongings and
wedding gifts while the ceremonies were taking place.
Dwayne had meticulously chronicled the bandits' activities,

from their basic modus operandi to the homes they'd targeted. It appeared the Wedding Bandits hit Roland Hatchmere's home the day of his daughter's wedding, but whether that was before, during, or after his death was undetermined. At least for Dwayne and me. Dwayne had been sidelined by his accident and his client, a onetime father-of-a-bride Wedding Bandit victim, had let the police take over rather than have the case turned over to me. Which was just fine. I was glad I didn't have a second client breathing down my neck. Violet Purcell was enough.

Dwayne picked cautiously through the salad with his fork. Apparently he didn't believe we were raisin-free. "You got that e-mail I sent you about Hatchmere's business partner?"

"I put in a call to Dr. Wu. He's out of the country for a few weeks, working with a medical relief team."

"Who's in charge of the clinics while he's gone?"

"No one person, apparently. They're owned by a consortium," I reminded him, though Dwayne was the one who'd secured that information in the first place. "I've been waiting for Wu to return."

Dr. Daniel Wu was the head plastic surgeon of a group of four clinics previously owned by Roland Hatchmere, who had once been a very well known plastic surgeon himself until his personal cocaine use got in the way. With his license revoked Roland turned his talents to business, capitalizing on his still valuable reputation and garnering patients to his clinics in droves. Dr. Wu had become his business partner, though Roland held on to the lion's share of the business until it was sold earlier this year to the consortium.

"Wu's the one to talk to," Dwayne agreed.

"It just means I'm stalled," I said.

"Things'll break."

Like that advice was going to help me. I wanted to shout, "When? How? Would you stop looking through those damn binoculars?" Instead I just finished my meal. Dwayne was nice enough to thank me and even pay for the food. I tried to demur, but he smiled faintly and ignored me, so I pocketed the bills. I'm pretty sure I should be embarrassed by my cheapness, but I can't stop considering it an attribute. Thriftiness is a good thing, right?

I watched him pick up the *Review* and start reading.

Feeling frustrated, I complained, "Wu's not the only issue. I'm having trouble getting the Hatchmere clan to talk to me. I've left messages. I even dropped by Roland's house once, but I got the door slammed in my face."

"Who slammed it on you?"

"The daughter. Gigi Hatchmere. Or, wait . . . Popparockskill . . ."

"It's still Hatchmere. Ceremony never came off when Roland didn't show." He shook the paper and opened to another page as he headed back outside.

"Have you got any bright ideas on what I should do next?" I called, but Dwayne was outside and either he couldn't hear me or he didn't care.

Annoyed, I pulled up my file on Violet and wirelessly sent its meager contents to the printer as I slid another look Dwayne's way.

He'd put down the paper and was standing in the strange darkness created by the storm, staring up at the sky. I followed his gaze and saw a crack between clouds where sunlight spilled through, looking like a sheer, glowing curtain of white and yellow, the kind of odd illumination that, as Dwayne moved in front of it, surrounded him with a brilliant aura.

"Saint Dwayne," I muttered.

"What?" he hollered.

Oh yeah, sure. Now he hears me? "Nothing."

I headed to the printer, which is currently set up in Dwayne's spare bedroom, and looked at the pages. It was disheartening how little progress I'd made. Nobody, but nobody, wanted to talk to anyone associated with Violet. I'd placed a few calls and gotten a few polite no's and a few more "you've got to be kiddings." One guy, some Hatchmere family friend known as Big Jim, just laughed like a hyena and hung up on me.

Gathering up the two pages of potential interviewees, I sensed a nub of anxiety tightening in the pit of my stomach. For all his inattention, Dwayne wasn't going to wait forever. He would expect some hard answers. But Violet was anathema. And no one wanted to talk to a friend of Violet's—*friend* being a stretch of the truth of our relationship—but I suspected Dwayne wasn't going to see it that way.

"Come on out here, Jane," Dwayne called, apparently sensing I'd returned to the living room as his eyes were once again glued to his binoculars.

He was back on the lounge, though I suspected there might be some moisture soaking into the seat of his jeans. The outdoor furniture and dock were still wet from the hail blast.

Squeezing back outside, I felt a frigid huff of wind whip beneath my black suede vest, press my shirt to my skin and generally bring me to goose bumps. Dwayne's cowboy hat, never far from his side, was now scrunched on his head. His long, light blue denim-clad left leg, and casted right one, stretched toward the small, slatted-wood table we'd knocked over on our scramble to get back inside. I righted the table and put it beside his chair. Apart from his shirt, there was no protection against the elements, but it didn't look like he cared much.

My eyes followed the line of his legs and I felt a twist of sexual interest. I gritted my teeth. And him being a semi-invalid. What did that say about *me*?

"Take a look here," he said, handing me the binoculars. "Straight over there is Rebel Yell. . . ." He pointed at a white two-story house across the bay and a little to our left. I looked through the lenses. "Parents, two teenage girls, lots of drama."

"You've named another one?"

"Named 'em all. It's next to Tab A and Slot B, just to the west side."

I gazed at Tab A and Slot B, where all fall the man and woman had been cavorting into every sexual position known to humankind, and tried to keep my mind off Dwayne. He and I had done a bit of that mating dance not so long ago, nothing too serious, and then Violet had entered our world. Sometimes, late at night, when my mind whirls on a repetitive track, I remember those moments with uncomfortable inner jolts that seem to hit my heart and parts down south as well. "We've watched them before," I said neutrally.

"Mm," he agreed. "Tab A'll be home in a couple hours. Lately they've been turning on their outdoor fire pit and then heading just inside the slider door and getting to work. Love-making by the fire. Guess it's what you do when you don't have an indoor fireplace."

"Can't wait for that."

"Next to Rebel Yell is Plastic Pet Cemetery, where old lawn ornaments go to die."

"The Pilarmos. With the dog."

Dwayne nodded. "Thing howls and looks like a wolf."

I centered my binoculars on the Pilarmos' tired, dark blue bungalow. Kinda looked like my cottage, only worse, if that was possible. Probably worth a small fortune. I could make out gnomes and plastic pink flamingos and faux cement birdbaths decorating a large portion of the backyard. A grayish wolf-dog cruised around the corner and disappeared from view.

"Then there's Do Not Enter."

I moved my glasses to aim toward a shell of a house where the beams and a skin of plywood constituted the walls. The roof was covered with plywood, and half the composition shingles had been nailed on. "Why is it Do Not Enter?"

"It's where the high school kids party. They try to keep their flashlights dimmed, but every Friday night, some Saturdays, there's something going on. And that last house before the road curves toward North Shore is Social Security. He's deaf and she's bedridden and neither of 'em is too worried about Do Not Enter."

Hearing he'd named more houses worried me anew. I had to remind myself that this, too, would pass. It was a harmless pursuit on Dwayne's part. Something to entertain him while he recovered. If it smacked a little too much of Jimmy Stewart's character in *Rear Window*, well, it wasn't like he was going to ask me to solve a murder over there.

I handed him back the binoculars, murmured something about getting back to my job, then squeezed inside the cabana and headed to my laptop. My job—the job I was getting paid for—was to prove Violet Purcell's innocence. Besides the fact that no one will talk to me, the bigger problem is I kinda think Violet might be guilty. She's sensed this and has yelled, "Things aren't always what they seem, Jane!" more times than I like to recall. And actually, I think that's a crock anyway. Most of the time things are *exactly* what they seem. We just can't accept them as they are. We want to make them better, or different, or meaningful.

But . . . I must remember, innocent until proven guilty. It's difficult with Violet. She's late forties, appears and acts over a decade younger, possesses more good looks than good sense, and has a family who took the "health" out of "mental health" in a big way. I would like to forget that she made a play for Dwayne, but I can't. It's only been a few weeks since I met Violet—basically a little over a month— but it feels like the proverbial eternity. First I thought she was a breath of fresh air. Then I decided she was a femme fatale. Now I'm thinking she might be a murderer.

I mean, couldn't she have killed ex-husband number three? Couldn't she? Why does Dwayne find that so impossible?

I shook my head and stared up at the fir beams that line Dwayne's cabana's ceiling and thought back. Upon first meeting I'd been intrigued with Violet's tell-it-like-it-is, take-no-prisoners attitude. But she was a Purcell and I had learned, by then, that they were a secretive, squirrelly bunch, so I wasn't sure what to think of her. It had been refreshing to be faced with a family member who initially exhibited none of their odd family traits. Key word here being *initially*. Violet's definitely got her own issues.

Luckily, since Dwayne's accident, things seem to have cooled off a bit between him and Violet, but that doesn't mean it's over. And okay, they haven't progressed to much more than friends, but I know she hauled off and kissed him once. I got to witness that. Dwayne is my mentor, boss, partner and friend. I cannot have him mean anything more to me and stay sane. I know this, but I have to keep reminding myself anyway because there's a part of me that just can't quite leave the whole possible romance thing alone. I would like to be disgusted with myself for being so nauseatingly hopeless. I mean, why *can't* I just get over it? It's interfering with my job and my life and I don't even think I really like Dwayne.

That memory of Violet pulling him into a kiss crossed the screen of my mind again and I had to clench my teeth.

I waited for the moment to pass.

"Are you growling?"

I jumped. Dwayne's voice was loud. Glancing back, I saw he'd stuck his head inside the slider door.

"Yes."

"Why?"

"I like to."

We looked at each other. I would rather suck on dirty socks than admit my feelings for Dwayne.

He let it go. "Violet's on her way over, right?"

"Yep. She wants us to talk to the police. Find out if they're going to indict her."

"Larrabee would have already if he could prove she was guilty," Dwayne said.

Detective Vince Larrabee was a homicide detective with the Portland police and a longtime acquaintance, sometime friend, of Dwayne's. I'd heard his name once or twice before Violet's case, but now it was part of our daily dialogue, though I had yet to meet the man.

"Violet wants that information directly from the big dog. I'm a mere lackey."

Dwayne snorted and returned to the dock. He sank into the hail- and rain-soaked chair again without comment.

It had been a lot sunnier the day Violet walked out on Dwayne's dock and announced that she might have killed her ex-husband. I'd been so giddily happy that she and Dwayne seemed kaput that I'd let myself be talked into helping her.

She'd showed up in true Violet fashion: looking beautiful, and . . . well, lusty. Her hair is blond and shoulder-length, her eyes that crazy electric blue color most of the Purcells seem to share. My own hair is a little longer than shoulder length, light brown, straight and wouldn't let itself be styled if I bought a truckload of Vidal Sassoon products. I don't possess Violet's curves, but my eyes are hazel and sane-looking. I'm thirty and Dwayne's about thirty-five. I figure that evens the score.

But that day Violet hadn't been thinking about Dwayne, not in any romantic capacity. She'd needed help.

She plopped down in one of the dock chairs and announced numbly, "My ex-husband's dead." I'd questioned which ex-husband, since she had a few, and learned it was Roland

Hatchmere, ex number three, the only one who lived in the Portland area.

"He was killed yesterday," she went on. "On his daughter's wedding day. Roland was still at the house, and these robbers showed up thinking he was gone, I guess, and he wasn't, and they killed him."

"Wedding robbers?" I asked, looking at Dwayne, since he'd already been investigating the Wedding Bandits.

"What happened?" Dwayne asked her.

"I don't know! The police came to see me today," Violet said, her eyes huge. "God, I don't believe this. They seem to think *I* did it." We asked her why that was and after hemming and hawing, she finally admitted, "Because he was killed with a heavy metal platter that has my fingerprints on it."

"Did you kill him?" Dwayne asked her.

"I don't think so," she responded in a small voice.

And that's when Dwayne checked out completely, picked up his binoculars and returned to his perusal of his buddies across the bay. If I'd known then he was going to make a serious job out of it, I might have been more concerned, but instead after he told Violet I was the lead investigator, I started thinking about how much money I could make and I agreed to take the case.

Since then my job had been mostly about keeping Violet calm and focused. She lived in a certain amount of fear the authorities were going to swoop down and haul her criminal ass to justice. I soothed with words about needing real evidence and motive and whatever else I could draw from the criminology classes I'd taken and my own vast repertoire of bullshit that I like to dress up as fact.

I'd managed to piece together the events of the wedding day from Violet's disjointed recitation. Apparently Roland's daughter Gigi had been slated to marry Emmett Popparockskill at the Cahill Winery in Dundee, Oregon, which is about an hour's drive from Roland's house in Portland's West Hills District.

The wedding was scheduled to be outdoors with the requisite flowers, arches, ring bearer and flower girl—two additions I always cheer for since they pretty much rip focus away from the bride by screwing up somehow. I swear to God they are the best part of any wedding, beyond the champagne, alcohol and food.

Violet was not invited to the ceremony as she and Gigi were not on the best of terms, but she'd stopped by Roland's house to drop off a gift for the bride and groom—the metal platter. While there, she and Roland got into some kind of fight, which culminated with Violet whacking him alongside the head with the platter and leaving in a huff.

Roland never showed for pictures and a search went out. He was found dead on the solarium floor from a blow to the head. Murder weapon, the tray.

Violet insists she didn't kill him. "He was perfectly fine when I left him! He was moving. Breathing. Swearing at me! I didn't kill him. Those robbers must have. After I left, they came in and murdered him. I didn't kill him!"

I've gotta say, she's quite convincing. I would probably believe her, but . . . well, Roland Hatchmere died from head trauma. And Violet hit him in the head with the tray. And the police only found one set of fingerprints on the tray: Violet's.

Now I heard the loud purr of a sports car and figured the woman in question had arrived. She gave a perfunctory knock on Dwayne's door, then pushed in, calling loudly, "I'm letting myself in!"

"Dwayne's on the dock," I greeted her.

She burst inside loaded with packages from several major department stores. A cloud of perfume wafted into the room, trailing in her wake. Catching my look, she held the bags higher. "I just couldn't stop. Am I spending all my funds to fill a need? I'd bet on it, hon. I have too much money and not enough friends. Look, I bought you something."

I tried hard not to react as Violet dug inside one of the bags. Scary, scary thought. I don't want to owe Violet *any-thing*. Working for her is one thing, but friendship. Clothes buying . . . ?

To my consternation she pulled out a dress. "Purple," I said faintly. I didn't want to be ungrateful but the thought of Violet buying me clothes . . . I just know it's not going to work somehow.

"It's my signature color," she said unnecessarily. "It's more amethyst, don't you think? It's like voile, really sheer in that sort of netty way? I just love it. I could just see you in it. Here, try it on." She held it out to me.

I instantly turned back to my screen. "In a minute, I need to finish this."

"Oh, come on, Jane."

I finally really looked at Violet. I'd been spending so much time on the dress and dealing with my internal horror that I hadn't given much thought to Violet herself. Now I saw clearly that this was important to her. Even worse. There was no polite way out.

"Sure," I said, taking the proffered garment and heading toward Dwayne's bathroom.

I stripped off my clothes and pulled it over my head. The dress, actually a gown, hung to my ankles and hugged like a second skin. I'd been wearing jeans and boots and had left dark socks on. Taking them off, I gave myself a studied look, turning to capture a view of the side and back.

I looked . . . well . . . good.

I'm not a clothes shopper. It's just so darn much trouble. I get irritated at salespeople and nothing ever seems to work the way I think it should. How could Violet pick out some-thing like this just by deciding it would be right?

"Okay, I like it," I admitted after I changed back into my clothes and I returned to the living room. "How much do I owe you?"

Violet's gaze was out the sliding door to the back of Dwayne's cowboy hat. Her face was wistful. "It's a gift," she said distractedly.

"No," I argued without much strength. I'd been afraid to look at the price tag.

"Just wear it sometime when we're out together," she said, turning back to me and smiling.

Here's the thing—I think she really likes me. Not in a weird way, just as a friend. Which makes me feel like a heel because I don't want to like her.

She didn't wait for more arguments but headed outside. I glanced toward the sky, but the clouds were holding back further precipitation. As she moved into Dwayne's line of vision, she smiled at him even more warmly than she'd smiled at me.

My cell phone buzzed.

"Hello," I answered, my gaze zeroed in on the two of them.

"This Jane Kelly?" a flat male voice asked.

"Yes."

"Hey, it's Sean Hatchmere. You called?"

Unbelievable. Dwayne was right; I'd just gotten my first break. Sean was Roland's son. I'd left messages on his cell phone explaining who I was—just like I'd left messages on Gigi's phone and Roland's wife Melinda's and many others'—but I'd assumed Sean wasn't interested in me any more than any of the rest of them were. "I sure did."

"You're trying to help Violet, right? My sister said you were."

He didn't bring up Gigi slamming the door in my face, so maybe he didn't know about her response. I said cautiously, "More like I'm trying to figure out what happened."

"Isn't that what the police are doing?"

There was noise in the background. Some kind of uniden-
tifiable music? Techno-rock? I couldn't tell. But it was loud
and Sean's flat voice was mere microdecibels above it,
barely enough for me to make out what he was saying.

"Yes." One thing I've learned in my brief foray into the
P.I. business, answer as truthfully as you dare but don't offer
up any more information than necessary. Let whomever
you're talking with develop their own conclusions. Those
conclusions might surprise you, more often than not.

"Yeah, well, if you wanna see me you can come down to
the Crock pretty much any night."

"The Crock?" I repeated, surprised.

"You know it?"

"Sure do. How about I stop by tonight? What time will
you be there?"

"We start about midnight and go till two or three."

I paused a beat before saying, "Okay."

I hung up, my momentary excitement at finally breaking
through the Hatchmere wall taking a nosedive. The idea of
starting anything at midnight made me inwardly groan. I'd
been a bartender for a number of years, but I'd lived a different lifestyle then, becoming by necessity a "night person"
and sleeping during the day. I'd effectively switched fully to
the daylight hours in the time since, so I knew I would struggle to stay awake tonight. Napping always sounds like a
good alternative, but, except for that bartending era when
my days and nights were completely flipped, I've never been
able to master it.

But Sean Hatchmere had given me a gift.

As I squeezed my way to the dock, I was just in time to
hear Violet say, "What is it with you and those binoculars?"
in a peeved voice.

I smiled inwardly, seeing Dwayne's obsession in a positive light for the first time. Especially when he answered,
"Darlin', you have no idea what you can learn. See that house

over there? The one under construction? Do Not Enter's got some serious teen parties happening every weekend."

"Teenagers," Violet responded derisively.

"Can't decide whether to report 'em to our local law enforcement, or head over there myself and score whatever they're sharin' amongst their secretive little selves." Dwayne grinned up at Violet from beneath the brim of his cowboy hat.

Violet threw a look my way. "I can't get him to take me seriously."

"Jane's your lead investigator."

"I know, I know." Violet sighed.

I broke in. "I just got a call from Sean Hatchmere. I'm meeting him at the Crock tonight."

"Good," Violet said with feeling. "That's what I'm paying for! Still no luck with Gigi?" I shook my head. "Well, maybe Sean can help you there. He doesn't like his sister much, though. Nobody does—did—except Roland."

Violet and I left Dwayne on the dock as we headed through his cabana and out to our cars. A brisk breeze whipped past, running like a ribbon through the tree boughs. I paused to look around me, waiting for Violet to get into her car, a white Mercedes convertible, which she did after searching in her purse for her cell phone. I watched her unlock the vehicle by remote while she connected to her housekeeper, outlining what she wanted done with the red wine stains on the carpet. As she drove away I had a mental picture of her alone in her mansion, drinking wine, worrying about whether she would be indicted for murder.

She'd married a series of husbands and never improved her financial situation with each divorce. She'd married for love, I guess. Or the hope of love and companionship.

It was ironic that the wealth had come to her from her own family, a group of relatives she'd been separated from for years. She might be facing a murder trial in her future, but at least she could pay for it with Purcell funds.

I climbed into my Volvo wagon and headed home. Another blast of hail came at me like a round of artillery. It made me wonder what I was going to wear to my midnight rendezvous with Sean at the Crock. I found myself beginning to look forward to the event, now that I'd mentally conditioned myself.

And there was always the chance that I might see Megan Adair, one of the Crock's bartenders and the woman who'd dropped The Binkster, my newly adopted pug, on my doorstep.

Who knew? If I wasn't careful, I might learn something.

CHAPTER TWO

I arrived back at my cottage around four o'clock, realizing I had a full eight-hour shift of waiting time till midnight and my rendezvous with Sean. There's a lot of waiting in this job, and I'm not all that good at it. Maybe I should take up a hobby. Like crossword puzzles or that Sudoku rage. Currently my pastimes appear to be coffee and wine consumption. I'm going for the gold in both pursuits, and I think I could actually get a medal. For exercise I jog from my cottage to the Coffee Nook.

Binkster, my adopted pug, met me at the door, wriggling wildly. I picked her up and we sat down on the couch together, where I petted her and she flopped across my lap as if to say, "Mine." This pleased me to no end. Unconditional love. Who knew it could be so good? I've only had the dog a few months, but she's become this integral part of my life in a way that still stuns me. I suspect this must be what motherhood's like—a new addition to your family/life that wasn't there before, and suddenly is too important to even quantify. She tangled with a car recently and still has the shaved hind leg to prove it. It looks a little like she's wearing stockings.

Well . . . stocking. I feel gut-wrenchingly bad about the accident, both because Binks was hurt and it was partially my fault. The great thing about Binks, though, is she neither holds it against me, nor probably even remembers. Except when she sees the grill of a vehicle. Then she tends to shy away and who can blame her? She feels the same way about grates over storm drains. She always eyes them warily and gives them a wide berth. I don't know what that's from, though I suspect there may be some buried trauma there from puppyhood.

After a few minutes I dislodged the pug who heaved a disappointed sigh and pressed right against my leg as I reached for my laptop. I decided I might as well edit my notes. I'd made a timeline of the events that read:

FRIDAY
6:00 p.m.—Rehearsal dinner at Castellina, forty people invited, Roland was there. Everyone invited is in attendance except Sean (the bride's brother), who has previous plans of unknown origin. Violet is not invited to any wedding event.

SATURDAY
10:00 a.m.—Gigi (the bride) and Melinda (the bride's stepmother) at Castellina early for hair and makeup. Various bridesmaids arrive. Female bonding all around. Emmett Popparockskill stays at apartment he and Gigi shared before the wedding day. (Roland is apparently at his house. Never made it to the winery/ceremony.)
1:00 p.m.—Gigi and bridesmaids head by limo to Cahill Winery for pictures, wedding and reception.
2:00 p.m.—Pictures scheduled at Cahill Winery. Emmett drives himself to winery for pictures. His parents arrive, David and Goldy Popparockskill. Various

*groomsmen arrive. Concern grows when Roland nei-
ther shows nor answers his home or cell phone.
3:00 p.m.—More guests arrive. Wedding is slated for
four, but by now the atmosphere's tense with worry.
People leave in search of Roland. Gigi stays, breaks
down. Emmett heads to Roland's house. The bridesmaids and groomsmen hit the bar early.
3:30 p.m.—Emmett discovers Roland's body. There
are items scattered around, wedding presents dropped
in the front yard. Suspicion grows that the Wedding
Bandits were interrupted by Roland and killed him. Violet's prints are the only ones on the tray.*

My timeline didn't offer much more than a listing of the
events as they occurred. I'd grilled Violet about her own
timeline for that morning, and Violet was forthcoming about
the fact that she and Roland had gotten in an argument and
she'd hit him with the silver tray. But that information was
documented fact from the police report, something she
couldn't deny. Obviously, there was a hell of a lot left unsaid.
She'd been pretty cagey about her relationship with her third
ex, acting as if they were just reunited friends, but we're talking about Violet here. She's not known for platonic relationships with men.

At the time of his death, Roland was still married to
Melinda McCrae Hatchmere, though they were living apart.
I believe Violet reconnected with Roland and they started a
steamy affair. Let's face it: some pretty powerful feelings
caused Violet to hit him with the tray. Maybe the relationship had started to sour. Maybe he decided to stick with
Melinda. Maybe Gigi got in the way of her father's new romance. Whatever the case, I'd taken to calling him Rol-Ex,
which I think is screamingly hilarious but other people seem
to find lame. Violet sure does.

Sometimes I think I'm the last person left on the planet with a real sense of humor.

So, whether she cops to it or not, I believe Violet and Rol-Ex were hitting the sheets together. It's almost a given. There's just something ripe, luscious and ready to pick about Violet that can't be missed. And she's not the type of woman to spend time mourning the death of a previous relationship, such as the one she was working on with Dwayne. Nope. More likely, Violet would simply zero in on the next opportunity and head that direction. I admire her ability to get over bad stuff. She says there's no time to dwell, regret, rue or wallow. She's supercharged in a sultry, throbbing way that reminds me of Mae West or Marilyn Monroe.

And she's nobody's fool.

I come by my paranoia over Violet's chances with Dwayne for good reason. I don't care that she's ten to fifteen years older. It didn't stop Demi Moore, and it would never stop Violet.

And I've grown pretty sick of her evasions, to tell the truth. No "amethyst" gown is going to change my feelings. After I talk with Sean I plan to have a serious tête-à-tête with my client and hopefully an exchange of information. I'll offer up what I learn from Sean, and she'd better come completely clean with a full account of what went on between her and Rol-Ex before she hit him with the platter.

I got ready for the evening early, more out of boredom than an urge to be ahead of the game. I opted for a pair of expensive brown pants—something my friend Cynthia had made me buy in a weak moment—a white, silky shell and a black leather jacket. The weather was unpredictable. Hail one minute, followed by surprisingly warm wintry sun the next, followed further by gale winds that shook the windows and rattled the branches. Whatever the case, Oregon nights in November require layering. It was going to be cold, cold, cold once that sun went down.

I threw a longing glance toward my sneakers; I like to be ready to move, if need be. The Binkster was curled up in her little bed in the corner of my bedroom watching me as I pulled items from the closet, tried them on, discarded them, then put them back. When I was finally dressed to my satisfaction I turned around and looked at her, splaying my palms up to ask for her opinion. Her little tail whipped into a curl, the only movement I could discern apart from her eyes. I've come to recognize this as "Hi, there."

"So, what do you think?" Her tail jerked into a speedy wag. "I have to go out tonight, so you need to head outside and take care of business." I moved to the kitchen door of my cottage, which leads to a back deck. Stairs descend to the backyard and a body of water known as West Bay. At the eastern end of the bay is a bridge, and once beneath the bridge you enter Lake Chinook itself.

Binks's toenails clicked against my hardwood floor. I opened the back door, then followed her down the steps, waiting patiently while she nosed around the yard. She can let herself out through her doggy-door cut into the wall, but I wanted to get the job done and lock her inside for the rest of the night. She looked up at me once, her wrinkly black face comically quizzical. I motioned for her to get at it and she got right down to business. I cleaned up after her as I can't stand dog doo-doo littering my yard and flushed the remains down the toilet.

Binkster looked at me expectantly. She seems to think everything she does requires a reward. Have I created this expectation? Undoubtedly. Do I regret it? Well, yeah, some. Did anyone tell me how to train a dog that was dumped on me unceremoniously? Hell no. I figure Binks is lucky to be alive, at this point.

I reached over and grabbed her face and leaned down and

let her half jump up to lick my lips. These kisses used to gross me out. The idea of dog germs is a very real thing. But now I don't know . . . I just sort of go with it, which is surprising because I have real Seinfeld-ish problems with that kind of thing.

My cell phone started singing. I dug in my purse for it. Why are those things so damn hard to find? When I finally corralled it and looked down at its brightly lit LCD and recognized the name and number, my brows lifted in surprise. It was my landlord, Mr. Ogilvy. This is not a man who calls me up. Our communication is by mail. I write him a rent check and send it to him. He responds by cashing the check.

"Hi," I answered.

"Jane?"

"Yes."

He didn't waste time. "I've decided to sell the place. I'm putting a sign up tomorrow."

My legs sagged beneath me and I had to sit down. Selling? My cottage? I'd been renting from Ogilvy for over four years. I couldn't imagine living anywhere else. I can afford the rent. The house is on the water. There's nothing like it anywhere in my price range. I don't want to leave. Ever. "Selling?" I repeated faintly.

"You don't have to move till it's in escrow," he said magnanimously.

Well, la-di-da. My mind immediately searched for a way to buy the property myself, but it wasn't possible. It was too much money. The property's value had to be in the stratosphere by virtue of the lakefront land beneath the cottage. The one-bedroom building itself wasn't much, but it was my home. I was horrified.

"You're going to have to take your stuff out of the garage," I said in a voice I barely recognized as my own. I couldn't think of anything else to say. I'd never been able to use the garage because of all of Ogilvy's junk that was padlocked inside. I guess I hoped this might deter him, but apart from an unhappy grunt of acknowledgment, he didn't react.

I left the cottage with that bad feeling that comes from unresolved issues, the kind that stays in your head, never quite put aside, remembered with a jarring lurch and a pit in your gut. I couldn't think about moving. I couldn't. I was pissed off at Ogilvy for even suggesting I should.

In a funk, I drove to my friend Cynthia's art gallery, the Black Swan, located in Portland's chichi Pearl District, and hung around until she closed at nine, and then even later, sharing a glass of red wine with her in her office. She looked sharp in a short forest-green skirt, a matching double-breasted jacket and a pair of silver heels. I asked her to go with me to the Crock.

"Can't," she declined. "Got to get to bed early. Much to do tomorrow. And I'm short-staffed, as ever, since Ernst left, which isn't a bad thing because the last thing I needed was to look at his ugly face every day."

Ernst was an ex-lover and ex-employee.

I walked her to her car, then climbed back in mine, heading east toward the Willamette River which feeds into the Columbia River, the dividing line between Oregon and Washington. The Willamette bisects Portland whose city center lies on the west side. The Crock, short for Crocodile, is located on the east side, not far from Twin Peaks, the two bluish glass towers that are perched atop the Convention Center. I crossed the Morrison Bridge and began a kind of haphazard journey down narrow streets in search of the bar. I'd never been to the Crock and I wasn't all that familiar with this area. It's a part of Portland that was once, and is largely still, industrial, this close to the river, but there are cubbyholes of trendy restaurants and nightclubs tucked here and there. In a few years it will probably be blocks of urban hot spots. I'd been to several of the clubs around town to see up-and-coming bands at a number of these joints: they were, to a one, dark, bare, crammed with young people and loud noises.

It had been a number of months since Megan Adair left Binkster in my care. She'd made noise that she might actually give the dog a home since Aunt Eugenie, Binky's original owner and a friend of my mother's, had departed this world, leaving her beloved pet in my mother's care. The fact was, Aunt Eugenie was not my aunt. She was, however, Megan Adair's. In our one meeting, when Megan dropped off the dog, I'd learned that Megan worked at the Crock and that she was in between places to live. I'd hoped she would come back for the pug soon, but now I felt completely different. If anybody were to try to take Binkster from me, they were in for a fight. It was like a bad love affair, really; the dog belonged to me and only me, and by God, I'd go to any means to keep her.

So it was with a slight chip on my shoulder that I entered the bar. If I saw Megan I was going to make it clear straight up that the dog would not be leaving my care. Which was just another reason why I couldn't be ousted from my cottage. My heart karumphed hard, hurting. I had to have a place that would take me and my dog. Had to.

"Five dollars," the bouncer manning the door said on a bored yawn. He was broad, shiny bald and wore all black.

"Five dollars? Really."

"Five dollars." He gazed at me hard, his left hand knotted into a fist that he lightly pounded atop a narrow podium.

"The cover's for . . . music?"

He just stared at me. Normally this kind of thing totally intimidates me, but I hate parting with money, especially when I can't see any discernible value to a potential purchase.

"I'm meeting Sean Hatchmere here? He's a musician?"

He mouthed, "Five dollars." The way he did it sent a

shiver down my spine. I forked over a Lincoln and he stood aside. I could feel my heart beating inside my rib cage like it was trying to escape. Sheesh. Sometimes it feels like the whole world's in a really bad mood.

I was too early for the bands, even though they were already charging a cover, so I headed around a corner—I swear the wall was simply a sheaf of black cardboard—and turned into a room with a circular bar in the center. It was all corrugated metal and chain link and spotlights that sent silver cones of illumination down upon a motley assortment of patrons.

I saw Megan immediately, her short, spiky blond hair taking on a bluish tint. She wore a tight T-shirt in some gray tone, if the lighting could be trusted, and a pair of darker cargo pants. She was rattling up drinks in a silver shaker, straining a dark red liquid into two martini glasses that looked to be made of molten silver. Everything had that urban, hard, cold feel to it, which I guess was the point. I could think of a million different names more suitable than The Crocodile, but no one asked for my opinion.

A barmaid in black pants and a gray top studded with rivets swooped down on me as I pulled out a metal stool and settled myself at the bar. I ordered a Mercury, and hoped I wouldn't be poisoned.

I watched as Megan assembled my drink. Something cool and grape-colored disappeared into the shaker with some sugar solution and premium vodka. I sweated the cost. Sometimes they'll charge you damn near ten dollars for a martini. I'd been so intent on slipping inside without Megan seeing me that I hadn't registered the price. Or maybe I just didn't want another fight like with the bouncer. I am kind of a chicken.

I worried that I'd obsess over the cost. Then I worried that I would worry about obsessing over the cost.

Life's hellish when you're cheap.

The silver martini glass was pushed toward the barmaid, who in turn carefully put it on her tray, and carefully brought it to me. "Three dollars," she said, much to my grateful surprise. To my look, she said quickly, "You paid the cover, right?"

"Oh yeah."

"Then you're okay till midnight. Price goes up then."

"Really."

"We get a lot of good musicians here. A lot of 'em. Nothing gets going till late, though."

I sipped away. The drink tasted more pomegranate than grape and it was good. I slurped it down so fast I pretended to keep drinking long after the last drop was absorbed. Thank God for opaque glasses. But then I remembered I could probably put this on an expense account, so I ordered another, and this time Megan herself brought it to me as my barmaid was busy elsewhere.

We locked eyes. I could tell she registered that she knew me from somewhere, but she was having a hard time placing it. I said, "Hello, Megan. I'm Jane Kelly. You brought me the pug this summer. Your aunt Eugenie's?"

"Oh, Binky!" Her eyes widened. "Is everything all right with the dog? Can't you keep her any longer?"

"Oh no, she's fine. I'm . . . well, I've grown attached to her. Honestly, I'd have a hard time giving her back now."

"Oh, good. I'm just struggling with my apartment, y'know? Good roommates are like hen's teeth." She smiled. "One of Aunt Eugenie's favorite sayings."

"Good old Aunt Eugenie."

"I've got a guy living with me now who tried to tell me he doesn't spank the monkey. This after he ate a bag of Cheetos. Your Honor, I saw evidence to the contrary."

In my mind's eye, I witnessed what she'd seen in all its orange glory.

"I don't care what he does. Masturbation's supposed to be healthy. It's the lying I can't stand. You know what I mean?"

I nodded. I hate being lied to. Lying to others, however, is what I live for. An unfair dichotomy that rarely bothers me.

"Gotta get him out and someone else in." She eyed me some more. "You looking to move? It's a nice place. Not far off Hawthorne."

Her words had the power to almost pierce me. It was like the whole world knew I was being kicked out. "I'm pretty happy where I am."

"I don't doubt it," she said a bit ruefully. "That's a nice cottage. I was just hoping."

Aren't we all?

"So, what brings you down to the Crock?"

"I'm meeting Sean Hatchmere here."

"Who?"

I half twisted in my chair. "I think he's with a band . . . maybe?"

"Oh. Yeah, the musicians. They're all stoned or worse. That's a stereotype and a fact. I've smoked some weed, but that other stuff'll kill ya."

Megan, I remembered, smoked Players as well. Sometimes I like the scent of a freshly lit cigarette, but the environs of the Crock were saturated with that stale, musty scent of old cigarettes, dust and, drifting from the kitchen, overused grease. I imagined boiling oil somewhere beyond that turned out jalapeño poppers, clam strips, chicken fingers and assorted deep-fried appetizers at an alarming rate.

"Didn't you say you used to tend bar?" she asked.

"In Southern California. A place called Sting Ray's."

"If you ever want to moonlight, we're always looking for someone to fill in."

"I'll keep it in mind," I said as Megan went back to fill another barmaid's order.

I tried to put myself in the picture as an employee of the

Crock. I liked the dress code. Pants, as opposed to shorts or short skirts. Easier to work in. But the hours, and the lingering smells, and the drunks . . .

Not that process serving, one of the offshoots of my business, doesn't have its perils and pitfalls. While Violet's case was on stall, I'd delivered a few notices with varying risks to my person. Three days ago I'd damn near gotten run down by a guy I'd served with divorce papers. The asshole got in his car while I was heading toward mine, suddenly shifted in reverse and stamped on the accelerator, roaring backward straight for me. I'm always a little more on my toes when I deliver people bad news, so I nimbly leapt out of his Porsche's path. He reversed right into the street and broadsided a passing sedan, luckily catching it at the back wheel well, so no one was seriously hurt. Everyone started screaming and shrieking and a man the size of Greenland unfolded himself from the sedan's driver's seat and glared down at the prick in the Porsche. I gave Greenland my phone number, told him I'd seen the whole thing, then climbed into my Volvo and calmly drove around them. I'd really wanted to flip the Porsche driver off. He'd tried to kill me, after all. But it looked to me like justice would be served, so I just rolled down my window and whistled the theme from *Rocky* at him as I cruised past.

Maturity may not be my long suit. Doesn't mean it didn't feel good.

I finished my drink but held on to my silver glass as I strolled away from the bar and toward the back of the room where scruffy men in dark T-shirts and wrinkled pants checked the sound and lights. I watched a guy unroll a wad of thick electrical cable, his movements so deliberate I wondered if he was in a zone. A drug zone, possibly, although I've known other people who moved at the speed of sloth.

There was a grouping of two-person café tables in front of the stage and I snagged a chair. The lighting was dim, which was probably a blessing as I tend to get anxious when I see the accumulation of dirt and crud that seems to go hand in hand with small nightclubs. I can live with a certain amount of dog hair clinging to my clothes. But true dirt? Inside, not outside? Uh-uh.

My eyes narrowed on the dusty footprints layered upon each other atop the dark stage. *Get a broom, somebody.*

"Sean, get up the catwalk and check that spot."

The speaker was an older guy with a frizzy, gray ponytail. He was pointing to a track light attached to a crossbeam above the far end of the stage. Sean was the guy slowly wrapping up the cable.

Could there be two Seans? I wondered hopefully. This one was slight with shaggy hair to his shoulders and a dopey expression on his thin face. Either he was under sedation or there was one very long neuron between sensory input and brain processing. He was, however, about the right age. Twenty-five, maybe?

Sean slowly balanced a tall ladder against the aforementioned catwalk. I held my breath as he climbed upward, his movements at a steady pace of .002 miles per hour. He trudged across the walk to the light, which he fiddled with and fiddled with while Frizzy Ponytail barked orders. Eventually they were both satisfied and Sean crept back down the rungs and returned to coiling cable. He'd sounded a lot more energetic on the phone.

I checked my watch. Eleven-thirty. Maybe I could get this interview over early and skedaddle before the witching hour. The thought of my bed was an invitation I wanted to accept sooner rather than later.

"Sean Hatchmere?" I asked, as he walked across the stage in front of me, his sneakers and pant legs passing by at eye level.

He stopped, shading his eyes against the lights to look down at me. "Yeah?"

"Jane Kelly."

It took a moment. "Oh. Yeah. Ya wanna come on back?" He veered toward the rear of the stage and after a brief second of hesitation, I hauled myself onto the dusty apron and followed, brushing off my palms.

Behind the enormous speakers and false walls was a rabbit warren of alleyways fashioned from more enormous false walls and black set boxes. I could see the bright green of an EXIT sign through a slit between black curtains. Sean stopped ahead of me and motioned me into a room with a haphazard selection of folding chairs. The greenroom, apparently, where the performers waited before going onstage.

Sean took a folding chair and I pulled up one beside him. The light was dim enough that I couldn't tell if his eyes were unfocused or not. "You wanted to talk about Dad," he said. His voice was a near monotone, but I thought that might be just his natural way of speaking rather than a passive-aggressive kind of compliance, the kind I might have used in the principal's office once upon a time.

"Violet didn't kill your father, either purposely or by accident," I said, forcing myself to sound positive. "She wants to find who did, and I'm trying to make that happen. I'm just gathering information. You're the first person interested in talking to me."

"You're a private eye?"

"Something like that."

"What does that mean?"

"It's a work in progress." I explained about the steps it took to be licensed, and Sean listened with apparent interest.

"That's cool." He bobbed his head. "You can't, like, bust some-one for something, though, huh? Like drugs, or . . . stuff . . ."

"I'm not the police."

"I dunno what I can tell ya. Dad was a control freak. Really wanted me to be a doctor, like he was. But y'know how that turned out." He peered at me through hanks of hair.

"He got his medical license revoked," I said.

"He was a lot more fun before that." His tone was wistful. "All of a sudden he's, like, climbing down my throat, turning my room upside down, sniffing around like a drug dog, y'know? Found a little stash of weed and thinks I'm a crackhead. Sends me to this rehab place with, like, these old people. Everybody's got a prescription drug problem. I mean, really. Like housewives and businessmen and lawyers and shit. They are really messed up. If these people had had a little weed, y'know? They'd be a lot better off."

"Did you tell your father that?"

"You bet. I told him lots of stuff. All that hypocritical shit. I kinda laughed at him, if you want the truth," Sean said sheepishly. "He just, like, blew a blood vessel. Really, really out of control."

I decided Sean might be stoned. His emotions seemed detached from his narrative. "So, were you and your dad having a problem when he died?"

"We were always having a problem. I was his problem. Well, and Gigi, too. I always kinda thought he wanted other kids, y'know? Smarter kids. Better athletes. More motivated." He shrugged. "Some parents are just like that. My friend Dillon? His dad's a total fuck wad. Told Dillon that if he didn't get a job, he wasn't invited to Thanksgiving. That's cold, man."

"How old is Dillon?"

"Twenty-four."

Sometimes I worry about the state of America's youth, but then I remember what I was like at his age, which although different—I wasn't a drug user—was kind of the same. I hate to use the word *slacker*. It's just got too many bad connotations. I prefer motivation-challenged. I didn't know what the hell to do with my life, and I spent my time stumbling through some college courses that still have the power to cause me moments of intense puzzlement. I remember one class titled Strategic Achievement in Common Socioeconomic and Cultural Workplace Situations in Conjunction with, or without, Today's Technological Advances. I dropped out after a week of obscure lectures. The only thing I remember is great bandying about of the term *utopic model*. My strategic achievement was getting the hell out.

"So, you're working for Violet, huh?" He sounded more curious than appalled. "Wow. I hear she inherited a ton a' money. Maybe that's what killed Dad." He barked out a laugh. "He hated not being in control."

"He controlled with money?"

"Oh, shit yeah. Totally. I don't mean to, like, talk bad about him. I'm sorry he's gone. He was . . . my dad." Sean stopped short. It took him a couple of tries to get started again. Clearing his throat, he finally said, "But he really got upset when we didn't follow the plan. 'The blueprint,' he called it. Y'know?"

"The blueprint." I was getting a bigger picture of Roland Hatchmere beyond Violet's description of him as a good father and an excellent plastic surgeon. "Sean, have you thought about who might have killed him?"

"Besides Violet . . . ?" He looked away, staring into space for long moments. "Those robbers, maybe?"

"Maybe."

"Nobody hated him, if that's where you're going. He didn't make enemies. No botched surgeries, when he was practicing. And he didn't screw anybody over in his business dealings. I mean, I don't think he did. Y'know Gigi and I had our problems. Like all kids, right? But everybody else thought he was great. Just ask 'em."

"Can you give me some names?"

"Like of his friends? Sure."

Quickly I pulled a small tablet and pen from my purse.

Sean scribbled down a list of people. "Is there anyone else? Other relatives? Businesspeople?" I tried to jog his memory.

"Oh yeah." He added a few more scratch marks to the list.

When he handed it back I felt jubilant. With Sean's tacit endorsement, these people might actually talk to me. "Thanks."

"Who do you think did it?" he asked.

"I'd have to get a lot more background before I could venture a guess."

"You don't think Violet did it."

I shook my head.

He grinned. "You don't like her, do ya? What happened? She screw you over, too?"

"Did she screw you over?"

"Oh, sure. Tried to get Dad to change his will, leave it all to her. He balked and they fought, and he lost his license and she was gone. But then she was back. You should talk to Melinda." He gestured at the list. "Dad's wife. You know she had to be really crazy, thinking about Violet returning to Portland, probably worming her way back in. Violet's like that. She just doesn't give up."

"Mm."

"You should talk to my mom, too," he added. "I put her name on the list."

I glanced down, pretending I didn't know whom he meant, though I'd practically memorized the names of the main players. "Renee?"

"Yeah. She doesn't live around here. She came up for the wedding, but, well, you know how that turned out."

Actually, I didn't. Violet had mentioned a minor brouhaha at the rehearsal dinner between Roland and his first wife, but she hadn't been there and I hadn't been able to gather any more information.

"What happened with Renee?"

But Sean, having realized I was fishing, decided to shut

down. He shrugged and said, "She didn't like Violet, either, I guess."

I thought of my timeline and said, "What time did she get to the wedding? Was she with Gigi at Castellina, getting ready?"

"I don't know . . ." He glanced over his shoulder. "You know, we're gonna be playing some good stuff. You wanna get ready?"

"I'll stay for some of it," I promised. He was clearly trying to get me off track and I wasn't ready to give up.

"No, I mean. Ya wanna *get ready*?" He inclined his head toward the rear of the building.

I looked in that direction. "You mean, get high?"

"Hey, alcohol's way worse than weed," he said, apparently hearing some condemnation in my tone I hadn't meant to voice.

"I've got my poison, thanks." I hoisted my empty glass.

"Well, okay . . . I guess we're done, then." He made a face and headed toward the back.

I hesitated a moment, then returned to my seat. Apart from some leftover questions concerning Renee Hatchmere, I felt I'd gotten all I could from Sean. I managed to stay through the first set before heading for the door. Either I'm growing old or my tolerance is shrinking, but I couldn't handle the pounding beat and roaring, amplified electric guitar. Everything inside my head was throbbing with the music. I slipped out into the icy night air and drew a deep breath. Outside, the din was muffled and almost okay.

I walked quickly to my Volvo, climbed inside, switched on the key and shivered until I was almost home. Hurriedly, I ripped off my clothes and threw a T-shirt over my head. When Binkster gave me a blinking, hopeful look, staggering to her feet, I threw back the covers in an invitation and we both settled into bed with a sigh.

I fell asleep with doggy toenails planted against my back.

* * *

In the night I heard a peculiar ringing sound I didn't associate with any noise I knew. I lifted my head reluctantly and saw it was after 3:00 a.m. Vaguely I discerned that the noise, now silenced, had come from my cell phone, which was lying on my nightstand, being charged. I grappled for it and knocked an empty plastic glass onto the floor. "Shit," I muttered as Binky snorted loudly but refused to lift her head.

I punched a button to light up the dial and saw that I had a text message. Aha! That was the undefinable ring. I pressed the button with the little envelope on it, and a message popped up:

> *party at Do Not Enter broke up at one. Since then, lots of crying at Rebel Yell. Something's definitely wrong. Need you to investigate.*
> *DAD*

I set the phone down and drifted back to sleep. Dwayne's initials are DAD for Dwayne Austin Durbin. Now he wanted me to *investigate* what was happening across the bay?

"He's around the bend, Binks. Completely around the bend," I mumbled.

She answered with an inhaled doggy snort that I swear made the bed thrum as if it were equipped with Magic Fingers.

CHAPTER THREE

The next morning I made my usual run to the Coffee Nook and poured myself a cup of basic black coffee while Julie, the shop's proprietress, and Jenny, Julie's number-one employee, served up a rush of customers. One of the regulars I know only as Chuck had been to a charity auction and had bid on, and won, a ride-along with the Lake Chinook cops. I was slightly amazed anyone would be interested. I pictured the cops racing out, sirens screaming, to rescue a cat from a tree. Of course with the current sensibilities of Lake Chinook, it would probably be rescuing a tree from a cat. Either way I was glad it was Chuck who'd parted with his hard-earned money for this treat rather than myself.

"The cop's name is Josh Newell," Chuck said, reading from his "certificate," a page with a glued on gold seal that said he was a WINNER!!! "Ever heard of him?"

Jenny shook her head, but I said, somewhat surprised myself, "I have." Everyone turned to look at me. "I gave his sister Cheryl a ride from the airport. She told me Josh was with the LCPD."

"I thought you avoided the police," said Julie.

"I've never met the guy. Just his sister." I'd tucked the information away for future use, but hadn't expected it to pop into my world so soon.

"Wanna go with me?" Chuck invited eagerly. "It's for two." He waved the certificate in my direction.

No . . . thank . . . you . . . please . . . God . . .

"I don't think I could fit it into my schedule," I demurred.

"Hey, it's not for any specific time. Any time next week work?" Chuck looked at me hopefully. He's around sixty with a barrel torso and close-cropped Homer Simpson hair.

"Not really."

"Thursday?"

"No."

"Yeah, right. Weekends'd be better. Friday. I'll take you to dinner, and then we'll ride around with Josh."

"Take her to Foster's on the Lake," Jenny said. "Her favorite place. She won't say no."

I gave Jenny a long look. She was grinning.

"Foster's it is," Chuck said merrily. "I'll pick you up at six."

"I'll meet you there," I said. He threw an arm up as a good-bye and I turned to Jenny as soon as he was out the door. "Judas."

"You could have said no."

"Free food at Foster's? Yeah, that's gonna happen."

"We'll come and meet you. Right, Julie? Jane, tell Jeff Foster to comp us a meal."

I laughed. We all knew Jeff Foster was a major cheapo and ice cubes would freeze in hell before he comped the likes of me a meal.

"Tell him it's for me and Julie."

I snorted.

"Come on, Jane. Go with Chuck. It'll be fun."

Right up there with root canals.

"We'll all meet at Foster's," she said. I could practically

see the wheels turning inside Jenny's head as she planned to weasel a meal. I appreciate this about her.

"All right," I said on a sigh.

My cell phone rang as I was taking a shower. I don't know what it says about me, but I have a hell of a time letting a phone ring, any phone, and I half debated on jumping out and running naked for it. It was with a supreme effort of self-control that I let it go to voice mail, and so I was perturbed when there was no message and the number on caller ID was one I didn't recognize.

I threw on my jeans, a blue V-necked, long-sleeved T-shirt and my black jacket, then punched in the digits to see who'd phoned. A woman's voice answered in irritation: "Yes? Who is it?"

"Jane Kelly, returning this number's call." I grabbed for my brown boots and encountered the wriggling body of The Binkster as she decided she needed some attention right then and there. I began petting her and she grabbed my hand with her mouth, a surefire sign she would prefer food over attention.

"Oh." A pause. "This is Gigi Hatchmere."

"Oh," I repeated in surprise. The last time I'd seen her was on the opposite side of her quickly shutting door. I'd had a brief glance of short dark hair, angry brows and a mouth turned down in what looked like perpetual displeasure.

Binkster gave a sharp yip when her ploy failed. I ignored her so she grabbed my pant leg with her teeth and growled. Her growls sound like they were made by Mattel: cute and puppyish. I pushed her aside but she came back for more.

"Sean told me you went to see him last night. What a dope head. I hope you didn't listen to anything he said. He should be committed, he's so screwed up. And he has no family loyalty!"

"He seems to want to know what really happened to his father." Not exactly what he'd said, but she didn't have to know.

It incensed Gigi. "Well, of course he does. We all do. What do you think? Violet killed him! And she gets to just walk around with all her money? That's just plain wrong! Why don't you stop harassing us and put her in jail where she belongs? Jesus, I can't believe this. The police are doing nothing. *Nothing.*"

That wasn't exactly the truth, either, but I saw an opportunity to push my own agenda. "I've been hired to investigate your father's death and find out what really happened."

"I know! By Violet. You're working for *her*."

"If I learn Violet's involved at some level, I'm duty-bound to report that to the authorities." Again, not exactly the truth.

"Violet *killed* him. And she's paying *you*."

What a stickler for detail. "Are you interested in finding your father's killer?"

"Absolutely."

"Then talk to me. Meet with me. Let me get some background. It may be just as you think, Violet could be guilty, but my loyalty's to the truth."

I heard the ring of conviction in my voice and was impressed with my skills of persuasion. I crossed my fingers that Gigi was impressed, too.

"You would really turn on Violet even though she's paying you?"

"What do you care, as long as justice is served?"

"I don't, I guess . . ."

"Who knows how long it will take the police to follow leads? I'm working on the case right now. I want to know what happened that day."

"Hunh," she said, rolling that around. My quest for might

and right seemed to have mollified her somewhat. "Where do you want to meet?"

"I could come by the house?" I suggested. I was taking a chance, as my last trip there hadn't ended well. But Gigi and Emmett had moved into her father's house after Roland's death, and, as it was the scene of the crime, I wanted to see it for myself.

"I guess we could meet here," she said reluctantly.

"Terrific." I pounced on it, afraid she might talk herself out of it.

"Maybe the end of next week?"

"Well, yes . . . that would work. But . . . any chance I could stop by today?" I pushed. "I'd like to get moving on this and I'm sure anything you could tell me would be helpful."

"I don't know about that. Violet was the one who was here that day. I was at my wedding. Or, my almost wedding. When Daddy didn't show I just couldn't go through with it. Ohmygod, I still can't believe it. I mean, isn't your day supposed to be perfect? Isn't this the *one day of your life* that's perfect?"

I thought about all the divorces that occur after that one day but decided to keep quiet on that, too.

"And then Violet kills my father and he can't come and everything's ruined," Gigi went on, sounding as if she was working herself up. "I was waiting and waiting and he just didn't show."

"It sounds—traumatic."

"You don't know the half of it." She sniffed. "Can you be here around four?"

"You bet."

"I really could use someone to talk to," she said in a teensy, little girl voice.

"It's been a trying time," I assured her as I hung up. I found myself already worrying that she might cry, hug me and need the kind of support I'm terrible at giving.

I looked over at Binkster, who'd given up biting my pant leg and had retreated to her furry little bed, gazing at me with an injured expression. "Chicken strip?" I said, and she raced over to the cupboard where I keep her treats.

My dog, I understand.

I had to stop by Dwayne's before heading to Gigi's though I was reluctant to learn what he wanted me to do about his friends across the bay. I brought Binkster with me because I feel guilty leaving her alone in the house too many days in a row, and I had an inner hope that I could talk Dwayne into keeping her for a few hours and that the dog might divert him from his new obsession.

Binkster loves Dwayne. Just loves him. It could seriously hurt my feelings except I'm a bigger person than that . . . most of the time. I watched her race up the sidewalk to his front door and dig one paw at the wood, scarcely able to contain herself. As soon as I opened the door she charged inside straight down the hall to the gap in the sliding glass door and out to the dock. I heard Dwayne exclaim as he saw her and I purposely took my time joining them, letting their bonding ritual run through its paces. By the time I stepped onto the dock, Binks was on Dwayne's lap, giving his lips some doggy licks. He was laughing and I think she tried to French him 'cause he scooped her up and put her on the ground, his laughter even deeper while she wriggled beneath his chair and began barking, her tail wagging furiously, totally into the game.

The game is simple. For Binkster it's: I will squeeze myself beneath your chair, the bed, the couch, the bar stool or whatever and then bark my silly head off like I'm stuck. When you come to rescue me, I'll pretend to snap at your hands, not to hurt, just to be a happy idiot. You, in turn, will laugh and pretend to drag me out, but you won't really, because then I'll just have to squeeze back in somewhere else and start the game again.

The game is dumb, but we all play it.

"I got your text message last night," I told Dwayne.

"Took you long enough to respond."

"Didn't know I was on the clock for Slot A and Tab B."

"Tab A. Slot B," he corrected. "Basic human anatomy, Jane. He's Tab A. She's Slot B."

"I get it."

Dwayne always says that everyone has secrets they don't want someone else to know about. I agree with him. I just wondered why he felt compelled to learn the secrets of the people across the bay.

He stretched and levered himself out of his deck chair. I leaned forward but resisted the urge to help him. I find myself shying away from physical contact, which really pisses me off at myself, but for the moment it's how things stand between us. At least how it stands for me.

I said, "Ogilvy's selling my cottage."

Dwayne tipped his hat back and gave me a penetrating look. "He tell you that?"

"Kind of announced it. Called me up and dropped the bomb. Looks like I'm going to be hunting for a new abode whether I want to or not."

"Why don't you buy it?"

"Great idea. With all the money I have."

"You have enough for a down payment."

"Look who you're talking to."

"I'm looking."

We stared at each other for a full ten seconds. By God, I wasn't going to turn away first. I said firmly, holding his gaze, "Inactivity has addled your brain. I'm Jane Kelly. I have nothing. Half the time my refrigerator's empty enough to use as an extra room."

"You're cheap. You're not poor."

I narrowed my eyes. "I'm luxury-challenged, not cheap. Since when do you get to call me 'not poor'?"

Dwayne smiled in that knowing way that sometimes intrigues me. I gazed over the bay, deciding I'd had enough of this meeting of the eyes. I wasn't up to this challenge right now, and though I didn't know where it was going, how it had begun and what it meant, I wanted to step out of it before something altered between us. Sometimes you recognize those moments when you're in them with just enough time to save yourself; sometimes you don't.

"You own a fourplex unit with your mother in Venice. You horde every dollar you make. I've heard you barter with Ogilvy on the rent more times than I can count. You have enough for a down payment, and if you don't, I'll help you."

"I don't barter with Ogilvy. I don't even talk to him."

"Yes, you do."

That stopped me for a moment. "You're thinking about years ago, when he was trying to jump the rent a hundred dollars a month. A hundred dollars!"

"I believe you set him straight."

"You bet I did," I harrumphed. I'm not sure what I think of rent control. My mother and I deal with it in our Venice four-unit. In some ways, it sounds great, but when costs spiral upward, repairs start becoming more and more expensive and pretty soon you realize you can't afford the upkeep with the amount of rent you're receiving. But I sure as hell didn't want Ogilvy gouging me. There is no rent control in Oregon, as far as I know. There's certainly none in Lake Chinook, and I don't think it generally counts on single-family dwellings anyway. But if he was selling the place, none of it mattered. Any way around it I was screwed.

"Did you say you'd help me?" I asked, reviewing our conversation.

"Afraid of what that might mean?" He lifted one brow.

"Yes."

"Tell me how much money you've got."

"Hell no," I said. "It isn't polite to ask, don't you know that?"

"Politeness ain't my strong suit, darlin'."

"Oh yes, it is. You can be as polite and charming as a politician stumping for votes. Worse, even."

"Tell Ogilvy to give you a price."

"I can tell this is a bad idea. I don't know why I even told you."

"'Cause you want me to rescue you," Dwayne said equably, and that sent me into overdrive. Every time I think I like him, he makes me crazy. It was far better when we were just compatriots. Buddies. Partners. And the hell of it is, I fear deep down I might be the only one of us who truly feels all this angst. I think Dwayne likes me fine, trusts me, is attracted to me, in fact. He's just not as worked up about the whole thing as I am.

"I'm not even having this talk," I said, walking away from him, toward the edge of the dock. "You want to tell me about what's going on over there, then tell." I swept an arm to encompass the south side of Lakewood Bay.

"Maybe I'll buy your cottage," Dwayne said as if the idea had just struck him. "Then I can be your landlord."

"What fun," I snarled.

He started laughing so hard I thought he'd split a gut. What is it about men that makes them goad me? Maybe it's not just me. Maybe it's the whole female gender.

No, it's probably just me.

When I didn't think it was a full-on laugh-riot, he finally pulled himself back from the edge of hilarity. Taking off his hat, he swept a hand through his hair, sank back on the lounge, then turned his attention back to his new friends. I watched the transformation as he gazed across the bay, his expression sobering.

"There's trouble over at Rebel Yell," he said. "They have

two teenaged girls. The younger one's been crying her eyes out. The parents alternate between trying to talk to her and losing patience and yelling. She hasn't been yelling back, which is a change."

"For the better, it sounds like."

"Not so sure. Something's eating at her. I think the gal's got some big secret."

I should add that Dwayne says all this with a drawl and a lot of "g" dropping, like he's from the South somewhere, although that hasn't been firmly established yet. Sometimes my vast ignorance of Dwayne's history bothers me. He seems to be on a need-to-know basis only, when it comes to talking about his personal life. Since the Violet thing, I've steered clear of any discussion about his history that might provide more insight into him. I've known Dwayne for nearly five years as an acquaintance, and our friendship has developed largely because Dwayne wanted me to come work for him. A part of me thirsts for more information—bits of data that I can obsess over whenever I start thinking maybe, just maybe, Dwayne and I could be a "thing." But that other part of me— the sane part—wants nothing to do with him. He could be bad for my mental health.

"High school secrets," I mused. "Test cheating, alcohol stealing and drinking, pot smoking, pregnancy . . ."

"I vote pregnancy," Dwayne said seriously.

"Who's the daddy?"

"That's what I need you to find out."

"Hell no."

"She's a good kid. Gets good grades. Plays soccer. Or played. I think she quit the team. Lots of yelling over that. Her older sister's a piece of work. Bossy. The parents are always trying to get her to behave, but you can tell she just tunes them out. Reminds me of Tracy." He grimaced.

Tracy is Dwayne's niece. And yes, she is a piece of work. Luckily, she lives in Seattle and neither Dwayne nor I have seen her since a spectacularly horrible few weeks last summer.

"But she's protective of the younger sister. When she thinks of it, anyway."

"This is a family problem between Mr. and Mrs. Rebel Yell—the Wilsons—and their two daughters. Not for me to get involved."

"You're good with teenagers."

"Do you hear yourself?" He reached for the binoculars again, but I snatched them away from him. "So help me God, Dwayne. I can't have you look through these one more time. Now, what did you mean by that? I'm not good with teenagers."

"They're your best sources of information. I wish I had your gift," he said, and with a muscular twist from his deceptively relaxed position, he grabbed my arm and the binoculars and wrested them from me. "Steal a cripple's binoculars," he muttered.

He was lucky I didn't smack him alongside the head with them. No one makes me want to act infantile quicker than Dwayne Durbin. It's like a bad sitcom where you just know the man and woman are going to get together because they're either acting like they're going to throttle each other, or they're goofily trying to one-up the other, or they're each trying to set the other one up with their best friend with hilarious results.

Half the time I cannot believe my own embarrassing thoughts.

Dwayne's blue eyes assessed me. "No witty comeback?"

"Teen pregnancy? Dwayne, I'd be useless to the girl. She needs to talk to her parents about it. Maybe she already has. Maybe that's what the yelling's about."

"They're always yelling. If she'd told them, something new would have happened."

"You're making up a soap opera. You don't know anything."

"She's been hanging around at Do Not Enter with a bunch of other kids. They're drinking and sneaking around. Pretty cagey about it, but I've kept an eye on them. They string colored lights. Little ones. Just enough to give themselves some illumination, but not draw too much attention."

"Do the parents have any idea?"

"No one does, otherwise they'd be busted. There are a lot of guys hanging around. The girls seem to wait to be picked."

"You have kept an eye on them."

"I've had to watch from inside," Dwayne admitted. "If my leg were better, I'd go up to the attic and watch from there."

Dwayne's cabana has a steep set of stairs to an attic whose roofline makes it hard not to hit your head against the slanted walls. To my knowledge, it's full of boxes and junk, like Ogilvy's garage.

"If your leg were better, you wouldn't have started watching them in the first place," I murmured.

"Probably."

"Look, Dwayne, I'm meeting with Gigi later today. I met with Sean last night. I'm finally moving on the Hatchmere case. You were right when you said things would get going. I'm busy, and anyway, it's not my place to step into some teen scene with sex, drugs and alcohol."

Dwayne said, "You know those guys, the ones who smile and act responsible and polite in front of parents. The ones who lie through their orthodontia-perfected teeth. Who play sports and give talks on the responsibility of today's youth. Who denounce drugs and alcohol, then get wasted every Friday night after the football game. The ones who lie to their parents and feel powerful about it. Who promise that they'll take good care of their younger siblings, then damn near kill them with alcohol poisoning the first chance they get. You know those guys, Jane."

"Ye-ess . . ."

"Those are the guys at Do Not Enter. The ones who tell a girl she's special, say they love her, say they're her boyfriend to talk her into sex. They're the same ones who turn their back when she tries to talk to them and whisper and snigger to their friends."

I'd never seen this side of Dwayne. He was dead serious, and it made me wonder what had happened to him when he was a teenager. Was there a girl from his past who'd been used and abused by some guy? A girl he'd cared about? Someone he couldn't save?

"What do you want me to do?" I asked, engaged in spite of myself.

"Find out who these guys are, Jane. Get me their names."

I gazed across the water. Was I really thinking about helping him? "I suppose I could go to Friday night's football game."

"It's the civil war between Lakeshore and Lake Chinook."

"You've done your homework, haven't you?"

"I'm an investigator."

I gave Dwayne a sideways look. He was smiling, but he looked more relieved than pleased, which made me decide his motives were in the right place. "Okay, Jimmy Stewart. I'm sure I'm going to be sorry, but what the hell? I'll try to meet them."

"Hal Jeffries."

"What?"

"The character Jimmy Stewart plays in *Rear Window* is Hal Jeffries."

"It worries me that you know that," I said, but I was committed all the same.

Roland Hatchmere's house was at the end of a cul-de-sac in a development where all the streets were named from the Tolkien fantasy novels: Elf Lane, Hobbit Drive, Aragon Avenue. His home was a tri-level on Rivendell Road; street level being the main floor with an upstairs over the garage and a basement at the sloping western end. There was a lot of glass, a lot of decks and a sweeping entrance lined with impatiens that had been beaten down under the torrential hail. The house itself had an early seventies look and feel, not my favorite architectural era, but the grounds and view up the Willamette River toward Portland's city center were spectacular.

I parked my Volvo under the dripping branches of a large maple. As I climbed from the car, soggy yellow and red leaves floated onto the hood. A breeze shook through the limbs, sending a cascade of water onto me as I hurried for the front door.

Ringing the bell, I huddled under a narrow overhang, which, I learned, served more for looks than function, then tried to push myself inside when the door opened. It hadn't worked last time. It didn't work this time.

Gigi Hatchmere stood in the way with her patented scowl. "You're dripping," she said.

"Sorry."

My boots were soaked and leaving little wet puddles. I slipped them off and, though reluctant, she finally allowed me entry, across a mahogany-lined foyer to a living room with wide windows and no discernible walls. The view was amazing, a wide screen of sky over the roofs of houses down the hill. Portland lay spread across both sides of the river. I could almost count all the bridges and in the far, far distance was the mesalike crown of Mount Saint Helens, which had blown its top in 1980.

Gigi was about my height, five foot seven, and she was slim and serious. Her hair was dark brown as were her eyes, and she wore it straight and parted down the middle like a child of the sixties. She might have been pretty if there were any joy in her expression, but mostly she just looked pissed off.

"So, you're working for that woman," Gigi said again, as if telling herself enough times would finally hold the information in her memory. She stood in the center of the living room, which seemed to have acres of cream carpeting. I wiggled my toes into its warmth, admiring the room in spite of myself. Maybe I was just growing envious of other people's homes because I felt like I soon might be without one. I wanted to practically drop down and roll in the carpet. I would have, too, except I needed to massage Gigi Hatchmere's bruised feelings if I hoped to learn anything from her that might help Violet.

She stared down at my socks, which were slightly damp. I wondered if she worried they would leave dark stains in the carpet. I wondered, too, if it would be polite or rude to offer to take them off.

"Would you like something?" she said grudgingly. "I was going to open a bottle of wine."

"Anything's fine," I said affably.

"Well, come on in." She turned around a partition that left a twelve-inch gap at the ceiling into a kitchen decked out in dark brown granite and darker brown cabinetry. The appliances were trimmed with matching wood veneer panels. Gigi gestured to a solarium that ran along the south side of the house and opened into a garden. The room was basically a walkway with a sloped, windowed ceiling and glass walls that looked onto an inner atrium. Wet leaves lay limply against the overhead glass and I looked up at them as I walked along the solarium. An Asian-influenced buffet, ornately carved, sat at the end of the walkway. On a warmer day, the benches inside the atrium looked like they'd be a nice place to settle in and read a book or just commune with the foliage.

I wondered if Gigi meant for me to stay in the solarium, but as there was no place to sit, I decided she'd simply given me an invitation to look around.

I returned to the kitchen where Gigi had pulled out a bottle of cheap white wine. I know this because it's the kind I buy. She saw me glance at the label and said, "Daddy's estate's in probate. It's not like we have *any* money. Want something better, ask Violet."

Had I made a judgment call? I shrugged. "That's my brand."

"Poor you."

She scrounged around on a lower refrigerator shelf and found a plastic party tray with cubed cheese in varying flavors. It might have been opened for a while. Certain sections of the tray looked picked over. I checked my inner "yuk" meter and decided I didn't care. Free food and drink? That's an automatic yes. I have my priorities in line.

Though slightly lactose-intolerant, today I was willing to take a chance on the cheese and go for broke.

The crystal stemware was Waterford. When, and if, Gigi inherited, she would get some nice things.

"That's where Emmett found him," she said, inclining her head toward the solarium. "I thought you'd want to see."

"In the solarium?"

"Uh-huh. The tray was on the floor beside him. Violet didn't bother to wrap it, just put a ribbon on it. The ribbon was still on it."

"Was anyone else there, when Emmett found your father?" I asked as Gigi handed me a glass.

She eyed my hand, watching me like a hawk. Her expression revealed she was already regretting giving me the good stuff. "It's crystal. Don't break it. No, Emmett was alone."

"I'll be careful. That must have been hard."

"It was terrible!" She tossed back a gulp of her drink. She had all the finesse of a stevedore. Apparently the worry over the stemware only applied to me. "The whole thing was terrible. And it started out so great!"

"Tell me about it," I encouraged.

She gestured for me to sit down at the glass-topped kitchen table. I took a chair, which was molded white plastic and surprisingly comfortable.

"We got to Castellina around ten. That's where we were doing hair and makeup. It was just Deenie and me, and my hairdresser, of course—she did my makeup, too—but Melinda, my stepmother, stopped by and brought mimosas. It was so fabulous. Do you know Castellina?"

"I've heard of it."

"It means 'little castle' and it's just so pretty. It's owned by the Buganzi family, too, like Cahill Winery. It's kind of a package deal for weddings, if you want to go that way."

I nodded. Castellina was the Portland estate used as an entertainment venue by the Buganzi family who also owned Cahill Winery just outside the town of Dundee, in the center of Oregon's wine country. Before the Buganzi family purchased it, it was a rambling, slightly tired, turn-of-the-century old maven of Portland's West Hill's architectural scene. Buganzi razed the old home much to a horrendous outcry and a ton of city fees, as he did it gleefully and without permits. Then he built Castellina with its fairy-tale castle design. I'd only seen it from the outside, but people either gush and rave or roll their eyes and wail about its design. Nevertheless, it's become as popular a place for weddings and parties as Cahill Winery itself, which is about forty-five minutes from Castellina on a Saturday afternoon. Apparently Roland Hatchmere had reserved both venues for his daughter. I've heard Cahill produces a more than respectable Pinot Noir, but I've never put it to the taste test, its price being outside my budget.

"The weather was just beautiful. We didn't know how it would be, October and all, but it was just such a great day."

Gigi gulped again and topped off her glass. I chewed on a piece of cheddar and sipped. "I had this great dress, too. It's a Millie V.," she added in an aside, looking for my reaction. I had no idea who this designer might be, so I just nodded enthusiastically and sipped some more. I love wine for this reason. Not just drinking, but a whole host of social moves. I can drink and nod and it won't appear as if I have nothing to say.

"Anyway, everything was perfect. The veil was kind of sucky, actually, but I got rid of it pretty quick. We were having a great time with the mimosas. Melinda brought the champagne, and it was nicer than I expected of her. I mean, we don't *hate* her, but she's not our mother. She never let me have a drop before I turned twenty-one, so I just didn't think she had it in her."

"You're twenty-one now, right?"

"I turn twenty-two in April. Sean's twenty-four, but I've always seemed older than he is. I mean, he's a complete fuckup, but he is my brother. He used to buy for me before I was legal. We gotta look out for each other." She said this rotely, without emotion, as if she'd heard it somewhere and thought it might be a good time to trot it out.

"So, Melinda brought the champagne. And . . . Deenie . . . was with you?"

"Oh, Deenie's my maid of honor. We call her Deenie even though her name's Denise. Everybody does. I've known her since third grade. We were having such a good time. I tied my hair up in a chignon but it looked like shit. Had to rip it all out and let it be down. I almost made Shari cry, she was the hairdresser. How was I supposed to know she was so sensitive! God, it was my wedding. Anyway, we got it all straightened out."

"What about your mom?" I inserted casually. "Was she there?"

"Renee? No way. We don't get along that great. I mean,

"The Ferrari guy got real upset. Told my dad he was no
nd of man. They'd driven all the way here, they'd been in-
ed, well, Mom had, anyway. Who did he think he was?
ah, blah, blah. It was a real scene. If I'd been sober I would
ve been even more mad, but we were knocked out by those
lian punch drinks they serve there. They got Campari or
nething in them? Makes them red? We drank tons of
m. It was really the only way to get through that night,
ugh Daddy did make a nice toast to me." Fresh tears filled
eyes. "He said how I was his little girl."

smiled encouragingly, thinking that was pretty standard
f for the dads of brides.

Gigi stabbed a piece of cheese with one of the ruffled
hpicks, then twirled it thoughtfully around. I wondered
e was rethinking putting it in her mouth. "I was kinda
over in the morning, but by noon I was okay. The mi-
s sure helped."

lair of the dog," I said.

uh?"

rugged, not wanting to sidetrack her with an explana-
bout why more alcohol was supposed to cure a hang-
'm not sure I believe it anyway. Gigi went on, "I guess
till hoping Daddy would show and we'd get a few pic-
aybe after the ceremony. People started arriving. It
t awful. I mean, it was getting close to four. Where
We told the caterers to open the champagne, so we
rinking some more. We even called my mother then,
nd the Ferrari guy came right over."

ou try to call Violet?" I asked.

not stupid. Of course we did. She never picked

kind of moved around the grounds, staying out of
think they were embarrassed. Deenie and I were
nobody knew what to do. Finally, we had to say

she lives in Santa Monica and that's just fine. I love her.
She's my mom and all, but when Sean and I moved to Portland with Daddy, she just stayed there. I haven't lived with
her since I was a kid."

"But she came up for the wedding."

"Yes." Gigi's jaw tightened stubbornly. She didn't like
being directed. She wanted to tell the story her way and that
was that.

"So, you changed your hair and had mimosas with Deenie and your stepmother."

"Melinda. Deenie and I had a limo and we were going to
meet the other bridesmaids at Cahill for pictures at two.
Melinda had her own car, so we all drove off around one
o'clock. Deenie and I took a bottle of champagne in the limo.
We turned the music up really loud and we were singing. It
was *so* much fun."

She stopped short, remembering. I could see her face
start to squinch up and get blotchy. "So, we got there," she said,
her voice getting small and teary. "And everybody came for
pictures but Daddy. It was almost two o'clock. The photo-
grapher took some photos of me and Emmett, and then the
bridal party, but Daddy wasn't there!"

"Emmett's parents were there," I said, sensing she was
about to collapse into sobs.

"Uh-huh."

"And your mother?"

"Why do you keep saying that! *No!* She wasn't invited to
the wedding." Gigi looked like she wanted to throw her glass
at me.

"I thought she came up from Santa Monica," I answered,
confused.

"She was disinvited, okay? She *was* invited. But then she
was a bitch at the rehearsal dinner and she was disinvited.
Melinda was there and she was being nice so I figured she
could be in the pictures. I didn't care if she and Daddy

weren't living in the same house. They really love each other. In fact, they'd be back together if it weren't for Violet!"

"Okay," I said, hoping she'd calm down.

"Want another glass of wine?" she asked, sniffing.

"Sure."

I handed her my glass and she gave me a refill. It was kind of eerie the way she could throw a fit and then turn around and act like it didn't happen. Maybe she'd been drinking before I arrived, although it didn't seem like it.

"So, then . . . Daddy never showed at all. He wasn't answering his cell phone, either. Honestly, I was kinda mad. It was my wedding day!"

I shook my head in commiseration, trying to look properly upset for her.

"And then it was three o'clock! Three o'clock! Deenie and I were just crying, holding each other up. It was like . . ." She shook her head, her nostrils quivering with remembered hurt. "It was like he didn't care. We didn't know what was wrong. That's when we had to call my mother. Just in case she knew something."

I waited.

Gigi shrugged. "Okay, look, I don't like talking about my mother that much. It's no big deal. She just doesn't know how to act. The rehearsal dinner was a disaster. Big fight between Mom and Daddy, but then what did I expect? They've always been that way."

"They fought at your rehearsal dinner?"

Gigi gestured impatiently. "She brought up Violet in front of Melinda and me and everybody. Asked where Violet was. Why wasn't Violet there? Wasn't Daddy seeing Violet? It was all just to bug him. That's what my mother always does. You'd have to know her to understand. She's kind of self-involved," Gigi said with a straight face.

"Ah."

"We were all at Castellina for the rehearsal di a package deal—book the rehearsal dinner and preprep at Castellina, then go to the wedding ar at the winery and it was a much better price. Yc expensive weddings are? Daddy got really ups end. I mean, I thought Clarice, our wedding going to quit. It was *awful.* I really thought he throw something at her. And Enzo, our florist' he ever got paid.

"Anyway, Mom shows up at the rehearsal d brings a date that she didn't mention. Some hair and a Ferrari. Can you stand it? They Santa Monica together, but did she tell any o have a place for him. It was just rude.

"And then she started in about Violet. Me tervene. She's such an idiot sometimes. A 'Stay away from me, Mel,' real coldlike. N Melinda looked like she was going to cr says, 'He gets like this every time he star should know.'"

"Did Violet break up your parents' wondering if Renee still held a grudge

"Well . . . no." Gigi sounded disapp tell the truth. "They were split up a upset Mom when Daddy and Violet moved away from Los Angeles."

"Was there any thought of stayin time?"

"I don't know what this has muttered, looking away.

I took that as a no. "But it sov let for a lot of what happened ir

"Yeah, I guess."

I could tell I was losing G disinvited your mother to the

there was an accident and the wedding was postponed. Emmett's parents, Dave and Goldy, were upset." Her lips compressed, and she started to say something, then cut herself off. I got the feeling it might have been something not all that nice about Emmett's parents. She went on instead, "We didn't really believe something bad had happened to Daddy. Not then . . . but then Emmett found Daddy and called his dad. He didn't want to tell me over the phone." She swept in a breath. "It was David who told everyone Daddy'd been in an accident. He didn't tell me the truth until everyone had left."

I heard a car engine and looked through the window to see a dark blue Mercedes convertible pull into the driveway and park. Emmett Popparockskill climbed from the driver's seat, removing a pair of Ray-Bans. He glanced toward the heavens, but the rain had briefly abated and rays of sunlight stabbed downward through black-bottomed clouds. Emmett was lean and dark like Gigi, and I watched him run a hand slowly alongside his hair, then do it again, a narcissistic habit that said a lot about him. Then he tucked his hands together in that way golfers do, as if they have an actual club in their palms, swept his arms back and made a deep swing. He finished, arms upward, staring in the direction the "ball" had gone. His clothes were golfers' togs: tan chinos, collared black T-shirt with three-button placket.

"There were just a few of us at the end," Gigi went on distractedly. She, too, was watching Emmett's swing. "I remember Melinda making a point to try to be nice to my mom even though she'd been such a bitch the night before. Renee was really quiet. I think she was scared. Like she knew something really bad had happened. I guess we all knew, just didn't want to face it."

Emmett entered the house and Gigi suddenly broke into action, running to him, juggling her wine. She managed to keep from sloshing, but after planting a smack on his mouth, she slurped some more from her glass. Emmett regarded her with a look threaded with both indulgence and annoyance, as if she were a bratty child, which wasn't that far from the truth. "Watch the wine," he said.

"Oh, pooh. Let me get you a glass." Gigi twirled back into the kitchen and grabbed another Lismore. She filled it full, saw that the bottle was empty, and after placing the stemware in Emmett's somewhat reluctant hand, plucked a new bottle from the fridge.

Emmett clearly hadn't expected visitors and his expression was long-suffering.

I stuck out a hand. "Jane Kelly."

"Emmett Popparockskill."

What a mouthful. He shook my hand and it was a decent handshake.

"She's here 'cause I invited her," Gigi said quickly. I shot her a look, not sure if she was hiding my true agenda for reasons of her own or not. "Have some cheese."

Emmett popped a couple of squares of pepper jack into his mouth and started drinking with more enthusiasm. "I quit my job today," he said.

Gigi's mouth dropped open, then shut, then dropped open again. She looked like a beached fish. "What? *Why?*"

"We'll talk about it later." Which was couple-speak for "after the guest leaves."

But Gigi was having none of it. "How're we supposed to pay our bills? Oh my God. You're kidding, right?"

"It'll all be okay."

"Oh my God . . ."

"Nobody knows what they're doing there. The other salesmen don't know fuel injectors from wiper blades." He flicked a look my way. "I work—worked—at Miller-Kennedy, the Mercedes dealership. Mike Miller's my uncle and there is no Kennedy anymore."

"A family-owned business," I said politely.

"You got that right. My dad's the account manager."

Something about his tone suggested he thought his father wasn't much of an employee, either. I got the feeling Emmett thought the place would fall apart without him.

Gigi was going through a rapid thought process. "She's still there, I take it."

"Everybody's still there. Except me." He leaned over and gave her a quick kiss on the lips.

I wondered who "she" was. Emmett's mother?

"Well, you can't quit now, Emmett! My dad's estate isn't even close to being settled. We gotta wait."

"Too late. I walked. Mike was yelling and screaming. I think he scared two customers out of the showroom."

"You should have that dealership," Gigi stated flatly. "But Mike'll leave it to those morons, you know he will."

"His sons," Emmett said for my benefit.

"But you're the only one who knows anything. Y'see?" she said, turning to me. "And then there's Violet. She gets her family's money? And she's awful. It's just not fair. Unbelievable! She hit Daddy with that tray and killed him and it's like it never happened! Why haven't they arrested her?"

Emmett gave me an assessing look. "You know Violet?"

Gigi apparently decided to come clean, saying, "She's working for her," then proceeded to put her spin on my role in searching for Roland's murderer, making me sound like I was just using his death as a means to suck off some of Violet's money.

"Violet's paying me," I admitted. "She's fully aware that if I find out she's at fault, I'll turn her in."

He looked skeptical. "She's a liar," he told me.

"Daddy used to call her *Ultra*-Violet, like it was a pet name," Gigi revealed. "Made me want to puke! She always tried to be so nice to us. I never liked her. I just know she slithered back into Daddy's bed." She shivered all over. "They were probably screwing while I was supposed to be walking down the aisle." Her face was suffused with color.

"She killed him," Emmett said.

"I'd like some proof, before I go there," I said.

"She hit him with a silver tray in the head and he died. What I wonder is, why aren't the police doing their job? She should be in jail."

His sentiments and Gigi's were one and the same. "She says he was alive when she left."

"But she admits she hit him." Gigi pounced on that one. "Who says he was alive? Emmett's right. Violet is a liar!"

"Can you think of anyone else who might have a reason to want him dead?"

"Violet hit him," Gigi repeated stubbornly. "That's a fact."

"The Wedding Bandits were there, too," I reminded her.

"Who says? Violet?" Gigi crossed her arms over her chest. "She could have stolen those things."

"The police are pretty sure the bandits were interrupted." I didn't feel I needed to go over all the particulars. The fact that items had been scattered around the house and yard was well documented.

"I found the body," Emmett reminded me soberly. "I know the crime scene."

Gigi tossed her head. "I don't care what anybody says. Violet killed Daddy. I hope she goes to jail forever. I hate her." She turned to Emmett, her nose turning red, angry tears welling. "It's so awful!" Emmett cuddled her into his arms, but Gigi turned her head toward me, her cheek pressed up against his shirt. "You're going to find Daddy's killer?"

"I'm gonna try."

"Good luck." Emmett didn't sound convinced of my abilities and I didn't blame him. They thought I was wasting my time. Neither of them liked Violet. And both of them thought she was guilty.

Hell, she probably was.

CHAPTER FOUR

I spent the next several days making phone calls, going down the list Sean had given me, trying to connect, or reconnect as the case might be, with various wedding guests. Big Jim answered his phone straightaway and this time, when I told him Sean and Gigi had okayed talking to me, he became garrulous to the point of mind-screaming. And he had *nothing* to contribute. I finally laid my head down on my kitchen table, the phone to my ear, mumbling an occasional "Oh," "huh," and "I see." I was practically in a coma by the time he finally wound down. The other bridesmaids, groomsmen and assorted guests I reached couldn't offer any further information or insight, either, so I was left knowing little more than I had before. I never reached Deenie but I left her a message, and I put in another call to Dr. Wu's, where I was told rather curtly that Dr. Wu was out of the country, Ms. Kelly, and he would contact me when he returned.

I also phoned Melinda Hatchmere, Roland's widow, and Renee Hatchmere, Roland's first wife, asking each of them in turn to call me back. To date, neither of them had responded. At another impasse, I wrote up my billable hours for Violet and temporarily dusted my hands of the case.

Friday evening I joined Chuck and Officer Josh Newell for a ride-along expecting the evening to be an uneventful waste of time. I was right about the uneventful part; wrong about the waste of time. While I rode around in the police car I watched the reactions of the people who noticed our vehicle. It broke down pretty evenly: twenty-five percent looked stricken, as if they'd been caught in some nefarious act; twenty-five percent pretended they didn't see us—like, oh, sure, that's gonna help; twenty-five percent reacted as if the police were their good buddy-buddy, waving frantically and smiling and generally being the kind of brownnosing suck-ups that drive me crazy; and twenty-five percent acted cool and hard-eyed and tough, mostly teenagers whose smoldering demeanors were for their friends' benefits and caused Officer Newell to chuckle low in his throat.

For my part, I'm sure I would fall in the looking stricken category. I always feel guilty when dealing with the authorities. I kept quiet in the backseat while Chuck prattled on about how he'd always thought he was going to be a police officer but could never quite break away from his daddy's business, which, from the hints he broadly threw out, appeared to be quite lucrative and given Daddy's nearness to the brink of death, could be Chuck's business soon.

Listening to him, I congratulated myself in forcing a change of plans: I'd boged out of dinner. Yes, he'd offered free food at Foster's on the Lake, my most favorite restaurant around, but . . . again . . . it would be dinner with Chuck. I hadn't been able to picture myself enjoying a meal with him, with or without Julie and Jenny, as every impression I'd garnered of the man was that he was overbearing, loud and deaf to anything but his own plan. Sometimes a free meal isn't . . . well . . . free. I hadn't figured out how to squirm out of the ride-along, however, so I met him at the police station parking lot instead of Foster's. Chuck hadn't liked the idea but I'd been firm. Either skip dinner, or I was out altogether. Grudgingly, he'd agreed to the plan, so I'd parked my Volvo in the station lot next to various black-and-whites, feeling vaguely uneasy, as if I were in the middle of a criminal act. What does it say about me that merely being around police cars—even when they're parked in their own lot—makes me uncomfortable?

Anyway, I'd begged off dinner, saying I had to be somewhere later and though Chuck had pressed me, I'd managed to get things the way I wanted them. I was still planning to meet Jenny and Julie at Foster's, but much later. Chuck just didn't have to know.

"Hey, Jane," Chuck hollered now over his shoulder. "So, I was reading on AOL that sausages can be good for you. Ease stress." He leered through the grate that divided my seat from his and Josh's. "I can think how they ease stress. How about you?" His laughter came from behind his nose, a dirty, snorting toot.

Chuck is enough of an Oregon Duck fan to only wear green and yellow—a virulent combination that should be outlawed if it isn't game day. I realized, belatedly, that I only tolerate Chuck because he frequents the Coffee Nook. This is definitely not enough to form a friendship on. I thought about several responses, chief among them being "Shut up, asshole," and decided to smile tightly and keep my own counsel. If you can't think of something clever to say, don't say anything at all.

I'd read that article, too, as it happens, and it was about the *sound* of sizzling sausages being something comforting as we headed into winter with all its bleakness and cold. But I kept that information to myself, deciding I could play passive/aggressive with the big boys.

"You still meeting Jenny and Julie at Foster's?" Chuck tossed into the silence.

You would have to torture me for hours to make me give up that information to Chuck. I reminded him, "I've got business to take care of later. Can't meet them." Before he could press the issue, I said to Josh, "Somebody told me that their sister smashed her car into a tree, and the tree savior people arrived before the ambulance."

"Was your friend all right?" Josh asked.

"Concussion, I think. Tree had extensive damage. Might have had to be put down."

Josh said mildly, "I take it you don't agree with the city's tree ordinance."

"I just struggle with people who use the tree ordinance to further their own political agenda."

"Whaddaya mean?" Chuck asked.

"Like that neighborhood association that tried to stop the guy building that huge house on the lake? They tried everything to stop him. Used the tree ordinance as one means to delay. Had nothing to do with the trees themselves."

Chuck said, "Who cares? Let's go hang around the bars, see if we can give somebody a DUI."

"It's a little early," I pointed out.

"Hey, my friend Sonny got picked up at nine-thirty. Jesus, he blew like a .16. Shit hit the fan, I'll tell ya. Wife kicked him out and now he's got all these crappy classes where he has to say he's got a problem. My day, the cops caught you, they just drove you home."

I gazed at the back of Chuck's head. "You wanna bust somebody for DUI, but you're grousing about your friend's luck?"

"Sonny's a good guy."

Josh said to me, "Have you thought about joining your own neighborhood association? Then you'd have some say in the decisions. You could make a difference." He looked at me through the rearview mirror and I hoped my horror didn't show on my face.

"I may be moving," I said. Like, oh, sure. Me in the neighborhood association. I had a mental image of do-gooders of all ages, earnestness oozing from their pores. "And I'm a renter."

Chuck singsonged, "Bor—ing."

I decided that Chuck was right and changed the subject. But Josh regarded me thoughtfully in his rearview for the rest of our trip. I found this unnerving. It was lucky Chuck was so all about himself that he neglected to bring up that I was a private investigator. Somehow I didn't think that would go over well with Josh. Unless his sister Cheryl had already spilled the beans, which was highly probable the more I thought about it.

I said good-bye to them both at the Lake Chinook Police Station. Josh headed inside the building and I gazed after him. It wouldn't be a bad thing to know someone on the force, but he struck me as one of those by-the-book, ultra-sincere types that never seem to get me.

Chuck ambled over to his car, an even older Volvo than my wagon, a sedan in pretty decent condition. I'd just about written Chuck off, but now I thought I might have to reevaluate. Volvo drivers feel absurdly like kin to me. I might have to give him a second chance, but it wasn't going to be tonight.

After Chuck drove away, I ignored my own car and walked from the police station, which is on A Street to Foster's, which is on State, the street that runs parallel to the Willamette River. There's terminally difficult parking near Foster's, so I figured I wouldn't bother. It's not a long walk, but it was windy and chilly and I was shivering like a plague victim by the time I blew into the front bar. The back patio's closed this time of year, for obvious reasons, so I entered the low-ceilinged front room with its bloodred Naugahyde booths, cozy tables with flickering, votive candles and sunken bar at the west end. Patrons sit at room height around the bar, while the bartender and servers are working several steps below. This is because the bar is street height and the restaurant slopes down a half-level toward the rear dining room and patio, which are lake height. In February 1996 the greater Portland area flooded from a massive amount of rain. The Willamette River crested at the top of its banks, and Lake Chinook, which is fed by the Tualatin River, ran more than a few feet beyond its highest point, spilling water through the businesses that lined State Street and running across the road to damn near meet up with the river. Sandbags around the buildings saved them from devastating ruin, but from all accounts, it was one massive mess. Fortunately, Foster's was saved.

Julie and Jenny were in a booth near the pane windows that look onto State Street. Those windows have exterior white lights surrounding them all year and illuminate passersby, so Julie and Jenny had seen me coming. They waved at me and I realized Jeff Foster, owner of Foster's, was flirting outrageously with them. I pulled up a chair and asked for a Screaming Orgasm. Foster smiled at me and left.

"What's in a Screaming Orgasm?" Julie asked.

"Vodka, Bailey's and Kahlua. You need high-quality vodka or the Bailey's may curdle. We'll see what Foster brings." My days as a bartender serve me well from time to time.

Jenny said, "Oh my God, bring me two."

Jeff Foster served me up a Screaming Orgasm himself. No curdling. Unfortunately, he expected me to pay for the drink, which I grudgingly did. I let Jenny have a taste and she upped her order to three. I looked around for Manny, my favorite bartender, the one who sometimes comps me drinks when Foster isn't looking, but the bar was being tended by a young woman deep into eyeliner and red lipstick and a metro sexual guy whose shirt and hair were military perfect. A gas fire, faced with that layered narrow rock that is so popular it's everywhere, was heating the place up like an oven. It was cheery, though, and I felt myself relax in that bone-melting, apres-ski way that seems to only come from a combination of warmth and alcohol.

They wanted to know about my evening with Chuck and I gave them the pertinent details. Jenny finds Chuck funny in that I-can-enjoy-an-ass way, but I think he just gives Julie a headache though she's too polite to say so about a paying customer.

A group of men and women suddenly exited together. I overheard something about the civil war game between the two Lake Chinook high schools and I remembered my promise to Dwayne. "I'm going to have to go," I said regretfully, swigging down the end of my drink and standing.

"What? You just got here." Jenny pointed at my vacated chair. "Sit down."

"I've got a job to do."

"Oh, sure."

"I know it's hard to believe, but I really do."

"Then you have to give us the details Monday."

"I'll make a report with pie charts."

Jenny picked up one of her drinks. "How about I make a bar chart?"

"Jenny," Julie said with a laugh.

"I'm counting on it." I sketched them both a good-bye and took off. If Dwayne wanted me to infiltrate the high school group at Do Not Enter, I was going to have to figure out who they were. All Dwayne had been able to give me was a description of one car—a tomato-red Taurus—which he thought one of the Wilson girls drove. The guys all showed in black macho SUVs or BMWs or something of that ilk. Dwayne had been able to catch part of one of the SUVs' vanity license plates through the mask of bushes and trees that hid the drive access to the construction. DOIN had been visible.

Tonight's game was at Lake Chinook High's football field

and I saw the stadium lights long before I encountered the tons of cars parked for a good half mile all around. There's a small war going on between the nearby residents and the school about those lights. The residents scream light pollution and general blinding annoyance; the school is relatively mum but I've heard grumblings from athletically minded kids' parents, the gist of which is: what part of living next to a football field didn't you get when you moved in?

I couldn't remember the last time I'd been to a high school football game. Had I *ever*, since high school? Even then I'd steered clear of the jocks as a rule. Their obsessive dedication to sports worried me, like there was nothing else on the planet that mattered. Not that I'd been any kind of role model. I'd spent most of my time wondering how my twin brother, Booth, could ace tests when I worked harder than he did and only managed to cough up a B. I learned much later that he had phenomenal retention, which only goes to show you how unfair nature is. I mean, why should Booth get that attribute? He also got the great hair.

But I got the snarky attitude, sense of irony and excruciating self-awareness, so we're probably even.

I cruised around the cars in the stadium lot and found four possibles on the tomato-colored cars, but only one of them was a Taurus. I memorized the license plate. My retention might not be as stellar as Booth's, but I'm not a complete slouch, either. There were simply too many black cars to check them out one by one, so I left that for later.

I headed into the game, which was nearly over, and so therefore no one was at the gate, asking for my ticket. Lake Chinook was ahead of Lakeshore High and there was much discussion about some highly disputed call that had the Lakeshore fans growling and booing. I ordered a hot dog and was pleased that it was cheap and hot. I really could have used a beer, but it wasn't on the menu and there were a whole lot of Don't Drink and Drive ads plastered about.

There were also some warnings about the evils of underage drinking.

In the end Lake Chinook High beat Lakeshore by a field goal with seconds left. The Lake Chinook fans ran out onto the field and the Lakeshore fans left quietly or with suppressed rage. The referees were escorted off the field by a burly-looking group of men in black rain gear. Some kid named Keegan had played "flawlessly, just flawlessly!" and there was speculation about a girl on the dance team who seemed to have either (a) an anorexia problem; (b) an obsessive/compulsive disorder; or (c) was top student in the Talented and Gifted program—TAG. She might have been all three. I wasn't paying close enough attention.

I moved back toward the tomato-red Taurus and pretended to be talking on my cell phone as I watched the crowd surge into the parking lot. My own car was a couple of rows over, close to the road, so I stood on the balls of my feet, ready to sprint to it as soon as I got a visual on whoever claimed the car.

It was a high school girl who'd done up her long hair in pigtails on either side of her head, one tied with a blue ribbon, one tied with a white ribbon, Lake Chinook High's colors. She was with two friends, a boy and a girl. The girlfriend was hanging on the boy and giggling. I suspected alcohol might be the culprit, regardless of the warning signage. The boy was grinning like a goofball, one hand around girlfriend's waist, though it was sitting a little low on her hip. They all wore blue jeans and hooded light blue sweatshirts monogrammed with a big white L. The driver of the Taurus wasn't near as giddy as her two friends. In fact, her eyes looked big and solemn and though she tried to smile in response to the friends' antics, there was no joy anywhere. Her mouth wanted to be an upside down U. I figured she was one of the Wilson sisters, but I wasn't sure which one. I was going to have to learn their names.

I was sprinting for my car when I nearly ran down a group from Lakeshore who were hauling a large box of sweatshirts and caps to a waiting black Hummer. "Hey," I said, slowing to a stop. "Can I buy one of those?"

"I guess so," one of the guys slamming the box into the back of the car said. He looked unsure.

"How much?" I pressed.

"Umm . . . I dunno. The sweatshirts are fifteen, I think."

"Thirty," a prim, female voice corrected him, shooting him a glare. "Jesus, Carl, why don't you give 'em away for free?"

"Thirty?" I rued the fact that I'd had to purchase my drink at Foster's on the Lake. Damn. I didn't think I had the cash. "Any chance on a discount?"

The girl made a face. "They'd be worth more if we'd won. They're going on sale next week anyway. I guess I could sell one to you for twenty," she said reluctantly.

I quickly pulled out the cash and forked it over. As soon as I had my prize I dragged it over my head, running the rest of the way to my car. This sweatshirt was navy blue with a red and white sailboat over the left breast, Lakeshore's colors.

I was barely behind the wheel when the Taurus whizzed by, traveling fast toward Lake Chinook proper. I had to jockey the wagon as I'd been boxed in pretty tightly, but my turning radius is about the best thing on my car and I was after the Taurus in less than a minute. I had to push the speed limit, which is dangerous in the heavily patrolled area around Lake Chinook. I swear to God they've got more traffic cops per square mile than's legal.

I caught up with the Taurus in the center of town. At this particular intersection two lanes are forced to turn south, so I pulled up right next to the car, both of us ready to make the turn, and slid a sideways look at them. They were on my left side and the girlfriend was in the passenger seat. Her boyfriend was in the back, leaning forward, his head between the bucket seats. The driver's eyes were on the road. She was disengaged from the goings-on, but her friends either didn't notice or didn't care.

To my good, and bad, luck, they drove all the way around Lakewood Bay and took the turn off on Beachlake Drive. I was pretty sure this was the road across the bay from Dwayne's cabana. I didn't follow them onto Beachlake as the road's kind of a boxed canyon, and I didn't want to have to turn around where they could see me. Also, I wanted some time to pass to allow the members of the football team to join the party. I kept on going up McVey, then parked in a deserted parking lot. Nearly an hour later, I drove down Beachlake and past the houses in Dwayne's sights, trying to figure out which was which from this view. It's surprisingly hard to tell. The lakeside view is vastly different than the street-facing facades. However, Do Not Enter was easy, the entry staked out by a temporary electrical pole and a Honey-pot Porta Potti. From there I could count back and match the lakeside view to the street frontage. I should've paid more attention to the house colors, but I got it figured out in the end.

I saw taillights winking red down the lane to Do Not Enter's construction site and could just make out the house's plywood and black Visqueen covered roof. A black Jimmy with the license plate DOINOU sat cheek to jowl with the red Taurus. It took me a moment; then I got it. The license plate was an abbreviated acronym for Do I know You?

Hmmm.

I didn't think I could crash the party. I wasn't exactly sure what to do. I parked the Volvo down Beachlake a ways, hoping I wouldn't get rear-ended or sideswiped as there wasn't much of a shoulder, then walked back. I had this nebulous plan about acting like I was a senior at Lakeshore. Would the fact that I was their rival eject me from the group? I knew better than to try to pretend I attended Lake Chinook High. And what if they asked me why I looked so old?

With that in mind, I pulled my hair into two pigtails like the Wilson girl, one on either side of my head. I didn't dare look in a mirror because I was afraid I'd scare myself. I didn't have any cute bows to add to the "look," but I didn't think it would matter. I put my cell phone on vibrate, slung my purse strap over my shoulder, then walked from my car to the party. Another car pulled into the drive as I approached, and a young guy glanced out his window at me. I smiled shyly and waved and he slowed to a stop and rolled down the window.

"You guys played good tonight," he said, checking out my sweatshirt. "Just not good enough." He grinned.

"Well, you know, Keegan was just so great."

"Yeah, he is. Surprised you guys don't hate his guts."

So Keegan was on the Lake Chinook High team. I hadn't been sure. "Well, you know," I said with a shrug of my shoulders.

"You here with anybody?"

"Nah . . . I . . ." I looked down the road. "My best friend and her boyfriend are fighting, and I kinda wanted out of the car. I've been walking around." I shrugged a bit woefully. "Maybe they forgot me."

"Where do you live?"

"Actually, I don't go to Lakeshore. I'm just staying with my dad," I improvised, waving toward the north. "Just got the sweatshirt for fun." This was a better idea all the way around. Sometimes I awe myself with my inspired lying.

"Hey, well . . ." He looked down the drive. "We got a party going. What school you go to?"

"Sunset," I said, pulling out the name of a Beaverton high school.

He was already past that and onto other things. "Well, get

in. I'm not a psycho. Or you can walk down the driveway but it's wet."

"I'll get in," I said, heading around the front of his car and climbing into the passenger seat. I don't carry a gun and I'm kind of a wimp, but I'd picked up a rock on the way and my fist closed around it inside the pocket of my sweatshirt. My first instinct is always to flee, but if someone attacks me I'm going to come out swinging. This kid looked like he weighed about a hundred pounds. I thought I had a good chance.

But he simply drove me down a long, curving gravel driveway that opened up in front of the construction zone. Several cars were angled around. We parked next to the red Taurus. I climbed out as another car pulled up behind us. I could see that pretty soon there would be no backing out unless the cars behind moved first. It was interesting, however, as I saw no one parked behind DOINOU. "Who's got the Jimmy?" I asked my friend.

"Keegan. Of course." He smiled. "Don't want to piss him off."

"Guess not," I said.

"I'm Brett."

"Ronnie. Short for Veronica."

We shook hands. I have this alias I trot out whenever I can, Veronica Kellogg. I know it's best to use an alias similar to your own name so you respond to it correctly, and I did all right with the Kellogg part—not too far from Kelly. But Veronica is nothing like Jane and I don't care. So sue me. I like Veronica.

I could tell Brett was warming to me. I wondered what his social status was, and why he seemed so eager to include me. Maybe it's that I'm older and have a strong sense of self-preservation, something missing during the teen years, but I never include people into my life so quickly. Maybe I would've in high school, but looking back, I don't think so. I'm just naturally suspicious.

Or maybe he was one of the guys Dwayne wanted to nail. Maybe his affability was all an act.

The car behind us unloaded five kids and they tromped up to us, loudly reliving the game, loving the fact they'd beaten Lakeshore. Spying my sweatshirt, they all had something to say to me, mostly about how Lakeshore sucked and Lake Chinook was the best, all the while eyeing me as if, as the enemy, I might suddenly whistle to a hidden army and take them out in a giant, bloody melee.

Brett explained how I was visiting my dad and that I'd just picked up a Lakeshore sweatshirt for fun. One of the guys, Glen, long-haired and kinda dopey looking, instantly stripped off his Lake Chinook sweatshirt and handed it to me. It was about two sizes too big, but he insisted I wear it. I traded my Lakeshore one for it and was horrified to watch the group of them drag it through the mud puddles surrounding Do Not Enter until it was crusted with brown goop; then Glen balled it up and hurled it skyward where it unfurled to catch in a thin overhead limb of a bare-leafed maple. The group of them all saluted it with their middle fingers, stumbling around. I figured they'd been imbibing awhile. I was burning inwardly. I'd paid good money for that shirt and now I had Glen's castoff, the arms of which hung to my knees. I scrunched them up and pretended to think it was a great joke. If Glen thought he was getting his shirt back, he could damn well think again.

It turned out most of the kids normally wouldn't be caught dead in school rah-rah gear, but on game day anything went. The rule wasn't that much different from when I was in school. Half of them wore the light blue and white colors of their school; half were in black and denim, the tacit colors of general teen acceptance. They also were about the only two colors that were safe for outdoor use in rainy Oregon weather. Forest green and navy can work, too, but tonight the kids were all about black jackets and jeans.

I picked Keegan out without any trouble. He sat on a tree stump someone had hauled inside the house, situated at the end of the room. This would be either Do Not Enter's living room or great room. A string of red lights wrapped around the two-by-fours that made up the wall behind him. I could see the heavy-duty extension cord they'd jerry-rigged to the temporary power pole located at the far end of the drive. Must have been sixty feet long. A half rack of beer was being watched like a hawk by a thin boy with lank, dark hair that fell in his face. He looked out of the locks with a grim, dark-eyed stare. I had to fight the urge to tuck the strands behind his ears. It made me keep wiping imaginary strands of hair from my own face.

Keegan wore a black jacket over a black shirt, thick denim trousers and work boots. The other kids wore work boots, too. This appeared to be a fashion statement as I doubted any of them had jobs in the great outdoors or anywhere else. Keegan was coolly smoking, dragging smoke into his lungs, then dropping his arm to lazily flick ash onto Do Not Enter's plywood floor. Bad form all around, especially for QB One. I wondered what transpired on Monday mornings when the construction workers came on the job and found the evidence.

That question was answered when a subservient female minion made it her job to clean up after Keegan and the others whenever they were involved in other pursuits. She kept darting in to clean up or disguise the evidence, rubbing mud over the ash, picking up cigarette butts and empty bottles or cans. Very interesting caste system they had going. The men—at least some of them—were the rulers. Like Dwayne, I found the guys in charge disturbing. A better-than-thou attitude percolated from Keegan on down, and it felt like there was some big secret, some inner joke, that escaped the rest of us but fueled the amusement of the elite guys at the top of the pyramid.

I didn't like it one bit.

The talk centered on the game. The Keegan worshipers kept bringing up his best plays. I learned his last name was Lendenhal and that he'd broken a few school football records already and was expected to break them all.

"You want a beer?" Brett asked me. He'd settled us to one corner, cross-legged on the cold plywood, then gone in search of refreshments. Now he handed me a can of Bud, which I opened and sipped at, wondering how many laws I was breaking by drinking with a slew of minors. I hadn't bought them the stuff, but I thought that might be a technicality if we were raided. I got a shiver all over as I pictured Officer Newell's frowning face, and could practically hear him saying, "I'm disappointed in you, Jane Kelly," right before he cuffed me and hauled my ass off to the Clackamas County Jail.

I suspected claiming I was working undercover wouldn't cut it.

The answer, then, was to not get caught. To that end I searched the faces of the knots of kids, hoping to find the driver of the Taurus. She didn't seem to be in the "house." I thought she might be on the grounds, maybe down by the lakeshore. There was a stairway leading to the basement, which was an OSHA nightmare—no rails, rickety boards slammed up by a carpenter to gain basic access, no lighting—but my bigger problem was how to extract myself from Brett. Because he'd introduced me to the group I was apparently now officially his.

To underscore this, Brett slipped an arm over my left shoulder, his hand and arm hanging over loosely. Golly, gee whiz, it looked like we were on the verge of being a couple, at least for the evening.

"So, you go to Lake Chinook High," I said, feeling the need for conversation. "What grade are you in?"

"I'm a junior," he said, belching loudly. He really threw

himself into it, in fact, and as soon as it was heard, it started a volley of belching from all the strutting roosters.

"Shut the fuck up," Keegan said without heat, and the immediate silence was deafening.

"So, you're seventeen?" I asked. Great. Just great. He wasn't even an adult.

"Just about. Next February. How about you?"

Sixteen. My heart sank. "A senior," I murmured.

"You eighteen?" he asked.

"Yep."

"I thought you looked older."

"Yeah?"

"Just something about you," he said. He tilted his head and gazed at me thoughtfully. "You seem . . . wise."

"Huh." I inclined my head toward the stairs. "Wanna go down to the lake?"

"Brrrr. No. Much better here."

"I'm kind of ready to take a walk," I said, easing from beneath his arm. The damn thing was like a lead weight.

"Oh, come on," he said grouchily, trying to struggle to his feet.

"I'll be right back," I promised, easing away.

He let me go but he didn't look happy. It didn't seem like many of the girls argued with these guys. I couldn't get it. What did they see in them? Most of them were the kind of guy I've avoided my entire life: self-important, narcissistic, nefarious and self-serving. I sensed it in that age-old way men and women have possessed since the beginning of time. I wasn't safe here. Brett might not be one of the true baddies, but if mob mentality prevailed, he would side with Keegan. I had no doubt.

I felt my way down the stairs and through the hazards of the lower level of construction. Chunks of wood had been tossed around. Lots of nail heads showed on the subfloor, dark spots visible in the uncertain red light that glowed through cracks from the upper floor. The only other illumination was from a three-quarter moon fighting off fast-moving clouds.

As I stepped onto the back grounds I listened to the low moaning of wind through nearby trees, the soft lap of water against the shore and the metallic clang of a flagpole's tethering chain. I glanced over to the Pilarmos' yard. They not only possessed a wolf dog and a menagerie of plastic lawn ornaments, they proudly displayed the Italian flag, now fluttering madly in the stiff night breeze. Either the flag was a new addition, or, more likely, I hadn't paid near enough attention while looking through Dwayne's binoculars. It occurred to me I'd focused way too much attention on Tab A and Slot B, but then, there was a lot to see there.

Three figures stood at the water's edge. The three friends from the Taurus, I determined, as I walked toward them. I kept about thirty feet between us; didn't want them to think I was horning in. But the girlfriend and guy were still all over each other. She of the giggles, he of the roving hands. Both hands were beneath her sweatshirt as he gave her a series of kisses on her mouth, cheeks and neck. She just kept right on giggling.

The other girl kept moving away from them. She was about as far as she could go, nearly pressed up against Social Security's chain-link fence. I gave a glance over to their house. A yellow outdoor light was the only sign of human habitation. The place could have been abandoned for all the life it showed.

I was still trying to figure out how to start a conversation when the kissing couple bumped into their friend, nearly knocking her off her feet. She caught herself before she slipped, said, "God, you guys. Stop it," then huffed around to my side.

Giggler singsonged, "Sorreee . . ."

The boy was too busy rubbing himself against her as best

he could to bother with a response. He was going to get as much body contact as he could before she shut him down, though she didn't seem even close to that yet.

Now the Taurus driver was only about five feet from me. I looked from her to the struggling couple. "They could fall right into the lake," I observed.

"I wish to God they would," she said with feeling. "Judd is such a horndog."

"She doesn't seem to mind."

"Glory? Oh, she's just being stupid. She never goes all the way, though. I mean, she's not in love or anything," she added quickly.

"I'm Ronnie," I introduced.

"Hi." She'd been studying Glory and Judd, but now she shot me a quick look. "I'm Dawn."

"You go to Lake Chinook?"

"Yeah. Oh yeah." She gazed at my Lake Chinook sweat-shirt. "You don't, though, do you?"

"Sunset," I said. "A senior."

"Oh. I'm a sophomore." She shivered and pressed her chin into her neck, hunching her shoulders. "Where'd you get the sweatshirt?"

"A guy named Glen." I told her about my Lakeshore one in the trees and how it had gotten there.

"Glen's a big dummy, but he's okay." She sniffed. "God, it's cold."

"I know. I gotta go home and get warm."

"Me, too, but I'll never get my car out."

"You need a ride?"

"No, I live just down the street. I shoulda parked at the house, but my parents get all weird when I come home just to leave again. So I'm stuck. Unless I get a chance to talk to Keegan." She glanced over her shoulder to the partially fin-ished structure. I couldn't read whether talking to Keegan might be a good thing or a bad.

"What'll Keegan do?"

"Get 'em to move their cars. But it's kinda early. I don't know. I gotta be home by midnight, though."

"It's after eleven," I pointed out.

"Yeah, well . . ."

Glory and Judd stumbled and fell, not into the water, into the mud. Glory started shrieking for all she was worth and Judd shushed her loudly. "You'll wake the fucking neighbors!" he yelled.

Dawn ran over to them and motioned them both to be quiet. Glory was good and steamed about ruining her coat. Judd wanted to pick up where they'd left off, but Glory was over it. She came whining and swearing to Dawn, who immediately went into girl-protection mode.

My chance to really talk to Dawn was over. It had been unlikely she would confide her problems to me on first meeting anyway. I'd made contact and that was as far as it was going to go.

They headed for the stairs and I trooped up behind them. As I reentered the main room I saw that Brett had lopped his arm over another girl's shoulder. She'd leaned her head into his chest. Some of the other kids were coupled up as well. There was a tight group of young women near one wall. To a girl they'd either taken off their sweatshirts or unbuttoned their black coats. Their backs were arched, their breasts projecting like arrows. All they needed was a "Touch me here" sign. Their collective attention rested on Keegan Lendenhal, who tortured them with the way he alternately sent them knowing looks, or ignored them completely. I felt his intense gaze skim over my body as if he were an MRI machine. I was mapped out and catalogued so fast it almost gave me a rush. Wow. This guy knew how to ratchet up the heat.

His teen magnetism was both scary and off-putting, but by God I *felt* it. I wondered who his parents were. If I were a religious person I might pray for them. This kid was serious trouble in a way I had yet to define, even to myself.

Judd, spurned, walked toward Keegan and said something in an aside. Keegan shot a look at Glory, who was still fighting tears over the ruination of her clothes. He reached inside his pocket and handed something to Judd. A packet? Drugs?

"Hey, you," Keegan said suddenly.

He was looking right at me. My heart squeezed. Did he know I'd been watching?

I pretended not to know he was addressing me. Instead I smiled at Brett, waved and said, "Gotta go. Thanks."

Brett gazed from me to Keegan, clearly unsure how to react. The girl he was with was now sprawled across his lap but his attention wasn't on her.

I headed down the plank that led from the front door to the ground, glanced up at the sweatshirt in the tree, then hurried away. I didn't look back until I was down the lane, nearly to the power pole. When I did, I saw that Keegan Lendenhal was standing in the open doorway, staring in my direction. Could he see me through the dark, from this distance? Impossible.

But I had the uncomfortable feeling he saw a whole lot more than I wanted to portray.

CHAPTER FIVE

The following day was Saturday and I slept in, The Binkster curled up beside me. It's okay when her back's facing me, but when she flips over she hits me with those doggy claws, pushing off me as if she's heading for a springboard dive. Painful. I have to keep turning her around and adjusting her. It takes way too much energy for a bedmate. Sometimes I settle her back in her bed on the floor to which she gives me the dejected, unfurled tail. She can make me feel like a heel, but sleep is all important to me, so tough.

I'd had one of those nights where thoughts tumble and tumble around inside your skull, seemingly mega-important, yet fade away when true consciousness hits. What I recalled mostly was the impression that I needed to put Violet's feet to the fire about her relationship with Roland. Her "I didn't kill him" mantra was all fine and good, but wasn't exactly helping me move forward. I needed background. Details. If she wanted me to believe in her, I needed some insight into Roland and who else might have killed him.

Which reminded me . . . what about the Wedding Bandits? Where did they fit in? And how could I get the police to share more information on them? During their previous burglaries the bandits had apparently never encountered anyone. There had been no physical harm. Their m.o. was get in and get out fast. It didn't really jibe that they might stop and whack Roland with Violet's gift. More likely, they'd found him already dead or dying and had run from the scene, dropping some of their loot. One report had mentioned one of the gifts dropped in the yard—the candy dish within the box in smithereens.

What are smithereens? I asked myself as I brushed my teeth, staring at my image in the mirror. Straight wet hair, hazel eyes, my purple toothbrush stuck in my cheek. I pulled it out and looked at it. Maybe it was amethyst, I thought with an inward snort.

Binkster sat on the bath mat, staring up at me. "Doesn't that hurt your neck?" I asked her. She cocked her head from side to side. She actually doesn't have much of a neck. Pretty much her head connects with her shoulders, and her collar disappears beneath a thick, furry roll.

She's on low-cal dog chow, but she can hang on to weight better than my aunt Ginger and that's saying something.

In the kitchen I opened the refrigerator door. Sometimes I surprise myself, forgetting that I've actually taken a trip to the store and purchased groceries. Today there was no surprise. All I discovered was a bag of Coffee Nook Black Satin blend, freebie little buckets of cream I'd helped myself to at Mook's, a local burger place that also serves breakfast, the heel of a loaf of wheat bread, carefully wrapped in its plastic packaging, a sprig of mint and a quart of lemonade from a powdered mix.

I could have a heel of bread, a cup of coffee with cream and a glass of pseudolemonade made pretty with mint leaves. Sounded like a feast, so I started up the coffeemaker.

Binkster eyed me carefully, but when I didn't immediately scoop dog chow into her bowl she toddled outside to do a perimeter check and her morning ablutions.

"That grocery shopping thing," I said to her when she returned. "It's way hard."

Binkster looked in her bowl, then up at me. I filled up the bottom with kiblets. She inhaled them and licked the sides of the bowl with her tongue. Feeling guilty, I let her snuffle up the crumbs off the plate that had housed my piece of bread.

We finished breakfast, both slightly dissatisfied.

I decided to take Binkster over to Dwayne's and let them keep each other company for the day. On my way I gave Violet a call on my cell, but I was forced to leave a message on hers, asking that we meet later in the day. She might or might not get back to me right away. She's even worse than I am about answering cell calls in a timely manner. I'm normally pretty good, but if you're not immediately important to me, I'm not so good. I get pissed off, however, when I'm treated the same way. Ergo, I was already a little pissed at Violet.

It was raining when we left, pouring actually, and my wipers were having a hell of a time keeping up. I'd thrown on my windbreaker and left the hood up, which was a little like wearing blinders. Plays hell with the peripheral vision.

I pulled up next to Dwayne's truck. The cabana boasts a one-car garage and that's where Dwayne stores his nondescript tan sedan, the one he uses for surveillance jobs and any time he wants to travel incognito. The truck, his usual mode of transportation, was therefore relegated to the parking pad and today it was getting drenched in rain.

I let myself in and Binkster tore through the cabana to the opening in the sliding glass door and out to the dock. I hadn't expected Dwayne to be outside in the rain, but he'd pulled over the green canvas umbrella normally used for his four-person outdoor table and placed it over his chair. His cowboy boots were taking the brunt of the rain, but the rest of him was dry. And he had the binoculars pressed to his eyes.

"Hey," he said in greeting, dragging squiggling Binkster onto his lap.

One house over from Dwayne a medium-sized black and white dog with a long snout started barking. It was standing beneath the back door overhang. Called to arms, Binks looked over at it and started barking and growling back. I couldn't tell if they were saying "happy to meetcha" or "get the fuck outta here." Coulda been either.

The owner of the black and white dog stepped out and grabbed it by its collar, dragging it back inside and slamming the door. Binkster gave a few more barks, delighted that she'd scared it off, apparently. A few muffled woofs sounded back. Binkster looked at Dwayne for approval and he petted her head. She then splayed herself across his stomach, about the only way she could balance herself on Dwayne and the chair. I stayed just inside the gap in Dwayne's slider door, my nose and face catching the brunt of the moisture.

"So, I made contact with your friends across the bay last night."

Dwayne lowered the binoculars and looked at me. "And?"

"I didn't learn if the girl from Rebel Yell is pregnant. Her name's Dawn Wilson, by the way. I didn't see any sister, but I think she might be the younger one. She was driving the red Taurus."

"What's she look like?"

I described Dawn as best I could: five-four, short, dark hair; serious expression.

"She's the younger one," Dwayne confirmed, frowning a bit. "Her older sister has longer hair. How'd she seem?"

"Like a high school kid." I shrugged. "I don't know."

"What about the guys?"

I made a face, then told him about my impressions and escapades of the night before. I tried not to completely give away my feelings about Keegan Lendenhal, but Dwayne picked up on them anyway.

"You think Lendenhal's a dealer?"

"I don't know," I admitted. "This kid's the quarterback and apparently a hell of an athlete and it's hard to believe he'd risk all that, you know?"

"People do stupid things."

"It just didn't feel like drugs. I'm no expert but nobody seemed totally wasted. They were drinking beer. They were making out. It was more like I remember high school parties, but . . . I don't know. Something was off. I didn't like it. And I didn't like him."

"He's the man," Dwayne said, dropping the binoculars to give me a look.

"He's a pain in the ass."

"You think he's screwing the girls?"

"Yep."

"One girl . . . a girlfriend? Or many?"

"More than one," I said, although I didn't have evidence to that effect. "The guys get the beer and cigarettes, or whatever else he wants, and they all go to Do Not Enter after the games and they bow to the king."

"He's Lake Chinook High's quarterback?"

"Uh-huh."

"Think we should alert the cops?" Dwayne asked.

"Maybe. I don't know. Makes me feel like a rat." I stepped into the rain and let it pour onto the top of my hood. I'm not good at turning people in for what I consider minor crimes. Was there something more than teen partying going on at Do Not Enter? Or had that been a product of my overactive imagination, brought on by both Dwayne's description of the guys and a need to put an egotistical teen in his place?

I deliberately changed the subject. "I've called a number of the guests on Sean's list. Waiting for some callbacks. Nobody seems to be able to pick up the phone. And Violet's holding out on us. She's not being entirely truthful about her relationship with Roland. Probably thinks we'll start thinking she's guilty."

Dwayne didn't respond. He was petting Binkster and staring into the middle distance.

"You're not listening," I accused.

"Yes, I am."

He was making me crazy. I ran my hands through my hair in an effort to buy time and keep myself sane, then said, "And what about the Wedding Bandits? We haven't heard anything in weeks. Nothing on the news. What do you think's going on?"

"There hasn't been a high-profile burglary since Roland Hatchmere."

"Not one? How do you know?"

"Larrabee."

"Larrabee just hands out this information to you?" I asked the back of Dwayne's cowboy hat. "What's the deal with you and him?"

"Let's go inside," Dwayne said. He set Binkster on the ground, then levered himself to his full height. I never know quite whether to offer help, unless the sky's raining hail. He didn't seem to need me, so I squeezed back through the gap and he and Binkster followed me inside. Binks jumped onto the couch and I scolded her for her wet, dirty feet, but Dwayne waved the issue aside. "I'll have the cleaning people take care of it."

"The cleaning people. Who are they? Slaves you keep in the attic?" I knew he didn't have "cleaning people."

"The lady next door, Mrs. Jansen, decided to sic her maid, Darlene, on me. Darlene needs more work. Something about her kids moving back home and bringing their kids with them. Sounded grim."

"This is altruism on your part?"

"I do what I can."

"Bullshit."

Dwayne smiled. It's a lazy smile, guaranteed to melt female hearts, but it's not just for show. It represents real amusement on his part. "The woman needs a job. She comes in every other week or so. Sometimes more. You looking for help?"

"Always. I just can't afford it."

Dwayne let that pass. "Speaking of the attic. What do you think about making it an office?"

"For midgets?"

Dwayne's attic is accessible only by an outside stairway, and as I've said before, it's not exactly adult-friendly. The few times I've been up there, shoving boxes around, looking for past data, I've been lucky I didn't concuss myself on the rafters.

"I'll bring the walls in, so there's some headroom. Make it smaller but more functional."

"You think about a lot of things when you're sitting on your dock."

"Not much else to do. When Ogilvy kicks you out, you can move upstairs for a while."

"No bathroom? I don't think so. Stop depressing me."

"Got a timeline on that?"

"No. I don't want to think about it."

"I know a mortgage broker—"

"*No*. What is this? I don't have the money. I'd have to rob a bank. Or maybe I'll join the Wedding Bandits and sell stolen toaster ovens, wine refrigerators and food processors. Make a fortune."

"Let's buy it together."

"I *can't*, Dwayne."

"Can't and won't have two different meanings," he said.

I clapped my hand to my forehead. "Wow. I was really confused until now. Thanks for explaining that. *Can't* isn't the same as *won't* . . ."

He crossed his arms over his chest and waited, faintly amused. It really torques me when he won't rise to the bait.

"Let's get back to Detective Larrabee. Bring me up to speed," I said.

"Larrabee's helped me out a time or two. I've done the same for him. He knows we've been hired by Violet, so he's been careful about the Hatchmere case. But we exchange information. Have for years."

"Huh . . ." I said.

Dwayne shrugged lightly. "Sometimes he needs something I can get for him."

"You mean something outside of the law. Not strictly legal."

"I'm a law-abiding citizen, Jane."

I snorted. Strictly speaking, Dwayne was. But neither one of us stood on ceremony if a more effective, quasi-unlawful means to further our ends presented itself.

"Larrabee's steered me in the right direction a time or two when I've needed it. And I've procured information for him."

"He's on the Hatchmere case, and that entails the Wedding Bandits?"

"Inside the Portland PD there aren't specific departments for crimes like burglary and robbery. Larrabee sometimes works cases besides homicide, anyway."

This I know, as Booth, my twin brother, works for the Portland police and has been trying to work his way up to detective. I hadn't heard from him in a few weeks and figured he was hard at it. That, and/or taking care of his fiancée: black, beautiful, high-powered, high-maintenance criminal defense attorney Sharona Williams.

"So, Larrabee told you there's been no bandit activity since Roland?" I asked.

"Says they're lying low. Probably scared shitless. They came into the place, scattered through the house, grabbing gifts, money, electronics. Then somebody stumbled over the body, sounded the alarm and they were outta there."

"No one believes they're responsible for Hatchmere's death?"

"Not so far as I can tell," Dwayne agreed.

"So we're back to Violet."

I half expected Dwayne to argue with me, but all he asked was, "Have you called her?"

"Left a message."

Dwayne was looking at me, so I phoned her again. This time she answered on the second ring, surprising me.

"Violet, it's Jane. Can we meet today? I stopped by Gigi's, well, Roland's, the other day for an interview. She gave me some background on the wedding day."

"Yeah? How was the sweet young thing?" Violet asked dryly.

"About what you'd expect."

"Sure. Let's meet for lunch. Where do you want to go?"

"Uh . . . Dottie's?" I suggested a local sandwich shop in Lake Chinook that was within my budget. Violet might be paying for my information specialist services, but if she didn't offer to buy lunch, I didn't quite see how I could put it on her tab. Dwayne might act like I had money to burn, but Dwayne spied on his neighbors with binoculars, so was I going to listen to him?

"Twelve-thirty?"

"Great." I clicked my cell phone closed. "Wanna join us?" I asked Dwayne.

He shook his head. "Binks and I'll keep the Border collie in line."

"I take it, that's not Mrs. Jansen's place."

"She's on the other side." He inclined his head toward the west wall.

"Who're the people with the dog?"

"Renters. Just moved in." He shrugged.

"Haven't turned your binoculars on them?"

"All they do is watch TV. And yell at their dog."

"Bummer," I said and headed for the door.

Dottie's is a teeny shop with teeny chairs clustered around teeny tables. You mark your selection on a plastic-coated menu right down to the type of mayonnaise: plain, garlic or blue cheese. Shaking rain off my jacket and hair, I chose roast beef and Havarti cheese, opting for tomatoes and onions and romaine, eschewing the alfalfa sprouts. Can't do 'em. I have this mental image of fields of grass and cows chewing their cud. I'm from California, originally, where the alfalfa sprout is king, but I just can't make them work for me. Makes me feel like a traitor somehow.

I swept my hood from my head but kept my coat on. I paid for my sandwich and my chosen beverage, a soda, which I then grabbed from the serve-yourself glass refrigerator at the end of the counter. I snagged the last postage-stamp-sized table, beating out a kid who was running ahead of a family of five. Who were these people, anyway? They didn't deserve a place to sit if they couldn't figure out this wasn't a family restaurant. Why weren't they at fast food? Or a Denny's or Shari's? Something with revolving pies in a case next to the cash register. How did they expect to all sit together here?

The kid was about seven. He gazed at me in that scary, unabashed, wide-eyed way that says nothing and everything at the same time, dripping water from the hem of his coat to the floor. Mom was carrying a baby on her hip, its face hidden behind the brim of a yellow, plastic duckie cap. She came up beside her goggle-eyed son, laying a hand on his shoulder. Dad and another little brother were grabbing plastic menus and trying to order for everyone. Water flew off their clothes, as if it were raining inside as well as out.

I looked through the window to a sheet of rain just as Violet sailed in, snapping closed an umbrella. She took one look at the clientele and said loudly, "Jane. Let's go to Foster's. I'll buy."

"I already ordered."

"Make it to go," she said and turned back outside.

I couldn't be happier. I graciously gave up my table and watched as the family tried to squeeze around it. "Good luck with that," I told them. There were only three chairs and that was two too many for the table size. I swept up my sandwich and soda and hurried outside to catch up with Violet.

She'd parked her Mercedes illegally on one side of the wide drive that leads to Lake Chinook's only multistory (three-level) parking structure. I have serious parking issues, so I'm reluctantly impressed by those who threaten the parking gods and get away with it.

I was intrigued to see what she would do when she got to Foster's as there's never any good parking available. Violet cruised to the nearest bank's parking lot and squeezed her Mercedes into an end space that looked like it was made for golf carts or Minis. I had to suck in my gut and hold my breath to climb out.

"Don't let me forget my sandwich," I said as we hurried toward Foster's street-side door. "It's dinner."

Violet didn't answer, just held her umbrella against the wind and rain like a shield. I stayed close to her as it was getting really nasty out. We entered Foster's in a whoosh of rain and wind, closing the door behind us quickly as other patrons looked up in panic at the blast of wet weather.

"God, I need a drink," she said, and set about talking directly to the bartender about her signature drink. Something amethyst, I recalled, as she'd tried to foist this concoction on me once before. I'd opted for a beer instead. I did the same thing now, but this time I asked for it to come with a lemon slice, just to be fancy.

he was a plastic surgeon from Beverly Hills. That was the best reference he had. The location. The land of everlasting youth and beauty.

"It was weird being near my family again," Violet admitted. "Though I didn't contact them. Except my mother, a couple of times, but you know all that."

I nodded. "Gigi and Sean moved with you?"

"They begged to come with us. I wasn't so keen on it, but they were Roland's kids. You don't know Renee. She's whacked."

"How so?"

"Totally into plastic surgery. A junkie. You know how women who do too much eye surgery start looking like Siamese cats? That's Renee. She kept after Roland for more surgery. He tried to put the kibosh on it. Finally did. Wouldn't help her. She got somebody else to do it and now she looks like a scary feline. That's really what broke up their marriage, her obsession. They stayed friendly, but it was never the same."

She tossed back the remains of her drink as the waiter came over for our order. Violet ordered a blackened salmon salad and I ordered the ten-dollar avocado cheeseburger. She'd said she was paying and I was starving. "How do you stay so slim?" she marveled.

"I jog to the Nook. I have to make quick exits from Jesse's serving on a regular basis, so I sprint, too. I have a fast metabolism. I come from good genes."

"Wait till you get to be my age. I have to diet and work like hell to look this good."

"I don't know your age," I said.

She smiled. "I was thirty-eight when Roland and I got married. We've been divorced two, almost three years. You do the math."

"Thirty-eight, plus seven years of marriage, plus three years of divorce. Forty-eight. I said, "You're like a medical marvel.""

"So, tell me more about Gigi," Violet said as she joined me by the maitre d's stand down the steps toward the rear of the establishment where the tables and circular booths resided for main dining. Beyond the pane windows lay the patio, currently being blitzed by slanting, furious rain that bounced off the pavement.

The hostess showed us to a table next to another of Foster's gas fireplaces. I could feel warmth on my left shoulder but couldn't quite shake off the shiver that hit me from head to toe. I gave Violet a quick recap of my visit to the Hatchmere house, then drew a deep breath and said, "I've been dinking around with this thing for nearly a month. I finally got to talk to both Sean and Gigi, and I've left messages with other wedding guests and friends. But it seems like a roundabout way of gaining information when you're sitting right here."

Violet's eyes are that amazing shade of electric blue that serves a lot of the Purcell family. She was gazing at me hard and there's just something unnerving about being captured in those twin, aqua laser beams. The sensation made me uneasy. Just like I'd been throughout my dealings with her family. "What are you asking?"

"I need background," I told her. "Something more than 'I dropped by Roland's to deliver a gift, which I then hit him with'."

"I didn't kill him. I told that detective that, but he just sat there and waited, hoping I'd suddenly throw myself across the table and confess, I guess."

"Why did you hit him?"

"I told you. We had a fight." Her drink was delivered along with my beer. "Thanks, hon," she said, then twirled the stem of her glass between her fingers, the silvery, lavender liquid sloshing up the sides. It looked like it was going to centrifugally launch itself into a purple wave, but she managed to keep it from going airborne. She picked up the glass and gulped gratefully, eyes closing.

I liked her better with her eyes shut. Much more restful.

"What was the fight about?"

"I don't know. Yes, I do." She opened her eyes again. "Do I have to tell you this?"

"You don't have to do anything. Except possibly go directly to jail without passing Go."

"Roland . . . and I . . . have a complicated history. We're better when we're not married."

I kind of thought that might be true of Violet and all her ex-husbands, but I kept it to myself.

"But we can't leave each other alone. This isn't the first time we connected since we've been divorced."

"What exactly do you mean by connected?"

"You know what I mean." She gave me a sidelong look.

"You were having an affair."

"It was more than that. Jesus, Jane. You make everything sound so tawdry."

"Was he married when you first met?"

"See what I mean? You have to go right there, don't you? No. He wasn't married. Except mentally, you could say. In that, he's always married to someone. He really never knows how to let go," she said with a trace of bitterness.

"Okay . . ." I said.

"Are you going to sit there and be all judgmental? Because honestly, I'm just so over that."

"Then, give me something to go on."

She scooted her chair closer and hunched over her drink. This near, I could see the faint cracking of her skin beneath her makeup, but she was still remarkably youthful looking.

"Roland was already divorced from Renee, Gigi and Sean's mother, when we hooked up, but it wasn't like he really was, if you know what I mean. Roland and Renee did all kinds of things together. They just didn't live together. They had a

piece of paper that said they were through with each but they weren't."

"Meaning?"

"They'd been living apart for ages. But they were each other's lives."

"Like Roland and Melinda."

"Except they're not divorced." She sighed. "It's ju Roland does. You know, he and I didn't actually ju divorce when we split up. It was only after Melind him that the deed was finally done. I should have w turned out. Those clinics paid off and they were a g *C'est la vie.*" She laughed and waved a hand.

"You met Roland in Los Angeles?" I knew so background.

"Yes. I was twice divorced by the time Ro hooked up. He'd been divorced from Renee for a

I nodded, recalling what I knew of Violet's ready. She'd gotten married at nineteen the fir done some modeling and film work, mostly as a ried and divorced a second time, worked as met Roland on one of those "dates."

"I don't know why Roland married me," denly, as if the idea had just struck her.

Looking at her now, I had a pretty good i have been a knockout when she was young "How old were you when you got married long look. "How old were Gigi and Sean?"

"Gigi was twelve, I think. So Sean wo teen. Roland and I were married seven ye

"Really." I was surprised she'd made of them.

"I almost believed I was going to ge down with Roland. We lived in L.A. th but then Roland wanted to launch h moved to Portland. He had a name fo

She smiled. "Thanks." She gazed at the fire. "You know it's funny. Gigi and Sean always blamed me for Roland and Renee's divorce, but that was such a crock. I guess kids just want to blame someone. Makes more sense than their parents just couldn't stand living with each other."

"I didn't get the feeling Gigi was close to her mother."

"Oh, she's not. She just likes to play both ends against the middle." Violet shrugged. "Neither one of them could really ever abide me. I never really cared because I thought they were both spoiled and shallow. Gigi . . . Lord, what a piece of work. Twelve when I met her, twenty-one going on thirteen now. She's hardly matured one iota. And Sean . . . he's really twenty-four? Twenty-five? What did you think of him?"

"Well, I thought he was using."

"He is. At least, he's smoking dope. Maybe more. Probably more. Roland was upset with him. Cocaine took away Roland's practice and it drove him crazy that Sean didn't learn by example. What a dope, so to speak." She smiled faintly. "Although it sure turned out well in the end for Roland, didn't it? He was a great plastic surgeon, but he was even better in business. Who knew?"

Our food arrived and conversation ended, more on my side than hers. I love a good hamburger and Foster's on the Lake does it right. I wondered if Jeff Foster was on the premises but thought it might be too early for him. He keeps a watch over the dinner hour and beyond.

Violet picked at her salad, her eye on me and my hamburger. I hoped she wasn't going to ask me to share, though if she did, I wasn't sure I could refuse her.

She said, "So, are you and Dwayne an item now?"

CHAPTER SIX

She damn near made me choke. I had to chew really carefully and hold in a cough while tears filled my eyes from the effort. My success rate was only so-so. I started hacking like I would toss up a lung. Other patrons turned to look at me with concerned eyes. I swear to God, if one of them came at me eager for a Heimlich maneuver, I would kick, flail and throw myself to the floor to scare them away. I might even be able to fake rolling my eyes up. But that would send them scrambling to call 911 on their cell phones and I didn't think I could take that kind of scene.

I managed to discreetly cough a few more times into my napkin and chug water like it would save my soul. Our waiter glanced over, looking scandalized by my disruptive behavior. I had a feeling he wouldn't serve me another beer if I asked.

Throughout, Violet just waited.

I said in a squeaky voice, as if I'd just sucked helium, "I'm okay."

"It didn't look serious," she said.

Easy for her to say. Perversely, now I wished I'd thrown myself around in my chair, clawing at my throat.

"I know you didn't like it when I started to get with Dwayne." She lifted one shoulder in a feminine "I just can't help myself sometimes" gesture. "You could have told me he was spoken for."

"He's not," I squeaked.

"Don't bullshit me, Jane. If we're going to work together . . . if you expect me to lay all my cards on the table . . ." Another shoulder lift. "Come on."

"Give me a minute." It was all I could do to get the words out. I drank some more water, nibbled off a tiny bite of the remains of my burger, sucked down the dregs of my beer and waited about thirty seconds. In a more normal voice, I said, "I'm not with Dwayne."

"But you're interested in him."

"I don't know where you're getting this."

"When it comes to male/female relationships, I'm an expert. You're in my rice bowl on this. You've got something going on inside you about Dwayne. You think he's yours. Maybe not as a lover, yet. And maybe you've convinced yourself you can just be friends. But it's radiating off you. I ignored the signals at first but you're flashing them in neon."

"I'm not in your rice bowl."

"Yeah, you are. What's so hard about admitting your feelings for Dwayne? We're not in junior high here."

"Dwayne's my boss."

"Partner," she corrected.

"Boss," I repeated. "He owns Durbin Investigations. I'm not even licensed completely yet."

"He treats you like a partner."

"I'm just saying, I work with him. We're friends. I'm not going to screw that up with sex."

"Oh, please," Violet said.

"What about you and Roland? Why were you at his place the morning of the wedding? I know, I know. You dropped by with a gift." Inspiration struck, one of those clear zingers from out of the blue you just know is true. "You didn't just stop in. You spent the night with him."

She didn't answer, and that was an answer in itself.

"Does Melinda know?" I asked. "Did she know then?"

She waved a hand. "They all suspected. How many times do I have to say it? Roland and Melinda weren't together. It's not like I swooped in and stole him away!"

"What were you and he fighting about?"

"Oh, you know." She flapped a hand at me, clearly uncomfortable reliving it. "The usual stuff. You know . . . what are we doing? Is this going anywhere? Do you love me?" She sighed. "I am so tired of that same scene. I've played it out so many times, I should get a lifetime achievement award."

Our waiter finally returned with the check. He asked me if I was all right and I said I was fine. Violet handed him her credit card, but after he left she didn't pick up the thread of her narrative.

It was hardly a revelation that she and Roland were seeing each other. With Violet, sex seems to always be the crux of the matter. The signs had been there. The passion she'd displayed in hitting Roland with the tray. The way she referred to him as her favorite ex-husband. The way she'd dismissed my Rol-Ex nickname. I mean, come on, that's funny.

"Roland's gone," Violet said into the silence that had developed, as if she were still coming to terms with the news. "I've been asking myself, 'what now?' What's next? How many chances do you get? It wasn't perfect between us, but it was good."

I hadn't credited her with really caring about him, I realized, which was maybe unfair.

"I called him. Looked him up to say hello." Her smile

was ironic. "I'd been asking myself where I could meet men. It gets harder as you get older."

"It's always hard," I said.

"Yeah, well, you've got yours."

We left the restaurant in silence. I did remember my roast beef and Havarti sandwich from Dottie's as Violet dropped me at my car, which made me happy. I drove home lost in thought. Contrary to Violet's conviction, I did not *have* Dwayne.

As I headed up Iron Mountain Boulevard I nearly missed recognizing the pod of hooded teenage girls walking along the designated pathway. I wouldn't have at all, except two of them were hoodless in the rain. Dawn and a girl with longer hair who looked a lot like her. The sister.

There were several other girls in the group whom I thought I remembered from the evening before, though the cinched hoods worked like a disguise. Most of the girls were engaged in animated conversations, but Dawn and the sister walked along silently.

I drove past them, thinking hard. At the turnaround circle where Iron Mountain divides and sends you either to Lakeview Boulevard or Upper Drive, I circled all the way around to head back the way I'd come. This circle is one of those bright ideas from some transportation expert who crows about its incredible design. But it never quite works the way it's supposed to. Nobody signals, nobody stops, nobody knows what the rules are. We all look at each other like hungry dogs, each waiting for the other to make a move. Every time I make it around the circle without incident, I count it as a win.

I drove past the girls again. It was going to take them a while to reach a road or turnoff point, so I zigzagged through the winding streets and screeched to a halt at Dwayne's from the back way. I ran inside. Dwayne was splayed on the couch—his injured leg stretched in front of him. The cowboy hat was off and his blondish brown hair was tousled. Binkster lay beside him and her head popped up when she saw me enter.

"I need Binkster. Quick," I said, ignoring my own reaction to Dwayne's unconscious sexuality.

Binky leapt to her feet and wagged her tail upon hearing her name. But she didn't jump down from the couch.

"Come on. Come on," I said urgently to her. Reluctantly, giving Dwayne a longing look, she thunked down and toddled over to me. I swooped her up.

"Did you see Violet?"

"Just finished lunch. I'll tell you about it later. Bye."

I tucked Binks in her doggy bed in the Volvo, then drove back toward Iron Mountain like a maniac, slowing down before I approached the area I expected to find the girls. The girls were still moving as one, keeping close together, like an amoeba that sprouts a leg and then absorbs itself into it.

Driving more sedately, I turned toward Lake Chinook proper and parked on the street. I clipped Binkster's leash to her collar, cursed the rain again as I cinched the hood of my jacket, then headed in the direction they were coming from. Maybe the rain was a plus. With all that water, it was likely they wouldn't notice I was a decade older than they were. At least that's what I was hoping for.

Binkster didn't think much of the rain, either, and the wind lifted her ears from her head a little like the Flying Nun.

It was one hell of a nasty day for a walk. Fortunately, or unfortunately, depending on how you look at it, dog owners head outside in all forms of weather. Dogs need to be walked. Maybe not all dogs. The little teeny ones work off enough energy just being wired and territorial. But big dogs and dogs with weight problems gotta get their daily constitutional or they're just not happy and healthy. Hence, I see dog walkers out when the winds are typhoon force and the rain is a monsoon.

And dogs are a fabulous ice breaker.

The girls saw Binkster from a football field away. I heard the excited rise in pitch of their voices. The amoeba moved toward me more swiftly. Only Dawn and her sister lagged behind.

The girls swarmed on. The Binkster, petting her wet head, squealing with delight and horror when she propped her wet and grimy paws on them. But they didn't really care. I was asked tons of questions about her, then heard about every acquaintance, long-distant relative, and celebrity who also owned a pug. I told them her name and pretended I was bored out of my skull with my "dog-sitting" job. While I was dutifully answering, Dawn moved in, her eyes on Binkster. She looked at the dog, her face long, her eyes wet, from rain or tears, I couldn't tell.

Finally, she glanced up, her gaze half meeting mine, then zooming back as if yanked by force. "You're . . . ?"

"Ronnie. How weird. I saw you last night, right?" I pitched my voice faintly higher than normal. It makes me sound younger. I hadn't bothered last night and I kicked myself for that.

"I guess." Dawn's eyes darted around the group, but no one seemed to be paying attention to our conversation except the sister. The rest of them were squatting down and petting the dog. Two were in a debate on who could hold her. I handed over the leash to a girl with short, blondish hair who didn't give a damn about her clothes. She grabbed Binky and held her up, "oofing" at the unexpected heft.

"Is he your dog?" Dawn asked.

"I'm just kinda taking care of her," I lied. The less they knew about me, the better.

"Our neighbors have a wolf," the older sister said with a sniff.

"He's not a real wolf," Dawn said.

"He looks like a real wolf."

"Yeah?" I said. "What's his name?"

"Lobo."

Ah. At least now if I ran across the Pilarmos' dog during my investigation, I could yell its name and hope it would respond appropriately.

"So, your dad lives around here?" Dawn asked.

"Over that way," I said, waving my arm vaguely. "Do you have dogs?"

"Nope. We did have a cat but it got in a fight and its eye bugged out. Dad said the vet would charge a thousand dollars to close the eye permanently, so he left it as it was. He said the cat wasn't in any pain."

"Caesar looked like an alien," the sister said with a shudder. "I hoped he would die or run away and he finally did. Run away, anyway. He's been missing for about a year."

"Half a year," Dawn corrected. "He left on my birthday. This is my sister, Dionne," she added for my benefit.

"Hi," Dionne said without much enthusiasm. She ran a hand under her hair and flipped it away from her neck.

"Hi," I answered, tossing a look toward the girls still cooing over Binkster. The dog's gaze was pinned on me. Maybe it was time to rescue her.

"I'm glad Caesar's gone," Dionne said. "I hated that cat."

"Caesar was my cat," Dawn answered. "He's all I had. I miss him."

"You never took care of him."

"Yes, I did."

Dionne regarded her sister for a long moment. She seemed to want to argue the point, but there was some kind of overriding governor on her tongue, like she didn't want to get into a full-scale battle over an issue they were clearly on opposite sides of.

"I better get Binkster home," I said.

"Are you going to be around next weekend?" Dawn asked. "The game's away. I think we play Clackamas. But we always get together afterward."

Dionne's brows formed a line. "You're not going there again," she declared.

"I might be," Dawn retorted.

"Dad said not to make plans."

"No, he didn't."

"You've got things to do," Dionne said meaningfully. "You know you do."

"Oh, thanks. I have things to do, but you get to be with Dylan."

"You know what I mean."

"Whatever." Dawn cut her sister off. Dionne was clearly trying to give her a message, and it was pissing her off that Dawn wasn't listening.

"Well, I'm not letting you go there again," Dionne said huffily. To me, she added, "They're all a bunch of delinquents, you know. And Keegan's the worst. I know he's all your big idol, but he's a prick!"

"You didn't feel that way before he dumped you," Dawn said with a sly look from the corner of her eye.

"Yeah, well, I didn't sleep with him!"

The two girls stared at each other. It was Dawn who looked away first and she seemed utterly wounded and miserable.

"I'm going," she said stubbornly. To me, she said, "Are you?"

"I'll be there," I said, though I kind of wondered what the hell I was doing.

Dionne gave me a hard look and I feared she would finally realize I was over a decade older. But she seemed to be responding more to her inner vision than her eyes. That's the great thing about teenagers; they're so self-absorbed you can get away with murder.

"You got a number? I'll text you," Dawn said.

"Okay." I was going to have to get better at it whether I liked it or not. We exchanged cell phone numbers and I in-putted hers into my phone under DWDNE, code for Dawn Wilson Do Not Enter. I have this fear of losing my cell phone and having my friends, sources, allies and favorite restaurants discovered by some villain out to do them harm, or order pickup and not follow through. I'm pretty sure I'll be blamed somehow, and besides, I like codes. Sometimes I forget what they mean, but most of the time I'm okay.

I recaptured Binkster and we let the girls move on. Unfortunately, they were heading in the direction I planned to go and I didn't want them to start asking more questions about where my dad's house was, so I continued walking in the sleeting rain in the opposite direction for another quarter mile.

By the time I got back to my car my jeans were absolutely soaked. Bink's double coat of fur looked bedraggled, too. When we got back to the cottage I gave her a toweling-off, which is another one of her favorite games. This consists of me rubbing her hard with the towel and her grabbing it with her teeth, growling and trying to shake the life out of it. This is accompanied by much jumping and twisting. Very acrobatic for Binks.

I took a long, hot shower and thought about Violet. Okay, that's a lie. I thought about Dwayne. Violet's perception felt like an invasion of my secret, secret self. Clearly this self wasn't so secret. In fact, I feared this self might be out-and-out overt.

"How do I get over him?" I asked the warm, mist-fogged air.

I didn't want to like Dwayne as more than a friend. I really didn't. I wanted to be cool and in control and remote. That woman who wears only black and sneers and is mysterious, yet beautiful, in an extraordinary way. I wanted to be *Ultra*-Jane.

My landline rang as I was getting out of the shower, so I let it go to voice mail. My pulse jumped, however, because only three people call me at home anymore: Mom, my twin brother and Dwayne. My thoughts were circling that third possibility, and I felt annoyed at myself enough to refuse to listen to the message for a good ten minutes as a form of punishment.

At the end of the time I swore at myself for being so juvenile, then punched in my voice mail code. This is the same code as the one for my cell phone: 2222. A lot easier than the confusing anagrams I concoct for my friends' names.

But it wasn't Dwayne, it was Booth and his message was terse: "Call me."

Well, okay. Booth wasn't one for keeping in touch on a regular basis, so I found the command interesting, to say the least. I picked up my cell and punched in Booth's number, only to get his voice mail in return. Figured.

"You called?" I asked after the beep, then hung up.

A few minutes later my phone made that strange ring that had brought me awake the other night. Texting. I grabbed my phone and checked the messages, wondering if Dawn was already my new text message buddy. But the missive was from Booth. I was impressed as he's not in love with technology the way Dwayne is. In fact, I'd say he's on a par with my own skills.

need to talk to you. will call later. rbk

RBK was for Richard Booth Kelly. There was something urgent in there, something unwritten, that sent worry gathering in the pit of my stomach. My twin and I have an uneasy relationship though we're connected deeply. I try to deny it, or minimize it, or laugh it off, but it's a true phenomenon, that twin thing. Booth and I aren't connected to the same degree shared by identical twins. I mean, those people are from the same egg and sperm, like the *same person* in two bodies, and therefore I figure it's like they share one brain. They're bound to have extra abilities, you know? Booth and I aren't like that, but we seem to have an awareness of each other that defies explanation. We understand each other, even if we don't each always like what the other one's about. It's that *I know you* thing that some people never seem to experience.

But for Booth and me, it sometimes works against us, like we're both battling for our own identity.

I decided not to dwell on it. Whatever it was, he would explain all soon enough.

I spent the remainder of the afternoon making more phone calls. I didn't always leave messages. Don't want to freak my would-be sources out, like I'm a stalker or something.

I hit the jackpot late in the afternoon when Melinda suddenly answered the phone and agreed to my stammering request to meet with her. She couldn't make a date till later in the week, however, as Sunday wasn't going to work and she had the bake sale on Monday. Questions hung over my head. Bake sale? When I asked, she became wildly animated, telling me about the Lake Chinook Junior League's annual preholiday event. Would I care to come? We could talk afterward . . . ? No problem, I told her, and we made a date for Monday.

I watched TV till midnight with Binkster snoring softly beside me. I fell asleep as if drugged and had trouble getting up the next day. The sky was dark and a light drizzle kept coming down incessantly. November in Oregon. I felt a pang of longing for Southern California weather that held me in its grip all of Sunday. In fact, I didn't leave the house. Binkster ate kiblets and I enjoyed some semistale Wheat

Thins and tap water until dinner when I had the second half of my leftover Dottie's sandwich. I ate the first half for breakfast. The bread was a little wet and mushy on one side by then, so I ate it open-faced.

I called my mother. I gotta say, this is almost a first for me, initiating conversation. Usually I'm phoning her back after I've worked up the energy to engage in one of her convoluted conversations. But today the weather was making me blue, so I sent out a message to her and the warmer climate where I grew up.

Mom is all about her landline. She'll use a cell phone if she has to, but it's not her thing. She and I own a fourplex in Venice together, which is where all my money's tied up. The opportunity to purchase this fourplex occurred while I was still living in So Cal, working as a bartender. Through some wangling, my mom found a way to horse the deal home. This is the property Dwayne keeps reminding me that I own and could sell, or use somehow, to buy my cottage. What he doesn't, or won't, understand is that I'm in this for the long haul with my mother. I like thinking I have this incredible nest egg. It makes the daily scrounging worthwhile. I'm thrifty—okay, okay, cheap—by nature, but I love knowing I have Mom and renters down South, a solid investment perking right along under my mother's watchful eye.

She picked up on the third ring. "Hello?"

"Hi, Mom. It's Jane. How are you?"

A studied pause. "Is everything okay?"

"Everything's fine." I ignored the tacit worry I could hear forming inside her head like a distant roar. "It's really lousy weather here. What's it like down there?"

"Sunny. About seventy-two. Have you heard from your brother lately?"

It defies any known ability beyond ESP the way Mom can zero in on underlying tensions within seconds. Takes my breath away sometimes. And though Booth wasn't why I'd

called, his text message had undoubtedly helped spur my
need to make contact with my family. If not my brother, my
mother.

"He left me a text message. Said he's going to contact me
later."

"Text message?"

"On my cell phone." When she didn't respond, I said, "It's
typing a message so it appears as text on the LCD, the screen?"

"Why doesn't he just talk to you?"

"Lot of people text, Mom."

"Do you think he's in some kind of trouble?"

"No," I responded heartily, but her words were like darts,
puncturing holes in the balloon of my denial. Something was
going on with Booth, but I didn't think it warranted the kind
of all-out hand-wringing my mother was warming up to.
"Actually, I understand he's trying to make detective. Sometimes that can happen sooner, rather than later, if he takes a
more challenging job."

"Dangerous job, you mean?"

"Not necessarily."

"You're lying, Jane. Minimizing."

Why is it that I can lie to nearly everyone convincingly
except my mother? Well, and Dwayne. Maybe Booth, too.
But otherwise I'm seriously good at it. No looking away, no
hemming or hawing, no guilt. The trick is to believe you're
telling the truth, easier to manage some times than others.
But with Mom . . .

"I don't know what Booth's up to," I said. "I got a text, he
said he'd call. When I hear from him, I'll let you know."

"Do you think he and Sharona are okay?"

My brother and his fiancée were planning a summer wedding. I would have liked to jump on that and allay Mom's
fears, but she's too smart for that. In a half-assed attempt to
mollify, I said, "I don't think it has anything to do with

Sharona. Booth's just busy. So's Sharona, I'm sure." I knew of a few cases she was involved in. A criminal defense attorney's life isn't exactly uneventful. Sometimes your clients are scared enough to call you every minute of every day. I know for a fact that if I were ever in serious trouble with the law, I would be parking myself at Sharona's front door, beating it down, begging for help.

Now I wanted off the phone. I'd reached my mother and learned the weather in Southern California was nauseatingly terrific. Mom was clearly fine as well, so now I was done. Unfortunately, Mom wasn't. She continued to worry about Booth and after a fashion, started in on me.

"Mr. Densworth? In the upper back unit? He hired a private investigator to look into his daughter-in-law's background, because she married his son, but then was with some other man, and I don't know what else, but all of a sudden this private investigator shows up dead. Shot twice through the head."

This was not what I wanted to hear. "Mom . . ."

"I know you're careful, Jane. I'm not saying that. But the daughter-in-law's gone, and she took Mr. Densworth's grandson with her. Sounds like she was involved in something really bad. Bad people."

"Was the private investigator killed over this particular case?" I asked. "Was that verified?"

"I don't really know. But this is the business you're in."

"Mostly I write up reports and process-serve," I said.

"But didn't your friend get hurt? Got his leg broken?"

I had not told my mother about Dwayne. She had to have heard this from Booth who normally laments loud and long about my foray into the "information specialist" business, which is a benign, catchall term for private investigation. Booth must have relayed this information. I questioned my mother on this and she admitted as much, which only served to irk me. Booth has absolute no faith in my abilities, which really ticks me off, especially since I question those abilities in myself all the time. I can do that, but Booth can't.

"Don't worry about me, Mom. When things look bad, I'm gone."

"Good. Keep to that plan."

"I'll call you later," I said. "After Booth calls."

"Try to make it down for a visit."

"I'll see what I can do," I said and hurriedly hung up. I turned to Binkster, who'd been snoozing on the couch, but seemed to understand I needed her attention as she lifted her head and looked at me expectantly.

"Sheesh," I said, and plopped down next to her. We spent the rest of the day doing next to nothing together and it felt great.

The Lake Chinook Junior League Bake Sale was being held at the Lake Chinook Community Library. I parked my car in the lot, luckily grabbing a spot being vacated by one of the slowest drivers on record. While I waited, drumming my fingers on the wheel, the older gentleman and his wife backed their cream-colored Chrysler out of the spot, then slowly turned it around and herded it toward the exit. A woman in a green Mazda made as if to outscore me for the spot, but I lay on the horn like I was announcing Armageddon. She glared at me with true bitchiness, but I kept my face neutral, as if I didn't realize what a pain in the ass I'd been. Inside I was happy, happy, happy. There are unwritten rules that must be adhered to in any culture. Parking issues are at the top of my rule list. Anyone who steals, or attempts to steal, a spot from someone who clearly has dibs on it, is the lowest of the low. Bitchy Lady was lucky to get off with a warning.

I locked my car, just managed to avoid stepping into a serious puddle, then bent my head to the rain again, one eye watching the green Mazda circle the lot as I headed for the library, a two-story brick building with a front portico. I ducked under the portico, then quickly hurried inside, finding a niche for myself by a rack of paperbacks with a good view of the front windows. I wanted a good look at Bitchy Woman before I started meandering around. I'd caught a glimpse of a black and white scarf around her neck, dark hair and pinched lips.

Pretty soon she appeared, stopping under the portico, hauling down her umbrella and shaking rain onto the ground. For a moment I panicked. What if this was Melinda Hatchmere? Not a great way to earn myself points. Another woman joined her, going through the same umbrella routine. They walked inside together and I heard them call each other by their names: Anne and Kathleen. Relieved, I pretended to peruse a book while they headed toward the main area, which was set up with tables for the bake sale. I realized they, like Melinda, were part of the Junior League.

There was a coven of Junior Leaguers hanging around several rows of tables loaded with baked goods. They wore slacks with matching sweaters or silk blouses and jackets, or skirts and blouses and scarves and jewelry. It looked like an Ann Taylor convention from where I stood. My jeans, soaked boots and damp gray windbreaker were regular attire for a large percentage of the Oregon population, but these ladies were a couple of notches up the fashion ladder. Didn't mean those clothes might not get ruined in the blasting wind and rain. One thing I know how to do is dress for the weather.

There were quite a few prospective customers milling about. I wondered if Bitchy Anne had given me the hard stare like I'd given her and therefore might recognize me. If she did I would have to brazen my way through it. I have a penchant for making these little wars happen; I don't know why. I must be really hard to get along with. This idea pleased me far more than it should.

There were about six tables all lined up with Junior League ladies standing near the ends, ready for all questions. I wandered amongst the crowd, examining the plates of cookies, cakes, pies, brownies and breads. My mouth watered over a pan of apple bars, the scents of cinnamon, nutmeg and hot fruit making me want to part with my hard-earned money as if I were a philanthropist. I dug out thirty dollars as it was a big pan and paid for it before I could stop myself. The ladies smiled at me as if I'd make a fabulous purchase.

"Jody makes those," one of them said. "Oh my gosh, the peach bars! It's enough to make you swoon."

"Where are the peach bars?" I asked with trepidation. I feared I might have to fork over some more cash.

"Oh, gone already. Out the door by ten-thirty. Her stuff just flies off the table. It's almost criminal."

Her tag read LEIGH. I'm never sure if that's pronounced Lay or Lee. I was about to inquire when the question was answered by a woman with blondish, chin-length hair swept away from a delicate face that was softly peach-colored. Her petite figure was swathed in a chic, silvery blue pantsuit and white silk shell that sported a plunging decolletage. A pewter chain was looped several times around her neck and her earrings were tiny silver and mother-of-pearl birds. Doves, maybe. There was something dovelike about her. She said, "Leigh, could you help Mr. Early restock Table Four? Jody's fruit bars are all gone, but we've got extra cookies in the back." She pronounced it *Lee*. I read her name tag. Melinda.

"Melinda Hatchmere?" I asked with a smile.

She looked at me blankly, trying not to stare at my less than stunning outfit. "Yes?"

"I called you. We're planning to meet? I'm Jane Kelly."

"Oh! Oh yes. I'm so sorry." She broke into smiles. "I forgot. We've been getting this bake sale together and it's just taken over. I see you bought some of Jody's apple bars. You won't be disappointed."

"Good to know." I couldn't remember the last time food had actually disappointed me. Availability is all that matters.

"I'm going to be about half an hour more," she said, looking around.

Leigh broke in, "Don't worry about it, Melinda. We can finish up."

"Wouldn't dream of it," she answered back. "Do you mind waiting?" she asked me, but it was just for show. This was her baby and she wouldn't leave it to someone else's care.

But Leigh was up for the challenge. "No, no. Go on." She flapped a hand at Melinda. "Jody's going to be back any minute with that rum cake she promised. She had to go make another one today," Leigh said to me in a low voice that said she was imparting "big news." "Five were sold by noon, and Mrs. Merker nearly had a hemorrhage when she learned she couldn't get one. So Jody headed home to make her another one. Just like that. Jody's amazing."

Melinda's peach complexion turned a rosier shade. "Jody's our star," she agreed through a stretched smile. "I'll be out in about thirty minutes."

Dismissed, I turned away but I kept them in my peripheral vision. I could feel the wall of ice building between them. God help me if I ever do something like that, I prayed; then I remembered my own battle with Bitchy Anne. Maybe I wasn't so different after all.

Bitchy Anne and Kathleen were chatting up a storm at the end of one table. They didn't appear to have any serious function apart from offering support to their Junior League buddies. Customers were buying the baked goods at a regular clip, and the working Junior League ladies kept bringing out more and more delights. I could spend my life savings in nothing flat at a place like this.

I ran to my car, shielding the apple bars with my body. The ladies had put a sheet of plastic wrap over the bars when I'd made the purchase, but I wasn't going to chance anything ruining my bounty.

Inside the car I pulled out one of the bars and with apple filling dripping warmly on my fingers I chomped it down in seconds flat. Leigh was right about the swooning. I let my head fall back against the headrest and made moaning sounds as if I were in pain.

I ate another one and made it halfway through a third before I felt slightly ill. Setting the pan aside, I waited for Melinda but she didn't appear. I had to dodge more rain and puddles as I went back inside to see what was keeping her.

Near the library front door I smacked directly into Bitchy Anne who'd been yakking away with Kathleen under the portico and turned into me just as I rounded the corner. Anne's umbrella went flying and I grabbed her hard to keep us both from tumbling onto the concrete apron.

"Jesus," Anne spat. "Look out next time." Then her expression tightened as she recognized me. "Oh," she said. She didn't know what else to do or say.

Kathleen, unaware of everything, said on a laugh, "It's hell getting out of this rain, isn't it?"

"Sure is." I smiled, just to show how amiable I was.

"Parking sure is tough," Anne said snarkily.

"You got that right."

Kathleen chimed in, "I had to beat out somebody for a spot. They were kinda mad." She giggled.

"Really?" I smiled some more.

"Oh yeah. It was this young girl? And she wasn't very nice. I could see her through the windshield. She was swear-

ing a blue streak! Her mother should wash her mouth out
with soap!"

"Stealing someone's parking spot . . ." I shook my head.
"Dangerous stuff."

Kathleen blinked. "It's not like they're numbered or anything. It's a free country."

Anne said coolly, "Come on, Kathleen. We've got some
important things to do."

They glanced back at me as they took off. Anne was talking rapidly in Kathleen's ear. I turned back and another gal
came hurrying up to the library, carrying a large box. As she
swept by I saw a dark cake inside and the smell of sugared
rum ran by with her. Ah. This must be Jody. I wondered pen-
sively if I could talk her into making one more rum cake beyond Mrs. Merker's.

Melinda was manning her table with no apparent desire
to leave any time soon. I wondered if she'd forgotten about
me. She spied Jody and stretched her smile even wider.
"There you are," she said. "We were beginning to wonder if
you forgot us."

Jody was thin, small and harried. "Traffic," she said, then,
"Has Mrs. Merker come back?"

"Not yet. Don't worry," Leigh said. "You made it in time."

"It must be incredibly gratifying to have so many happy
customers," I said.

All three of them looked at me. Jody smiled uncertainly,
as if afraid to take the compliment. "We all work hard."

"Yeah, but you're the queen bee. That's all I've heard
since I got here. Jody, Jody, Jody. Your apple bars . . . oh my
God." I held my stomach. "I had to stop myself from eating
the whole pan."

Jody flushed with delight but Melinda and Leigh went
silent. Deciding I'd better stop before Melinda gave me the
old heave-ho, I said, "I was standing outside. All of you are

getting rave reviews. Everybody who came from the bake sale thought it was the best ever. I heard somebody say something about better than the Food Channel's recipes."

"Really?" A tiny line formed between Melinda's brows.

"That must've been about Noreen's shortbread," Leigh said. "Somebody said she copied that recipe, but she acts like it's her own creation."

"She did the same thing last year with the Christmas decorations. I saw those yarn Santas on TV," Melinda reminded her.

Jody pretended her rum cake needed further arranging on the table, even though it was still in its box, waiting for Mrs. Merker.

Now that Jody was back I was hoping to snag Melinda away from the event, but she was bound and determined to stay until the last crumb was either sold, eaten or swept away. I kinda kept hoping Mrs. Merker would be a no-show, but she finally blew in just as they were disassembling the tables, pouncing on Jody's rum cake and throwing a hundred-dollar bill on the table. The ladies were all agog about the size of Mrs. Merker's donation. I kinda thought it might include a tip for Jody, but hey, this event was supposed to be a fund-raiser for permanent Lake Chinook art, so I guess Jody was going to have to live with it. Based on the selection of art that's currently lining the streets of Lake Chinook, some of which are obvious phallic symbols, I feel maybe the art procurement committee is either blind or collectively getting a huge inner laugh. Either way, Jody was screwed.

"Are you . . . about wrapped up here?" I asked Melinda.

"Oh. Yes." She looked around. "Ummm . . ." She sidled away from the group, touching at her hair and licking her lips as if she were getting ready for a television interview. I wondered if I should remind her it was just little old me but decided against it. Whatever works to get you ready. I followed after her.

"Let's go to my place," she suggested, throwing a glance toward Leigh, Jody and the rest of the Junior Leaguers still hanging around. "More privacy."

"Is it far?"

"Just around the corner. I have one of those new condos on B Street. I'll just be a minute." Her heels tippy-tapped quickly across the linoleum and to a door in the back where she disappeared.

I'd been wondering how she'd been involved with the Lake Chinook Junior League when Roland's address was Portland. I hadn't realized when she and Roland split that she'd moved to Lake Chinook.

She returned in a long, white wool coat with a white fur collar. "It's faux," she said, pulling out a red umbrella. "You ready?"

I nodded.

CHAPTER SEVEN

I followed her outside. She popped the umbrella and tippy-tapped to her silver Lexus, skirting puddles with ease.

I didn't even try to dodge raindrops as I headed to the Volvo again. Pulling out behind Melinda, I drove about four blocks before she turned into the Chinook Villa Condominiums' parking lot. I looked around with interest, as I had a friend/acquaintance who was converting apartments to condominiums in this same area of town, a section of Lake Chinook known as First Addition. This particular project was brand-new, the smaller, older homes that had once sat on these parcels of land gone to make way for chic, new condominiums and offices.

A row of garage doors lined the backs of the buildings. One door started lifting and Melinda aimed for it, while I found an empty visitor spot in the lot. I climbed out of my car, feeling damp to the bone. The Lexus's brake lights blinked out and a minute later, Melinda exited the garage, and the door slowly descended behind her. She entered a wooden gate that was fancied up with some filigree wrought iron arched across the top and led to a sidewalk shared between her building and the next one over. I saw she was waiting for me under her umbrella and I scooted over to meet her. Melinda walked quickly to one of the tiny porches that jutted out like soldiers at attention down the row. Each entryway had three concrete steps and a wrought-iron rail that matched the gate's design. Melinda had arranged two pots full of rain-soaked, spindly-branched plants on the top step that looked like they'd been completely forgotten. Maybe they were supposed to be that way in winter. Deciduous azaleas was my guess.

She opened the door, shook out her umbrella, stepped into a hardwood entry and delicately removed her shoes. I followed suit. Beyond the entry was a hallway, kitchen, living/family room with a fireplace centered on the far wall. A glass door exited to a small, fence-enclosed patio. A stairway ran up the south end of the room, to my right.

Melinda was examining her white coat as she hung it on a hanger and placed it in the entry hall closet. "Don't want it to drip on my floor. It's Brazilian cherry. It's my favorite thing about this place."

"It's beautiful."

"The kitchen's okay," she said, as if I'd asked for a review. "A little modern. All that stainless steel. I know it's popular but honestly, it's everywhere and I think it's overdone. I asked for the marble counter. For baking. Nothing better than marble for rolling out dough. Cold, clean, beautiful."

I decided to forgo telling her how much I liked my chipped laminate. No need for a cutting board; the surface was already marked with knife wounds when I moved in, so I continued the tradition with pride. I'd sprayed the laminate down with bleach water on a steady basis ever since my mother pointed out that the little cuts in the surface didn't look all that clean. Germ phobia took over big time. I might not have had groceries, but I was pretty stocked up on cleaning supplies.

Ogilvy would probably have to redo the kitchen when he sold the cottage, I thought with a pang of regret. I'd got him to install new floors for me when I moved in, though it was no mean trick to get him to part with some dough for upgrades. The kitchen is the last room that needs serious attention. I've never worried because, apart from assembling sandwiches, my use for it is limited. I've never fretted that it wasn't the dream kitchen touted in all the women's magazines.

But Melinda possessed the magazine kitchen, whether she liked its style or not. The cooktop was against one wall and sported one of those overbearing stainless steel vents that crawls down the wall and looks like some kind of medical apparatus for staring through skin, cartilage and bone. To the left of the cooktop was the white, gray-veined marble counter she so loved; the right side was black granite. A center island was topped with the same granite and Melinda had dotted the whole area with touches of red: serving platters, a colander holding fresh fruit, oranges and red apples; a pitcher that bristled with kitchen utensils, most of which I couldn't guess at their function; a set of hot mitts.

Melinda removed her silvery jacket and her breasts about fell out of the white shell. There was something eye-popping about her. Not in the overtly sensual, naughty-girl Violet way, more like Donna Reed behind closed doors . . . a kind of "come into my kitchen, big boy, and let Mama show you how to cook . . ."

I did a mental check of my own athletic body with its straight lines and broad shoulders and decided I would never have had to worry about Roland Hatchmere looking my way, if he were still alive, even if I'd been in the right age bracket. His taste in women ran to soft, curvy and luscious.

She turned on the oven, then opened the refrigerator and pulled out a tray of crescent-shaped hors d'oeuvres, ready to bake. "Would you like white wine, or a soft drink? Sparkling water?"

"Whatever you're having," I said, delighted I'd fallen into this bonanza. This interviewing thing was taking on a whole new light. Far cooler than process-serving. Polite conversation, food and drink. Nobody hurling things at me.

Melinda said, "I'm having some sparkling water."

"Great."

She popped the hors d'oeuvres in the oven, handed me my glass and invited me to sit down on the cream-colored couch in front of the fire. Her cell phone rang and she opened a dark red leather purse and pulled it out. Glancing at the caller ID, she switched it off and it abruptly stopped singing. "I don't even know why I keep one," she muttered, then flipped on the gas fire and curled into a matching cream armchair, tucking her feet beneath her. I shivered a bit and she gave me a look. "Maybe I should have made it coffee and rum."

Whatever she saw on my face—hope, probably—sent her to the coffeemaker. I gazed into the fire, then outside to the drifting rain as it came down in curtains, plip-plopping onto the concrete patio outside the glass door, slapping against the windows.

I was doing a mental calculation on how much the condominium must have cost. "How long have you lived here?"

Melinda pulled a bottle of Myer's rum from a narrow cherry cabinet. Okay, I'd lost out on Jody's rum cake, but this was looking promising. I saw her lips tighten as she said, "I suppose you know that Roland and I were having some problems. Violet wasn't the reason, although I'm sure she'd like to believe she was. I'd told Roland that we should buy one of these condos while they were going up, for investment purposes. I didn't know I would end up here."

"Not a bad place to be."

"You interviewed Gigi at the house. What did you think about it?"

"The house? It's spectacular. What a view."

"It was designed by Monroe Jessle-Tate, the architect. Have you heard of him?" I shook my head. "He was famous in small circles, mostly Northwest homes built in the late sixties."

There was a soft, cheery *ding* from the timer and Melinda turned to pull out the hors d'oeuvres with one of the bright red mitts. "This place is nothing like the house, of course. I don't even know that I'll get to keep it. Roland had me sign a prenup, and I don't know what that entails."

"But if this was purchased while you were married, the prenup wouldn't be in effect."

"You would think. But Roland was cagey. He was always having me sign documents. By the time I realized I needed a lawyer to look out for my interests, it was too late. I'd signed and signed and signed." She gave me a cool look. "I'm not entitled to any part of the clinics' sale. I know that. But I really thought Roland would take care of me."

"Maybe he did," I said lamely. What did I know?

"Oh, it's all decided. Gigi's got the house. Or maybe it's split with Sean, but he's not interested in anything but cash, anyway. And the business proceeds go to them, of course, although Daniel Wu's a wolf in sheep's clothing. Have you met him?" I shook my head again. "He was only supposed to get twenty-five percent, tops, but there's something fishy there. Of course, no one talks to me. I'm the third wife." She poured the rum into the bottom of two coffee mugs and picked up the coffeepot, topping off the drinks. She then pulled a silver pitcher from the refrigerator and added real cream. "I can't believe you're actually working for Violet," she said, carefully balancing my mug as she walked toward me. "I can't tell you how furious I am. She fools around with my husband, then she kills him. And it's always poor Violet.

She's so misunderstood." Melinda gave a very undignified snort as she returned to the kitchen. "She's trash. I don't care if she's a Purcell or not. Trash is a state of mind." While she ranted, she placed the crescents on a plate, added some icicle radishes and a wedge of blue cheese and brought the platter to the coffee table, handing me a red cocktail napkin. "You're *really* helping her?"

Her eyes were hazel, a little darker than my own greenish gold ones. Her hair, like Violet's, was light brown, artfully streaked with blond both for beauty and to hide the encroaching gray. I sensed steel in her. A determination that belied her soft, homemaker exterior.

"Maybe the Wedding Bandits killed him," I tried out.

"You believe that?"

I shrugged. My hand hovered over the hors d'oeuvres. There was a tiny pot of some kind of jelly beside them. I picked one up, dipped it in the jelly and took a bite. "Oh, my, God," I said around a mouthful. It was an explosion of flavor, sweet and savory and just plain damn good.

Melinda smiled. "Bacon, cream cheese with curry, smoked almonds, and the dip is chutney. I'm trying them out. I'm in charge of the Neighborhood Association's fall, really preholiday, get-together just before Thanksgiving. Well, it's really an all-community event to establish better communication as some of the associations are jealous of our presence in Lake Chinook. So, they'll work?" she asked, indicating the hors d'oeuvres.

"If I cooked, I'd ask for the recipe," I said sincerely.

Melinda seemed to take this as her due. "Roland never really appreciated my culinary skills. Oh, he praised me, but he wasn't really into food. A shame. Maybe if he'd cared about something other than sex he wouldn't have needed Violet. And just for the record? Those apple bars. That's my recipe. Jody's just taken it over as if it's hers."

"Well, they're fabulous." I eased another hors d'oeuvre

from the plate, wondering how many I could take before it became rude, wondering also if I cared. I was surprised at how aware Melinda was about Roland and Violet's relationship.

As if she read my mind, Melinda said, "They were having an affair."

I didn't argue with her.

"I know Violet's guilty," she stated positively. "She took my husband's life. She blew back into our lives at the worst time for us and took advantage of the situation, moving in on Roland. Poor, poor Roland who was having trouble with his wife," she singsonged, parodying Violet. Rolling her eyes, Melinda added coldly, "She's like a fungus. You can't get rid of her."

"Maybe someone else was at the scene. The Wedding Bandits were there. Maybe they weren't the only ones."

"Violet beat him to death with the tray. She admitted to that, right? That's what I heard."

"She hit him once. He was alive when she left."

"Once?" She gave me a "get real" look. "I can't believe she actually brought a gift over. She and Gigi hadn't spoken in years. But maybe Roland was trying to get them to make up. That would be just like him. And Gigi would do whatever he wanted, because otherwise she could be cut out of the will." She grabbed a crescent, touched it to the chutney, then bit into it, chewing hard. Frowning, she took another bite. "A little light on the curry, I think," she said. Dusting her hands, she added, "Roland's kids might act like they cared about him, but I'm the only one who really misses him. And financially, I'm the only one who loses there, too."

I sensed that Violet missed him a bit, too, but I kept that thought to myself. If Violet weren't so concerned about clearing her name, I felt, she might show even more sorrow over Roland's death. Or was that wishful thinking on my part? Something Violet wanted me to feel?

Scamming another hors d'oeuvre, I said, "I'm making a timeline of the rehearsal dinner and wedding day. Could you tell me what time you got there? Who was there? What happened . . . ?"

"To help get Violet off?"

"Just to help."

She went back to the kitchen and poured us each another cup of coffee, liberally laced with more rum. Handing me my cup, she recurled herself into her chair. "I was curious to meet you. You're helping Violet. That's what you're doing. You don't have to lie about it."

"I told Violet if I found out she was guilty, I was going straight to the cops. She hired me anyway."

"I'm not sure if I believe you." I waited, sensing it was best to let her work it out. She seemed to come to some conclusion, because she said, "If I help you, I'd like you to keep me informed."

"I can't promise that."

"Can you at least tell me if you've got a different lead? Someone that's sending you away from Violet?"

"So you can send me back, so to speak?" She smiled at me over the rim of her cup. "If you've got something to say, now's the time."

"Maybe you should look more into Violet's past," she suggested.

"Anything particular you want me to find?"

"She's had a number of husbands. Two before Roland." I could have responded that Roland had had a number of wives, two before Melinda, but I was hoping she would tell me something I didn't know. When I didn't bite, she looked a little annoyed. "Fine. You're working on a timeline. You want me to tell you what I was doing at the wedding and when."

"That would be great."

"I was at the rehearsal dinner the night before. Everybody

was happy. Roland was there, making a toast to his daughter. Violet wasn't invited to that, thank God."

"What time was the rehearsal dinner?"

"Six-thirty. Roland had rented Castellina, the Pinot Noir Room." She smiled faintly. "Roland and Emmett's family being cheap. It was a package deal for a better price."

I would call that being thrifty, but what do I know? "I've been meaning to call Emmett's parents . . . I wrote their names in the timeline but we haven't connected yet."

"You mean David and Goliath?"

I'd been digging in my purse for a pen and the notepad I always carry, but I looked up. "Goliath?"

"Okay, it's Goldy. But she's huge. I mean *huge*. She's gotta be close to six feet and she's just as wide. Luckily Emmett takes after his father."

"Who else was there?"

"The bridal party, some close friends of Emmett's. Gigi doesn't really have any friends besides Deenie. She was lucky to have four bridesmaids. Sean wasn't there. A conflict with his *band*," she said scornfully. "But Renee showed." She made a face. "She was invited to the wedding, but she and Gigi got into a huge argument at the rehearsal dinner and she was told not to come."

"I thought she argued with Roland."

"First Roland, then Gigi. Renee had brought this heavyset man with a beard, her date, and she hadn't told anyone. They drove up in a Ferrari, if you can believe that. I mean, a thousand miles? You wouldn't catch me doing that! Roland let Renee know it was bad form in plain terms, I'll tell you. But her date gets all huffy with Roland. It was almost taken care of, until she and Gigi started sniping at each other. After that, Roland just roared, 'Don't come tomorrow. You're not invited.' "

"After they drove all the way from Santa Monica?"

"Bad behavior's bad behavior," she dismissed. "Renee's

something else. She looks like a cat, you know. You probably heard that already. All that plastic surgery. And she decided to wear this leopard-print skirt out of faux fur with a matching leather jacket, also trimmed in leopard. I couldn't believe it! She thinks she's so funny but it's just too weird." Melinda gave a mock shudder. "And she had on this black pillbox hat with a veil, but it couldn't cover up that face. Gigi was embarrassed. Not that she's much better. Her bridal gown accentuated everything wrong—her hips, her arm fat, her short neck. She's an attractive enough girl, but she looked terrible. I tried to give her some advice, but she acted like I was criticizing her."

Imagine that.

"And Renee can't stop," Melinda said, returning to her earlier subject. "I mean, sure, a little freshening. Who wouldn't? But it's surgery after surgery. She still hasn't stopped. It's a sickness with her."

"How did you meet Roland?"

The abrupt change of topic stopped her short. She looked as if I'd slapped her. "Why do you need all this? What are you trying to do? Am *I* a suspect?"

"I'm just filling in," I said. It was just a question I'd put on my list, though I was a little surprised at her offense.

She flushed. "You're an amateur. Acting like you know what you're doing. I don't even know why I agreed to this."

"If you don't want to talk about it, that's okay."

"I did not break up Violet and Roland's marriage, no matter what anyone says!" she blasted back at me. "And I have every right to feel like she was trying to break up mine!"

"I wasn't suggesting that," I assured her. "Violet never said you broke up their marriage."

"Roland was single when we met," she wanted me to know. "He'd been single awhile because Violet ran off when he had his substance abuse problem. She just bailed. And Roland being Roland, he forgave her. He didn't blame her for leaving him when he needed her most. He just picked himself up, went through rehab, then set about putting his name and expertise behind the clinics. I met him when he was opening the third clinic. He was so upbeat. I fell in love with him instantly." She swallowed hard and looked toward the fire, tears glittering in the corners of her eyes. "I can't believe he's gone."

"You were already living here"—I gestured to the condo surroundings—"when Violet returned to Portland a couple of months ago?"

"It was temporary. Roland and I were working things out. I don't need to tell you this, but we'd been fighting about the kids, Gigi and Sean. Roland just indulged them so much and I made the mistake of telling him he should stop bankrolling them. He really took that the wrong way." Her mouth worked. "But by the wedding, things were better. We were virtually back together and were talking about going to it together. But then Violet got in the way. She kept calling him and calling him. I caught Roland on the phone with her a few times, and I got really upset. Then he started lying about it. It was just awful. Roland told me he loved me and not to worry about Violet, but you know her. Of course I was worried. Things really were improving between us, though," she reiterated, as if saying it enough times might make it true.

"Renee came up from Santa Monica. On that Friday? Or earlier?"

"Earlier, I think. You'd have to ask her. I don't remember."

"So, the rehearsal dinner was the first event where people gathered . . . most of the family and friends."

"Gigi had some luncheons or something earlier in the week, I think," Melinda said with a shrug, losing interest. "Of course, we all got to see each other all over again at the memorial service. Renee was there. I think she sent her friend back and just stayed on. Gigi was a wreck and Sean was utterly useless. I had to make the arrangements, and it was really, really hard. I called the Lake Chinook Country Club and they put on the event, but I had special items brought in from Blackbird Pie Catering. They make bite-size tomato tarts that are indescribable. Everybody just loved them."

She fell silent, recalling happier moments. I hadn't even thought about a funeral or memorial service for Roland. Violet hadn't mentioned any, and I wondered if she'd even attended. Maybe she'd missed the memo. She was outside the family and friends loop, and everyone thought she was guilty of killing him. Not exactly party guest number one on the list.

I quizzed Melinda on the schedule of events on the wedding day. She gave the time she arrived at both Castellina and the winery, and how she and Deenie had stalwartly held Gigi's hands when the search for Roland began. Beyond that, she didn't have much more to add. She started looking at her watch and I realized my interview was over, so I rose to my feet and thanked her for everything before she got antsy and pushed me out the door. Better to leave on a high note, just in case you need something more later.

"Would you like to take these with you?" she asked, indicating the six leftover hors d'oeuvres.

"Are you sure?"

"Oh, I'm making dozens more." She grabbed a disposable plastic tub and carefully arranged the crescents inside, adding dabs of chutney to their toasted tops. Then she snapped on a blue plastic lid and handed it to me. I thanked her and she said, "Maybe you'd like to join us at the neighborhood get-together. It's at the Village Shopping Center the Saturday before Thanksgiving."

"Definitely," I said.

At the door, she had one more interesting thing to add.

"Now that you've met Gigi, what do you think of her?" she asked as I gauged the distance to my car and the extent of rain that would drench me as I hurried to the driver's door.

"Well . . ."

Melinda smiled faintly. "Gigi doesn't think much of anyone besides Gigi. I've asked myself a thousand times what Emmett sees in her. Maybe she's a good lay."

Those last words ran around in my head all the way back to the cottage. Melinda was so tidy and precise, the phraseology seemed oddly crude for her. Her feelings for Gigi didn't appear all that far from her feelings for Violet.

I spent the next several days filling in my timeline, reviewing my impressions, wondering if I was wasting everyone's time and money. In this I wasn't sure I cared. Violet was paying and didn't appear overly concerned about the cost.

I did a bit of uneventful process-serving, uneventful except for the barrage of epithets thrown at me from a heavyset man who shook a brass candlestick at me he happened to have in his hand when I served him the eviction notice. I kept my eye on the candlestick, worried he might chuck it at me, but apparently he considered it too valuable and just kept up the four-letter words as I retreated to my car.

Sticks and stones, buddy. Sticks and stones.

I put in calls to Renee Hatchmere and David and Goliath Popparockskill, but none of them answered and by Friday not one of them had returned my call. David and Goliath lived in southeast Portland, on the east side of the Willamette and far enough from downtown to make me think of visiting them as a "trip." I also tried calling Deenie again to no avail. I figured she'd give me the same information as the rest of the wedding party bridesmaids and groomsmen: the color scheme sucked, the wedding cancellation sucked, the bachelor party rocked, Roland's death sucked.

Okay, the best man had had a few other things to say as well. I caught an inkling of his feelings regarding the bride when he referred to Gigi as a "hysterical, whining train wreck." Yes, I'm quick to pick up on these seemingly benign comments. Being the clever investigator I am, I told James it sounded like he was happy the wedding never came off and James very succinctly said Emmett's head was up his ass because Junie-Marie, his last girlfriend, was the most lovely, sweet, voluptuous, down-to-earth woman in the world. Junie-Marie? I asked. Named after her grandmother June Marie, I learned. Junie-Marie's only problem appeared to be that she did not enjoy the Hatchmere wealth. James thought that was a poor excuse indeed to throw her over for the wealthy, bitchy, vicious, skinny, ugly Gigi Hatchmere.

Gigi wasn't ugly, and she wasn't really skinny. I wasn't certain about the vicious part, either, but I pretty well concurred with James on the wealthy and bitchy parts. I asked how to contact Junie-Marie, which made James highly suspicious of my intentions. He told me he didn't have that information at hand, but promised to get it for me later. Like, oh, sure. I had a feeling he was the kind that spoke loudly and freely, then wished he could cut out his own tongue later.

All of this background material was interesting. Maybe some of it might actually have some meaning someday. I wrote it up in a report for Dwayne, making sure all pertinent information was recorded.

Violet called me daily. I'd given her Sharona's name in case she needed an attorney any time soon, but so far she hadn't called her. I think she had her fingers crossed that the court wouldn't indict and she wouldn't need representation. I kind of thought it would be good to get Sharona up to speed just in case, but then I don't have a lot of faith in innocent until proven guilty.

Friday dawned gray and bleak and wet. It dampened my spirits, so to speak, and the thought of meeting Dawn and company at Do Not Enter in this weather sounded like a total drag.

I ran to the Coffee Nook in the rain, cinching the hood of my blue windbreaker so tightly that only my eyes, nose and mouth were exposed to the elements. Even so I thought I could drown before I blew inside with a gust of wind that caused everyone standing by the door to shriek with surprise and irritation.

"Shut the damn door!" Chuck growled.

I was trying to do just that but it took some effort. One of the other regulars helped me thrust back the wind, just as another customer blew in with the same wildly flinging door entrance.

"What a bunch of idiots," Chuck said, dolefully shaking his head. My interest in knowing him slid even further down the scale into negative numbers. He added the icing to the cake by asking me, "Do you always wear the same thing?"

"I try."

"Oh. Did I offend you? Sorry." He tried to look apologetic but it appeared more like a smirk.

There was a girl in my high school who allegedly, every month, mapped out what she would wear to school each day for that month, just so she wouldn't repeat herself on what was apparently a popularity-killing offense. I never saw the point of this and wore whatever the hell I felt like. I consequently was not elected to any high school court, nor was I hugely popular with members of the male sex, so maybe there was some validity to her obsession. My noteworthy high school achievement was burning the cinnamon rolls in Home Ec class and setting the overhead sprinklers off from the boiling smoke that filled the room. So, okay, I thought they weren't getting done fast enough and I figured five hundred degrees was a better option. The sugar carmelized, blackened and turned the rolls into charred hockey pucks. Though I was willing to take the blame, my Home Ec partner, Michele, jumped in and said it was all her fault before I could fess up. At the time I was taken aback, but as I watched the events unfold I learned Michele loved to be the center of attention, either bad or good. She apologized contritely to the administration and teachers and said she would do whatever needed to be done to make it right, all the while slyly smiling at her friends when no one was looking, who in turn thought she was the coolest. Nothing ever bothered her. I helped her on the cleanup but she really didn't care. She thought the world was one big joke and enjoyed her own niche of back-asswards popularity because of it. I think there's a lesson in there somewhere, but what I really came away with is that baking's a lot trickier than it looks.

Billy Leonard was seated on one of the Coffee Nook's stools, so I slid onto the one next to him. Billy is one of those guys who looks like he was meant for pickup trucks, rusted fishing trawlers and evenings spent with cheap cigars and long yarns. Surprisingly, he's a CPA. I find I learn a lot from Billy although he made an allusion to the fact that we were raising our kids as "hatchery fish," coddling them, not preparing them for the harsh realities of life, which had me worried about my own abilities a few months back. I've come to peace with that, pretty much, now that I'm working for Dwayne. I'm pretty sure now I'm not a hatchery fish.

Billy was drinking coffee and talking to some of the people across the way. He said in an aside to me, "Chuck's the fashion police now?"

We both looked over at Chuck's wrinkled slacks and gray pullover. There was a tiny moth hole near the underarm where we got a peek of his white undershirt. "Billy, if I asked you about one of your clients' net worth, would you tell me?"

"That wouldn't be ethical."

"So that's a no?"

"Who are you trying to find out about?"

I shrugged. "Roland Hatchmere, I guess."

"He's not my client. And I hear he's dead. What do you mean, you guess?"

"I was thinking about the Wedding Bandits. How they pick their targets. I mean, sure there are engagement and wedding announcements that list the venues and dates, so I guess it could be pretty easy to know where the ceremony's going to be, but how do you know who has the money? And how do you know where they live?"

I hadn't really realized I'd been thinking in these terms. Sometimes the mind is a strange and fabulous thing, working, sorting, plotting while we sleep, or watch TV, or play with our dogs. Seeing Billy, thinking about his job, had sent my mind down the financial path and I slammed into the Wedding Bandits without thinking.

"You know Dr. Hatchmere of Hatchmere Plastic Surgery has money because you just know," Billy said. "Read the paper."

"How do you know where he lives?"

Billy shrugged. "You follow him home from work one day."

I nodded. That was as good an answer as any.

The thought circled my mind as I jogged back to the cottage. I was still thinking it as I stripped off my wet clothes and headed for the shower. As soon as I was toweled off and in dry jeans, my brown boots and a black, ribbed V-neck sweater, I phoned Dwayne on his cell. "Hullo," he greeted me, sounding distracted.

"Does your buddy Larrabee know how the robbery victims are targeted?"

"He's not keeping me in that loop."

"Could it be that the bandits just follow the primary target home from work? Like Roland. It wouldn't be hard to figure out who he is."

"Sure."

I could tell I wasn't quite engaging him and it kind of pissed me off. "Am I keeping you from your binoculars?"

"The damn rain's keeping me from my binoculars," he groused. "You wanna meet Larrabee?"

That stopped me. "Yes."

"I'll give him a call. See if I can set something up. I wanna know what's going on with that investigation, too."

I could hear the frustration in his voice, which I thought was a good sign. Dwayne had seemed way too relaxed for far too long, so I inwardly cheered the dissatisfaction. "Great," I said.

I told him that I'd added to my written report and I mentioned my meeting with Melinda. Dwayne asked me if I had any apple bars left over. I visualized the two sitting on a plate in my refrigerator, silently mourned the loss, and generously told Dwayne I would bring them over to him.

"That hurt, didn't it?" he said, barely holding back a laugh.

"I get one and you get one."

"Get over here, then."

Something about his warm tone got to me. I assured him I would be there, then got off the phone and looked at The Binkster. She cocked her head, ready for a deep discussion.

"Let's not go there now." I went to the refrigerator and pulled out the plate of apple bars. I felt slightly guilty that I hadn't mentioned Melinda's fabulous hors d'oeuvres at all. This was mainly because they never made it into my refrigerator. I pretty much took care of them on the ride home that day and their existence didn't make it into my report, either written or oral. But I'd hoarded the apple bars and sharing was the price I would pay.

Dwayne was standing in his kitchen when I arrived, and I did the proverbial double take. "You've got a new cast on." I set the plate on the counter and gave him the once-over. The full-length cast had been replaced by what looked like wrapped splints and Dwayne was in tattered denim cutoffs, revealing the tight, damn near fused bandage holding the pieces in place around his right thigh and across his knee. His attire suggested a sunny day on the lake. Like in August.

"Violet drove me to the doctor," he said.

Pissed me off to no end. As many times as Violet called me on the phone, had she once mentioned this? Oh, sure. I "have mine." It certainly didn't look as if she was giving up on Dwayne completely any time soon.

Dwayne's way too aware of mood to let my silence go unremarked. "Didn't want to disturb you," he said in his drawl. "You were meeting Roland's wife the time of my appointment. Violet stopped by so I asked her for the favor."

And she was happy to help. I didn't say it. I didn't say anything at all.

Dwayne chose to ignore further comment on the issue and eyed the two apple bars. "Should we nuke 'em?"

"Go ahead."

He put the plate in the microwave and we both watched the apple bars spin around for a minute as if we would be tested later on how they turned out. We ate them in silence and mine could have been sawdust for all the attention to flavor it presented, but Dwayne smacked his up. "God, those are good," he said with real admiration.

I shook myself out of my mood with an effort. This is exactly why I don't want to feel anything for Dwayne. I don't want to be driven crazy, and though nothing—*nothing*—has transpired between us of a serious nature, certainly of a sexual nature, it's already affecting my sanity.

"Did you talk to Larrabee?" I asked.

"Left a message on his voice mail. He hasn't gotten back to me yet."

"It's an epidemic," I grumbled, explaining that I, too, had left messages all over the place that hadn't been returned yet.

"He'll get in touch with you," Dwayne assured me. "When he does, offer to buy him lunch. Or dinner."

Dwayne's suddenly careful tone caught my attention. "Something you're not telling me about Detective Larrabee?"

"Be careful of him," he said with a faint smile.

"Oh, great. Why?"

"I've known him a long time. He's—thorough."

"Meaning?"

He shook his head. "The guy has a lot of levels. You'll be fine. Women love him."

Like they love you? I turned away from him. Nope. I was not going to go there. "You lost your little red heart with the initials," I pointed out, gesturing to his cast.

"Darlene's eight-year-old'll probably be upset."

"Your cleaning lady's daughter?"

"Yeah. Why? Who'd you think drew it?"

I decided a change of subject was in order. "I'm going over to Do Not Enter tonight. Gotta meet Dawn."

"Darlin', don't go if you don't want to," Dwayne drawled. "It's rainin' buckets out there."

"Oh, don't give me that."

"What?"

"The 'aw, shucks, it's no big deal' act. You started this, Hal Jeffries. I'm just along for the ride."

He smiled. Then he picked up his cell phone and placed a call. "Call me," he said and clicked off. "Larrabee," he told me. "Might as well keep after him."

I nodded and glanced out to the darkening sky. Though I wanted to rail about it, I really felt the same way about Dawn and the kids at Do Not Enter. I wasn't sure what to do, but I figured I could make another appearance before ratting them out. "Any ideas how to make myself look younger tonight?"

"Show more skin."

I gazed at his tattered shorts. "It's November and the weather is crap."

"Doesn't stop 'em. The girls wear skimpy tops under their jackets. Always showin' off a bare shoulder or a patch of skin at the waistline. They hook up and disappear with one of the guys, come back all bundled up again."

"I've got a V-neck on. That's as bare as it goes."

"You asked."

"And how am I getting compensated for this, again?"

"I'm paying your rates. Don't worry about it."

I shivered involuntarily. "Thanks, but I've got a sweat-shirt that should do the trick."

Five hours later, I drove toward Beachlake Drive wearing Glen's Lake Chinook sweatshirt, which I'd washed and dried and shrunk some. The hem had crept up a little, but the sleeves still looked like they'd fit an orangutan and the shirt's width was wide enough to fit two of me. I'd brought my anorak but it was in the backseat. Rain or no, I wanted to show up in the sweatshirt.

I found a parking spot a bit farther away this time, closer to the dead end of the road, as there were quite a few more cars parked along the road's narrow shoulder. Apparently there was a bigger group tonight.

I gazed at my reflection in the rearview mirror. Tonight I'd snapped my hair into a ponytail, my usual jogging style, and I'd added more makeup than I can usually stomach. I'd really laid it on thick. Makeup's supposed to make you look older, but I tried to kind of dumb it down, like I really didn't know what I was doing, to make it appear that this whole makeup thing was new to me. This meant the eyeliner was a teensy bit crooked and the mascara was on both my upper and lower lashes and thick enough to be the *great, greater, greatest!* lashes of all time. I looked like a reject from a Maybelline commercial, eyelashes sprouting all around my hazel irises, giving me a surprised look. When coupled with a vacant stare, I was pretty pleased with the results. Still, high school would be a stretch to most anyone who saw me in the light of day. Do Not Enter's uncertain illumination was a definite plus.

I placed a last call to Dwayne. "I'm going in, Coach."

"Taking your cell phone?"

"Putting it on vibrate and keeping it close."

"Call me when you're leaving."

"If my parents come looking for me, tell them you haven't seen me. No matter what they do to you."

"I won't give you up," he said, the smile sounding in his voice. "The team's behind you."

"Later, dude."

"I'm right across the bay."

Somehow that was comforting. I clicked off and stuffed the phone in my pocket. Bending my head against the driving rain, I picked up another rock and stuffed it in the sweatshirt pocket, then picked my way through the mud and dirty water toward the construction site.

CHAPTER EIGHT

The kids who'd gone to the game—either playing or watching—hadn't arrived yet, but there were more than a few others hanging around. My buddy Brett was there and upon my arrival, grinned like a goof and came over to me, throwing an arm around me. This seemed to be the usual form of greeting, and I tried like hell not to let on that I'm not a huge fan of the full body hug. There are only three reasons to connect so fully with another human body, in my opinion: sexual foreplay, grief comfort and as a way to stave off death in freezing temperatures. I didn't think any of the three applied, but I smiled at Brett anyway, as if I'd been waiting all day just for this.

"Hey, sorry about last time. I didn't know you were still around. Tina just kinda came over."

"No problem," I said. "We're still friends."

"We could be more," he pointed out.

I smiled crookedly and let it pass. The way I saw it, when he and Tina hooked up, it had taken the onus off me being his exclusive find. I figured I could now do whatever the hell I wanted with impunity. It would have been trickier had he somehow marked me as his and then I backed away. Hard feelings might have surfaced. These dating rituals are complicated and it's hard to skirt around them, but some of the rules are sacrosanct. Brett had thrown his arm around another girl while I was out meeting friends. I was a free agent.

He released me long enough to find us both a beer. I was chilled and thought beer wasn't exactly going to do much for me, but I dutifully accepted it, popping the top. He flung his arm over my shoulder and again the dead weight of it drove me nearly insane. I wanted to scream and fling it off.

Note to self: work on relationship skills.

One of the girls, shivering in a short furry coat over a miniskirt, puffed on a cigarette, sucking smoke in and spitting it out like it was a speed event. Though not a smoker myself, I felt she lacked a certain style, and isn't that what it's about at some level? Coolness? Sophistication? She could really use a remedial course. Another girl leaning against a post knew how to do it, inhaling slowly and deliberately, her eyes half closed, her throat arched, exhaling a soft cloud of smoke.

"Gonna take 'em a while to get here from Clackamas," Brett said by way of explanation. He lifted his beer and clinked it against mine. "Have to start without 'em."

I'd been wondering where Keegan was. And Dawn. With an inward sigh, I settled in for a wait. They hadn't strung the red lights yet and it was dark and cold, rain pounding on the roof.

Brett started telling me all the reasons he hadn't made it to tonight's game. I listened with half an ear, wishing I'd timed my arrival a little better.

A flash of light strobed through. White. Then red.

"Fuck," a male voice whispered from somewhere outside the front door. "The cops."

I was on my feet and shooting downstairs to the backyard before my brain was in full gear. My heart jerked wildly in my chest. Behind me I heard the kids bumbling around and swearing, running into each other, but I was out the back and across the yard to Social Security before you could say, "Halt, you're under arrest."

I threw my purse over the fence, then climbed with an agility that surprised me later, practically vaulting over the top. As I've said, fleeing is my first response and I'm damn good at it. I dropped into the gushy muck on Social Security's side of the chain-link. Their yard was a mire that sucked at my shoes. Glancing back, I saw flashing illumination from Beachlake, an aurora borealis lighting up the area. Quickly, I scooped up my purse and hurried to the farthest side of their boathouse. Their canoe lay upside down, exactly as I'd seen it from Dwayne's dock. I flipped it over, rain running down my neck.

I set my purse down, searching the canoe's interior. No oars. Panicked, I turned around in a rapid circle, scanning the surrounding grounds. Nothing. Tiptoeing to the end of the yard, which ended at a concrete skirt, I peered around the wall of the boathouse into its yawning black mouth. The skirt turned into a narrow concrete ledge that ran around the inside edge of the building. An old motorboat, suspended by canvas straps, groaned slightly as my hand touched the side of it for balance. It rocked gently. I steadied it and tried to get a handle on my rapid breathing.

The oars were hung on the wall. I squeezed inside the boathouse and grabbed them. One slipped from my hand and clattered to the concrete, sounding like gunfire. Swooping it up, I morphed myself back around the edge of the boathouse, daring one glance toward the rear yard of Do Not Enter. Kids were running stealthily across Pet Cemetery toward Rebel Yell and Tab A/Slot B. The lights still flashed and then I heard the first whine of a siren from the direction of Lake Chinook.

I could not be caught.

With an effort I shoved the canoe into the water. It splashed loudly. I held on to one end, leaning over the water, sure I was going to fall in. Precariously balancing, I grabbed my purse with my free hand. After a moment the canoe steadied and I stepped inside, wobbling a bit. I sat down quickly. Glanced up at Social Security. Lights blazed on.

Oh God. They'd heard me.

I paddled west, quietly but with an inner urgency. *Hurry, hurry, hurry.* I could practically see Josh Newell's face. I pictured handcuffs. A ride in the back of his police car for real.

I dipped the oars as carefully as I could, opting for silence over speed. My jaw was clenched. My head bent to the driving rain. I slipped past other houses along Beachlake Drive, trying to calculate where the road dead-ended. It's hard to tell because the houses continue past Beachlake's final cul-de-sac, their access from a tangle of roads that delta off North Shore Loop. If someone hoped to follow me, they would have to head back to a main road and find their way to wherever I decided to pull in.

I hoped to God they hadn't seen me.

But if they had . . . My mind was filled with images of a Lake Chinook prowler, silently creeping along the narrow roadways, tracking my progress.

The siren grew louder and louder, its *wooOOOOOO ooooooo-OOOOOOoooo* splitting the still night air.

I kept moving west. My vague plan had been to eventually circle around and cross the bay to Dwayne's. But I couldn't make myself do it. Too exposed. Too dark. Too dangerous.

I struggled with the oars, clumsy and awkward. It felt like I was treading water. My teeth chattered, more from fear than cold, though there was plenty of that, too. The rain beat on me. I had to shake it out of my eyes. I thought about my car, parked on the street. Were they searching it? It could belong to any of the residents on Beachlake, couldn't it? My purse was still over my shoulder, banging against me as I oared, but I wouldn't set it down. I would rather drown with it than let it get away from me.

I hugged the seawall, moving steadily away from Social Security. About six houses down, I glanced back. Were the police after me? Did they know I'd taken the canoe? I stopped oaring and simply slid my hand along the seawall, propelling the canoe toward the end of Beachlake. *Hurry, hurry, hurry.* Sweat ran down my back.

A loud alarm sounded from the house I'd just passed, one of those spiraling screams that blare over and over again. I practically jumped from the boat and my gasp was a bitten off scream. My skin lifted in fear. Any minute I expected a searchlight to pin me in its glare.

Lights burst on in more houses along Beachlake. I gave up stealth and oared like mad to the footbridge that marked the end of the cul-de-sac. The bridge crossed over a tiny stream that fed into the bay. I kept paddling past the footbridge, past another house that wasn't on Beachlake, past another. *Get away*, I whispered inside my own head. *Get away.*

The siren cut off with an abrupt chirp.

I was four houses past the end of Beachlake Drive, four houses into the next neighborhood. I didn't know what street their addresses were, or how one would find them. I pulled up to a house that looked empty. It had a yawning boathouse that was four poles topped by a slanted metal roof, kind of like a carport for boats. There was no boat in residence, so I slid the canoe under its shelter, listening to the rain pound and ping on its hard roof. There was a rope at the end of the canoe, and I tied it carefully to a rusted cleat, then stepped onto a narrow dock whose boards were rotted and soft. My legs shook. I was soaked to the bone. Carefully I peeked from beneath my shelter toward the dark, gloomy house. Not one light. And the two houses on either side weren't waking to the alarm, either. I hoped to high heaven this house was as abandoned as it seemed. Carefully, treading as lightly as I could, I edged my way through the thick laurel hedge on the home's eastern side, looking for access to the front.

There was a wrought-iron gate between me and freedom. My heart nearly stopped until I realized it wasn't locked. It creaked as I pulled it open, so I squeezed through and left it ajar.

Head bent, I scurried forward, my purse held tight to my side. My Lake Chinook sweatshirt had been worse than useless in this weather; it stuck to me, a sodden deadweight. I found my cell phone, comforted by its welcoming light, as I put a call into Dwayne.

"Hey," Dwayne answered, obviously recognizing my number.

"Can you come get me?" I whispered.

"Where are you?" He was all business.

"Not sure. You know where Beachlake Drive ends? The houses that are further west, but you reach them by some access road? That's the road I'll be on."

"I hear sirens."

"No shit."

"They're coming from Social Security."

My heart clutched. Had they seen me steal their canoe? "Better hurry, Dwayne."

He clicked off and was gone.

I counted it a blessing, practically a miracle, that he'd gotten his full leg cast off and was more mobile. Mobile enough, anyway, to drive his surveillance car.

I reached the road, which was covered by a canopy of fir branches high overhead, both from the trees lining the road and from a screen of Douglas firs that marched up the hill, nearly obscuring houses farther up. Pinpricks of light showed through the foliage, like tiny stars, illumination from

the houses hanging on the cliffside with views of Lakewood
Bay. I trudged along, moving ever farther west, away from
Beachlake Drive but also from Dwayne's cabana on the
other side of the bay. The road curved to the left and circled
to the right and I finally came to where it T'd into North
Shore.

There are no streetlights along these curvy lanes and for
that I was grateful. I stayed outside the circle of illumination
offered by a lantern on a stone entry post at the end of a
drive and shivered convulsively. I could have been the only
person on the planet. It was dark, wet, cold and miserable.

I heard a car's engine, quiet, and the glow of headlights
approaching from around a corner. I stepped back and
pressed myself to the side of a detached garage, sliding
around to the back as the car neared, keeping myself well out
of detection. The car purred past me but I didn't dare look
immediately. I managed a peek as its taillights turned the
next corner. A black, unmarked police car. Jesus. Haven't I
said the Lake Chinook police have nothing to do? *Haven't I?*
They were treating Operation Teen Drinking like an FBI
sting.

Five minutes later another car's engine sounded, also
quiet. I kept to my hiding place and hoped the homeowners
didn't wake and see a figure crouching behind the back of
their garage.

This time the car that cruised by was a beige sedan. I
punched autodial for Dwayne's number. He answered on the
first ring.

"You just went past me," I said. "A police car's somewhere ahead of you."

"I'm stopping."

I ran from my hiding place and hurried to the car.
Dwayne had pulled to the edge of the road and I jumped into
the passenger side. He was already in motion, smoothly

moving forward. We drove around North Shore for a quarter of a mile, then took a turn that eventually landed us on Iron Mountain Boulevard. As we headed back toward Lake Chinook proper we passed the unmarked prowler going the other way.

"The lights are on at Social Security."

I nodded jerkily. "I'm free–ee–zeeing." I couldn't get the word out through teeth that had a mind of their own.

"There's a jacket in the back. Can you reach it?" He was trying to twist around but it wasn't easy for him.

"Uh-huh."

"You all right?"

"I'm ohhhh–kayyy." I grabbed the denim jacket with clammy hands that scarcely had feeling in them. I wrapped it around my shoulders. It smelled like Dwayne.

"Your makeup's kind of scary," he said.

I refused to give in to the almost pathological desire to look in a mirror. Instead I told him what he could do to himself in vivid terms. He grinned, and I instantly felt better.

We made it back to Dwayne's without incident. The alarm from Social Security had finally been silenced and activity had diminished. We kept Dwayne's lights off but looked through the binoculars and his sliding glass doors. Through the bay window on Social Security's main floor we could see an older gentleman in a robe and pajamas talking heatedly with two policemen.

"I don't know what that's about," Dwayne said. "But I think the wife went to the hospital. The ambulance showed up, lights flashing, no siren."

"So it wasn't a raid on Do Not Enter."

"No. Kids started pouring onto the backyard as soon as the ambulance showed. Someone must have reported them running, because the police came but the kids were gone. Then the house alarm started."

"Maybe the old guy thought someone was stealing a canoe from him," I ventured, hugging Dwayne's coat against me.

"Hunh," Dwayne said.

"Yeah. Hunh."

We watched for a while more. The police left and the old guy changed his clothes and headed to his car. I felt a little nervous for him driving through this miserable weather, but his wife was at the hospital, so I guess that's what happens.

Dwayne put me in his shower to warm me up. I tossed my clothes in a pile on the floor. Behind the shower curtain, I heard the bathroom door open and stood frozen in place.

"Got some clothes here for ya," he said, and let himself back out.

I peered around the shower curtain. I could see a pair of gray sweatpants and one of his denim shirts.

I scrubbed my face and stood with my head under the hot spray until my muscles began to thaw. It took a while before I felt warm enough to turn off the taps and step from the shower. I toweled off and put on my cold, wet underwear before sliding into Dwayne's clothes. A few minutes later I padded barefoot to the kitchen, where he was leaning against the counter, watching coffee brew, a stream of dark liquid bubbling into the coffeemaker's glass pot.

"How do I look?" I asked.

He examined me from the top of my wet head to the peek of my toes beneath the folds of his sweats. "Warmer."

"I was really afraid I'd be caught contributing to the delinquency of minors."

"You wanna give this up?" He poured me a cup, handing it to me, our fingers brushing.

"You mean drinking beer with teenagers, running from the police, stealing canoes, freezing in the rain?" I drank the coffee, feeling it run hot down my throat. "I don't know.

Dawn wasn't there yet, and neither was Keegan. You think they'll still meet at Do Not Enter after this? I wouldn't."

"It's a perfect place for them. Yeah, I think they'll be there next week."

"They'd be nuts."

"They're teens. They don't have many options. It's parent-free and has a roof against the rain."

"The police know about it."

"Do they?" Dwayne pulled a bottle of Jack Daniel's from the cupboard above his head and raised it up to me in a question. I held my cup out to him and he gave me a liberal dose. "I think the kids left before they were raided. The cops responded to a call from the neighbors when they saw them running over their yards. I'm not sure any of 'em were collared."

"So, what are you saying?"

He made a face. "I don't know. Maybe it's time for Hal Jeffries to put away his binoculars."

I should have been thrilled to hear it. Should have wanted to dance in the streets. But Dwayne, blast him, had hooked me on Dawn's problems and I wanted to bring down Keegan Lendenhal in a bad way. I murmured something about that being a good idea, finished my coffee, then asked Dwayne to drive me to my car.

It turned out the old guy had simply hit his home alarm by accident after he called for an ambulance for his wife. The police followed up on the alarm and Mr. Social Security had been so upset over everything he'd bawled them out. They had not, apparently, chased the high school kids. Mrs. Social Security had suffered chest pains and a minor heart attack and was home by the end of the weekend, apparently okay.

I, on the other hand, came down with the sniffles after my

damp and chilly escape. Sure, okay, you can't catch a cold from the cold; you catch a cold from another person. But if you're around people who manhandle you and get too close, and their friends are around, too, and they're all touching each other and packing into tight places, then your chances of catching a cold greatly increase. And then if you run around in the dark, damp cold you might get your resistance down and voila, you got yourself a cold.

I made it through the rest of the weekend wrapped in a blanket with The Binkster pressed to my side on the living room couch, watching whatever came on TV. I learned to my horror that Binks was nearly out of food. I had enough stale saltines to last me a good week and a half, but I wasn't sure what to do about my dog, so in the end I called my friend Cynthia for help.

The great thing about her is she can take orders, mine being, buy something cheap and low-cal for The Binkster. I gave her the name of my usual brand and she showed up with a hefty bag of the stuff. She also picked up some mochis, a frozen Japanese dessert that is basically a ball of ice cream enclosed in a rice gum so that you can hold it in your hands. This set Binks dancing on her hind legs and twirling. I wasn't sure if dogs can catch people germs, but I figured I wouldn't take a chance sharing with her. I just gave her teensy bits and put the rest back in the freezer. Binks pathetically sat down in front of the refrigerator and whined. Cynthia couldn't stand it and pulled out a few bites more.

"You're spoiling her," I said, my voice all cloggy and dull.

"I brought you something, too," she said, digging into the large grocery bag she'd dumped on the counter.

I hadn't asked for anything for myself because I'm old school enough to want to get well without the aid of over-the-counter drugs. I'm so damned drug sensitive that the least little thing can make me stupid, crazy and seemingly on a bender.

But Cynthia pulled out a quart of some goldish liquid. "Chicken soup," she told me. "From Zeke and Jake's Deli."

"Cool," I said with enthusiasm. This sounded more like "Gull," but I think Cynthia got the message.

She stuck around long enough to serve me a bowl of soup and a couple of slices of baguette smeared with butter, but she tried to stay out of range of my germs. I just thanked my lucky stars that I had friends who actually liked me and wanted to do nice things for me.

I'd been all set to spend the afternoon sniffing and feeling sorry for myself, but Cynthia's soup and the baguette gave me enough energy to go over my notes on the Hatchmere case again, adding and tweaking and bringing them up to date. I swept my hardwood floor clean, pausing for long draughts of water from my kitchen tap, and then I plumped up the pillows on my couch and made the place presentable instead of some nest of sick germs. After doing a check for dog fur I hauled out the awkward vacuum cleaner, a canister type that I drag along like a ball and chain, and gave all the furniture a thorough cleaning. Finished, I found I was in a sweat, so I showered and redressed in fresh jeans and a light brown sweater. I felt almost human as I was combing the water from my hair, except my nose was red, swollen and dripping.

My cell phone vibrated noisily and I hurried to the front room to answer it. I'd left it on my coffee table and it was spinning around like it was trying to make itself dizzy when I snatched it up. Caller ID was unavailable, which generally means: wrong number. However, I had a lot of callbacks from people who might or might not have blocked their numbers.

"Hello?"

"Is this Jane Kelly?" a male voice rumbled. There was some kind of distortion on the line that made the timbre go in and out.

"Last I looked. And you are?"

"Vince Larrabee."

My mouth formed an O. I decided he must be outside and that was what was creating the audible interference.

"Durbin said you wanted to talk to me about the wedding day burglaries."

"The Wedding Bandits."

He didn't respond. Maybe he was one of those who obstinately ignored any name the press might ascribe to the culprits.

"I don't know what I can tell you that hasn't been printed already," he said, and I heard that tiny bit of judgment in his voice. Clearly he was doing his duty and trying to fob me off before things went any further.

"Would you mind if we got together and I just picked your brain a bit?" I asked. Lame, lame, lame. From what I'd gleaned, the guy wouldn't want some wet-behind-the-ears private investigator dogging his heels.

"Pick my brain?"

"I could meet you. Let me buy lunch." I held my breath.

He hesitated. "You sound like you've got a cold."

"Allergies," I lied.

I could almost hear him debating with himself. He didn't want to bother. He really didn't. "There's a place in southeast called Tony's, off Holgate," he said with a noticeable lack of enthusiasm.

Thank you, Dwayne. "I know it," I said, which wasn't exactly the truth but I was pretty sure I could find it.

"I'll be there at two."

He hung up before I had a chance to ask how I would know him. Glancing at the clock, I grabbed my windbreaker, threw the hood over my head, patted my dog on the head good-bye while she stood stiffly, staring from me to the door hopefully. She jumped down but I hurried out, telling her not this time.

The wind hit me with a rain-filled blast, slapping my face. "Peachy," I muttered, and scurried to my car.

When it rains, it pours, so to speak. The weather was a case in point, the gray skies throwing down an endless supply of precipitation. But also in life sometimes, like now. I'd been complaining that no one returned my phone calls but now the phone was ringing off the hook. Larrabee phoned as I drove to meet him, followed by calls from both Renee Hatchmere and my brother, Booth.

I didn't have time to talk to either of them, but I had to work hardest with Renee—who seemed thrilled to learn I wasn't available—to get her to even allow me a second phone call. She was intent on doing her duty, but that, apparently, was the extent of what she considered good manners. I could hear the wheedling tone in my voice that begged her please, please, please with sugar on top let me phone her back later. She didn't say yes, but she didn't completely say no, either.

Luckily, Booth wasn't much interested in talking, either. There seemed to be something on his mind, but when I told him to "Spit it out" he retreated into his shell at top speed, mumbling something about his job and he was too busy to spend time trying to make me and Mom happy. I thought that was just plain rude and told him so, but he'd already hung up.

If that wasn't enough, the phone rang again and Deenie identified herself. Ah yes, the hard-to-reach maid of honor. Her tone was petulant as she said the only reason she was returning my call was that Gigi had said she should. I checked my watch. Two p.m. straight up. Anxiously, I scanned the buildings around, realizing the area appeared a little bit too industrial for a restaurant. To Deenie, I said, "I'm walking into a meeting. May I call you back in an hour?"

"Well, I guess . . ."

"Thanks." I clicked off and drove over the speed limit, searching the area. Finally I saw TONY'S scrawled in black cursive along the cream-painted cinder block back wall of a building in a tired-looking commercial center, tucked up against a lumberyard and some kind of scrap metal operation.

I hoped to hell I wouldn't be the only female in the joint, gathering my courage as I stepped past the scarred front doors whose only decoration was a large NO MINORS ALLOWED sign.

I was hit by the cigarette smoke before the doors closed behind me. If the day had been any brighter I would have had to allow time for my eyes to adjust. As it was, I could see the bar was populated by a smattering of middle-aged men in varying degrees of decay, a woman behind the bar with a belly large and tight sporting a T-shirt that said *Beyond Bitch,* three young men in dirty jeans and plaid shirts holding up the bar, all attempting to grow facial hair without serious success, and a guy in a booth facing the door whose gray overcoat and serious expression signified the long arm of the law.

I walked straight to him. "Detective Larrabee?"

"Ms. Kelly."

I slid in across from him, feeling like we were playing some scripted part in a film noir. I wasn't sure what my line was, so I waited, hoping for a cue.

His face was lean, his liquid-brown eyes filled with an underlying amusement, as if life were just one long joke of which only he understood the punch line. His skin tone was much darker than my own. He had a De Niro look about him that was both magnetic and spoke of barely leashed energy. He wasn't wearing a hat and moisture had coalesced in his dark brown hair, darkening it further, leaving dampness at his temples. He didn't have a spare pound on him. I suspected he was hard as cement.

"So, you're Durbin's friend," he said.

I heard more in his tone than was probably there. Some kind of stress on "friend" that suggested a lot more. It bugged me, but I chose to ignore it. I mean, I was trying to get in the guy's good graces. No need to start out by questioning his meaning.

"You're a friend, too," I responded, pretending there was no subtext at all.

The amusement deepened. "Known him long?"

"A few years," I said.

He was drinking a tall glass of water, which he picked up, never losing eye contact with me. Taking a long drink, he set the glass back down. "He said you were interested in the . . . Wedding Bandits."

"Violet Purcell is afraid the police think she's responsible for Roland Hatchmere's death. I'm looking into other options."

"She admitted to hitting him with the metal tray," Larrabee said mildly.

"She says she didn't kill him."

"You trying to pin this on the burglars?"

"I don't think they did it. Not in their m.o., unless there's something the press hasn't been telling us."

"Not in their m.o.," he agreed.

"I'd like to know what the police think. What *you* think," I stressed. "I'd like to know the current status on the investigation."

"Not exactly public information."

"I get that. What do you think about the Wedding Bandits?"

Larrabee held my gaze. I hoped he would share something, just throw me a few crumbs.

Our waiter arrived, a big, beefy guy wearing a white

apron, and handed us each a menu. Mine was splatted with grease stains. I glanced down the selections, glad to break eye contact with the detective. There was something magnetic about him that made my pulse beat hard and affected the neurons traveling through my brain. The air between us felt dense. I wouldn't call it sexual tension. I wasn't feeling that way . . . well, not exactly. But I was completely aware of him, like I'd sprouted antennae all tuned to his channel.

When Larrabee ordered, I said I'd have the same. The waiter brought us each a Reuben and a large diet cola that I at first thought was dark beer.

We ate in silence. The food was really good. And I mean, really good, which explained why he'd suggested this place. After the chicken soup and bread I'd thought I wouldn't be able to eat much, but I managed to tuck in like I'd been on a deserted island for weeks. What is that axiom? Feed a cold, starve a fever? Feed a fever, starve a cold? Whatever the case, I smacked that Reuben down in record time, though Larrabee beat me. A pile of french fries had been placed on a platter between us and I selected a few carefully, wondering if they were really to share. Larrabee grabbed a fistful and ate them slowly, watching me. I grabbed a few more and shoved them in my mouth. I had an insane urge to chew the food and then open my mouth to show him. I managed to tamp it down, but I sensed we were in some kind of pissing match, a hazing of sorts, to determine whether we could ever speak again or if the loser should just leave in silence.

"Allergies, huh?" he asked.

"Or possibly a raging, unidentified, lethal pathogen that will take us both out."

The corner of his mouth lifted. "How did Durbin find you?"

"We had . . . mutual friends," I said.

"How much do you know about him?" he asked curiously.

Not enough, I decided right then and there. But I'd be damned if I'd let Larrabee know that. There was some kind of chess game going on between him and Dwayne, I realized. Currently, I was one of the pawns.

I gave myself a hard mental shake. I'd offered to buy lunch, so I pulled out my credit card. I'd barely scanned the menu and I'd been afraid to check the prices, but a deal was a deal. Tony's wasn't a happening, trendy place, but one never knows. I'm one of those people so afraid of debt that I pay off my credit card every month. The idea of paying interest makes me ill.

Larrabee wiped his mouth with the tiny paper napkin they'd allotted him. I did the same with mine. After a long, long moment, he leaned forward. "You don't have much to say, do you?"

"I have a lot to say," I responded. "I just haven't started."

He lifted a hand in a "go ahead" signal.

"Who are the Wedding Bandits? Do you have any idea? Do you think they accidentally killed Roland Hatchmere, or are you focusing your investigation on Violet, like she thinks? Or . . ."

"Or?"

"You tell me. Is there another 'person of interest'? Someone keeping you from indicting Violet?"

He thought a moment. "Durbin asked me to talk to you. That's why I'm here. I'm not duty-bound to tell you anything. If I don't feel like keeping you in the loop, you're not in the loop."

"Check," I said, holding his gaze.

He leaned back. He seemed to consider a number of responses, discarding all of them one by one. The waiter came and scooped up my credit card.

I was signing the receipt when Larrabee finally revealed, "Your so-called Wedding Bandits have diversified. They are also Funeral Bandits now."

I looked up in surprise, more that he'd confided in me than the news he'd imparted. "You have any leads on them?"

"Maybe."

"That's all I get? Maybe?"

"We have the make and model of a van seen in the area."

"So you were doing surveillance," I said, pleased that my own thoughts traveled along the same line as law enforcement's.

"Been a number of notable weddings since the Hatchmere homicide. No 'Wedding Bandits' anywhere near them. But homes have been burgled while the mourners were at a loved one's funeral." He finished the rest of his cola and slid his water glass in front of him again. "These burglaries weren't planned as well, and the victims weren't well known, wealthy families. Not as much money involved and therefore not the same dollar recovery per item." He spoke slowly and carefully, clearly picking his words. "Then recently, another wedding was targeted. First one since Hatchmere. The groom's parents' home in Beaverton was burglarized. A van seen in the area was similar to one reported outside the home of the man who died in that six-car pileup on 205. Did you read about it? His house was burgled during his funeral. Stole their TV and DVD player."

"That's low," I said with feeling.

"Not the same caliber of crime as the 'Wedding Bandits' pulled off. Certainly not at the last wedding. No expensive presents, silver, crystal, envelopes of cash. The groom's parents lost their TV, like the man who died in the pileup, but it was an older model. Quite a bit older. Either we're dealing with a different group of burglars, or they've lost their connection to the money."

"Why do you think that is?"

"If it's the same group, their targets shifted after the Hatchmere homicide. I can make a guess," he said cautiously. Again, I waited, figuring the less I said, the better. I sensed eagerness would be a serious turnoff to learning more. "I think they stumbled across Roland Hatchmere's dead body and it scared 'em. Whoever was their inside man, cut out. They lost their connection to the moneyed families when he or she left. Now they're scrambling for whatever they can find."

"So you don't think the Wedding Bandits are responsible for Roland's death? And you don't seem to be focused on Violet, either."

"Violet admitted to hitting him with the tray."

"And it's definitely the murder weapon?"

He nodded.

"How many times was he hit with it?"

"A number. I see why you're Durbin's girl. We're not publicizing that fact yet."

"So you don't want me to tell Violet, I take it." I was struggling to get over him calling me Durbin's girl.

"I'd rather you didn't, but I can't stop you. Roland Hatchmere was hit twice. The first blow didn't kill him. Did it contribute to his death? Possibly. Possibly not. The second one crushed his skull. Violet Purcell has maintained she hit him with the tray. Once. Either she's very clever and actually hit him several times, hoping we'll believe her and search for some other killer, or she's telling the truth. In that case, we have a different killer."

I nodded. "But not the Wedding Bandits?"

"Do you see the burglars stopping their looting to grab the tray and hit Roland Hatchmere? It could have happened, if he'd caught them in the act and tried to call for help. But he was likely lying right where Violet left him. I think Hatchmere was already dead. The burglars came in, grabbed a few things, discovered the body and took off. They've never killed anyone, as yet."

"Someone else, then," I said.

Larrabee said, "Learning the motive would go a long way to identifying the doer."

I nodded slowly, realizing I had only considered two possible motives: Violet's anger at Roland, or the Wedding Bandits' need to silence Roland to keep him from identifying them.

"Do you have a theory?" I asked.

"I got a lot of theories," Larrabee assured me. "When we catch the 'Wedding Bandits,' maybe we'll get some answers."

"Is that going to happen soon?" I asked.

"Hard to say."

"Will you let Dwayne, or me, know?"

Larrabee flashed a smile. He had very white teeth. "What's going on between you and Durbin?"

"We're business partners."

"Uh-huh."

"That's about it."

"Quid pro quo, Ms. Kelly. This is how the information game works. I give to you. You give to me. Dwayne understands that."

I nodded, but I felt nervous inside. I couldn't tell exactly what he wanted from me. Dwayne had warned me to be careful and that, at least, I understood.

"You have a brother with the P.D., don't you?" Larrabee said into the silence.

I felt heat rise up my cheeks. Could Dwayne have given him a healthy dose of my background information? Or had he done some research on his own? "Booth," I said. "I haven't spoken to him about this case."

"Your brother's ambitious," Larrabee said.

I wasn't sure I liked the sound of that. I let it pass, deciding I would dissect all the little nuances and meanings later.

"You haven't asked him for help."

"No."

"Why?"

"Booth thinks I'd be better off bartending again. It's that overprotective brother thing. Or maybe he just thinks I'm inadequate. Either way, I lose."

"Durbin seems to disagree."

My smile was noncommittal, though I was curious to know what Dwayne had said about my P.I. skills. He has a tendency to sing my praises and though I appreciate his faith in me, I sometimes think he's full of shit.

Larrabee walked me outside. We stood under the roof overhang for a moment, adjusting our rain gear. I swept my hood over my head. He simply bent his head to the rain and we both race-walked to our respective vehicles, his being a black Crown Vic. As I climbed into my car, he said, "Good luck, Jane Kelly."

I watched him back out of the lot and drive into the pounding rain.

CHAPTER NINE

The rain was becoming an entity.

I tried to count up how many days it had rained in a row and failed. We were living in a miasma of dreariness that just went on and on and on. This is a perception of Oregon weather that generally pisses me off because it's not accurate. Well, even a stopped clock is right twice a day, so I guess, the law of percentages being what it is, those who claim "Oregon equals rain" are bound to be right sometimes. Still, I was getting pretty annoyed by the weather people gleefully pointing out how right they were. Wasn't the weather just awful? Hadn't they said it was? Wasn't this what Oregon's reputation was all about?

It was Tuesday morning. I'd forgone my jog to the Nook because of the rain. Now, driving there for my morning coffee, The Binkster tucked into her fuzzy car bed in the passenger seat, her nose and face squished into the side, so wrinkled up she looked like a grub, I thought back to those hot nights the previous summer when I was drifting around the lake in either Dwayne's boat or my neighbors and bickering friends', Arista and Lyle Mooney.

My cold was basically gone. Well, apart from an occasional wracking cough that sounded like I was hawking up a lung.

Pulling out my cell phone, I dialed Deenie's number again and left yet another message. What is it with people? I'd clearly missed the window of opportunity she'd allotted me because she would not pick up her phone. I should have taken her call when I was on my way to meet Larrabee. I wasn't sure what Gigi's maid of honor could offer, but I wanted to cross her name off my list if for no other reason than to make my report complete.

At the Nook I poured myself black coffee from the help-yourself counter, glancing over the varying carafe choices of cream, two-percent and skim milk. Throwing caution to the wind, I tossed in some skim. Lactose, schmactose. My body's reaction to it is unpredictable. Sometimes milk products send me into a purge. Sometimes nothing much happens. Black coffee is a safe bet but I was feeling reckless.

I'd called Dwayne and told him about my meeting with Larrabee. He'd absorbed the information with a grunt. I don't know what I'd expected. Some major "Aha!" I guess, but he'd given me his usual "Put it in a report." I tried to get him to talk about his friendship with Larrabee some more, but Dwayne clammed right up. Learning anything more about either one of them was going to be like pulling teeth.

I didn't stick around the Nook long. Heading outside, I tossed my hood up and pulled Binks reluctantly from the dry warmth of the car. Clipping on her leash, we took a stroll around the parking lot and up some concrete stairs along a bark-dust-covered hill toward the residential district behind the shopping center. I had a baggie in my pocket and Binkster snuffled her way through the drizzle nose down. She started circling around, looking for the perfect place to off-load. I dutifully cleaned up after her. She watched me, making little jumping movements, as if she were about to charge into a race. It's a kind of "I feel so *great* now that I've pooped" thing, but with the leash, rain and mud, I had no interest in indulging her. I tugged on the leash and she got all recalcitrant, the collar squishing her skin and fur up her neck so that I could scarcely see her eyes for the wrinkles.

"Come on," I urged.

Something about her attitude set something loose in my brain. Some memory or recall or synapse that I tried to latch on to, but it was slippery and amorphous and my brain couldn't make the connection. I shook my head and tried to pick up my dog. She started leaping sideways and trying to run, but I held her fast. By the time I actually got her in my arms, her feet were covered in mud and her fur was soaking wet. Some of it flew off and stuck to my lips. I tried to spit it off but had to wait till I got her settled in her bed.

"The weather *sucks*," I told her with feeling.

We drove home. I toweled Binks off, though that became a game, too. We played tug-of-war with the end of the terry cloth towel and Binks growled like she was going to tear it in half. Fat chance.

I showered, changed into a clean pair of jeans and dark brown shirt, walked through the kitchen to the small adjunct that was my laundry room—basically a closet that was originally some kind of mudroom between the garage and kitchen but that has since been closed off and wired for a washer and dryer. Doing the laundry depressed me. Was I going to have to give this up, too? Find an apartment with community laundry facilities, if that?

Damn Ogilvy for making this place *perfect* for me, then deciding to sell!

The thought really put me in a black mood. If I'd had any food around I would have gone into one of those emotional eating binges I hear about from doctors on daytime talk shows. As it was, I knocked back the rest of my coffee, chewing angrily on the paper cup, and the tumblers in my mind suddenly slipped into place.

Binks's resistance while I'd pulled her leash was a metaphor for how I felt about Violet. About her lies, her obstinance, her prevarication. Sure, Violet doled out tidbits of information, but I was the one who had to come up with the right questions. Nothing was just offered up. It was all a fight.

And I was sick . . . of . . . it.

I grabbed the cell phone and punched in Violet's number, a little surprised by the wave of feeling that had overtaken me. I was really mad at her. Part of it had to do with Dwayne, sure, but a lot of it was that she'd been working me these past few weeks, crying about her innocence, begging for help, assuring both Dwayne and me that she was a victim. And what had she given me? A tentative admission that she and Roland had been seeing each other. Like that was big news.

In the back of my mind I sensed that I might be using Violet as a target for my own frustration, but I didn't much care. She was the source. She was at Roland's house the day he died. She hit him, for God's sake. At least once.

She answered her cell with a cheery, "Hi there. I sure hope you're calling with good news."

"Yeah, that's right. I've cracked the case wide open. It was Ms. Violet in the solarium with the goddamn silver tray! That's who did it."

A weighty pause. "If you've got something to say, maybe you should just say it."

"Tell me about that day, Violet. The whole day. Every minute. Roland died from a blow to the head. What time was that?"

"He definitely died from a blow to the head?" Violet asked, which damn near derailed me because she sounded so upset.

"Yes," I stressed. I wasn't going to give her more details, but it wasn't like this was exactly news. "What were you hoping for? A heart attack? Some kind of exotic poison? A gunshot wound that the pathologist missed when they autopsied his body?"

"I get it that you're mad," Violet said coolly. "I just don't know why."

"You're still withholding. You've been withholding from the get-go. If Dwayne were the investigator, if he were at the top of his game . . . you wouldn't have been able to bob and weave this long. He would have made you tell him every detail. He's good like that."

"Dwayne believes in me."

"Make me believe in you, too. Tell me about Roland."

"I'm going shopping," Violet said abruptly. "I'm not going to just drop everything so you can grill me. But if you join me, I promise I'll talk to you about Roland."

There might be a catch in there somewhere, but she sounded more irked than resigned, so maybe not. "Fine," I said. "I'll meet you. Tell me where."

Bridgetown is a new shopping center on the Tualatin/ Tigard border, just outside the Lake Chinook limits, half a block from I-5. It's one of those "lifestyle malls" where all the stores face sidewalks and streets and have different facades as if Walt Disney had designed it. The problem is parking, and in Oregon, of course, the rain. The center actually has valet parkers, but using them comes with its own set of problems. I knew someone who tried to get them to park her car last year during the holidays and they acted like a parker wasn't around. Like what the hell were the rest of them doing, standing around at the valet kiosk? Waiting for Godot? My friend, having seen an empty spot designated for "valet only," offered to park her car there herself, which sent them into a

Keystone Kops panic. One of them finally agreed to park her car, shooting his friends a "Can you believe this?" look. Sometimes I look at other employment opportunities and wonder why I'm not doing them because I could do a hell of a lot better job. Of course, this could be simply my way of looking around because I feel I'm falling behind in the information specialist arena.

I ignored the valet parkers and drove myself to the three-story parking structure at the far end. It's full a lot of the time and I hope to God the city planners and developer made structural plans for adding a few more stories in the future. As it is, even when you get a spot you've generally got a long, long walk to your destination.

Violet apparently had a whole list of stores she needed to visit. I was to meet her at one that exclusively sold cosmetics, The Face. I beat her there and when one of the salesgirls asked me if I needed help, I asked her if it seemed right that The Face also sold products for The Body, as there were creams, rough-looking sponges that looked as if they'd been scraped from the ocean floor and various clippers and scissors and awl-like instruments that worried me and convinced me they were *not* to be used on The Face.

My salesgirl did not find me amusing. In fact, she didn't find me anything at all, I guess, because she just hovered silently nearby. At first I wondered if she thought I was planning to shoplift, and then I realized I was simply *hers* and she was staking her claim, warning the other salespeople to keep their distance, accomplishing this by staying about two arm's lengths away from me but no farther.

Violet breezed in, shaking rain from her umbrella. The sales team's heads collectively turned her way, their faces brightening. My girl tried to dump me in favor of Violet, but a faster one jumped right up with a husky "Welcome to The Face" that sounded like she were auditioning for a role in a porn film.

My girl was crestfallen, but I could see her mentally taking notes. When Violet met my gaze and smiled, my girl perked right up. I might be slightly bedraggled in a soaked windbreaker, but I kept good company.

There was no way we could talk at The Face. Maybe Violet had counted on that, maybe not. Maybe this was her answer for "what's next?": Endless shopping. I tagged along behind her as she bought items for The Cheeks, The Mouth, The Eyes and one of those hard sponge-bricks that was one hell of an exfoliate for The Skin, generally not for The Skin on The Face. I pointed this out as well, since it wasn't exactly truth in advertising. This earned me scathing glances from my girl, who sidled up to her compatriot with the porn star voice, who in turn regarded me with tolerant benevolence as *she* had the *buyer*, Violet.

This is why I find shopping exhausting. The energy required is enormous, and though I sense I'm in the minority on the shopping issue, I believe there must be more women like me out there. Either that or I suffer from some deep-seated neuroses, which has to be just plain *wrong*, because I know I'm very well adjusted. Just ask my dog. She knows I'm perfect.

We left The Face loaded down with packages. I was amazed, based on how small the product sizes were, how full Violet's shopping bags were. I offered to carry a couple and though they weren't heavy, the bags bumped my hips and shins all the way to store number two, which was a fancy-schmancy furniture store called Interiors Italianate. I sat down on a tufted lounge that was situated on a raised dais by the entry, Violet's bags flanking me. I had the presence of mind to remove my jacket first and hang it on the wrought-iron rack nearby. Other coats were already on the rack, so I figured I wasn't committing some major faux pas. In this, apparently, I was wrong as a wiry gentleman in wire-rim glasses, a white-cuffed and collared shirt and a taupe sweater looked ready to scream, stamp and phone the authorities if I did not get off the furniture.

Violet interceded with a smooth "She's with me." The salesman sent me a look that was full of pleading, as if he expected me to wipe my feet on their expensive material, but then let me be. I thought about lying down on the lounge, staring at the ceiling and singing "That's Amore" but decided to act like a grown-up and merely waited dolefully like the long-suffering pack mule I was.

We made a trip to the parking structure to off-load our bags, stopping at a lingerie shop on the way that Violet insisted on entering. I was so over shopping that I groaned aloud and refused to pass the threshold. She practically pushed me inside and then wouldn't leave until I tried on a push-up bra to go with my new dress. She wanted to buy it for me, but I put my foot down, though the price of that piece of lingerie nearly caused me a coronary. I put another foot down when she insisted I purchase some thong underwear. Puhh . . . leeze . . . like I would be caught dead with a piece of material dividing my butt cheeks. I settled for some basic bikini underwear that was on sale and demure by comparison.

We left in a kind of annoyed huff with each other. I felt I'd been very patient throughout our shopping trip, and it must have shown on my face because once Violet slammed the trunk on her Mercedes, she turned to me and said, "Jesus, you're a pain in the ass."

"Why do you keep trying to buy me things?" I demanded.

"God knows. I keep thinking we're friends, or something."

"We can't be friends."

"Why not? Because of Dwayne? Come on, Jane. We're way past that now, aren't we?"

I wasn't as convinced as she was, apparently. "It's not because of Dwayne," I retorted.

"Then what?" She leaned against the side of her car, arms crossed.

"I don't know."

"Jane . . ."

I held up my palms to get her to stop. I don't know what it is about her that drives me so insane. In some weird way I'd like to believe it is because of Dwayne. That at least would be uncomplicated, even understandable, maybe. But it's more about Violet herself. And me. I have this sense that something bad could happen to me if I hang around her too much.

"What do you want to know about me and Roland that I haven't already said?" she asked on a sigh.

"Tell me more about the fight."

"What's to tell?" She pressed her lips together. "He wanted out, okay? He said he wanted to stop, and we'd barely gotten back together. I mean, I could count the times we'd been together and I was so *happy*. I just—" She shook her head and took a moment. "Maybe I just wanted to be in love. Maybe I put all that on Roland too soon and he panicked. I don't know. But we went to bed that night okay with each other. It was the next morning—Gigi's wedding day—that things really went bad."

"What happened?"

A car drove slowly past us, looking for a spot. The driver gazed at us hopefully but we ignored him. Beyond the concrete edge of the lot the skies opened up and rain poured down, a deafening curtain. Both Violet and I paused, staring into the deluge as a mist of precipitation whisked in and dampened our faces.

"I don't really know. He'd come home from the rehearsal dinner in a foul mood. Really mad at Renee about bringing this guy who wasn't invited. He'd driven Renee up from Santa Monica, so I guess she figured he'd earned a spot. Dumb. It doesn't work that way."

"Gigi and Melinda both mentioned him."

"I just wanted him to stop thinking about the whole thing. I mean, who cared, really? In a matter of hours Gigi was going to be married. So Renee infuriated him. So what?"

"You argued about it?"

"I just wanted to get past it. Roland had a drink. I tried to talk him into bed. He said something about sleeping on the couch. We had a fight. I almost left, and then we eventually did go to bed together." She smiled fleetingly. "And it was really sweet. I wished I'd known then that it was our last night together. I would have tried harder to be . . . less selfish. I wanted to make plans and he wasn't interested. I think he was thinking of breaking up with me. I don't know." She ran her hands through her hair, holding the ends at her nape and closing her eyes.

"Did he say something, or do something, that gave you that idea?"

"Not really. Not that night. Everything seemed okay again, but then the next morning he was brusque. Distracted."

"Did something happen?"

She thought about it and shook her head. "No."

"Anything at all. Maybe something that didn't have anything to do with you. He came home upset with Renee, and you had a fight," I repeated.

"More like a spat. A couple of comments and that was it," she corrected.

"Then you went to bed together and you thought everything was all right."

She nodded.

"Then what happened?"

"He just woke up on the wrong side of the bed. The phone started ringing. All that wedding stuff started. He didn't want to get in the tux. I actually laid it on the bed for him but he was so touchy. You know, being the supportive girlfriend be-

hind the scenes isn't my forte," Violet remarked candidly.
"But I was doing a hell of a job."

"So, then . . . ?"

"We got dressed and went downstairs. I was getting ready
to go home and leave him to it, but Roland hadn't put his coat
on. He was in the pants and shirt, and he was . . . oh, I don't
know . . . a pain in the ass, if you want to know the truth. He
wouldn't talk. He wouldn't say what was wrong. I tried to be
all fun and bubbly and act like I didn't notice. I joked that
he could call me at the reception and maybe I could sneak in
for a while, and he about bit my head off. I was getting fed
up by this time."

"What time was it?"

Violet shrugged. "Ten-thirty? Eleven? I don't know. It
was early. Roland was supposed to be at the Cahill Winery
for pictures at two. He was going to leave around one. I told
all this to the police."

"I'm just trying to get the timeline down for myself. So,
what happened between you and him between eleven and
one?"

"Nothing. We stopped talking. He'd made a toast to Gigi
the night before, apparently, and he was planning to say
something more at the reception. He said he wanted to go
finish writing his speech, and he walked outside to the garden beyond the solarium. I stayed in the kitchen, but I kind
of kept peeking at him. His back was to me. He was on the
phone. There wasn't a lot of writing going on."

"You know who he was talking to?"

"No. But I heard him say something about Melinda. I
was really trying to eavesdrop but he caught me, and that's
when we really started fighting. I wanted to know what he'd
said about Melinda. At first he wouldn't answer. Told me it
was none of my business, to which I said, 'Oh no. I have a
stake in this!' and I demanded to know what was going on

with him and Melinda." She looked down at the ground and I saw color creep up her neck. Violet was usually in such perfect control that it sent a frisson down my spine. "We said some pretty terrible things to each other," she admitted. "Things I wish I could take back. Roland was absolutely furious. He grabbed my shoulders and pushed me up against the wall. I couldn't believe it! He told me to stay out of his business. Said he had things to work out with Melinda. Said he'd misjudged her. But he was *roaring* this at me! *Shaking* me." The memory brought tears to Violet's eyes, which she dashed away in fury. "The tray was right there. On that Asian buffet in the hallway. I grabbed it and slammed it against his head." She pressed her knuckles to her lips and said around them, "I hurt him, but it wasn't half as much as he hurt me. He grabbed his head and yelled at me to get the fuck out of his house. So I left."

Her narrative cut off abruptly. We stood quietly, listening to the rain. After a moment I stirred myself. "What time was that?"

"Noon, maybe?"

"How much of this did you tell the police?"

"As little as possible. I said I'd stopped by in the morning, that we had a fight about the fact I wasn't invited to the wedding." Her lips pulled into a bitter smile. "I can't believe we were breaking up over Melinda."

"But she knew about you and Roland."

"Suspected, not knew," Violet corrected.

"Maybe that's motive enough," I suggested.

"Who? Melinda? No way. Melinda would never kill Roland. He was her meal ticket."

"She doesn't act like it."

"She had a chance to come out okay in a divorce settlement, but death? Uh-uh. The estate went to Gigi and Sean, almost entirely. She signed a prenup. Roland said so. Besides, she was at the wedding when he died, wasn't she? As much as I'd love to blame this on Melinda, I don't see how she could be in two places at the same time."

I nodded. The same thoughts had occurred to me. Like Larrabee suggested, I kept trying to think up some other motive for Roland's death.

"Well, who else, then?" I asked Violet.

She shrugged. "Some disgruntled patient?"

"But he was talking about Melinda on the phone."

"Talking about her . . . I don't know. Her name was mentioned, that's all. And he said something like 'your day'll come' or 'you've got it coming' or 'today's the day.'" Violet made a dismissive gesture. "Maybe he was talking about the wedding, and I got it screwed up."

"It sounds like a threat."

"Maybe," she said, cocking her head as if she was thinking that over.

Watching her, I recalled Melinda's comment about how I should look into Violet's past. I'd dismissed it, mostly because I knew the basics of Violet's history. I'd thought Melinda was just being snarky. But could something else have cropped up? Something about Violet that she still wasn't willing to share? And could this all be an act? A means to push me in another direction?

"And afterward, that's when things got physical," I said.

"We'd never fought like that before," she said. "I was stunned when he shoved me against the wall. It just wasn't like him." She searched through her purse for her keys. "It's just depressing to go over this. I really thought Roland and I had a chance. I wanted to remarry him. It sounds ridiculous now, but I fell in love with him. When we got married the first time, I don't know . . . I didn't really feel that way about him. I liked him. Sure. He was nice to me and I wanted out of L.A. I was not thrilled about his kids, and they were not thrilled about me, but it wasn't terrible. I even helped Gigi with birth control when she needed it. At fourteen! Trust me, that girl would have been pregnant before she hit high school if I hadn't intervened. And the drugs and alcohol? Roland may have had his problems, but drug abuse runs in that family. Look at Sean, and Gigi sure took her turn around that block when she was younger. So Roland and I split up. Too many forces dragging us down back then." She shook her head at the irony of it all. "But now was our time. It was just us. Somebody killed him, Jane, but it wasn't me."

For the first time I thought Violet looked her age. Every minute of it.

"Okay," I said after a long moment.

She gazed at me uncertainly.

"I get that you loved him."

Violet exhaled as if she'd been holding her breath for eons. "The Dwayne thing got in the way of you believing me before."

That was true, but I didn't feel like confirming it.

"Maybe it *was* those Wedding Bandits," she said. "Maybe they came to rob the place after I left, but Roland was still there and got in the way. Maybe . . . they hit him with something, too?"

My skin rippled as if a cold breeze swept over me. Maybe she was trying to lead me in another direction.

Something niggled at my brain. Another thought that swam just out of reach. I tried hard to catch it, but it seemed to leap away at the last moment, a teasing sprite I was going to have to ignore for now and hope it would draw near enough some time in the future for me to grab.

A different issue occurred to me. "You didn't go to the memorial service?"

Violet was opening her driver's door. "Oh, I went, though I know they all wished I wouldn't. I came late and stayed toward the back, but it wasn't really the way I wanted to say good-bye, so I left early." She looked at me over the roof of her car, her smile ironic. "I drank a toast to him by myself. To what might have been."

I nodded.

"Jane?"

"Yeah?"

"Find who killed him. Please."

I nodded again and climbed in my Volvo. As I drove toward the parking lot exit I watched her in my rearview mirror. She took a long time to thread her key in the lock. Sometimes it's weird how people age in an instant. Vitality one moment and then poof. Father Time swings his scythe and hourglass and knocks them hard on the head.

I thought maybe it was a good thing she'd damn near bought out The Face.

CHAPTER TEN

I drove straight to Dwayne's and we stood side by side just inside the sliding glass door to his dock. The slider was tightly shut for once, as the rain continued unabated. Balanced lightly on his crutches, his binoculars hanging from one hand, Dwayne silently watched the deluge while I recounted the gist of my latest interview with Violet.

When I was finished he digested the information for a bit, then said, "So, now what do you think about our client?"

"She's been lying to us. Okay, omitting. Amounts to the same thing."

"Think you squeezed her dry?"

"Pretty damn close."

Dwayne nodded thoughtfully. I waited for further instructions, but he just kept staring out at the weather. I was feeling frustrated and stymied all over again and asked myself once more if I was really cut out for this business.

"Who do you think called Roland that morning?" Dwayne asked finally.

"Someone involved in the wedding?"

"Roland was talking about Melinda during the call, so it

wasn't her. When you talked to Gigi, did she say she'd called him?"

"No . . . she must have been having mimosas about that time, and getting her hair and makeup done," I recalled. "With Deenie and Melinda."

"Doesn't sound like she'd take a break to call dear old dad," Dwayne said. "It was after the phone call, or calls, that Roland was upset."

"Yes, but Violet said he was distracted and they were having trouble the night before, too."

"But not like after the phone calls. That's when things got physical."

"True."

"Somebody set him off. Whoever called Roland gave him some information that sent him over the edge, enough for him to push Violet against the wall."

"Do you think he was mad at Violet?" I asked. "Or he was just enraged and she was there to take the brunt?"

"Could be either. We know that after Roland talked on the phone he and Violet got into a fight, and she hit him with the first available object, the silver tray."

"She says it was the first time they fought physically." When Dwayne didn't immediately respond, I asked, "You're not convinced Violet's telling the truth anymore?"

"I don't think she killed Roland, but I don't think she's giving us the complete truth, either. Was Roland going back to Melinda? Was he breaking up with Violet? Were he and Violet getting back together? There's no way of knowing. I'm not even sure Violet really knows. We've got to stick with the facts. And the fact is Roland took at least one call that precipitated the fight with Violet."

"Roland's cell phone," I said suddenly. "The police must have confiscated it. You think Larrabee might tell us about those calls?"

"Not unless it suits his purposes."

corner. The guy had a shock of gray hair and about the blackest, bushiest eyebrows around. He could give Scorsese a run for his money.

"You're starting to clear this out?" I asked, looking at the pile of old toys, circa mid-seventies, early eighties. Fisher-Price scored big. Lots of little, cylindrical people wearing big smiles. There were also a couple of yellow, red and blue Big Wheels, molded-plastic vehicles with pedals.

"Garage sale," he stated. "This Saturday."

We were practically shouting at each other to be heard above the rain as it pounded on the roof. I had a picture of would-be "garage-salers" blocking my driveway and trying to involve me in their purchases.

"You want anything, you can have it," he added generously. "Better tag it or get it outta here quick."

I want my cottage, I thought. Binkster snuffled on the ground, eye to eye with a group of displaced centipedes disturbed by Ogilvy. They gave me the willies as they moved like a wave to the nearest group of Fisher-Price people lying on their sides, having been tossed out of their faded Fisher-Price home.

I feel for you, I told them silently as I pulled Binks away from the centipedes. Aren't they supposed to be poisonous? Or is that something I learned from a video game that has no merit? Whatever—they're creepy. I had a picture of myself pulling one out of Binkster's mouth and it gave me the hee-bee-jeebies.

"I got an offer on the place," Ogilvy grunted. "No real estate commission."

I regarded him in horror. "I thought you weren't selling for a while. You said I had time."

He shrugged. "Can't ignore a good offer."

"I was thinking about trying to buy the cottage myself," I said, the words flying from my mouth as if I'd been put under a spell.

"What do you think we should do?"

"Stir things up."

"Okay." I waited. "How?"

"When you interviewed Melinda she asked you to keep her informed if the investigation led away from Violet," Dwayne reminded me. "Go ahead and do that. Tell her you're certain of Violet's innocence and you're looking in other directions. Maybe she'll tell you what she was hinting at before."

"Good idea."

"Tell Gigi and Emmett the same thing. Have you called Emmett's parents? Maybe it's time to check with them. I'll give Larrabee another call and push him."

I was thrilled Dwayne's brain was humming along. This was what I'd missed while he'd been recuperating. I could have shouted my joy to the skies.

"And the plastic surgery partner?"

"Dr. Wu."

"Damn convenient that he's out of the country right now," Dwayne muttered. "Go to one of the clinics. See what they're about."

"Oh yeah, sure. That'll be easy. Roland sold that business," I reminded him.

"Money's a big motive for murder."

"Melinda thought there was something fishy about the business sale, but she really doesn't have much nice to say about anyone or anything."

Dwayne snorted. "Do any of them?"

"Not really."

"What about after Thursday's game?" he asked suddenly. "Are you planning to meet Dawn?"

"Thursday?" I repeated, before I remembered that we were approaching Veterans Day, one of those holiday weekends that sometimes include a teacher in-service day, or whatever they call them now. "The game's on Thursday?"

Dwayne nodded. "You seriously think they'll meet at Do Not Enter after last week's fiasco?"

"Maybe not. But it's like their clubhouse."

I drew a breath, gazing across the bay. I let my eye travel along the shoreline. "I should return Social Security's canoe," I admitted.

The house where I'd docked was nearly out of sight from Dwayne's, tucked into a slight bend as far west as I could see. I took the binoculars from Dwayne's hand and adjusted them. I could just see the end of the canoe, peeking from beneath the shelter of the boat-port. Through the rain I could see it was a faded red, its tags barely visible. If I didn't move it back, someone might eventually discover it and learn it was registered with the Lake Corporation, so its ownership would be established. But how long would it take for someone to find it? It wasn't like there was a lot of bustling activity over there. I was doomed to take it back.

"Could it just stop raining?" I muttered.

Dwayne snorted in agreement.

Binkster greeted me at the door when I returned, wriggling around my legs excitedly, as if she hadn't seen me in a decade. I had stopped at the market and purchased several sacks of essential foods. I'd even gone so far as to buy hamburger, half price, a few days old, and had visions of spaghetti or lasagna or something. I was pretty sure I could stir in tomato sauce and pour it over pasta. Hefting my brown bags on the counter, I bent down to scratch Binkster's ears, which earned me a long, happy inhalation that sounded like a train rumbling over tracks.

"Guess what?" I told her, to which she cocked her head from side to side. "I bought groceries!"

She wagged her tail slowly, clearly trying to assess the importance of my words. Dogs apparently have about two

hundred words they understand. Treat, mochi, walk, she gets. Groceries, apparently not.

Note to self: increase dog's vocabulary.

I put a call into Melinda's cell, wondering if she would pick up or dismiss me as quickly as she had the caller who'd phoned the day I'd interviewed her. I got her voice mail fairly quickly, so I left a message, telling her that it appeared the Wedding Bandits were more at fault than originally thought. I added that she'd asked if I would let her know if the investigation was turning away from Violet, so I was following through, just letting her know. I topped off the lie about the Wedding Bandits by saying I'd talked with the police and though they hadn't come right out and said so, they, too, were concentrating on the Wedding Bandits instead of Violet.

I called Gigi and Emmett with about the same messag and then I tried the number for the Popparockskills, David and Goliath also weren't answering. I left my n and contact information with them, then Renee once just for the hell of it, since she seemed to have drop the planet. Finally, I gave Deenie another jingle, her voice mail. Then I took my dog for a walk in th

As I was returning, I saw Mr. Ogilvy's blue pic in my drive and my heart sank. Now what?

The side door to the garage was open, to my never really seen inside and since this could be only opportunity, I hurried to the open door Binkster pulled at the leash for all she was w her tight. She shook water from her coat an door while I stared past her at a huge pile furniture, rotting trunks, boxes of files s from the beginning of time, some bicycl and sundry other stuff. Above my head laid over the open rafters, and on tho boxes.

"Jane?" Ogilvy called, straightenin

He assessed me for a moment, checking to see if I was serious, I guess. "Better get it in writing soon," he muttered, bending back to his task.

I stumbled to the house with Binks in tow, practically falling through the door in my haste. Binks ran to her bowl, shaking off rain, and I skidded with wet feet onto one of the stools at my little breakfast bar.

I felt ill. Flushed. Feverish. I sensed a closeness moving into my peripheral vision, as if I'd been drugged or dealt a blow to the head. He was selling. *Selling*. It was real. I had to buy it. I couldn't buy it. Couldn't afford it. Needed to have it.

I charged to the refrigerator, yanking open the door. Miracles. I'd bought a jug of orange juice in my shopping frenzy. I unscrewed the top and gulped thirstily. Sugar. I needed sustenance. Energy.

I felt Binkster's paws on my leg and looked down to see her staring up at me. Did she understand I was stressed? Or did the orange juice look good? Hard to tell with her.

Soberly, I said, "We are about to be evicted from our home."

Now, there was irony for you: I made part of my living from evicting people. But it wasn't the same. Those people didn't pay their rent, whereas I paid on time, *every time!*

My cell phone bleeped. A text message. Expecting it to be Dwayne, I was a little surprised to see it wasn't. I thought it was Violet for a moment, when I saw the one line missive:

break in the case. vl

Then I realized it was Vince Larrabee.

I phoned him back immediately but the call went right to a generic voice mail. I left him my name and number, though he already had it, just in case that would speed his return call. I couldn't believe he'd taken the time to let me know. What kind of break? I wondered. Could the police have nabbed one or more of the Wedding Bandits? Larrabee had sounded hot on their trail when we met. I hoped like hell he continued to keep me in the loop.

I also hoped he wouldn't expect information on Violet I wasn't prepared to give. A faint hope, I know. Quid pro quo.

I called Dwayne and told him the news about Larrabee's call. "Did you ever get through to him?"

"Just by voice mail. But, darlin', you got him wrapped around your finger."

I made a disparaging sound. "Not so. He barely spoke to me."

"You did something right."

"It's probably an aberration. Like he'll remember he didn't like me, and this'll be the end of it."

"Nah."

"What's the deal with the two of you?" I asked.

"Nothing," he dismissed, then hung up before the conversation could take hold.

Dwayne's reassurances made me feel better, temporarily, but after spending the rest of the afternoon counting the hours, waiting for something to happen, I fell back into a dreary fugue, worrying about where my dog and I would end up. Worrying about my life. Worrying about the world . . .

I wrapped myself in a blanket and fell asleep on the couch, Binkster tucked in beside me. I swam up from sleep sometime deep in the night and realized it was close to midnight.

And the phone rang.

I jumped about a foot, the hair on my arms lifting. Binks caught my mood and started growling low in her throat. Snatching up the phone, I checked caller ID, my heart tripping wildly. *Not available.*

I answered with trepidation. "Hello." It's these weird moments of precognition that are the spookiest.

"Jane?"

"Booth?"

"Sorry to call so late. I'm on a job, but I need to talk to you."

At midnight? "Okay . . ."

"Would you talk to Sharona? Give her a call? Tell her I'm trying to reach her but it's tough right now. . . ." There was some yelling in the background, muffled as it sounded like Booth covered the phone with his hand. "Jane?" he said softly, a careful whisper.

"Sure. Is there something specific you'd like me to tell her?"

"This is just temporary," he said urgently. "Tell her that."

"You mean the job?"

More background noise. I heard a male voice bark out, "Get off the fuckin' phone!"

Booth responded coldly in my ear, "You wanna talk to me? Write my parole officer, bitch."

The line went dead.

I sat for a moment in silence, hearing the clock *tick, tick, tick.* Then I gathered Binks to me and took her to bed. We curled in together. I didn't even mind that her doggy breath was in my face.

The following morning I phoned Booth's home number, which was also Sharona's. I got their answering machine. The homey "Hi, you've reached Booth and Sharona" had been replaced with a flat, computer voice repeating their number. I left a message for Sharona, asking her to call me. This is what my life consists of, I thought. Leaving messages begging for an answering response. Sheesh. I could get a complex.

I bundled myself into my rain gear and ran to the Nook, grabbed a cup of black coffee, drank it down, then jogged back home. I was drenched by the time I returned and Binkster still hadn't roused herself. I had to prod her to get her out her doggy-door to the backyard, and then she simply sat on the deck forlornly under the little round, glass-topped table. It took her a long time to go down the steps to the yard and empty her bladder. As soon as she was finished, however, she bounded back inside, ready for breakfast. I toweled her off and this time she didn't bother playing, just went straight to her bowl. I gave her a smattering of kiblets while I toasted some wheat bread and spread it with margarine. She finished as I took my first bite and sat at my feet, staring up at me. I gave her the last bite of my crust, which she inhaled.

When we were both done we stared at each other. She was undoubtedly still thinking about food, but I was thinking about Booth. And Larrabee. And Violet. And the god . . . damn . . . rain.

My cell phone rang and I looked at the caller ID. A number I almost recognized but no name. "Hello?"

"So, you've decided Violet didn't kill Roland," Melinda said, her voice accusing. "That's convenient. And for the record, you're wrong!"

I pictured her all coiffed and peachy skinned, her kitchen smelling of cinnamon and vanilla. Kinda pissed me off. It was a little early in the morning to be attacked with so much venom.

But . . . stir the pot and this is what happens.

Her tone put me on the defensive and I had to edit my initial response, which would have been something like "Up yours, Betty Crocker." Her reaction was just what Dwayne and I wanted.

I said neutrally, "Violet and Roland were seeing each other. They had a fight, which got physical, but she didn't kill him." I decided to expand on the truth. "They were planning a future together. Talking of marriage."

"She told you that?" she sputtered. "*We* were getting back together. Violet was just a fling. Roland knew he couldn't trust her. He learned that when they were married. It was too late by then, he had to pretend to make the marriage work, but he never forgot what she did. He would *never* go back to her. Not like that."

"What did she do?"

"She killed her first husband," Melinda said like I was beyond belief. "Don't you know that? Don't the police know that? Why do I have to be the one to wake you all up?"

I squinted at the phone. Was that true? I thought she'd divorced both exes prior to Roland. "All I know is that she says she and Roland were planning their own wedding."

"She's a liar. *Do* you know how her first husband died? Roland knew. He considered himself lucky that he got out of their marriage with his life!"

"He must've had a change of heart." I tried not to sound feeble in my defense. I knew I would get more from Melinda if I stuck to my guns, taking a strong stand for the opposition. She would fight doubly hard to convince me I was wrong.

"Talk to Renee, if you don't believe me," she said. "Violet killed her first husband. Renee and Roland may have been divorced when Violet swooped in and turned his head, but Renee wasn't really over him. She found out about the first husband—God, what was his name? Bart something, I think—but by the time she did, Roland and Violet were already married. Roland wouldn't listen to her. But he did later. That's why he and Violet divorced."

There were a lot of reasons why he and Violet divorced, but I'd never heard this one. "Renee told you this?" I asked, deliberately lacing my tone with skepticism.

"Absolutely. Talk to her. Learn the truth about Violet. She'll tell you."

"Well, okay . . ."

She doubled her efforts to convince me. "Roland would never take Violet back again. Never. I'm not surprised they were having sex," she said with distaste. "Violet has one way of getting what she wants and that's it. But believe me, that's all there was between them."

There was a holier-than-thou attitude about Melinda that reared up whenever she talked about Violet. I thanked her for the call and considered what it meant. Then I placed a call to Dwayne and told him what she'd said.

"This Renee hasn't gotten back to you?"

"She—like everyone else—seems determined to put me off. What is it with cell phones? They're supposed to make communication easier, but nobody *calls back*!"

"Think you should go to Santa Monica?"

That sort of stopped me. "To see Renee in person?"

"A face-to-face is always better than a phone call."

Well, that's true . . . it's harder to ignore someone standing right in front of you, whereas a phone call can be easily fobbed off and ignored; I was living that minor hell right now. And an in-person interview makes it possible to witness the facial tics and expressions that are dead giveaways. Sure, there are accomplished liars who can escape the usual body language that reveals their true thoughts, but most people never have the reason or inclination to develop that fine art.

"I can get her home address from Gigi," I said slowly, thinking it through. The flight from Portland to Los Angeles is about two hours. If I left early the next morning I could make it a day trip. Or I could leave today, spend the night with my mother and return tomorrow afternoon.

"I'll take care of Binks," Dwayne said, solving that issue for me before I'd even asked.

"Violet paying for this?" I asked.

"Sure, why not?"

"Seems kind of wrong, since I'm checking on her."

"She hired us to learn the truth."

"She hired us to save her ass."

"She won't care," Dwayne assured me. "And if she does, we won't charge her."

My eyes strayed to the window and the beating rain. A trip to sunny Southern California. Why was I arguing? I knew my mother would be happy to see me. "I'll go," I said.

"Good."

I hung up from Dwayne and phoned Gigi, who thankfully actually answered before the call went to voice mail. I told her I wanted her mother's address and she got all huffy and protective. "What are you doing?" she demanded. "Violet murdered Daddy! Why does it take so long for everybody to get that!"

I realized she must not know about Melinda's accusations concerning Violet's first husband, which made me wonder about the story's validity some more.

"I'm looking into Violet's past. About some—inconsistencies—that may shed some light on your father's death. I think your mother can help."

"You're not trying to pin this on my mother?"

"This is about Violet," I assured her.

She thought about it, made a sound of annoyance, then spat out the address.

Next, I phoned my mother at work. She's a part-time office manager at a real estate office. She was thrilled to hear I was coming her way. I tried to bypass all the niceties of conversation that seem to take so long whenever I talk to Mom, but there was no hope for it. There seems to be a routine to our conversation that makes me chew my nails and pull at my hair in impatience. I was praying something would happen that would require her immediate attention at work, but no such luck. I pretended to listen as she rattled on about the doings of the four-unit that I co-owned with her. I decided right then and there I needed to take a look at that building as long as I was in the area. I couldn't remember the last time I'd been there to check up on the property, and I could make dual use out of this trip. Finally, she had to grab another call and I told her I'd see her later that day.

I booked an afternoon flight. Tomorrow I would return in time for the big home game between Lake Chinook High and Brookstone, which was the team from the town of the same name to Lake Chinook's south and a serious rival whether either team was any good or not.

I threw items in an overnight bag and remembered to pack my cell phone charger at the last moment. I bought an e-ticket on Alaska Airlines, dropped The Binkster off at Dwayne's, drove my car to the airport, then inwardly howled at the highway robbery prices for long-term parking. The airline ticket wasn't cheap, either, but if I have an expectation of what something costs I can generally live with it. Parking fees always send me into overdrive, so to speak. You have to practically leave your car in the next state to keep the daily rate reasonable.

It took me a while to get through airport security. The TSA workers pulled me aside, searched my bag and came up with a minibottle of water that had been given to me by one of the airlines on my last flight. I'd forgotten about it, which just goes to show how often I go through my luggage. They confiscated the water, gave me a hard once-over, then let me pass. I had my e-ticket in my hand, then had to stop to put on my coat, my shoes, gather my purse and my overnight bag. In the process the e-ticket slipped from my fingers and I had to chase it down. Two security lines over, another man was doing the same chase and grab.

"Move out of the way," an authoritative voice called to us all. My feet were only half in my shoes and I had to shuffle toward the concourse. A group of us dropped our gear on the floor and started putting ourselves back together. I know it's safer. I'm glad we're all checked to make sure we're not carrying weapons and explosives. But this traveling by air has become a total pain in the ass.

After all that screening the flight to L.A. was unremarkable except for the fact that there were only eleven pretzels in my minifoil snack pack. As if my diet weren't scanty enough.

It was two-thirty when we touched down at LAX. Through my window seat window I examined the tawny landscape: buildings, tarmac, vehicles, even the sky—were varying shades of tan, like someone had put a filter on a camera to make the setting seem hot, dry and forbidding.

After all the rain, it looked like heaven.

Mom had offered to pick me up and I'd gratefully agreed. Not that I enjoy traveling with her in L.A. traffic, but a rental car would have been worse, not to mention more expensive.

I saw her silver Volvo wagon pull up and I admired a much newer version of my own vehicle. My car had basically been a gift from my mother. She'd upgraded to a new car and I'd ended up with the dark blue Volvo wagon I still own. One of these days I might have to spring for a newer model. Or one of these days Mom might decide to buy new and leave me hers. I began to covet the car with the same desire Binkster eyes a mochi. With an effort, I pulled my brain back to the task at hand.

Mom stopped in the no-parking area right by the taxis. The whole area is no-parking. It's insane how fast you have to jump into a vehicle that's pulled to the side to pick you up. They're snotty at the Portland Airport, but they're their own militia in Los Angeles. Out of the corner of my eye I saw airport parking security heading our direction, so I hurriedly threw open the back door and hefted my roller bag inside. I thought about affecting a limp, just to buy some time, but we were okay as it turned out.

Mom merged into the god-awful airport traffic, barreling

in front of another driver, narrowly missing his bumper. He tooted at her and she pretended she was deaf.

My mother, Carole Kelly, is an older, softer version of myself with light brown hair and hazel eyes. Sometimes I wonder how we can be related. Other times, like now, I see definite familial traits.

"I left Binks with Dwayne," I said, as if she'd asked.

She was stuck in three lanes of traffic, all inching toward the exit. "Binks?"

"My dog. The one you made me take from dear, departed Aunt Eugenie?" If my tone was long-suffering, I should be pardoned. For reasons unknown to me, Mom cannot, or will not, remember that she's responsible for me being a pet owner.

"Oh . . . right . . ." Mom had lost interest. She was edging into another lane. I wrapped my fingers around the handle above the passenger door and tried not to press too hard with my foot against the imaginary brake.

With a deftness bordering on insanity, Mom cut off a stretch limo, which blared at her with its horn. She practically put a wheel on the curb to circumvent another car. I closed my eyes, hazarding a peek out of my right eye when we started speeding up. We were just about to enter the 405 freeway on our way north toward Santa Monica. Mom managed to fight off the traffic and merge us in. I held my breath as we took the exit ramp to 10 West, but we were okay. L.A. driving requires speed and decisiveness. Mom had both. It was accuracy I was worried about.

We cruised into Santa Monica without incident, turning on Lincoln, which runs parallel to the beach and is eight blocks in. We wound our way into the pricey neighborhood north of Montana, approaching on a street lined with tall, skinny-trunked palms, their ruffed tops all leaning toward the ocean. The city of Santa Monica sits on a shelf of land

high above the ocean. Access to the beach is down dizzying
stairways and a trip across Pacific Coast Highway. There are
several pedestrian overpasses, and I've taken them all, but
for practical purposes, the houses facing the Pacific mostly
have ocean views, not ocean fronts. Malibu, which boasts
amazing beachfront homes owned by many celebrities and
other wealthy Californians, is just north of Santa Monica.

Renee owned a Santa Monica bungalow with an ocean
view, which meant it could be three hundred square feet and
cost millions, land value being what it is. Unlike Violet, she
clearly had come away with something from her divorce.

Mom pulled into a parking spot across the street, a lucky
break as we saw it being vacated. Renee's house was actually
a bit larger than I'd expected. I calculated a thousand square
feet in a two-bedroom, one-bath cottage with a tidy, green
lawn and a brick serpentine walk to the dark, plank-wood
door with a tiny, iron-grilled viewing window. The bungalow
was tan stucco with a red tile roof, typical Southern California real estate fare. There was no garage, but two parallel cement tracks ran down one side of the house where an older
model, dark green Cadillac sedan sat waiting by a teensy
back porch with four red-tiled steps.

Mom and I walked up to the front door and knocked. I
could smell the jasmine and turned my face to a surprisingly
warm sun. November, and you'd never know it. I thought of
Randy Newman's song "I Love L.A." Yep. I was feeling it. I
know it's popular to denigrate L.A. and its glitzy, shallow
image, but hey, ya gotta appreciate the weather.

Renee didn't immediately open the door, so I pulled out
my cell phone and called her again. I could hear the sound of
it distantly trilling away inside the house, so I knew she was
probably home. She didn't answer its call, however. Figured.

Mom asked, "She a recluse, or something?"

"Or something," I agreed, knocking again. I was wondering about the wisdom of bringing my mother along for this trip, but I hadn't known how to say thanks for the ride and now get lost.

It took about ten minutes of impatient waiting until I saw a twitch at the front window's curtains. I waved at the movement and smiled brightly. Let her try to figure out who Mom and I were. Jehovah's Witnesses in jeans and sneakers? Not likely. I could be with Publishers Clearing House, though.

My cell phone rang as we were waiting. I debated on answering it, not recognizing the number. I snatched it up impatiently and demanded, "Hello?"

"Hi, this is Deenie. Sorry I couldn't talk to you before. My boyfriend and I are just—well . . . it's such a mess."

"Unfortunately, now I'm the one who can't talk. Let me call you back."

"Well, God . . . fine." She hung up.

"Who was that?" Mom asked.

Before I could answer, the door finally opened. Mom and I turned our heads and stared in astonishment. Catlike, they'd said? No shit. Renee's eyes were pulled into a slant that tilted upward at the outside corners, and she'd darkened the brows in a way that accentuated the feline look. Her whole face appeared stretched back and her mouth had lengthened into a flat line that seemed to go halfway around her head. Her hair lopped forward over her forehead in a tawny mane, then swept to a sort of fashionable mullet down her neck. The scariest part of it was that it wasn't unattractive. It was kind of arty and interesting. And, well, weird.

She was slim and dressed in a pair of black capri stretch pants and a sleeveless black top. She looked as if she were about to do some kind of performance art whereby she would scratch, claw and hiss. If I'd had Binkster with me I think she would have started whining, which is what she does when she encounters a feline. She likes them, but they worry her. I understood the feeling.

"I'm Jane Kelly," I said, thrusting my hand toward her. "I called you earlier. I'm the private investigator looking into Roland Hatchmere's death."

She cautiously accepted the handshake. My mother followed suit, smiling beneficently. "Carole Kelly." Renee shook her hand, too. Her face showed no expression. I doubted there were enough muscles left for that.

"I don't know how I can help you," she said in a normal voice. I had so expected a purr. "You didn't come all the way here just to interview me, did you?"

"My mother lives here," I said easily.

"I've been trying to get Jane to visit for months. Finally the time was right," my mother put in, just as easily.

It took all I had not to give her the proverbial double take. Sometimes Mom surprises me. Actually, oftentimes Mom surprises me, it's just that sometimes the surprise isn't exactly a welcome one.

Renee clearly didn't know what to do with us. Grudgingly she stepped back from the door, then suggested we go back outside through the rear door and follow the gravel path to the backyard. We followed her across a scarred oak floor scattered with area rugs in varying jungle prints. The kitchen was tiny and hadn't been updated since the fifties, but it was clean and tidy.

We went down the four steps, past the Cadillac, to a tall wooden fence, a portion of which was a gate with a hook on top. Renee reached up and unlatched it, swinging the gate section inward, and we entered an area that was more patio than yard, but nicely done. Swept concrete was surrounded by potted plants: a lush jade, a red bottle brush plant, some kind of ground cover flowing over one pot that perfumed the air. A round, redwood table with semicircular benches sat under the shade of a coral tree, the branches of which curved and twisted, reminiscent of an ocean reef. Tucked along the grassy edges were metal posts with hooks, and from the hooks hung lanterns with fat, white candles.

"This is lovely," my mother said admiringly.

It went a long way in getting Renee to thaw. She smiled, and that, too, had a cat-who-ate-the-canary quality to it. "I spend most of my time out here. The house needs work but it's peaceful here." She grabbed a red flame lighter and touched it to the candles, sending out flickering illumination. Shadows were beginning to spread across the backyard and patio as it was after four o'clock.

"I own a four-unit in Venice," Mom added. "Amazing what the property values have risen to, isn't it? This place, when it was built, when you think about it . . ." She shook her head, marveling, looking around.

Renee nodded eagerly. I watched in amusement as she jumped into the game. People love, love, love to tell you how much they've made on their real estate investments, as if it's a ruler for their business acumen and general smartness when in reality if you hold prime real estate long enough, and don't have an abyss of debt, you'll generally do fine and sometimes make out like a bandit. I was intrigued that my mother, whose age was probably close to Renee's, was deliberately getting Renee to warm to her, pulling down her barriers. It saved me a helluva lot of effort.

They talked price and location and the market for a good ten minutes. I listened with a growing sense of unease I didn't initially identify. I did an inner search and discovered the source of this dread was my soon-to-be eviction. I would be losing my own piece of real estate unless I did something about it.

Like what? I asked myself.

Renee offered to serve us some lemonade and went to take care of it. I gave Mom a look.

"What?" she asked, but her little smile said she knew exactly what I was thinking.

"I might have to bring you on all my interviews."

"You might," she agreed.

Renee returned with a tray holding a pitcher of pink lemonade and three glasses filled with cubes of ice. There was also a stack of hors d'oeuvre plates, an array of crackers covered with dabs of cream cheese, a wedge of cold, sliced salmon and a little glass bowl of different varieties of olives. It was damn good on short notice. Maybe not in Melinda's league, but better than I could ever hope to manage.

Mom selected a plate, filled it with salmon, crackers and a grouping of olives and accepted the glass of lemonade Renee poured for her. Leaning back in her chair, she eyed me expectantly.

Showtime.

CHAPTER ELEVEN

I mentally prepared myself for the interview, aware that I was slightly nervous.

Her odd looks just put me on edge.

Renee was gazing toward the back of her property. "Roland and I were madly in love once. The kind of thing that happens once in a lifetime, at least to me." She gave us a quick, wry look, which was a little disconcerting. Sort of like a cat with the power to be self-effacing. "He was an incredible surgeon. I've never been able to find anyone who could do work like he did."

"You've tried, then?" my mother asked politely.

Like, duh. How much surgery had this woman had?

Renee nodded, totally serious. "I've had some facial reconstruction since Roland retired. But it's never been the same."

"So, you've seen Roland—professionally—for years," I said.

"Absolutely. He used to try to talk me out of it, but after a while I think it was kind of peaceful for him. Familiar. We knew each other well." She waved a hand at me. "Violet hated it, when they were together. Wanted to get Roland away from me. That's why they left for Portland, you know. Oh, sure, Roland was expanding his business, starting those clinics, but Violet was all for it because it got him away from me. I did make a couple of trips to Portland for some touch-up, though, before Roland's problems got in the way."

"Naturally," Mom said.

Renee gave her a swift look, as if sensing something wasn't quite on the level but Mom gazed back, all innocence and interest.

"Violet and Roland lived here for a while before they left for Portland," I said, to put things back on track.

"A long while," Renee agreed.

"When they left, Gigi and Sean went with them."

"I suppose you think I'm a terrible mother," she said to me.

"Things happen for a lot of reasons," I responded vaguely.

Renee plucked an olive with her fingernails, which were long and bloodred. "Roland wanted Gigi and Sean and I fought him on that. I figured Violet would be a terrible influence. But . . . Gigi was such a daddy's girl, it became . . . problematic. And where Gigi went, Sean wanted to go, too. Believe me, it made everybody happier to have them all head to Portland together, except possibly Violet. Roland and I had a huge house in the valley with a swimming pool. We sold it and that's when I bought this bungalow."

"You drove to Gigi's wedding with a friend," I said, changing the subject. I wanted to get to Violet's background, but I sensed it wasn't time yet. Interviews typically have a life of their own and it's best to let them unfold on their own schedule. I've learned less by forcing questions than biding my time, even when I feel the clock ticking in my head, urging me to get going in all due haste.

"Ah, Aaron." She hesitated, seeming to have a debate with herself. In the end she shook her head and said, "He's

from some of my classes. I just couldn't bear to go alone and
he thought it would be a kick to drive up in the Ferrari. Actually, it was horrible. Drive a thousand miles to Portland,
and another back? My tush still hurts. Should have taken my
Caddy." She gave a disparaging laugh. "We've scarcely spoken since we got back. Some bonding experience."

"What kind of classes?"

"Pilates, spinning, low-impact aerobics."

"Are you an instructor?" Mom asked.

I kept myself from giving my mom a "look," but just
barely. I'd begun to wonder how to ask Renee what she did
careerwise, if anything, but Mom just popped up with a way
to get the information.

"Oh, sure, I help out sometimes. But I'm not really good
with a schedule. Mostly I just take the classes to keep in
shape."

I had this picture of Renee's life: one fitness class after
another. One plastic surgery after another. She'd as much as
said she hadn't been interested in another man since Roland.
She seemed to only care about her appearance, such as it
was.

I asked her about Gigi's wedding, which events she'd attended, how many days she'd been there, when she learned
of Roland's death.

"You probably know I was disinvited to the wedding,"
Renee said, her expression tightening with the first sign of
annoyance I'd seen. Either that or her stretched face just
couldn't handle any nuances of emotion. "You know I loved
that man, but Roland could be such a prig. He *hated* it that I
was there with Aaron. Just hated it." A tiny trill of triumph
rang in her voice. "I called him that at the rehearsal dinner. A
prig. I was kidding, really, but Roland never could take a
joke. Well, he got all heated up. Before that he hadn't cared
a whit that I'd brought Aaron to the dinner, but all of a sudden—holy mother of God, I've committed the faux pas of all

faux pas! He starts yelling at me. And Melinda . . . she's so damn stupid. She gets all fluttery and anxious and tries to make nice with everybody. I ignored her. I mean, give me a friggin' break. Aaron tried to talk reason to Roland and that didn't work. Then Gigi started that whining thing." She made a dismissive gesture and rolled her eyes. "I told them all they should change their diet. Less red meat, more whole grains and leafy green vegetables. It's not rocket science, now, is it? Turn on the Food Channel, for Pete's sake. Learn what a healthy diet is. Hello! But there they were, forks loaded with bloody meat." She made a retching sound. "Gigi just freaked. Told me I was ruining everything. Oh, sure, she's my daughter and all, but there's no denying she's a little bitch. Really, I was glad to have a reason to leave." Lifting the lemonade pitcher, she looked at my mother. "A little more?"

"Hit me," Mom said.

Surreptitiously, I glanced at my watch. "Was the rehearsal dinner your first event with the family?"

"First and only, except when they called looking for Roland. At first I thought it was funny that they'd lost him, the Father of the Bride. I was still pretty hot about the way they'd treated us the night before. But Gigi was just sobbing, so Aaron and I drove to Cahill Winery. Gigi threw herself in my arms. Kind of surprised me, to be honest. Then Emmett called with the news. . . ." She pulled her lips back in what I took to be a rueful expression.

"Was there any indication that anyone thought Roland might be with Violet? That she was the reason for the delay?"

Renee thought back. "Not really. I mean, Gigi was just shattered. Her wedding was ruined. She wasn't thinking about what was keeping Roland. She just wanted him there." She selected another olive, capturing it with her nails and dropping it in her mouth, chewing thoughtfully. "I don't think anybody really thought about Violet until Roland's body was discovered. Then, of course, it all made sense. It's the same thing that happened with Bart. She was the last one to see him alive, too."

"Bart . . . ?"

"Treadway. Violet's first husband. You don't know about him?" Her tawny brows arched.

"Melinda mentioned something about it," I murmured.

Renee looked at me as if she was doubting my ability as an investigator. I could scarcely blame her. "You know it's amazing Roland ever hooked up with Violet in the first place. I mean, he is a prig. And she's so . . . ripe. Once upon a time, I guess I was like that, too. Good old Roland. He never changed much over the years." She touched a hand to her cheek, looking mildly embarrassed. "We met at the same escort service, if you can believe that."

"You and Roland? The same one as . . . ?"

"Roland and Violet. I actually knew Violet first. We were both part of Landon Escort Services. Landon Ladies, that's what we were called. Then that scandal stopped everything for a while, and they came back as something different. Something generic. Connections, I think it was called. Didn't have the same ring."

"When was this?" I asked.

"Violet joined Landon's right after Bart's death. I was already there and we struck up a friendship of sorts. She wasn't there very long because she met her second husband right away. I cannot remember his name for the life of me. This is about the time Roland and I started seeing each other, so I wasn't really paying much attention. He'd spent all that time in med school and it was like he'd never had time for a girlfriend. We met in January and were married by June. Sean and Gigi came along and I guess we were happy for a while, then things just sort of fell apart. You know how that goes."

"My husband left me for his secretary," my mother said.

"Bastard," Renee said.

"Jane's father," Mom reminded.

"You can't hurt me with that one," I assured Renee. "I haven't seen him in years."

My father took off when Booth and I were still toddlers. My mother helped support him through law school; then he left her for his secretary, whom he promptly married and started a new family with. I believe I have three half siblings; I probably have a lot more by now. To date that's all I know about Richard Booth Kelly. My brother is Richard Booth Kelly Jr.

The shadows had lengthened and I was done with the trip down my own personal memory lane. "So, you met Roland at Landon Ladies, where Violet met her second husband."

"That's right. Then Roland went back to it after it became Connections, or whatever it was, and that's where he and Violet found each other. Isn't that just lovely?"

"Violet worked for the same company twice," I confirmed. "The one that had the scandal?" At Renee's nod, I asked, "What was that about?"

"A couple of the Landon Ladies were selling more than their sparkling conversation. Lucrative, but it was illegal, of course, and well . . ." She shrugged. No judgment. "So Landon Services became Connections."

I hadn't realized Violet had worked for the escort service more than once. She'd told me that she'd quit the job upon realizing her dates had expected more than a handshake at the end of the evening. It was a surprise to learn she'd gone back for a second try. It was also a surprise to learn that's how she'd met Roland.

"How did Violet's first husband die?" I asked.

"Bart Treadway was a hiker. One of those outdoorsy guys everybody just loves. I never met the man, personally. He was dead before Violet showed up at Landon Ladies, but she talked about him quite a bit in the beginning. She was upset that his family blamed her for his death. They had money, but everything was in trust for him, and it didn't pass on to Violet. She got nothing, and I suppose that's how come she was never indicted for his death."

"She was suspected of killing him?" Mom posed.

"I got this from Bart's sister, Patsy Treadway," Renee revealed. "I was kind of crazy for a while, after Roland hooked up with Violet, and so I looked up Patsy and became friends with her. She was more than happy to rank on Violet, which I needed at the time. She told me Violet never went hiking with him. Never, never, never. That sounds just like Violet, right? She's *not* a hiker. Then one day she decides to go with him and they take off together. But later that day she comes off the mountain alone. Says she left Bart to do more hiking. That she got tired. Two days later they find his body at the bottom of a ravine. He 'fell' from the trail above."

"He didn't fall," I guessed.

"Well . . ." Renee spread her hands. "Everybody knew Bart and Violet were having problems. She was pretty young in those days. Probably thought she'd get the money, but oops. Didn't happen. Bart's family tried to get the D.A. to prosecute, but the case wasn't strong enough. No money, no motive, was the way they saw it. Violet said she'd gone hiking with him because he'd asked, and she wanted to try and save their marriage. But she got whiny and he grew tired of her, so she walked back to where they'd left their car. She hung around awhile but finally took herself home. She called Patsy and said Bart might need a ride back, which pissed Patsy off but good. She went to collect him but he never came out."

"She still maintains that Bart's death was Violet's fault. What do you think?"

"I wouldn't put anything past Violet."

"And you told Melinda this."

Renee smiled fleetingly. "Oh, you know . . . Melinda's so easy to send over the edge."

It was interesting how Renee had stayed a part of Roland's life all these years, and not just through her children. In fact, she scarcely seemed connected to her children by anything more than happenstance. It was like she didn't know what to do with them.

"You can talk to Patsy," Renee encouraged. "I've got her address."

"What about Violet's second husband?"

"They divorced. That's all I know."

Mom and I left soon afterward. Renee pressed Patsy Treadway's number and address upon me. I put in a call to her as we headed for the car and was sent, as ever, directly to voice mail. The communication age. Like, oh, sure. Not that I was exactly panting to talk to the woman as I felt I'd pretty much gotten the gist of what had taken place from Renee, and I had a feeling I would hear a lot more theory than fact from Patsy.

Mom and I drove to our four-unit in Venice through heavy commuter traffic down Lincoln. It felt like we hit every light. Finally Mom eased onto Abbott-Kinney and then meandered through narrow beach streets until we turned on Baybridge. Venice is kind of a weird place. All this prime beachfront real estate yet everything has that musty, dank smell and peeling-paint appearance of an area gone to seed. There's a carnival, Coney Island–type atmosphere about the place: surf shops; wind socks fluttering; roller skaters in shorts zigzagging along the sidewalk that cuts through the sand.

My mother and I co-own a tan-colored rectangular box. Its front faces the ocean and if it weren't for the buildings on the three blocks between it and the water, it would have an excellent view. As it is, it pretty much looks at walls, roofs and sprouting antennae, though the tiny balconies on both front units have teensy, peekaboo views if you hang over the rails. They were originally apartments; my mother was savvy enough to convert them into condominiums shortly after she managed to buy the building, yet she and I still maintain ownership of all four units. At the time of the purchase I was working at Sting Ray's, a beach bar, as one of their bartenders. By my mother's wheeling, dealing and stretching the boundaries of financial security, I became part owner in the project. My mother actually lives a couple of streets over in the little three-bedroom house Booth and I grew up in. Now, when it was clear she was heading directly toward the four-unit instead of her house, I made a sound of protest.

"We're not dropping off my bag first?"

"I've moved to one of the units," she said, causing my jaw to drop.

"When?"

"Mrs. Cassleway died and so the lower front unit was empty. I started redoing it. She had dogs. Big dogs, and cats. It reeked. And then someone wanted to buy my house."

"You sold the house?" I asked in horror.

"No way." Mom gave me a sideways look, silently chiding me. "But I started thinking about its value, and then I decided to rent it. It's got a garage, you know. And a driveway. They're paying me a small fortune."

This made me happy. "So you moved into the four-unit," I repeated.

"Yep."

We drove past our building and circled toward the parking spots in the rear. The upper front space is the "owner's unit," which means it's slightly larger, and it's been rented to the same couple for two decades. Its grander space cuts into that of the rear upper unit, so we get less rent for that one.

Mom turned into the alley that leads to our building.

There's no garage, but there's enough land behind the structure to allow for four parking spots covered by a shingled carport. Signage across the back of the building warns would-be parkers that their lives will be in jeopardy if they so much as edge a tire onto one of our spots. Mostly, we're treated with respect by the beach people who come in droves on the weekends and circle the narrow streets in search of parking.

A row of exterior lights, each one covered by a stainless steel grid with a nautical motif, lined the back of the four-plex. Each light offered a pool of illumination against the dark cobalt sky. Mom pulled into her spot and we stepped into a brisk wind. I grabbed my overnight bag, my hair flying around my face. I'd left it loose from its ubiquitous ponytail to fly down here and meet Renee. Now I grabbed it in one fist, hauling my bag with the other hand, my purse bumping my hip and threatening to slide from my shoulder.

"Whew," Mom said as she slammed the front door behind us and switched on the interior lights. The room snapped into bright focus. I dropped my bag on the hardwood floor and looked around with interest.

I knew the property was valuable. I loved having an investment. If it weren't for Mom, I wouldn't have anything to call my own, and I could turn religious when I remember how she talked me out of using my hard-earned money to buy a better car, or take a luxury vacation, or consider investing with my first boyfriend, a surfer dude guy who was all California blond good looks and ideas that never materialized. She made me put my money in the four-unit instead. Booth didn't listen to her, though she tried to get him, too. He bought the car and took the vacation, though the only person I think he's ever invested money with is Sharona, and believe me, she's a sure bet. They have a house together in northwest Portland, so luckily Booth didn't completely miss the investing opportunity, either.

But his decision made it that Mom and I are in this together. Just the two of us. I said, meaning it, "This is great."

"I thought I'd miss my house more than I do. Of course, I've only been here a couple of weeks. Got the phone moved over and just settled in. I guess you can tell I redid the place."

The cabinets were painted a creamy, buttery color and the countertops were large blocks of a darker, taupe tile. The backsplash tile was another shade of cream, subway style, with a crackle finish. She'd put in a gas range, stainless steel, and a matching refrigerator with a freezer drawer on the bottom. She also had one of those two-drawer dishwashers, also stainless. The effect was contemporary yet warmer than Melinda's unit. Two hanging lights with glowing dark amber-colored glass shades hung down over the eating peninsula that jutted from one wall.

The kitchen opened into the living room, and down the hall was one bathroom, two bedrooms and an alcove with a built-in desk. I used the bathroom and took my bag into the spare bedroom, which she'd done in an olive green color trimmed out in white. The furniture was white, louvered and distressed, very beachy, and the bed sat on a fuzzy cream-colored area rug.

I returned to the kitchen where Mom had poured us each a glass of white wine. God, I love my mother.

"You remember me telling you about Mr. Densworth," Mom said as she picked up her glass and headed toward the living room. "In the upper back unit, whose daughter-in-law took off with his grandson?"

I dug my cell phone out of my purse and followed her. "Where the private investigator was shot twice in the head. I remember."

Mom settled into a rattan chair and I sat on the tweed-colored love seat opposite her. "Who are you calling?"

"Sorry. Just a sec." I phoned Deenie back. She didn't pick up, so I left her another message.

"You sound discouraged," Mom said.

No shit. I launched into a dissertation on the failings of cell phones and people who don't seem to understand the proper etiquette, to which my mother listened politely without the slightest bit of interest. When I finally wound down, she did the equivalent of patting me on the hand and saying, "There, there." She took a sip of wine and said, "Don't worry. You'll figure it out."

"Thanks, Mom. But it's possible I won't."

She smiled. "You will."

My mother has dimples that my cheeks only hint at. She's sweeter by nature. At least I think she is, although there's a steel rod up her spine that shows from time to time.

"You're not worried I'll get shot in the head?"

"I'm always worried. But that's what I was going to tell you. You were right. That investigator was killed from some other case he was on. It wasn't Mr. Densworth's daughter-in-law's. It was something to do with teenage boys. They were drunk or on drugs or something and they just killed him execution style. They'd seen it in the movies."

Teenage boys . . . I felt slightly light-headed.

"What were you trying to get from Cat Lady?" Mom asked.

I corralled my attention with an effort. "Background on Violet Purcell. What happened with her first husband."

"You think she killed him?" Mom asked curiously.

"I don't know."

My mother had met Violet's nephew, Jasper "Jazz" Purcell, the last time she'd visited and she'd been convinced that Jazz was the guy for me. Handsome, wealthy, gentlemanly . . . She'd let it be known she thought I should jump into the relationship with Jazz, but then she hadn't known the whole story. I had no intention of letting her know Violet was related to Jazz.

"Cat Lady's daughter, Gigi, calls her Ultra-Violet," I said, thinking aloud. "More like Ultra-Violent, the way people keep dying around her."

"You mean this Roland fellow."

"She hit him with a silver tray. The tray's the murder weapon."

"And she's your client?"

I nodded.

"Hunh." Mom buried her nose in her wineglass and looked concerned.

I decided to walk to Sting Ray's and see if Ray was around. I hadn't been back to the place in several years. When I made the move to Oregon, it was like I'd shed one life for another, a snake leaving its skin behind, unwanted and forgotten.

Hunching a shoulder to the stiff breeze, I kept to the lighted areas. I didn't feel like meeting eyes with the panhandlers and hecklers, an unfortunate section of the homeless population that loitered along the beachfront.

Like with any beach community, the weather takes its toll wherever you are. Even Venice's freshly painted apartment buildings looked abused somehow, their stucco sidings circa 1950 and showing the passing of time no matter how much fresh paint was slapped atop it. There are lots of homes that were purchased a long, long time ago and look like they've fallen on hard times, their owners unable to keep up with the high cost of maintenance. This same housing sits cheek-by-jowl with multimillion-dollar properties. You just never know what you're going to get, kind of like Cracker Jack, a surprise in every box.

Sting Ray's probably defies all kinds of city codes, meandering off its designated lot onto the beach as if it's slowly dragging itself toward the ocean. Its beachside eating area is a wooden platform atop the sand with a retractable awning in striped black and tan shading it from the sun.

I entered through the main entry, a Dutch door on the south side. The maitre d's stand was directly in front of me and a girl in tan shorts and a bright blue shirt with a tiny, stitched gray manta ray across the left breast pocket that sported "Sting Ray's" spelled out in yellow script gave me a look and then walked away. I saw that she was in some kind of altercation with another similarly dressed woman who looked about five years her senior. The older woman pointed to me, and my girl returned, her face flushed. The smile she gave me was little more than bared teeth. "Are you having dinner?"

"Just the bar, thanks." I strolled past her to the back deck. She gave the older woman a hard look that said, "See?" plain as day. The senior worker watched me with a baleful eye. I was taken back to a time when these little dramas played out daily while I worked the bar.

Ray wasn't around, as far as I could tell. I slid my rear end onto a black-and-tan-striped stool and ordered a Sting Ray, which is basically a mai tai with a few extra ingredients added and a clear plastic swizzle stick with a little jellyfish critter on top. The bartender was male and wore the same tan cotton shorts, but his T-shirt was gray with a three-button placket. The yellow, scripted Sting Ray's logo ran obliquely across the pocket. "Ray not around?" I asked.

"Nah. He only stops in at night."

Well, night was here. The sun wasn't even a paler part of the sky any longer. The breeze was an out-and-out wind along the beach, and it was blowing stiffly, making it possible to see hard, pinprick stars in between the moving clouds. It was turning the air downright chilly and I could feel gooseflesh rise on my skin. The hanging black and gold

Japanese lanterns that ran along the roofline were doing a little dance all their own. One of the employees untied the clear plastic drapes that are pulled shut when the wind kicks up. If it gets really cold, Ray closes down the back deck completely.

The bartender critically eyed some of the stemware hanging upside down from a wooden rack above his head. He slid out several rows, one by one, placing them in the dishwasher. "Blender explosion," he said, aware that I was watching. "Strawberry daiquiris. Happened last night and we're still finding it everywhere."

"Sticky," I said.

"No shit," he answered mildly. "You know Ray?"

"Used to work for him. Bartender."

"Yeah? You working somewhere else around here?"

I shook my head. "Followed a guy to Lake Chinook, Oregon. Relationship ended but I stayed on."

"If you're looking for a job, mine's going to be open. Got a callback on a new television series. It's time for me to give it my all, y'know? Now or never, that's what I think."

I'd almost forgotten that nearly all the waiters in Los Angeles were actors at heart. "Thanks, but I've switched professions." I picked up my drink and moved off to stand at the edge of the wooden platform and stare toward the ocean. There weren't many people left on the sand. They'd already packed up their beach paraphernalia—balls, flip-flops, kites, canopied strollers—and headed home.

Another wind gust sent a shiver down my back. I was still in the brown slacks and boots I'd chosen for my interview with Renee, but the thin, long-sleeved, dressy T-shirt wasn't enough for the coming night. I should have changed into my jeans and trusty Nikes. I could have sat myself down in the sand and contemplated life. As it was, I tucked myself into a table at the edge of the platform. A votive candle, its holder blue shark-shaped glass, graced my table, the little flame flickering wildly and threatening to extinguish with each new gust of energetic breeze. I moved it closer to me and it steadied.

I'd brought my purse with me and the notebook and pen I carry around at all times, just in case I have a sudden compelling need to write down information. The notebook was scratched with phone numbers and addresses. Sometimes it's just easier than plugging the information into my phone.

I wrote down Renee's timeline information, planning to add it to my computer later. I started doodling as soon as I got all the information notated. Renee acted like she wanted me to follow up on Violet, but it wasn't like she was dying for me to prove her guilt like Gigi and Melinda were. I hadn't gotten any real sense of vindictiveness or emotion on her part. The truth was, she didn't give a shit. Not really. Roland was dead and it was too bad and she would miss him, sort of, but that was about it. Though Renee gave lip service to Roland being the love of her life, it kinda appeared Renee pretty much loved Renee. There wasn't room for anyone else in her tiny little heart.

So, where did that leave the investigation?

I wished Larrabee would call me with more information on the Wedding Bandits. If any of them were caught and would talk, it could make a huge difference. I wanted to know how they'd targeted the Hatchmere wedding and how they'd learned Roland's home address. More than that, I wanted to know what the story was when they ran across Roland. Was he unconscious, possibly dead, and that's what scared them off, like Larrabee suspected? The trail of gifts, wrapped and unwrapped, across the front yard showed a very hasty exit. Something sent them scurrying and I thought Roland's dead body was a good guess.

That same niggling thought touched a finger inside my brain. This time I didn't try to grab for it. I stared through the wavering clear plastic curtain toward the dark waves, crest-ing and foaming white against the wet gray sand. The ocean looked as vast and dangerous as it was.

"Want another?" a young woman asked. She wore long pants, preparation for the chilly night. The girl at the podium was still in shorts and I could see she was shivering.

"Sure." To stay ahead of my alcohol consumption I ordered off the happy hour menu. Some cold shrimp and a salad. In my notebook I wrote down the cost. I was really getting into this expense account thing.

And suddenly the thought coalesced. It was the timing, yes, but I was concentrating on the wrong timeline. It was the Wedding Bandits who were off. From Dwayne's notes I knew they robbed homes while weddings were in progress. That was their m.o. and they hadn't varied from it even once while they were running and gunning.

But they'd shown up to the Hatchmere house early. Way early.

Basics from the timeline read:

12:00 p.m.—Violet and Roland get into a fight. She hits him and storms out.

2:00 p.m.—Roland doesn't show for pictures at Cahill Winery. Guests become worried. Emmett calls Roland several times.

3:00 p.m.—Emmett leaves to find Roland.

3:30 p.m.—Emmett discovers Roland's body.

4:00 p.m.—Scheduled wedding ceremony. Canceled. Gigi and remaining guests leave.

The police hadn't said much about Roland's time of death, but Violet told me she hit him around noon, so it had to be sometime around there. Therefore, Roland must have died at noon or shortly after. The Wedding Bandits must have burgled the house after noon, when Violet left, and before three-thirty, when Emmett arrived. But the wedding was scheduled for four.

Based on their m.o., they would not have arrived at Roland's house any earlier than three-thirty. They always robbed the homes during the scheduled ceremony.

Always.

Yet, this time they were early. Why?

What was different?

I gave it some thought, rolling the idea around in my head.

Had the Wedding Bandits known Roland was supposed to be at pictures at two? Had they received inside information? Giving them more time to rob the place blind?

Inside information . . . from the man or woman who was their leader? The one who'd apparently quit the team after Roland's death? Leaving them to their own devices . . . ?

Who was this person who had access to addresses, finances?

I wondered if Larrabee, who'd brought up the inside man, had an idea and just hadn't shared it.

CHAPTER TWELVE

I was booked on a 1:00 p.m. flight the next day and had thoughts of sleeping in when my cell phone caught me at seven-thirty. Groaning, I checked caller ID. An 818 area code, which is Burbank, the Valley and surrounding environs, and it also happened to be where Bart Treadway's sister, Patsy, lived.

"Hullo?"

"This is Patsy Treadway. You called and left a message on my phone about Violet Purcell."

Her tone was slightly aggressive. My hope for a relaxing morning grew dim, although I could hear Mom already puttering around in the kitchen and the scent of coffee and cinnamon wafted into my bedroom. Cinnamon what? I wondered. Rolls? Toast? "Um, yeah."

"Well, you came to the right person. I have a lot to say about Violet. Did Renee fill you in at all?"

"A little bit."

"You're a private investigator? Does that mean Violet's up to her old tricks again, luring men with her siren's call? I just hope you get her this time. She killed my brother, and if I can help you in any way, any way at all, just ask! When do you want to meet?" she swept on. "I'm in Burbank. Where are you?"

"Venice."

"Well, that's perfect. I'm heading to San Clemente this afternoon, so I'll be shooting right by you. I'll come your way. Maybe have lunch?"

I perked up. If anyone offers to come your way in the Greater Los Angeles area, it's a gift. "I have a flight at one. Could we meet around eleven?"

"Do you have somewhere in mind? Oh, wait. How about Encounter?"

Encounter is the mod, Lava Lamp–motifed restaurant situated in the spaceshiplike structure that is the symbol of Los Angeles International Airport. It has a futuristic nightclub feel any hour of the day.

"I'll be there."

It was cinnamon English muffins, black coffee and fresh tangerine slices. I made appreciative noises around mouthfuls. Today was one of those days when I can scarcely believe my luck: breakfast *and* lunch. Many mornings I'm relegated to coffee and Chap Stick.

Mom was disappointed that I was leaving so soon. She really wanted me to stay, but it wasn't going to work right now. As she drove me to the airport I promised again that I would come back and see her soon. She'd made noise about Thanksgiving, but she'd been invited to a friend's home, so I skated on that one.

I strapped my purse atop my roller bag as I headed up the elevator to the restaurant. Encounter feels like it's got its tongue planted very firmly in its cheek. It turned out eleven o'clock was as early as it opened, and I was led to a window seat for two, where I looked out at the hazy gray sky and the buildings and ramps and vehicles that make up Los Angeles International Airport. Inside, Encounter's Lava Lamps were in full swing and I watched as a purple blob goopily separated into several smaller blobs within the lamp's clear liquid.

I text-messaged Larrabee again, just for the hell of it.

don't leave me hanging. jk

Probably wouldn't do any good. People might not be calling me, but good old Jane was standing by, cell phone at the ready.

I pegged Patsy Treadway as soon as she stepped off the elevator. There were four arriving guests, two gentlemen in business suits, a woman in a simple green dress and sensible pumps and a middle-aged woman in a caftan. Had to be Patsy. Her hair was long, gray and wavy, and looked like it could catch and pull in the oversized hammered silver chandelier earrings that hung to her shoulders. She had that "life is serious, so don't laugh" and "I won't drink pasteurized milk" look. I tried to imagine Violet married to this woman's brother and failed. Sexual chemistry is a strange and incomprehensible thing.

She picked me out as well. I lifted a hand to indicate she was right and she said a word to the maitre d' and came directly to my table. She wore sandals that looked as if they'd been bought in Nazareth. I began to rethink my dreams of a BLT for lunch, afraid I might get the evil eye. But I'd be damned if I went for the alfalfa sprouts. Can't do it.

"Hello, I'm Patsy," she said, holding out a hand. Her nails were short and devoid of any kind of polish. Once in a great while I do the girly thing and get a manicure, but there was something so intimidating about her I wanted to curl my nails up and hide them, just because they looked more feminine.

"Jane Kelly."

We assessed each other. She said, "I hope Violet will finally get what's coming to her."

"Renee gave me some background on your brother's death, but she thought I should hear it from you."

Patsy nodded vigorously, waving a hand in front of her face as her skin grew red and blotchy. "Hot flashes," she said by way of explanation. "That's why I'm going to San Clemente. A famous herbalist lives there."

"Ah."

She then launched into the tale of Bart and Violet, with a lot of Patsy thrown in, and how Violet was the root of all evil, Satan herself, a gold digger, a murderess, a liar and a fraud.

I listened, but my hunch about her proved true: I didn't really learn anything new on the Bart Treadway death. Violet left him while they were hiking and he fell off a cliff and died. I tried to get to the timing of the whole thing. Did Patsy think Violet pushed him? Was that why Violet should be brought to justice? But Patsy couldn't be pinned down with specifics, and I got the feeling there was a large enough gap between the time Violet left Bart and he died that it was clear it was an accident. Throughout our lunch Patsy tried her damnedest to ignore the facts and convince me with rhetoric, but as I ate my chicken Caesar salad and listened I realized I was hearing an age-old, vitriolic song that had become lore in Patsy Treadway's world but didn't amount to much in mine.

While she talked, I compared Patsy to Violet. The two women couldn't have been more different, even though they were probably close in age. Patsy had called Violet a siren, and that was apt. Patsy herself was an earth mother.

About the time she wound down, our waiter brought our bill. She was very specific about what she owed and what I did. I watched her add, calculate and cipher several times. She told me my bill and how much to tip. I did as I was told.

As we got up to leave, she said, "I always thought there would be enough money, but that didn't happen. Violet got it all."

Violet? She must have read the confusion on my face, because she said, "Oh yes. She got away with murder and my inheritance, too." I watched another hot flash pinken her flesh and cause tiny beads of perspiration to form around her lips. I let her catch the elevator by herself, pretending I'd forgotten something at the table. In reality I just needed some time alone to think.

Could I believe Patsy? Was this another one of Violet's lies? She'd said she hadn't really profited from her divorces . . . but then this wasn't a divorce.

When I got off the plane in Portland it was just after three. I switched on my cell phone and learned I had two messages. One was from Sharona, returning my call. Took her long enough, I thought uncharitably. She'd probably already talked to Booth. The second was from David Popparockskill. In a stiff, rod-up-his-ass voice he said, "This is David Popparockskill. We got your message. This has been a trying time for all of us, as I'm sure you know. I've discussed this with Emmett and I don't believe there's anything more we can do to help you. My wife and I believe in leaving the matter to the police. Any further inquiries should be directed to them. Thank you."

I made a big raspberry sound aloud on the airport parking bus as I was driven through the Portland rain to my car. A young couple with a baby turned their shoulder to me, afraid to look me in the eye. The baby, however, stared at me over the father's shoulder, eyes wide and vacant. I made a couple of ugly faces and the baby stuck its thumb in its mouth and sucked for all it was worth. Kind of like popcorn at a movie. The mom looked at me over the child's head and whispered something to the father. She pulled the baby down and cuddled it close. I was gratified when it fussed and bobbed and tried to look at me again. Pretty soon it started into one of those siren howls that normally make me want to put my fingers in my ears. This time I kind of sat back and enjoyed it.

I called Violet on my cell as soon as I was pulling away from the lot, juggling the phone and switching on my wipers. She didn't answer and I had to work hard to make myself sound as if I were just checking in, instead of fulminating with suppressed anger. How many times was I going to let her fool me? I asked her to call me when she could. Just good old Jane, wanting to catch up on the case. No hurry. La-di-da.

I called Dwayne next and when he picked up, said, "I've come across a minor discrepancy." Then I told him about the Wedding Bandit's divergence from their m.o., half expecting Dwayne to tell me I was overthinking the whole thing. Instead he said merely, "Hunh," as he thought it over, then, "It's an anomaly."

"You think the Wedding Bandits knew pictures were at two? Maybe from an inside source?"

"Someone involved with the wedding? That doesn't explain how they targeted other places." Dwayne sounded skeptical. "More likely the information was posted. On their wedding Web site, or MySpace, or some other Internet chat room. People'll give away the most amazing info."

"I'll call Gigi and see if she posted her information anywhere."

"Good."

"I need to talk to Violet again," I said. "I've left her a message to call me."

"Renee tell you something?"

I recapped what had transpired with both Renee and Patsy. Dwayne absorbed the information, then asked, "If she got the money, why did she go back for second helpings at the escort service?"

"I didn't think she had until Renee said so," I admitted.

"Something's off," he muttered. "Violet should clear it up."

I sensed I was losing his attention. "Are you looking through those binoculars again?" I demanded.

"Things have quieted down at Rebel Yell. Maybe Dawn's talked to her parents."

"You think I should forget going to Do Not Enter tonight?" I asked a tad hopefully, although a part of me personally wanted to bring down Keegan Lendenhal and his disciples.

"I don't know." For the first time Dwayne sounded unsure. I knew the feeling. We were both feeling protective of Dawn, yet we wanted to get Keegan. "The weather's supposed to clear this afternoon."

I gazed out at the gray clouds and the drizzle. Fat chance. Neither Dwayne nor I seemed ready to make a decision about Do Not Enter, so I mumbled a few words about needing to keep my attention on the road and clicked off. I had the rest of the afternoon and evening to think about it.

Traffic was moving slowly down I-205. I drove onto I-84 with serious concentration because visibility was low and the rest of the drivers were *idiots*. By the time I'd crossed the Marquam Bridge and merged onto I-5 south, I'd labeled the drivers moving faster than I to be lunatics, the ones moving slower, morons. Faintly ahead I could see a break in the clouds, a lightening of the gray. I was afraid to call it sunshine, thinking I might scare it into remission.

Once I was heading into Lake Chinook I phoned both Sharona and Gigi. Ha, ha. Big surprise. Nobody picked up. I left messages and clicked off.

I drove directly to Dwayne's to pick up Binks and was gratified when my dog did her "I missed you so much" happy dance for my benefit, wiggling and jumping around on her toes. Mostly I get to watch her do this with everyone who walks through the door. She licked me twice on the end of my nose as I bent down to her, huge affection on her part.

Dwayne was perched on one of the stools around his kitchen bar. They're kind of rickety and I looked his way with worry. Today he eschewed his jerry-rigged jeans for a pair of shorts, his right leg thrust forward, the knee and shin visible below the splint-strapped thigh cast.

He swung around. "Feel this," he said, pointing to his good thigh.

"Thanks. But no."

"Compare it to this one." He depressed his finger into the band of muscle just above his right knee and below the cast.

I had no intention of touching Dwayne's flesh for any reason. I mean, come on. I'm not an idiot. "You losing muscle tone?"

"Pain in the ass," he muttered, punching his finger around the area. "I'm scared to know what it's like under this." He knocked his knuckles on the splint. "I'll be in rehab forever."

"Somehow I don't think so."

"Come on. Feel this, Jane."

Because it mattered to him, I stepped forward and touched a finger to his injured leg. The muscle didn't feel all that bad to me and I said so.

"Now feel this," he said, guiding my hand to his left thigh. Beneath my palm I felt tense, strong, sinewy muscles. "You see?"

Was he really so dense that he didn't know what I was really feeling? I didn't dare meet his gaze. Adopting a sort of Sigmund Freud, stroke-the-chin attitude, I said, "Okay, it's not as toned, but that's to be expected." I turned away and chased Binkster around the room as a distraction. The dog was surprised by my sudden interest and ran beneath the chair to play "the game." She started whining and acting like she was stuck. Worked for me. I squirreled around with her for another five minutes, and by the time we both lost interest, Dwayne had moved from the stool to the refrigerator in search of food.

I gazed over his shoulder. He never has much more than I do, and it was true in this case. I told him I'd go in search of sandwiches, but he said he'd go with me. I gazed down at his bare legs, and he headed for the bedroom to change into his jeans. He wasn't using his crutches at all, I realized. Instead he put most of his weight on his good leg and kind of hopped with the weaker one. Redressed, he slammed his cowboy hat on his head and shrugged into his beat-up leather bomber jacket.

We went out to the rain together, leaving a forlorn Binkster gazing after us.

Not so long ago Dwayne and I spent a night together. A night that did not include sex but did include nakedness. There was alcohol involved and a lot of guilt on my part over the near death of my pug, and I kissed Dwayne and blubbered on his shoulder and generally made a complete and utter fool of myself. If Violet hadn't come along and derailed things, I'm not sure where Dwayne and I would be right now. His broken leg and our circumspect carefulness of each other has made our working relationship a tad more distant, less familiar. But at least we're not facing any postcoital regrets.

We went to Mook's, a nearby burger joint. Both of us ordered cheeseburgers, and I filled him in more completely on everything and anything I could think of regarding Violet's case. I also mentioned how the Popparockskills had blown me off, and I even told him about my secretive brother's phone calls and his request for me to talk to Sharona.

Dwayne mowed through his burger, leaning toward me in the booth, listening hard. There were quite a few surrounding booths filled with lively discussions, so our conversation wasn't overheard. Still, I kept my voice fairly low. Maybe I'm paranoid, but you just never know whose ears are listening.

He swirled the crushed ice around in his empty root beer glass. "Your brother's working undercover and it's playing hell with his relationship with Sharona. You might as well kiss that engagement good-bye."

I reared back as if he'd struck me. "That's ridiculous. They're like glued together. They'll weather this."

"It won't last. It never does."

"You don't know Booth and Sharona."

"You haven't talked to her yet. When you do, feel her out on the subject. He's already worried or he wouldn't involve you."

I glared at him. I hadn't known Sharona long, but I knew what I'd seen between her and Booth. I'd been envious of the way they'd looked at each other, the silent messages between them. "You're really pissing me off."

"That's 'cause you know I'm right."

I gritted my teeth.

He noticed and grinned like a devil.

I held on to my annoyance with an effort. One thing I've learned is don't give in when a man switches from pig-headed to charming. It's a ploy. As soon as you roll over and forgive, you're had. I went on the attack instead. "I've been giving our relationship some thought and I've got some things that need to be addressed."

"Our relationship? Yours and mine?"

"We're working together. We don't quite have a business partnership, but we could. At least that's what I'm hearing from you. Let me know if I'm wrong."

"No, that's about right," Dwayne said equably.

"Okay."

"Okay," he repeated, watching me.

I was gathering my courage. Points needed to be addressed. Clarified. It felt as if the moment had suddenly arrived when I needed plain answers instead of suppositions.

"I need some background on you, Dwayne."

He lifted a brow. "I thought it was Violet you needed to interview."

"I'm talking about us now. You and me."

He spread his palms at my pugnacious tone. "All right."

"I know your father's name was Dwayne Durbin and you're not a junior. Your middle name is different. Austin. You don't get along with your brother, but you like his son, Del."

"Stepbrother," Dwayne corrected.

"You also don't get along with your stepmother."

"I'm difficult to get along with," Dwayne agreed.

"I don't know where you're from, but you've got that southern twang thing that you trot out when it suits you. Somewhere you got in the P.I. business and ended up in Oregon. You have a sister, Angela, and a niece, Tracy, who live in Seattle. Is she a full sister?"

"Yep."

"And she's got a workaholic husband. Tracy's a handful. Anyway, she was last summer."

"Still is, I'm sure. She started high school in September."

"So, that's it. That's the whole enchilada. The Dwayne Durbin bio."

"I wish they served beer here," Dwayne muttered, shaking the ice in his glass again and frowning.

"Are you trying to be a pain in the ass?"

He thought a moment, but didn't meet my eyes. "What brought this on?"

"I just need to know."

"Something to do with job security? Are you trying to buy your cottage? You're doing a good job, Jane. You've been the whole business lately. Eyes, ears, certainly legs."

"That's not it!" I sputtered.

"Well, what, then?"

"I just want to know about you. That's all. How did you end up in Lake Chinook? Let's start with that. You didn't grow up in Oregon. So, where did you grow up?"

He rubbed his chin. I was afraid he was going to fob me off some more, but he drew a breath and said, "All over the place. I was an Air Force brat. Product of Captain Dwayne Durbin and Naomi Durbin, deceased. One sibling, Angela. One stepbrother, Cal Riggert. Two stepsisters, Valerie and Patience." He snorted. "My stepmama is a real piece of work. Evelyn. She sent me to Catholic school in Beaverton to get me away from the family. I'd been in a bit of trouble."

"Where? What kind of trouble?"

"Outside of Grosbeck, Texas. I was hanging out with some friends. There was a vehicle with the keys in it, engine running. Decided to take it for a drive."

"You stole a car."

"A hearse, actually."

"A hearse," I repeated. Dwayne smiled faintly. "How old were you when you stole this hearse?"

"Almost fifteen."

"That would be fourteen."

"Yes, it would."

"What happened?"

"The funeral director and the family wanted to prosecute. But I was a minor, and there was no real harm done, so it kind of blew over."

I squinted at him. "What do you mean? Who wanted to prosecute? What family?"

"There was a body in the hearse. I took it for a ride. Didn't know it was in there."

Did I detect amusement? Undoubtedly. "You're not Catholic," I pointed out.

"Evelyn didn't care much about that. She heard of this school and she enrolled me and I went."

"A boarding school?"

He shook his head. "I lived with my mother's sister, Aunt Helena. Angela stayed with her part of the time, too. That's how she ended up in Seattle. My stepmama and the rest of them are still in Texas. Evelyn felt I was a bad influence on her girls. I never went back."

"So you've been here for years."

"Yup."

"And you started the agency how long ago?"

"Oh, I don't know . . . six years? I worked for a guy, an information specialist, for a few years before that. I had this idea of being in law enforcement, but things happened that interfered."

"Like stealing a hearse."

"Yeah. Things like that." He tossed back some ice and chewed on it. "This is probably a good idea. If we're in business together, you should know you've hooked up with an almost felon."

I leaned back in my chair. "Wow. I feel dizzy from all the information."

"I took criminology courses, like you," he admitted, sliding his glass across the laminate tabletop, smearing the sweat ring into a line of liquid dots.

"What about relationships?" I asked carefully.

"Business relationships?" His eyes smiled, daring me to be truthful.

"The other kind."

"Tab A and Slot B?"

"Yeah, that kind."

He turned to look out the window at the still falling, but merely drizzling, rain. I examined his profile, the masculine line of his jaw, the hint of a beard, the intensity of his blue eyes. Classically handsome, Dwayne is not. But he's lean and rugged, and his slow drawling style works like an aphrodisiac. I've spent a lot of time telling myself that I'm immune, that I only find Dwayne attractive after a few drinks. If I tell this lie to myself enough times, I'm sure it will become truth.

The moment was interrupted by my singing cell phone. I checked caller ID. Sharona. Her timing couldn't have been worse. I hesitated, wondering if I should click her off.

"You're not answering?" Dwayne asked.

Muttering, I twisted in my chair, giving him my shoulder as I hit the green button to accept the call. This shoulder thing is such a dumb thing. Like he can't hear me? Like he's been shut out? But it's the best I could do in the circumstances. "Hey there," I answered easily. "We finally connect."

"Sorry it took me so long to get back to you," Sharona apologized. "It's been crazy busy around here."

"Too many people committing too many crimes?"

"Luckily most of them are property damage. Angry neighbors who smash up fences, slash tires, that kind of stuff. It can get nasty, though."

I've often pictured Sharona, her being a criminal defense attorney, in a courtroom next to a hulking, menacing thug, pleading for leniency after he'd raped, murdered and plundered. The idea that she might represent your basic suburban homeowner with anger issues made me feel better.

"I got a call from Booth the other night," I said. "I got that he's undercover on some job that's taking all his time. He really wanted me to call you and let you know he was deep into it, and that he'd connect with you as soon as he could."

"He left me the same message on my voice mail," Sharona said. Was her voice a few shades cooler?

I could feel Dwayne's gaze on me but I just hunched my shoulder more. "He didn't tell me where he was or what he was doing. I got the feeling he couldn't."

"He can't say anything right now. This new . . . path he's taken." She snorted. "Booth just up and decided to further his career. Didn't ask me what I thought. He thinks it's a shorter route to making detective. Maybe it is. That's why he's signed up for hazardous duty. Drugs, gangs, assault weapons, teen murderers. It's loads of fun."

"I detect a healthy layer of sarcasm."

"Jane, I appreciate that you're trying to help Booth. And

it probably speaks well that he involved you at all. Means he's really worried. But he can't ask me to put my life on hold just because he's got to play Serpico. And just for the record, he's enjoying this far more than he should."

"It's hard to fault him for trying to get ahead," I said, feeling out of my depth.

"I'm not faulting him. But I don't feel good about it, either." She sounded tense. "He made a choice, and I appreciate that, but for every action there's an equal and opposite reaction. Things aren't the same between us, and they won't ever be again. They'll be different. Maybe someday they'll even be better. But not now."

"Okay." I felt chastised.

"He calls when he can. I'm just letting the voice mail pick up. I don't want to talk to him. Not now."

I sensed she was afraid and understood that most of her anger stemmed from that. "If he calls me again, I'll tell him that's why you can't talk to him."

"Tell him whatever you like. Sorry, Jane. I've got to go." She hesitated. "I love your brother. You know that. But this is too hard."

"Too hard?"

"I can't think about this now."

I heard someone speaking to her in a low voice. A male voice. She said to me, "I'll talk to you later." And she was gone.

"Well?" Dwayne asked.

"They've moved up the wedding date a few months."

"Liar."

"Fine. You were right. Things are not okay between them." It felt like a weight on my chest. I hadn't realized how much I was counting on Booth having a so-called normal life: wife, kids, picket fence. Now it felt like a personal hit.

My phone rang again, saving me from further explanation. It was Gigi. "Jane Kelly," I answered perfunctorily.

"You wanted something?" she said without enthusiasm.

"Yeah, I just wanted to clarifiy. Your pictures were scheduled for two p.m. Did you post that information on a wedding Web site? Or anywhere on the Internet?"

"We just told the people when to be there. Why?"

I couldn't see how it would do any harm to tell her the truth. "The Wedding Bandits arrived at your father's house earlier than was their usual m.o. It seems like they already knew Roland would be gone before two."

"Everybody thought the wedding was at two," Gigi declared, "because of the stupid paper. I had a hell of a time reminding them to look at the invitation. It was at four, not two!"

"The paper?"

"The *Lake Chinook Review*. They screwed up. Had the time listed as two, not four. Morons."

"So, the *Review* listed it wrong," I said for Dwayne's benefit. "Thanks."

"That all you wanted?"

"For now." I clicked off.

Dwayne looked thoughtful. "The Wedding Bandits got the time from the *Review* and thought the wedding was at two."

"That kind of blows Larrabee's theory about an insider getting information."

"They still had to get the home addresses," Dwayne pointed out. "You sure Gigi didn't post on the Internet?"

"She says not."

Dwayne shook his head. "Somehow they're getting the addresses. Maybe following principal players home from work. Let's say they followed Roland. They thought the wedding was at two. They showed up about one-thirty, maybe. Roland was already injured from Violet, maybe from the fatal blow, too. He was probably dead or dying, so the Wedding Bandits ran away."

"Someone came between noon, when Violet left, and one-thirty to two, when the Wedding Bandits showed," I said.

"They hit him with Violet's tray, mortally wounding him."

"There were no other fingerprints on the tray. So whoever hit him wore gloves, or used a cloth—say, a towel—some form of cover."

"That implies forethought," Dwayne pointed out.

"Which means someone meant to kill him," I conceded. "Went to his house specifically with that in mind."

"Why not bring a weapon, then? If I were going to kill someone, I'd sure as hell bring the means with me."

"Me, too," I admitted. "And what's the motive?"

"Money. Revenge. Jealousy. If we take Violet and the Wedding Bandits out, the field's wide open."

"I'll put in another call to her," I said, reaching for my phone.

"Let's widen the circle. Find out who was having problems with Roland, who the heirs are."

"Gigi and Sean are the heirs," I said automatically.

"Who's the estate lawyer?"

"God help me. Please don't let it be Jerome Neusmeyer," I said with feeling. I'd had more than my share of run-ins with that particular lecherous attorney over the past few months.

Dwayne smiled. He knows all the lurid details about my dealings with Neusmeyer. "I don't think you could be that unlucky."

"Yeah? Watch me."

"I'll shoot Larrabee another text. See if I can get him to open up a bit, save us some time. He's busy, but to hell with that. He can call back."

"Quid pro quo?"

Dwayne threw some bills down on the table. "Yeah, he's big on that. Might ask you on a date as payment."

"Funny." Dwayne smiled like he had me, so I said, "Well, okay, but I don't have sex until a second date. And I want dinner."

"Heavy petting?"

"Depends on how good dinner is."

"Taco Bell?"

I pretended to think that over. "Maybe we won't have to wait for that second date."

"I love that you have standards," Dwayne drawled.

The word I heard was "love." I could feel my attention screech to a halt in the direction it had been traveling and center on Dwayne. Rather than get myself in trouble, I pretended to ignore the direction the conversation had taken and started digging through my purse, mainly as a distraction.

"Looking for your rule book?" he asked.

"Rule book?"

He gave me that lazy smile that I find alternately interesting and infuriating. It took me a moment to recall that I'd proclaimed I could never have sex with someone named Dwayne. That it was written specifically in my rule book: no Dwaynes. This was at the height of our new awareness of each other, just before Violet's campaign to win him changed everything.

"I keep my rule book in a safe place," I told him.

"I think I'm going to find it."

"You never will."

He just looked at me in a way that caused my blood to surge through my veins. I could feel my face flush, which nearly sent me around the bend. "Bastard," I muttered with feeling.

Dwayne laughed. By sheer willpower I didn't kick his shin beneath the table.

CHAPTER THIRTEEN

I heard the now familiar ring that denoted an incoming text message as I emptied my overnight bag onto my red quilted bedspread and started separating the clean clothes from the dirty ones. My cell also lay on my double bed. I snatched it up and read:

meet us tonite dawn

I made an impatient sound in my throat. Wouldn't you know? Now that Dwayne wasn't pressing as hard, Dawn was after me.

Did I want to go? Glancing out my bedroom window, I saw the rain still drizzling, but it was more like a mist. A definite improvement. I didn't know what I wanted to accomplish at Do Not Enter, but I couldn't completely back away. I texted Dawn back:

okay will see you after game ronnie

This took me some time to compose and send, and then she wrote right back:

tonite!! d

Hmmm . . . two exclamation points.

I walked into the bathroom and looked at myself in the mirror, turning my head from side to side, examining my face. A teenager I was not. I couldn't even text-message with alacrity.

Once more I scrounged around for my Lake Chinook sweatshirt, which I'd wadded into a ball and thrown in the back of my closet after my escapades with the canoe. Now I pulled it out, gave it a good, long sniff, coughed a little at the mildewy odor, then ran it through the washer.

Binkster watched me go through my laundry routine from her favorite spot on the couch. While I worked I looked over occasionally and made smoochy noises. She invariably curled up her tail and wagged at me, even if she didn't lift her head from the cushions. A few months back, right after she was foisted on me, I spent an inordinate amount of time and energy trying to get rid of her. Now it would kill me to lose her.

The cell phone rang as I was leaning on my refrigerator door, wondering if it was safe to eat the hamburger I'd purchased, now nearly a week past its pull date. Aren't those dates just a guide rather than a warning? Like it's okay, just not as fresh as it could be? The idea of tossing out the meat was an anathema. Yet . . . there was definitely some off-color there. I suspected if I pulled off the shrink-wrap there might be some off-odors as well.

Not that I was hungry. It had only been a couple of hours since Mook's. Well, okay, I was sorta hungry.

I glanced hopefully at caller ID. Not Violet. Cynthia.

"What's up?" I greeted her, regretfully dropping the pack of hamburger into my trash bin. Why don't I know myself better? If it isn't frozen, microwavable and/or packed with preservatives, it's just not going to work.

Cynthia asked, "What are you doing for Thanksgiving?"

"Nothing. Hopefully." Twice now I'd been quizzed on this. As I said, I'm not good with holidays. For reasons probably buried deep in my psyche, my first reaction to affairs with lots of people, many of them relatives, is a desire to plead sickness or insanity, whatever works, to keep myself from facing some excruciating mealtime where everyone makes small talk and wishes they were *anywhere* else.

"I want you to have Thanksgiving dinner with me," Cynthia said.

"No can do. I have my own tradition. I wear my sweats and eat Swanson turkey TV dinners, both for lunch and dinner. Sometimes I open a can of cranberries just in case you need more than the little square of dessert they give you."

"I'm making a turkey and all the trimmings," she said smoothly, "and I'm inviting you, your brother and his fiancée to join me. You can ask Dwayne, too."

"Did the Pod People find you, suck out your inner self and leave behind a shell?"

"I'm not actually doing the cooking," she confessed. "A friend of mine, who's not a chef but should be, is preparing the meal. Free food, Jane. Really good food. And wine."

"This social event is still a couple of weeks away," I reminded her.

"I wanted to catch you early. Before you felt compelled to make up an excuse."

I thought about telling her about Booth and Sharona, just to get her off my back, but I didn't have the energy. I mumbled something about a spurious mental illness that runs in the Kelly family that's exacerbated by holiday gatherings, but I didn't think she was buying it.

"You can wear your sweats," she coerced.

I was compelled to tell her I would think about it. As I hung up, I began to wonder if I'd been wrong . . . maybe this "not calling back" epidemic wasn't such a bad thing.

Communication can be highly overrated.

Violet finally called me as I was getting ready for my teen fun at Do Not Enter.

"Ah, there you are," I said as I examined myself in my Lake Chinook sweatshirt one more time. This outfit was getting really old. I considered wearing something else, but Dwayne's comment about showing bare skin as an alternative was really off-putting.

"I talked to Dwayne," she revealed. "He said you went to Santa Monica to interview Renee."

"That would be true. I also met with Patsy Treadway, who insists you killed her brother, Bart. And Renee seems to think you did the escort service gig a few more times than you led me to believe."

She muttered a swear word or two. "I didn't kill Bart. I told him I'd go on one of his hikes. It was pure hell. He kept pushing and pushing, climbing and climbing. It was hot and miserable and I finally just screamed that I couldn't go on. So I left him. Twisted my ankle on the way back and it took me hours to find my way out! I was crying and scared and it was damn near night by the time I came across some other hikers who helped me find my way back. Patsy can't accept that Bart wouldn't lead me out. It couldn't be that he made a lot of mistakes, nearly getting us both killed in the process!"

"Patsy seemed to think—"

She cut me off. "You know, Jane, I don't give a damn. Patsy had one of those hero-worship things going for her brother. He could do no wrong. No wrong. But the truth is, Bart wouldn't come back that day, when he should have. He slipped in the dark and fell to his death, trying to prove what a man he was, what an awesome climber. He just *fell.*"

"She said you ended up with the inheritance." There was a faint trace of condemnation in my tone that I couldn't help.

"She's always said that!" Violet practically shouted at me. "What inheritance? Bart went through every dime we had. Every . . . dime. He was terrible with money. Just terrible! The man left me in serious debt. I came out better from my divorces, although it's not like I robbed them blind, either. Patsy will just never believe that. You should have told me you were going to meet her. I could have warned you."

I felt a slight headache coming on. Every time I think I have all the facts on Violet I'm proved wrong.

"Has she still got that Bohemian Granola thing going?" Violet demanded.

"Umm . . . yeah."

She made a disparaging sound. "Patsy wants to believe I'm responsible for Bart's death. She can't help herself. Bart was the only man in her life. Ever. She has to blame someone for taking him away from her."

I moved to the other issue. "But you did go back to the escort service. That part's true?"

"Okay, look. I had to. I had no money. Not every man who walked through the door expected sex. A lot, yes, but some honestly wanted companionship. I tried other jobs and I was terrible at them."

"And the escort service is how you met your second husband?"

"And my third. Roland."

"What happened with your second husband?"

"Divorce. You'll love this. His name was John DeBussy. Because of the escort service thing, you know, the image that they're only a front for prostitution, I called him my john. He had a great sense of humor. We enjoyed each other a lot for a while. Until he started an affair with a woman who looked just like me but was a few years younger. Twenty, I think," she said dryly.

It amazes me how often Violet stymies me. Just when I think I've got her. Just when she seems to be everything everyone accuses her of being . . . she slips away. And she does it with such aplomb.

"So, you met Bart, John and Roland through the escort service."

"Hon, when something works for you, stick with it. Roland's a case in point. He met Renee, me and Melinda the same way."

"He met Melinda through an escort service?" I asked in surprise.

"You bet. After he and I split up he 'went back to the well.' His exact words. It was that Millionaires' Club, oh, what's it called . . . ?" She paused, thinking. "Columbia Millionaires' Club. CMC. The male members have to be millionaires, and all the women are young, beautiful and educated. A selective dating service."

"Melinda and Roland met on one of these dates?"

"Yes." On a note of discovery, she added, "Maybe the women don't have to be all that young."

I couldn't think of anything else to add, so after a few moments, we hung up. I thought back on the events that had led me to this point in the investigation and all the people who seemed so desperate for me to believe Violet was guilty. I kept vacillating on the issue myself. Up, down, up, down. As I finished getting ready I told myself to listen to my gut instincts. Dwayne said he always listened to them, that relying on his instincts had saved him more than once.

I stared at my Lake Chinook sweatshirted self for a moment, didn't like what I saw, ripped the sweatshirt off my body. I traded for a forest-green short-sleeved T-shirt and my black leather jacket. A thin slice of skin showed at my midriff. I could possibly freeze to death but I looked better than usual.

I called Melinda, deciding I was through pussyfooting around with anyone any longer. "Hi, it's Jane," I told her voice mail. "I understand you met Roland at the Columbia Millionaire's Club. Call me back and let's talk about it."

After that I threw the Lake Chinook sweatshirt in the back of the car, just in case. I carry a small bag with a couple of changes of clothes at all times and various sundry accessories I feel I may need to use as a disguise from time to time. From experience, I've learned that I may need to quickly change personas without time to go home and re-group.

I drove to Taco Bell for dinner. My talk with Dwayne had started a craving of sorts. I waited in line, boggled by the rapid-fire, heavily Spanish-accented sell-up coming from the drive-through speaker. I have no ear for languages. It's almost embarrassing. "Um . . . how about *numero ocho* . . . three crunchy tacos and a diet cola?"

I think she agreed and gave me a price. I drove to the window and forked over a ten-dollar bill and was rewarded with my bounty and some change.

It was near 7:00 p.m. by then, but I had hours to kill before I was due at Do Not Enter. Since it wasn't raining cats and dogs any longer, I decided to attend the game, get a look at Keegan Lendenhal in action. But I didn't want any of the Do Not Enter crowd to recognize me, so I mentally searched through my bag of clothes while I chomped down my meal. Taco Bell's really hard to eat in the car without making a mess. McDonald's is easier. Everything kind of sticks together better.

A call buzzed through on my cell phone that went straight to voice mail. I was instantly annoyed. What's that all about?

The damn thing never even bothered to ring. The mysteries of wireless communication just keep getting bigger.

I punched in my code and listened to the message as I drove toward the Lake Chinook High stadium.

"Hello," a man's voice greeted me. "This is Dr. Daniel Wu, returning your call. You said you wish to speak to me about Roland Hatchmere. If it is urgent, I will be at the East-moreland Clinic tomorrow." He then left his office number and hours.

I was thrilled and surprised. Yeah! A loose end I might be able to tie up.

Once again it was tricky to find a place to park. I circled around the surrounding neighborhoods, counting the signs that screamed against the stadium lights versus the ones that shrieked the benefits of all athletics. Looked like an even battle for the moment.

When I finally got the Volvo squeezed behind a Volkswagen bug, I opened my back hatch and scrounged through my bag. I didn't want any of the kids to see me in the company of other adults. My age might show through despite my efforts to look and seem younger. I grabbed a baseball cap, a pair of wire-rimmed glasses with prescriptionless lenses and a plaid, flannel scarf that I tossed around my neck. I put on the glasses and tucked my chin into the scarf. I shut the back, stuck my head inside the driver's side to get a glimpse of myself in the rearview mirror.

I looked like I was about to go out on a fishing trawler in the North Sea.

Trudging to the gate, I paid for a ticket, deciding to stay on visiting Brookstone's side to steer clear of my teen buddies. Visitors don't rank covered seating, but there was no place left to sit anyway, so I hung at the end of the bleachers near a knot of middle-aged men who were deeply invested in the game. The score was 7-all at the end of the first quarter. I gazed across the field at the players whose uniforms were already smeared with mud and grass stains. Lake Chinook's light blue and white colors had really taken a beating. Brookstone's green and gold, reminiscent of Oregon Ducks' green and yellow, seemed to be faring better.

Brookstone had the ball and their quarterback threw a pass that fell short of the receiver's hands.

"Damn it, Ty," one of the men near me spat out.

"He's gotta do better than that," another man concurred.

"Jason doesn't have any idea where the ball's going," a third said. "Just runs like a goddamn horse heading for the barn."

I watched the team break from the huddle and go again. This time Ty connected with Jason and he went flying down the field. All was forgiven, apparently, by the now ecstatic shouting dads. It was all they could do to keep themselves from running onto the field.

Sheesh.

My cell phone rang. I only heard it because the din slowly died down. Whipping it out of my purse, I was surprised to see the call was Detective Larrabee. "Hello?" I said loudly, covering my exposed ear with my hand. "Can you hear me?"

"Ms. Kelly?" His smooth voice registered.

"Yeah, it's Jane," I said, turning away from the game.

"Is this inconvenient?"

"No." I was practically yelling. I explained that I was at the Lake Chinook/Brookstone game but that I could leave with no regrets.

Surprisingly, he said, "I'll come to you," so I told him I was on the Brookstone side of the field, then asked, "Did something happen?" before he could hang up.

"Our surveillance paid off," he said with a smile in his voice.

I did a little dance of delight. So far it had been a good night. Then I had a worry about my appearance, which I tried to dismiss—I mean, the guy's attractive, sure, but it's not like that has anything to do with anything. Dwayne's joking about Larrabee and me on a date was just that, a joke. There was no reason to think about him in any regard but professional.

But did I have to look so crappy?

I whipped off the glasses and stuck them in my coat pocket.

I spent the next forty minutes trying to keep my mind on the game, which had lost all interest for me. Keegan Lendenhal proved he was an excellent quarterback, throwing passes, reading the field, doing all that football stuff that I've never paid any attention to, but that I learned about play-by-play from the group of dads nearby, much to their disappointment and dismay. Ty just couldn't keep up with Keegan. He was good, yes, but Keegan was great. There was no denying it. A lot of college scouts had looked at Keegan already. The kid was bound to be All-State. He had a helluva future ahead of him. A helluva future.

I gazed across the field to the Lake Chinook side, wondering which knot of men over there included Keegan's father. What would happen if and when Mr. All-State's extracurricular activities came to light?

At halftime Lake Chinook was ahead 21–10. There was a lot of discussion about the upcoming play-offs. I went in search of a hot dog and ended up fumbling to put my glasses back on when I recognized some of the kids from Do Not Enter. I didn't see Dawn, but her sister Dionne was there, scowling, her arms across her chest. The guy she was with seemed to be trying to cheer her up, but she practically snapped his head off. My hot dog in hand, I sidled a little closer, taking a bite and pretending to be with a couple of families who obviously had come to the game together.

"Look, she's not your problem," the guy said to Dionne.

"She's totally stupid!" Dionne volleyed back. "He's already dumped her and she keeps following him around. He sucks it up. And she's . . . just . . . *stupid!*"

"She'll get over it."

"No, she won't," she muttered angrily.

"You did."

That earned him a scathing glare. They moved away from me. I took a few steps after them, but then they abruptly turned my way, so I had to twist on my shoe and mosey a different direction. The guy kept trying to mollify her, but Dionne was having none of it. I suspected she was talking about Dawn. Was the boy who'd dumped her Keegan?

The rain let up completely during halftime and I cautiously pulled off my hoodie, but kept the baseball cap in place. When I got back to my spot beside the Brookestone dads I removed my glasses again.

The third quarter had started by the time Vince Larrabee made an appearance. I'd expected to see him in the overcoat, but he was wearing jeans and a jacket like me so I didn't recognize him at first. He found me despite my baseball cap, flashing me a smile as he approached that heated me up in a way I could scarcely credit. Was I so desperate for a date that Dwayne's joking insinuations had given me hope? Or was I simply trying anything to get my mind off *him*?

"Why did you want to come to the game?" I asked after we said hello. As soon as he reached me, he gestured for us to move away from the dads, closer to Brookestone's end zone.

When we were out of earshot, he revealed, "I went to Brookestone."

"You're kidding."

"'Fraid not."

"Really?"

He nodded, more amusement flickering in his dark gaze. My heart did a funny little pitter-pat. I warned myself not to be an idiot. I wasn't attracted to the man. I wasn't attracted to Dwayne, either. I just . . . wasn't.

"So, don't leave me hanging," I said. "Did you get the Wedding Bandits?"

"Two are in custody. Two more identified."

"Fabulous. What did they say?" I asked eagerly. "Have they talked about Roland? Do you know anything yet?"

"A few things," Larrabee admitted. "What does Durbin want with the calls to Hatchmere's cell phone the day of the homicide?"

Ah . . . I should have known. Quid pro quo. I searched around for an appropriate answer and in the end couldn't see any reason not to be completely honest. "Violet told us he received a phone call, or calls, maybe around eleven or eleven-thirty that morning, that—altered his mood. Upset him. She tried to find out what was wrong and that's when they started fighting. He shoved her against the wall and she hit him with the tray."

Larrabee listened intently. "That's the reason she gave you?"

"Yes."

"You believe her?"

"Well, yes. Why? Did she tell you something else?"

"She was remarkably unhelpful during our interview."

"Sounds just like her," I said. "What did the Wedding Bandits say?"

"At first, nothing. Apart from the usual protests 'We had the wrong guys. We couldn't prove anything. It wasn't their van.' But with a possible murder charge, their lawyers finally got them to open up. One of their group, still missing, worked at the *Lake Chinook Review*. He's the one who got the addresses for the targeted homes. Took it from the billing for the cost of the wedding announcements. But he got cold feet after the Hatchmere murder. Quit the paper and took off."

"Ah . . . the inside man."

"He screwed up the time and sent the team too early. Not that it should have mattered as Roland was supposed to be at pictures at two."

"Was he—dead when they got there?"

Larrabee nodded. "That's what they say. Two of them ran to the bedroom looking for cash and jewelry. One of them took gifts off the dining room table. The fourth was heading down the solarium and nearly skidded into Roland. He yelled and they all started running. It nearly scared them straight."

"But then they turned to funerals," I said.

"And became less discriminatory about their victims."

A sudden roar from the crowd turned us both toward the game again. Lake Chinook's center had snapped the ball to Keegan on the Brookstone ten-yard line. Keegan stepped back, pretended to hand off the ball, then followed the offensive line into the end zone for a score.

The crowd jumped to its feet, screaming.

"Hmmm," Larrabee said.

"I'm glad you got them," I said to him. "Or at least half of them. You found the white van?"

"Surveillance is tedious, but it works." He gave me a long look.

"What?"

"I want something from you."

"O . . . kay . . ."

"I'm not trying to nail Violet Purcell. I really don't think she killed Roland. But I want on the inside track with her. I think she's involved, somehow. She's at the center of this thing, whether she wants to be or not."

I thought about it. "I agree."

"There were two calls to Roland Hatchmere's cell phone that morning," he revealed. "One came from a business called the Columbia Millionaires' Club. I want you to find out if Violet's ever been associated with it." He read something in my face though I tried to shutter my thoughts. "What?"

"I know about CMC." I filled him in on what Violet had said about Roland and Melinda. Larrabee absorbed the news, and I finished with "I put a call into Melinda, but she hasn't called me back yet."

"Let me know when she does."

"You think someone from the club has something to do with all this?"

He lifted his palms. "It's just one of the calls. The club doesn't have a record of who made that call to Roland, though. They've got an interesting operation. They rent space downtown," he said. "During the day, there's no one specifically slated for the front desk. They don't have many full-time employees and the employees that are there are manning the small restaurant and bar, which is available for the members, all male, mostly. Apparently, it's mainly an escort/dating service that floats from venue to venue. They have parties semimonthly."

"The women aren't members?"

"Didn't get into it with the president, George Tertian. I just was following up on the phone call. There's a phone for member use at the end of the front counter. Anyone could step off the elevator at the sixth floor, walk right up and use it. But I'm guessing it would most likely be a member."

"If it's an escort service . . . and Roland was married . . . maybe it was a 'secret' call?"

"Another woman?" He thought it over. "It would be tough for a woman to make that call and not be noticed. It's a men's club, at least during the day. They have parties and women are invited. Probably how they get around having only male members. I have a club roster."

"Anyone on that list I should know about?"

"Haven't checked it closely yet, but Roland's name is still there."

"How about the girl at the desk?" I suggested, although why I was traveling this path was kind of a mystery to me. Roland was already involved with Melinda and Violet. He seemed to have been a serial dater, not a juggler of numerous affairs.

"The receptionist is about twenty-three," Larrabee said.

I thought that over. Roland Hatchmere seemed to stick closer to his own age bracket. "Maybe it's not about a woman. The caller could have been a man. I mean, if that's what the club's all about, stands to reason, right? Maybe it was someone who wanted to use the phone when no one would be listening. Someone who didn't want the call traced back to him."

"Or it could simply be that someone made a call when the receptionist was busy elsewhere."

His casual attitude finally registered with me. He was only partially invested in the Millionaires' Club angle. "You said there was a second call to Roland's cell," I reminded him.

He nodded.

"Well, who was it? Do you know?"

"Roland's son. Sean Hatchmere."

CHAPTER FOURTEEN

"Sean?" I said.

Larrabee nodded again. "Those were the only two calls to Roland's cell that morning."

I thought about Roland's son, his laid-back, "let's get high" nature. Is that what had set Roland off? His anger over Sean's continued drug use? And had Roland simply taken out his anger on Violet?

It seemed anticlimactic, though. "Sean didn't go to the rehearsal dinner," I remembered. "I thought he was with his band, working that night. That was his excuse, anyway."

Another surge of screams from the crowd sent my gaze back to the game. I caught sight of the end of a spiraling pass. The receiver, arms out in a cradle, captured the ball on a full run for another Lake Chinook touchdown. I glanced at Keegan, who held both arms in the air, his hands fisted.

"What do you think of the quarterback?" I asked Larrabee.

He followed my gaze. "Lendenhal? He's good."

"At football," I agreed.

Larrabee checked his watch. "Time to get home."

"You're not staying for the end?"

"This is about all the beating I can stand to watch."

We smiled at each other. Larrabee cocked a brow and said, "You're not Durbin's usual type."

I tried not to react. "Yeah? What's that?"

"Ask him."

"Oh no. I deserve more of an answer than that."

"You pretty anxious for information on him?" He was truly enjoying this, and I found it just as irritating as when Dwayne did it.

"When it comes to Dwayne's past, I'm apparently on a need-to-know basis only," I said dryly.

"I'm here to help."

Like, oh, sure. That's what this was all about. But if he was going to pretend to "dish" with me, I was going to go for it. "How did you meet him?" I queried.

It was the fourth quarter and Brookstone was trailing by twenty-eight points. I fell in step beside Larrabee and we headed toward the gate and the parking lot. "We took criminology classes together at Portland State."

"You went into law enforcement and Dwayne apprenticed with a private investigator."

"We don't call each other unless we have to." The detective pulled a remote lock opener from his pocket and I heard the *chirp-chirp* as he depressed the button. From across the lot his car's lights flashed. It was apparently his personal vehicle tonight, a silver BMW.

"Dwayne never thought about law enforcement?"

We reached my Volvo first. Larrabee leaned a hip against my front fender and considered me. "Okay, screw Durbin. He's not gonna like me telling you this. He was under suspicion of murder once. Never convicted. No evidence. Kinda broke his faith with law enforcement."

I stared at him in disbelief. "Murder?" I repeated. "Oh, come on."

"It was more a case of him getting caught up in a large net of possible suspects. Pissed him off but good. Can't say I blame him." Larrabee held up a hand in goodbye as he headed out. In a dry voice, he said, "Still, I owe him."

"Yeah?" I was still absorbing these unlikely bits of information about Dwayne.

"He introduced me to my wife."

I tried to call Dwayne as soon as I was on the road. Wife? *Wife?* I knew Dwayne had been joking about the dating thing with Larrabee, but not for a single minute had I suspected the man had a wife!

And a *murder charge?* I still didn't believe it. Larrabee had enjoyed shocking me with that one. Dwayne clearly hadn't expected him to be so candid.

"Come on, come on," I muttered, but Dwayne didn't pick up his phone.

I drove by his place, but I didn't go in. I didn't really have time if I wanted to meet Dawn and my teen cohorts at Do Not Enter. Not that I was looking forward to tonight's tête-à-tête, but I wanted the task behind me.

I decided it was better to corral Dwayne when I had no other pressing engagement. As soon as my mission was accomplished, I would head over to his house and demand some answers.

Tonight when I parked my car down Beachlake, I positioned it nose out, just in case I needed a hasty getaway. I stayed in my car thinking over all the things Larrabee had said, more absorbed with what he'd said about Dwayne than anything to do with the Hatchmere case. I mean . . . wow. My brain felt overloaded. I wondered if too much information was a bad thing. I had this vision of neurons spontaneously combusting inside my head. *Phhhhtttt!*

With an effort I put everything aside and concentrated on

the task at hand. I stayed in my car for a while, watching as other teenagers arrived. It was interesting how quiet they were, their music subdued, their talk low, the only serious sound coming from car engines and tires crunching on gravel. Someone had laid down the rules since the events of last weekend. The party had broken up before Keegan arrived, but this seemed like his doing. This was Keegan's kingdom. Keegan's rules.

I still thought it was highly dangerous not to change their venue, but I'm a known chicken.

Stripping off my jacket, I grabbed the Lake Chinook sweatshirt and yanked it over my head. To hell with bare midriffs in November. Finger-combing my hair, I snapped it into a ponytail, smushed the baseball cap back down, tucked my purse under my arm, then zipped my ID and keys in a pocket, just in case somebody got snoopy and checked my license. After locking my car, I picked up yet another rock to hide in my pocket. Then I switched my cell phone to vibrate again as I headed toward the driveway. I'm getting a whole lot better at cell phone function. By the time I'm forty, who knows? I might be able to program rocket trajectories.

Everything was wet and wind shook water from the surrounding trees, but the rain was still on pause. I passed by Social Security on the way and felt the hairs lift on the back of my neck, as if accusing eyes were glaring down at me. My guilt, I knew. Maybe I'd feel better after I got them back their canoe.

Skirting mud puddles, I made my way to the plank that led up to the front of Do Not Enter. Work had been done on the property. More two-by-four walls had been erected and whips of loose, white electrical wiring hung down or were looped through bored holes. Tonight we weren't connecting to the temporary power pole, apparently, as no string of lights illuminated the house's interior. More caution. A good sign.

"Hey." A guy materialized from the shadows, nearly scaring me out of a year's growth. He was the lank-haired kid who guarded the alcohol stash.

"Hey," I responded.

He checked out the sweatshirt. "Oh, okay. Go on in. We're kinda on red alert here."

"Oh, I know," I breathed, throwing a wild look over my shoulder at Social Security.

"No shit." He'd been holding a cigarette down at his side, as if that could disguise it. I'd already smelled the smoke and seen the orange glow, but then, I'm a detective. Ha.

I walked carefully up the ramp and inside. The party tonight was in the basement. Again, better thinking. I eased myself down the hazardous steps and joined the group. They all stopped and turned toward me, like a herd of elk sniffing the air. The sweatshirt was an automatic access card. Spying it, they went back to their little groups within the group and paid me no never mind.

I'd half decided to steal outside and work my way to the canoe, but I realized it would be better to take Beachlake to its end, cross the footbridge, pick up the road to the empty house, sneak to the water, then paddle the canoe back to its home.

A girl detached herself from a group at the far end of the basement and came my way. Dawn. She gave the impression that she'd been on pins and needles, waiting for me, especially when she suddenly grabbed my arm and pulled me out to the slippery, muddy backyard, leading me away from the house. Her grip on my wrist was like a vise.

"Hey," I said uneasily. "What's up?"

"I just want to talk to you, you know?" She tried to sound pleasant, but something was going on beneath her tone.

"Sure."

She drew a breath, exhaled, drew another. "Keegan's been asking for you."

"For me? Is he here?" I twisted around to look, wondering if she was ever going to let go of me.

"He's on his way. Are you with Brett?" she demanded. "I mean, I don't really care, but Clarissa wants to know."

"I'm . . . not really with any guy. Who's Clarissa?"

She dragged me closer to the water's edge and for a moment I wondered if she planned to throw me in. Here I'd thought we were becoming friends, but it looked like I was mistaken on that. Dawn sure didn't act like she was overjoyed to see me tonight. She seemed intent on intimidating me. Because of Keegan?

I was trying to come up with the proper reaction to her high-handedness. Should I be cowed or snotty? These seemed to be the two main forms of behavior for the girls. There wasn't a whole lot of female bonding going on. Pretty much it was a dogfight over the menfolk, and what a stellar group they were.

Dawn and I were out of earshot of the rest of the group. She still had hold of my wrist like I was her prisoner, and I was waiting for her to make some kind of move when she started shaking all over as if from ague. "You okay?" I whispered, alarmed.

The sobs started from her core and came out in ragged gasps. She was trying desperately to hold them in, tamping back a spiral to a full-blown wail. Awkwardly I put an arm around her and she turned into my shoulder, her slender body racked and quaking. Were she to let out her feelings instead of clamping them back, I could believe it would be a scream-a-thon. No wonder Dwayne had named her house Rebel Yell. The emotional violence held in check was awesome.

I patted her on the back. Whatever was troubling her was deep and soul-consuming. "Are you pregnant?" I asked.

She clutched my clothes with fingers like talons, hanging on as if she would fall. I tightened my grip. "How did you know?" came her muffled response.

"An educated guess." My gaze drifted back to the half-finished house. Groups of kids had split off, some drifting back upstairs. Little pods of secluded lovemaking? Something . . .

"I'm not pregnant anymore," she sobbed. "I wanted this baby! I wanted her so much! I told my parents and they demanded that I give her up. But I wouldn't. I wouldn't." Her voice dropped to a barely audible whisper. "But I lost her. How could that happen? Why couldn't I have her?"

"You miscarried," I realized.

"My parents were *happy*! They tried to hide it but they were *happy*!"

"Well, relieved, maybe."

She pounded her fist on me. "Happy," she insisted fiercely. "Glad. They wanted her dead." She flung herself away from me.

I didn't believe she'd been far enough gone to actually know the sex of the child before the miscarriage. She was projecting, planning for a baby to give her unconditional love. A baby, to take the place of her missing, one-eyed cat, Caesar.

"Who's the father?"

"I don't know." She scrubbed at her cheeks like a child.

"Come on, Dawn," I chided softly.

"I don't know! Keegan . . . maybe? What does it matter now?"

"Did you tell him you were pregnant?"

"Dionne wouldn't let me. She said he wouldn't care, and I was better off without him. He'd moved on to Clarissa, by then. So I listened to Dionne, but I shouldn't have. He had a right to know." It sounded like this was something she'd rehearsed often, but hadn't actually been able to perform.

"Is there a chance someone else is the father?" I asked.

"No."

Oh, now she was positive? "Why did you say that you don't know for sure it's Keegan?"

"I just don't remember. I had too much to drink."

"But you're sure you were pregnant?" I asked, treading carefully.

Dawn sighed as if I were truly dense. "Yes. I didn't know at first. But then I started feeling terrible. Really, really gross. I puked up breakfast one morning and Dionne heard me. She, like, had a fit. Started screaming and yelling. I told her to shut up! Mom and Dad wanted to know what was wrong and Dionne told them she was pissed off because I'd ruined her favorite shoes. It was a total lie. Then later she brought back this birth control test, the one with the pink lines, you know?"

"Pregnancy test," I corrected.

"She made me pee on this stick and there it was. Two pink lines. I was just . . . I don't know . . . scared. And then, when I figured it was Keegan's . . ." She pressed her knuckles to her mouth while tears rained down her cheeks. "I thought he might, want me back, you know?"

I gazed at her in consternation. This was a whole lot more involved than I'd expected. "So, he still doesn't know?"

She shook her head violently.

"Have you told anyone else?"

"No. You think I should tell him?" she asked, suddenly hopeful.

"*No!*"

She recoiled from me. Okay, I didn't mean to sound so absolute. That wasn't what she wanted to hear. But subtlety didn't seem what was called for here.

"Okay," I said. "Okay." Like I was coming up with a plan.

I didn't like it that she couldn't remember having sex with Keegan. I didn't like it one bit. "Come with me," I said.

"Where are we going?"

I didn't answer her, just turned back toward the house. She followed after me like a puppy. We headed back inside and up the stairs, but at the front door ramp the King himself suddenly separated from the shadows. "Where are you going in such a hurry?" Keegan asked.

Both Dawn and I froze as if caught in a searchlight. She gazed at him as if he were a screen idol while I couldn't get past my sick smile. "I've got to move a canoe," I told him.

"A canoe?"

I grabbed Dawn's arm and hauled her down the plank. "We'll be right back."

"Don't make me wait long . . . Veronica," he said.

I didn't answer or turn around. I practically dragged Dawn behind me, though she started resisting and twisting her arm.

"Let go of me! Where are you taking me?"

"I need help," I said, increasing my grip. She didn't like it much that the tables were turned, but we bumped along that way until I thought we were out of earshot. I loosened my grip and she shook me off.

We were near my car but I didn't let on that it was mine. Dawn wasn't sure what to make of me. She'd wanted a friend but with Keegan's sudden interest in me, that wasn't quite working out.

"Where's this canoe?" she demanded.

"I'll show you."

We moved in silence for a while, the only sounds the faint, tinny noise from the television sets of different homes we passed as we worked our way to the end of Beachlake. In the distance, I could hear the faraway rush of traffic from a road far to our south. At the footbridge Dawn said, "Keegan's into you."

I didn't feel like an argument, so I said nothing.

"He was like that with me at the beginning of the season."

"That when you two got together?"

"We were together the first couple of games, I guess."

"You mean, having sex."

"No . . . just drinking. Smoking, a little. All the girls were envious," she said wistfully. "But then he kind of went for Clarissa."

"You must have had sex sometime," I pointed out.

"I guess it was after the Oregon City game . . ." she said. "I really don't remember. Dionne was there and she wanted me to go home. That's before she got so upset. She and Keegan dated a while back. Sort of, anyway. What are you doing?"

We were at the house where I'd left the canoe and she balked at crossing the lawn. I had to practically muscle her along the side wall. "No one lives here," I said in her ear. "I left a canoe here the night the paramedics showed up. That's how I escaped. I've got to take it back."

"What if we get caught?"

"We're screwed," I said.

"I don't want to go."

I ignored her. "How'd you get home the night you think you slept with Keegan? Do you remember?"

She didn't answer right at first, seeming to think there might be a trap in there somewhere. "Dionne said she helped me."

"You don't remember that, either?"

"Not really. Why? Is it a crime or something?"

Maybe, I thought, as we reached the water. To Dawn, I said, "Stand guard for a minute, okay?" as I slipped inside the boathouse.

"What? No. Where are you going?"

"Just wait . . ."

It took a lot of persuasion on my part, a lot of resistance on hers, but we finally got the canoe back in the water and began paddling quietly, keeping to the shoreline. I could tell she wanted to ask a million questions, but my threat that we could get in trouble kept her quiet. At Social Security I clambered out, then helped her to the seawall. I placed a finger to my lips and glared at her harshly, reminding her anew of the need for quiet. She glanced toward the house and kept her lips firmly shut. With an effort we hauled the canoe inside the boathouse, placing it upside down like I'd found it. I even hung the oars back on the wall.

Climbing over the fence to Do Not Enter was where things got tricky. She whispered, "I can't do it!" way too loudly.

"Yes, you can," I said through my teeth. She shook her head, but I added, "Do this," and wound my fingers in the chain-link, prepared to climb. I just wanted off Social Security's property.

Dawn whispered, "I don't think I can."

"You can. Trust me." With her grip, I figured she could hang glide without a harness and do fine.

She grabbed the fence, following my example, but my gaze was glued to the amber light shining from Social Security's living room. I just wanted to get the hell out. Now.

With an effort, she tried to haul herself over. I confess I gave her a hefty push. She made a strangled sound and plopped down into the muck on Do Not Enter's side. "Goddammit!" she yelled.

A light flashed on.

I leapt over that fence as if demons were licking my heels. Dawn was still struggling to her feet as I raced for the basement. I hoped she wouldn't get caught but now that I knew she was (a) not pregnant and (b) kind of a pain in the ass, I wasn't as concerned as I might have been.

Several couples had straggled outside in our absence and

they stopped and stared as I shot past, Dawn following after me, swearing in frustration.

Someone had finally dared to turn on the red string lights, which I thought might be a bad idea. I hesitated on the bottom stair and Dawn caught up to me. "I don't know why I told you everything. I must be crazy. And he wants you now. I guess I should have known this would happen."

"Yeah. Well. I'm not interested."

"That's what they all say," she said, snorting in disgust.

"I don't want to be with anybody I can't remember having sex with," I told her. "You shouldn't, either."

"Who are you? My mother?"

She was spoiling for a fight. I figured it was just a matter of time before the yelling started. "You should remember," I told her fiercely.

She pushed herself past me and headed upstairs. I was right behind her, anxious to get the hell away. As soon as we were on the main floor, it felt like kids materialized from the gloom, coming our way. Dawn moved out of the way and I edged toward the front door.

Keegan stood to one side, his shoulder propped up against one of the posts. "Hey, there," he said smoothly. He moved toward me with a conqueror's confidence, handing me a beer. "Got your canoe back, huh?" He inclined his head toward Social Security.

"Yep."

"You were here last week. Sorry I missed all the excitement." He smiled. "Glad you got away."

"Yeah, me, too."

"Come on over here. . . ."

Dawn had melted away. I tried to think of a way out, but Keegan was surrounded by his disciples, all of them looking as if they might wrestle me to the ground should I disobey. Man, oh, man. I was not okay with this. Was I being overly dramatic? Imagining danger from this high school kid that just wasn't there?

I looked down at my beer. Its top had been popped. I didn't see how I was going to fake being thrilled to be with him. I sure as hell wasn't going to become part of the harem.

As if noticing I wasn't imbibing, Keegan tipped up the brim of my baseball cap to look meaningfully into my eyes. "Drink up," he said, tossing back his beer, taking several long, healthy swallows. Then he held my gaze, waiting.

I tipped my beer and swallowed.

He gave me a knowing smile.

I stared at him, chilled. My cell phone suddenly vibrated in my pocket. Keegan heard the faint buzzing. I unzipped the pocket, pulled out the phone and looked at it.

Keegan snatched it away from me.

I held my breath.

"Your dad," he said, sounding pissed.

My dad?

Keegan quickly took back my beer. "Fucking parents."

I stared at the still vibrating phone. The word DAD stared at me from the liquid crystal dial.

Dwayne Austin Durbin. In a faintly trembling voice, I answered, "Hi, Dad. I'm still with my friends."

There was the faintest of hesitations, and then he said clearly, "It's getting pretty late, Ronnie."

"I'm on my way. Bye." I clicked off. "Gotta go," I told Keegan.

"I don't want to wait another week."

"Umm . . . I don't know."

"Give me your cell number. I'll call you."

"Give me yours. My dad's real strict. I'd better call you."

He didn't like the shift in power, but I wouldn't give him my number. No way was he going to have a link to Jane Kelly. Not that I expected him to be an expert on discerning information, but one never knows. I'm always amazed at what people are capable of.

He finally coughed up his number and I plugged it into my phone as I hurried away from him.

I drove toward Dwayne's feeling light-headed. I'd escaped by the skin of my teeth, on that I was sure. Once parked, I pounded on his door. I was incapable of searching through my purse for his key. When Dwayne opened the door, I threw myself into his arms. Luckily, he took my weight without a stumble.

My body shook in waves. Aftershock. I've been in tight spots before. I've been scared. But I never wanted the feel of human comfort more than I did right now.

"Jane . . ."

I shivered violently.

"What did he do to you?" Dwayne's voice was taut.

"Nothing." Dwayne smelled good and felt better. I wrapped myself around him, clinging to him as if my life depended on it. Distantly I knew I'd be embarrassed later. I was taking advantage of the situation, giving myself a reason to stay close to him, to feel my flesh against his.

Dwayne's arms were strong and supportive around me. I buried my face in his shirt, much like Dawn had buried hers in mine. "I'm okay," I assured him again, my voice sounding strangled. I cleared my throat and tried again. "I'm overreacting. I'm fine. Truly."

"What happened?"

I eased myself from his embrace. He regarded me seriously, his blue eyes intense. He was holding me up by my arms. I felt like kissing him. Really, really felt like it. That heavy-heartbeat, time-telescoping-to-this-moment kind of desire. Thudding. Needy.

"Why did you call?" I asked.

"It was dark over there. I couldn't see anything and it felt wrong."

"Gut instinct?" I said shakily.

"You sure something didn't happen?"

"I'm fine." Running a hand through my hair, I turned away from the door toward the living room and Dwayne's faded gray sofa. I stumbled to it. Dwayne followed, sitting down next to me. He was in shorts. His right leg wrapped, elasticized, strapped. His left leg lay against mine. I tore my gaze from his thigh and wondered if I was having some kind of strange attack, an intense desire I couldn't control. Reaction to fear. Panic. A primal need to assure ourselves that we're alive. I wanted sex. I wanted sex with Dwayne. It felt like a drug rushing through my system, roaring in my ears, heating my blood.

He was staring at me, concerned and perplexed. I pressed trembling fingers to my lips, begging my body for control. I mean . . . goddammn it! I couldn't do this. Not now . . . not in this way.

"It's date rape," I finally said, surprised by the normalcy of my voice. "Something like GHB or Rohypnol. This guy, who could have any girl he wants, prefers to drug them."

Dwayne made a sound low in his throat. Something animal that only increased my pulsing need. I wanted to grab Dwayne and writhe around with him. Like I had no brain. Like a sex addict with zero control.

With an effort I pulled my thoughts from him. I thought of icebergs. Frozen wastelands and frostbite. Crashing arctic waves and frigid temperatures. It helped. Enough that I could concentrate on my narrative.

"He gave me an opened beer."

"Lendenhal?"

"Yes. That's the first time that happened. Every other time I've popped the beer's top myself. But they were all there. The disciples. It's like they knew what he was up to. Like a big fraternity."

"No one tried to stop him?"

I shook my head, pulling myself together, thinking about the situation. "He's not the only one who uses Roofies, or whatever. The first time I was there, I saw him give a packet to Judd. Glory was mad at Judd for ruining her clothes, and she wasn't in the mood, so Judd went to Keegan for help. Keegan handed him the packet."

"Did you drink any of the beer?"

"Pretended to. Keegan grabbed it back from me when you called." I explained how he thought Dwayne was my father, then added, "Oh, and Dawn's not pregnant. She was. She miscarried. She's not happy about it, but her parents are."

"She told her parents?"

"She wanted the baby. It was Keegan's and she wants him."

Dwayne's jaw was stiff with suppressed fury. I thought of all the things Larrabee had said earlier. All the things I didn't know about him. What I did know was he possessed a strong sense of justice. "I want this bastard's balls in a wringer," he muttered tightly.

"Me, too."

"We can call the police on them. Next Friday."

I nodded. It was time for the police. "Keegan said he didn't want to wait another week. He wants me to call him."

"You have his number?"

"He gave it to me." I glanced out the window to the dark night. I thought about Keegan. Yes, it was time for the police, but I felt an irrational need—very unlike me—to see this through. "You know . . . if I saw him again . . . I think I could get one of those doctored beers."

"No." Dwayne was positive on that score.

"Keegan Lendenhal's practically a god. He'll slip out of the noose, I just know it. His parents, the team, the whole town . . . they won't be able to pin this on him without proof."

"The guy drugged and raped Dawn Wilson."

"And she'll never press charges. We've got to catch him, Dwayne."

He got to his feet as if compelled, shaking his head. Perversely, the more he fought me, the more I was sure this was the way to bring Keegan Lendenhal down.

"Dwayne, it's personal."

"Bullshit! You know better. That's what makes you right for this job, Jane. You're never irrational about the danger. This guy drugs girls and has sex with them. His buddies help him. He'll try it on you. And, Jane . . . he could succeed."

I had a vision of myself, out cold, being deliberately stripped of my clothes, Keegan Lendenhal climbing atop me.

All my muscles seemed to contract together. I couldn't think about Keegan Lendenhal anymore. "There's something else," I said. "Not the teenagers. Just something else that Larrabee said."

"What?"

"He said you—introduced him—to his wife?"

Dwayne didn't want to switch subjects. He looked like he was going to brush me aside. But he stopped himself, maybe realizing that I was the one who needed the change. "That's true," he admitted. "The marriage lasted four months. He still blames me."

I stared at him and then I started laughing. And then hiccupping. And then laughing some more. The tension went out of Dwayne's muscles as he watched me collapse into a sort of welcome hysteria.

"What is it with you two?" I asked him.

Dwayne shrugged.

"He also told me you were accused of murder."

"I was." Dwayne seemed about to say something more, then shook his head. "That bastard. I thought he knew how to keep his mouth shut."

"What happened?"

"It's old, old history. But right now? We need to concentrate on what to do about Lendenhal."

"How old a history?"

Dwayne ran a hand through his hair, fighting frustration. "High school."

"*That* long ago?" I said in surprise.

"A girl I knew went missing. This gung-ho homicide detective tried to charge a bunch of us with murder, but there was no evidence. After high school, I thought about law enforcement, but it wasn't going to happen. The girl was never found, and that detective was sure I was responsible. He wouldn't let it go, and it followed me around for a long while. Nobody wanted to trust me. So I changed my mind. End of story."

"And the homicide detective?"

"I don't know. Probably still stewing about it. It's long over."

There was a lot left unsaid, as ever with Dwayne. But the switch of subject made me feel more like myself, had shifted the focus off me and helped pushed Keegan Lendenhal's sick behavior aside for the moment.

"Wow," I said. "My life's really boring."

I could tell he wanted to close the door on this once and for all. *No way, buddy,* I thought, but I was willing to let him off the hook for the moment. After all, he'd restored my equilibrium—at least as far as Keegan Lendenhal was concerned. I was going to have to stick with images of icebergs and glaciers for a while on that other, sexual thing.

"That answer your questions?" Dwayne asked.

"I've just got one more."

He gave me a long, hard look.

"What are smithereens?"

CHAPTER FIFTEEN

The problem with unresolved issues is they keep you awake all night. From midnight to 7:00 a.m. I tossed and turned and generally disturbed Binkster's sleep, as she was stretched out beside me, her muzzle softly snoring right at my face, one front paw holding my restless body at bay.

Reluctantly dragging myself from my bed, I felt crabby and out of sorts. Lack of sleep'll do that to you. Stumbling into the kitchen, I examined the remains of my grocery shopping. I still had some coffee, but I didn't feel like making any. Glancing outside to my backyard, I registered the gray day.

But there was no rain.

I threw on my sweats and Nikes and tried to talk Binkster into joining me. She flipped over and ignored me, kicking her back legs a couple of times as she settled in again, just in case I missed the point. I decided she wasn't starving and she could let herself out her dog door if she needed to, so I locked up the house, tucked my key in the zippered pocket of my sweatpants, then jogged to the Coffee Nook.

In the light of day, my anxiety over Keegan Lendenhal retreated. In fact, as I jogged onward, it gave way to a healthy anger. Who the hell did he think he was? His actions were *criminal*. Yes, I could call the police on him, and I intended to, but I really wanted to be the one to bring him down. I wasn't quite sure how to do it yet. I needed a foolproof plan. But I'd give myself a week to figure it out, and Dwayne was just going to have to accept that fact.

It was Friday and the Nook was busy. Spying Chuck talking loudly with another older man—who looked as pained as I felt—I zigged the other direction. Julie saw me and handed me an empty paper cup without comment. I filled it up with black coffee and circled to the other side of the bar. Billy Leonard wasn't at his usual stool, but then I was later than normal.

Jenny said, "You look like you need breakfast."

"I do?" I was hunkered down in my spot, leaning forward over my coffee, blowing across the top.

"How about a sesame bagel with cream cheese?"

"Put it on my coffee card," I said. Coffee Nook has prepaid cards that are set up for ten drinks, but other items can be substituted in coffee's place. The great thing about the cards is, once you've been stamped ten times, you get a free cup.

"What's wrong with you?" Jenny asked, slicing the bagel in half and slamming it in the toaster.

"What do you mean?"

"You're sprawled across the counter."

It was true. My arms were spread out in front of me. I looked like I was going to lay my head down on the laminate and pass out. It sounded like a pretty good idea, too. Well, okay, maybe I was feeling some reaction from last night's events. Or maybe it was an overall malaise brought on by everything going on in my life.

"My landlord's selling my cottage," I informed her. "He's already got an offer. And he's having a garage sale tomorrow. I don't know what I'm going to do."

"How much was the offer for?"

"I don't know."

Julie looked up from the espresso machine. "Can you make an offer, too?"

"He hasn't accepted the first offer yet. Or at least he hadn't the last I talked to him. He said for me to get on it, if I were going to do it. But it's just not possible."

"What about that boss of yours?" Jenny suggested, handing me my bagel with an individual packet of cream cheese. "The cute one who owns the cabana. Have him buy it for you."

"Yeah, right." Dwayne was a last resort.

"Your cottage is on the canal?" Julie asked.

"West Bay," I corrected, giving her my address. "At least for the moment."

They commiserated with me while they went about their business making lattés, mochas and Nook-a-chinos, frozen coffee drinks that required a blender-type device that's loud enough to split eardrums. I was heading out the door for my run back, one eye on the low, threatening clouds, when Chuck sidled up to me. "That fellow you work for? Dwayne Durbin? Think he'd do something for me?"

No.

"What do you need?" I asked reluctantly. I try so very hard not to engage Chuck. I never want to meet his eye, never want to give him the slightest indication that I might be interested in speaking with him, because I'm not. Though he's been around the Nook for years, it's just recently that he seems to be everywhere. I don't know what's changed but I don't like it.

"I need a background check on a guy my daughter's marrying. Wanna make sure he's not after her money, y'know?"

I didn't have a business card on me, so I gave Chuck Dwayne's home landline, which is basically his office number. I left as Chuck was placing the call and was scarcely out of the Nook's parking lot when my cell phone buzzed. Pulling it out of my pocket, I guessed that it was Dwayne.

"Who's this Chuck character?" he greeted me.

"How should I know?" I responded, just to be ornery.

"He said you gave him my number."

Oh. I picked up my pace, knowing the two-and-a-half-mile trip was going to feel a whole lot longer on the return. "He's a guy who comes into the Nook."

"You're jogging. Call me when you get back. We've got things to talk about."

Yeah, yeah.

"And smithereens are extremely small smithers." He clicked off.

I smiled in spite of myself.

All the way back I felt the stretch in my muscles and when I let myself inside the cottage I headed straight for the shower, asking myself, as I often did, if exercise can truly be good for you.

On my way, I popped my head inside my bedroom. Dark, marble eyes looked at me from a tangle of covers and a tail wagged. No other movement. "Get out of bed!" I ordered the dog, but she was still there when I got out of the shower and changed into clean jeans and an oversized, ribbed black sweater.

If I didn't know The Binkster I might have thought there was something wrong with her, but she's a slug by nature. I said, "Breakfast," and headed to her bowl. Instantly I heard a thunk as she landed on the floor, and the click of her toenails as she hurried after me. When I turned to her bowl, dog food bag in hand, she was standing beside it like a sentry, one paw lifted just in case this was going to be one of those times I threw Kiblets across the floor for her to chase. I'm not the only one who should suffer through exercise.

This morning I just poured the crunchies into the bowl and she stuck her head in before I was finished, so the little brown nuggets bounced off her ears and onto the floor. Not a problem. She doesn't miss a single one.

I worked on my hair, brushing it down to my shoulders, then added some makeup, pleased with the result. I dug through some of my desk drawers till I found some more business cards, something Dwayne had ordered for me, just to look official. I didn't care that I hadn't had one for Chuck, but Dr. Daniel Wu might need some proof of who I was. He'd said he would be at the Eastmoreland clinic all day today, so I was determined to see him as soon as possible. Then I was going to call Sean and see if he could shed some light on that conversation with his father that took place the morning of Gigi's wedding day.

Melinda deigned to return my call as I was driving across the Sellwood Bridge to the east side of the Willamette. "Hi," I greeted her.

"What are you doing?" she demanded before I could say anything else. "Yes, I met Roland at CMC. Yes, it's how we met. I am so tired of having to explain it to everyone!"

Wow. Touchy. "I'm just following up," I said, negotiating the bridge. Is it a law, or something, that the lanes have to be narrower than the vehicle?

She made a disparaging noise. Clearly I hadn't given her a reason to believe I was any better at my craft than she'd felt before. "I don't know why you're still bothering."

"I guess, if you met him there, that Roland was a member of the club."

"You guess right."

"I'm just asking."

She relented enough to say, "He joined after he and Violet broke up, and let me tell you, he was a mess. That marriage nearly destroyed him. I mean, here he was, recovering from his problems, and she just aggravated everything."

"Were you a member, too?"

"Why are you asking these questions?"

"*Are* the women members?"

"It's a men's club, mostly," she said after a long moment. "But they have special memberships for women as long as you're interested in dating. Once you're married, that's it. Well, for the women anyway."

"The men can still belong?"

"Roland didn't," she assured me quickly. "Once we got together, that was it. I'd been going to the parties for a while and was about to chuck the whole thing. It can get really old, you know, meeting new people, going through all the same rituals. And then I saw him. He was standing by the fireplace, staring into it, and he looked so sad," she said wistfully. "We just started talking and we never stopped. He told me he was in the middle of a messy divorce. That's the first time I heard about Violet."

"How long were you part of CMC?"

"I went to enough parties to know most of the men were frogs."

"What's the procedure?"

"Oh, for God's sake. Why don't you go find out for yourself? I haven't been part of it for years!"

She hung up with a click.

"I just might," I said to empty air.

The Eastmoreland Clinic was a low, sprawling white stucco building with a gray tile roof. I pegged its era as early to mid-seventies with the architect vacillating between Spanish style and cheap industrial. There were four visitors' spots freshly marked with yellow lines. I pulled into one of two that were still empty, locked my car, walked to the swinging glass door that led to reception and pushed my way inside.

To my left was a low counter in fake wood grain that served as the receptionist's desk. The receptionist was young and attractive, but not an out-and-out beauty. She had great skin, though, a warm, peachy tone with smooth lines and no shadows around her eyes. Her name tag read CARLA.

Two women, one in her forties and one about my age, sat in the overstuffed chairs done in gray, taupe and black. They eyed me over the top of their magazines as I walked up to Carla's desk.

"May I help you?" she said, her smile practiced.

"I'm here to see Dr. Wu. He told me he would be here all day and to stop by when I could." I dug in my purse for my business card and slid it in her direction.

She ignored the card. I almost pointed out the gold letters that spelled out my name. I'm rather proud of those cards, even if I'm still working toward my license. "Today's Dr. Wu's first day since his trip with Willamette Medical Services to offer aid to weather-ravaged areas in Southeast Asia, specifically the Philippines," Carla said, as if giving a speech. There was admonition in her tone as well. The man was "too busy" to see me.

"That's why I came today instead of yesterday."

"I'm sorry. I don't believe he has time."

"Maybe you should check with him," I suggested reasonably.

Her face turned to stone. That fast, we were at war with each other. I don't know what it is about me, but I don't do authority well. I piss people off in record time, and it works the same on me. She glared and I met her glare.

"Dr. Wu is busy all day," she said coldly.

"Why don't you call him and verify that?"

The other two women in the room had dropped their magazines and were hanging on our every word. Carla's eyes darted their way. She really wanted to get into a full-blown battle with me, but she had witnesses.

She picked up the phone and bit out, "Alma, is Dr. Wu with a patient?" A pause. "That's what I thought. No, don't bother him," she said quickly. She slammed down the phone. "You can wait if you'd like," she said sneerily.

Read that to mean: you can wait till hell ices over and beyond.

"I'll be right over there." I pointed to a seat. "In case you should forget me."

Her face flushed.

As I took my seat the other women couldn't stop looking at me. I shot them each a quelling glance and they hid behind their magazines. One's was upside down for a good five minutes before she righted it.

Carla touched a finger to my card and slid it to the left side of her desk as if it were poisonous. Another woman entered the clinic and Carla got all perky and sweet again. The two women waiting before me were called inside by a nurse's aide who opened an inner door and read their names from the files in her arms. Time crawled by. When this newest woman's name was called, neatly bypassing mine entirely, I simply followed right after her.

Carla opened and shut her mouth like a fish as I passed by. "Excuse me." She tried to get up from her desk, but her phone rang.

The nurse's aide, whose tag read BUNNY, frowned at me.

"I left my jacket in room six," I said, brushing right past her and heading down the hall.

"Room six is the other way."

"That's right." I sent her an apologetic smile and turned around on my heel. Bunny was mildly concerned but the woman whose name had just been called was a pile of nerves and started firing questions like artillery. When was the doctor planning the surgery? Was it really awful? Was there lot of pain? How long would it take before she could be seen in public? Wasn't there any way to get her insurance company to pay for some of it?

I turned at the first corner, heading into a narrow hall with numbered doors on either side. Room six was empty, as luck would have it, and I stepped inside to get my bearings.

It wouldn't take long for Carla to be on my scent. As I stood there, another woman in a blue smock stopped at my

open door. Alma Lucas, RN. "Are you waiting for someone?" she asked, perplexed, her gaze on the rack outside the
door that would hold a patient's chart.

I started crying for all I was worth, hoping to God I could
actually scare up some tears. "Dr. Wu!" I wailed, burying my
face in my hands.

"What's this about?"

I just sobbed and sobbed. Okay, it wasn't the most sophis-
ticated plan, but she finally grew uncomfortable and hurried
off. As soon as she was gone I lifted my head. No tears. I was
going to have to work on that.

I left room six and walked swiftly down the hall, listening
at doors until I heard low, male tones coming from the other
side of the panels. From my conversation with him yesterday, I was pretty sure it was Wu's voice. I hesitated. I didn't
want to alienate him before I had a chance to talk to him, so
I decided to try and catch him on his way out rather than
barging into the room while he was with a patient.

Hearing approaching footsteps, I ducked around the corner, rattling the handles of a couple of doors. Most were
unlocked. I peeked inside. There were several more examination rooms and a storeroom. I really wanted the storeroom, but there was a paper smock laid out on a padded
table in one of the examining rooms. Quickly, I stripped off
my shirt and bra and slipped on the smock, then lay down on
the table, staring at the ceiling. Okay. This was a plastic
surgery clinic, not a gynecologist's office. Maybe they didn't
lie down. Maybe I should sit up.

I heard some discussion out in the hall. Carla's voice
squeaked with fury. She was going to *have* to get back to the
front. But they *needed* to find this Jane Kelly person before
she *did* something *criminal* like stealing drugs, for *God's sake!*

I was outraged. Stealing drugs?

The door to my room started to open. I flung my arm over
my eyes.

Dr. Wu said, "Excuse me. I thought this room was empty."

I dropped my arm and struggled to sit up. He gave me a quick look as he started to close the door. "Dr. Wu?" I asked hurriedly.

"Yes?"

"I'm Jane Kelly, the private investigator who called you yesterday about Roland Hatchmere. Your staff wouldn't let me in to see you. I'm not here for anything nefarious. I just needed to talk to you. Could you talk to me? Just for a few minutes?"

"Did you want an exam?" he asked, faintly confused.

I held the paper top close, clamping my arms to my side to pin it in place. It was my turn to flush. "No."

He shut the door behind him and leaned back against it. He was middle-aged, his shock of black hair shot with gray. He wore narrow, wire-rimmed glasses and I couldn't read his expression. He didn't seem to find my appearance unsettling or even particularly surprising. He seemed tired.

"I've been looking forward to talking to you," he admitted. "I was good friends with Roland. He was always fair and when we sold the clinics, he made certain I had a contract with the new owners. I owe him a lot. I'm sorry about the staff. It's been controlled chaos since I got back."

"I appreciate that," I said, thrilled that he wasn't going to toss me out on my ass. "I'm looking into a motive for Roland's death. I was hoping you could tell me about the clinics. Maybe there's some financial gain I'm not aware of?"

"I thought it was established that his girlfriend killed him."

"It may be something else entirely."

A storm was gathering in the hall outside. "Dr. Wu?" Alma called, knocking lightly on our door.

"I'll be right there," he told her. Strident voices surged, then purposely lowered to a murmur on the other side of the door. Dr. Wu ignored them. "Have you looked at Roland's children, Gigi and Sean?"

"Gigi and Sean?"

"If it's a financial motive, they would be the most likely, I would think. Roland was disinheriting them. Sean, because of his drug use. Roland couldn't bear watching his son go down the same path that had ruined his medical career. He and Sean had a serious argument about two weeks before the wedding, and Roland decided the only way to get through to him was cut him off completely. He planned to sever all financial ties. Permanently."

"Did he go through with it?"

"I don't think he had time to rewrite his will, but he was certainly planning on it. He told Sean not to contact him until he got himself clean."

I stared at him, processing. Maybe this was why Sean wasn't at the rehearsal dinner. "And Gigi?"

"Roland couldn't stand Emmett and Emmett's family," Daniel Wu told me. "In public he was nice to them, but in private he didn't bother. I'm not sure what it was exactly. Maybe he just didn't like them. He kept hoping Gigi would change her mind, but she's not known for making the best choices. Roland had a special account for her and she stripped it without telling him. She swore it was for an investment opportunity, something Emmett talked her into, but Roland was furious."

"Do you know how much money was in the account?"

"Somewhere in the range of a hundred thousand."

"Was the investment ever made?"

He lifted his palms. "I'm not really sure." Behind him, the voices were gathering force. He looked annoyed, then sighed. "I'm overscheduled. I didn't realize how much when I told you to stop by. Is there anything else? I'm happy to help any way I can."

"You've helped a lot," I assured him.

He grabbed a prescription pad from inside a drawer and scribbled on it. "This is my home number. If you need anything else, call me. I'll try to get back to you as soon as I can."

"Do you know anything about Roland's relationship with his wife?" I asked as he turned to the door, his hand on the knob.

"You mean beyond the fact that they were separated?" He peered at me through his glasses, the lenses flashing in the light. "I believe he was dating again."

"Violet Purcell," I said.

"She was one of them," he agreed, and then he swept into the hall. A sea of pinched female faces stared in at me before Dr. Wu closed the door behind him. He asked them all to get back to work in a cool voice.

Quickly, I grabbed my bra. I was reaching for my sweater when the door opened again. Alma looked in. Apparently she'd drawn the short straw from the group and was elected to show me the door.

Carla had won her over as an ally and she regarded me with a chilly expression. "I'm sorry, Ms. Kelly. We don't have any of your insurance information," she told me crisply. "When you're dressed, you need to stop by the front desk so Carla can photostat your card."

I pulled my sweater over my head and pretended to be concerned. "I don't have insurance," I lied.

"Then we'll send you a bill. We'll need your address, phone number and Social Security number."

I thought of a lot of answers, voted for passive-aggressive silence and just shrugged as I walked away.

I strolled up to Carla's desk. Her eyes narrowed and her lips grew pinched as I approached. She tossed a clipboard with about four pages at me. "You'll need to fill this out."

"No problem." I reached over and slid my business card back into my palm. She eyed me suspiciously. I walked straight to the door, saluted her with the clipboard and walked into the watery November afternoon sunlight.

I put in the call to Sean and ended up leaving a message. Big surprise. I doubted he would phone me back in a timely manner. I mean, why should he be different from anyone else? Maybe I should stop by the Crock later on. It was Friday. I could phone ahead and see if Sean's band was still on the playbill.

I went home and took Binkster for a walk around the neighborhood. It makes me kind of nervous because around this section of West Bay there aren't any sidewalks, and the streets are narrow and twisty with poor visibility. Still, I was feeling the need to move, so we wandered around with Binks smelling every leaf and twig, pressing her flat face to the ground, stubbornly ignoring my tugs on the leash. But the rain still held off. It had been nearly a day since it had precipitated. Almost a record.

Violet called as Binks and I reentered the cottage. Binks ran straight for her bowl as I answered my cell phone.

"Jane, I've got the greatest news," Violet said.

Instantly, I braced myself. Everything comes out of left field with Violet and I wasn't sure I was ready. "What?" I asked cautiously.

"Well, first let me tell you that I joined the Columbia Millionaires' Club. It's kind of like being a social member rather than a full-fledged one, if you're a woman, but it was great. I just walked in and told them who I was and what I was about—being a Purcell doesn't hurt around Portland—and voila!"

"Well, that's great." The wheels in my head were turning.

"And guess what? There's a CMC party tomorrow night, and I put your name down as my guest! Now you can wear that dress. It's perfect. You want to know about escort services? Dating services? Might as well check it out from the inside. Right? Best kind of investigation."

"Where'd you get this idea?"

"It just came to me. It's brilliant, don't you think?"

More than delving deeper into the circumstances surrounding Roland's death, I sensed this was one of her attempts to be friends. Just us girls . . . doing something crazy again.

"I'm guessing you didn't tell them about your association with the deceased Mr. Hatchmere."

"I left that off the application," she admitted. "And I had to be a little cagey about your occupation, too. I fuzzed up some details on both of us, but it's always kind of a game at these places anyway. Everybody lies."

"What did you say about me?"

"I said you were looking to meet a partner. I'll come over tomorrow and put you together before we go."

"You don't trust me to do it on my own?"

"No."

I stared into the middle distance, thinking hard. This was an unexpected opportunity for me to gain access to Columbia Millionaires' Club. "Okay, I'm in."

"Terrific," Violet enthused. "Good thing I bought all those products at The Face, huh?"

I had hours to kill before I could meet Sean at the Crock, so I spent the afternoon on my laptop writing up my notes. I put the facts in one file, my thoughts and impressions in another. If and when I could, I wrote down people's comments verbatim because sometimes what they said took on new meaning later—a trick I learned from Dwayne.

That finished, I took some time to chronicle my adventures at Do Not Enter, facetiously writing up a bill for Dwayne. I wasn't really after payment on this one, but it worked great as an exercise in laying out the information I'd gathered. It was clear to me Keegan Lendenhal would have to be caught in the act to make the charges stick as there was no direct evidence. Maybe Dawn's older sister, Dionne, would have some things to say about Keegan. Maybe Dawn's parents would chime in with their own suspicions. But getting Dawn to have a change of heart was something else again, and even on the remote chance she did, with no evidence it was a matter of "he said, she said."

However, a beer can with traces of a date rape drug and Keegan Lendenhal's fingerprints ought to be a good start. I didn't trust Lake Chinook's finest to procure that piece of evidence in a raid on Do Not Enter. Keegan would dispose of it first. On that I would bet. So it looked like it was up to me.

Since I had no intention of calling Keegan earlier, as he'd practically insisted, I had a week before the next, and last, game. Meanwhile, I could concentrate on the Hatchmere murder, so I whiled away Friday afternoon looking over the information I'd put in my notes, examining my timeline and considering the possible motives that Dr. Wu had given me for both Gigi and Sean. Roland's death had prevented him from changing his will. His estate was divided between them, except for concessions made to Melinda. Violet got exactly zero.

I glanced down the list of names of wedding guests and friends. Deenie was still incommunicado, but my interest level in her had nose-dived. What could she tell me anyway? That she and Gigi had cried and hugged and cried some more? Would her version be any more illuminating than Gigi's? I was betting on a big, fat *no*, but I circled her name anyway.

I paused at Emmett's name, then moved down the list to David and Goldy Popparockskill. If I believed Daniel Wu's account, which I did, then what had Roland had against them? Was it just a case of no one being good enough for his little girl, including the would-be groom's parents? Or was it something else?

Grabbing my coat, I decided to take a jaunt down to Wilsonville, about seven miles south of Lake Chinook, to check out Miller-Kennedy Mercedes. Maybe David Popparockskill wasn't interested in talking to me, but hey, I sure felt like talking to him. Emmett had said he was the accounts manager. Based on David's one uptight phone message to me, I suspected it was a good thing he wasn't in sales.

It was about four-thirty when I took off and I wondered if I might be too late. Did the employees leave at five? Six? Or did some of them stay around throughout the evening, catching the after-work customer? This might be an exercise in futility, but one never knew.

There was a faint misting rain sputtering on and off. I looked up at the heavens and silently pleaded for a drought. A fat plop of water splattered on my windshield and I turned on my wipers.

I considered how it might be going with Gigi and Emmett since he'd quit the dealership. What's that line about retirement: twice the husband, half the income? In Emmett's case, he wasn't even getting half the income. But then he wasn't even once a husband, strictly speaking.

The Miller-Kennedy Mercedes dealership was all bluegreen tinted glass hung on a soaring, silvery metal frame. The front windows formed a peak over the showroom, which made it look like a huge, futuristic church. The back of the building dropped a story or two into your basic tilt-up concrete walls painted a shade of ecru. All the cars sparkled like polished gems, lined up in rows with rain beading on their waxed exteriors: red, blue, gold and silver, shining under the stadium lights that lit up the place like day.

A salesman held open the glass-paneled front door for me, all smiles. I reflected on my black pants and boots, topped by my anorak. I was almost okay, though the coat was a little tired, but hey, it had gotten a lot of use lately.

"Weather's been a mess, huh?" he greeted me.

"The cars look great."

"They sure do, don't they?"

The showroom held three superfancy cars with every button and gizmo known to mankind. A dark blue convertible took center stage, gleaming and throwing back sparks of illumination from the overhead track lights. My new friend started talking car talk as if I'd pulled a string to his voice box. I waited politely for about three seconds, then interrupted. "Is David Popparockskill still here?"

He stopped abruptly, looking more surprised than crestfallen. "I'm not sure. He could still be in his office." He pointed to a hallway that turned a corner toward the back of the building. "It's down that way. Take a right after you pass the water fountain. Better yet, check with Junie-Marie. She's at the reception desk till seven."

"Junie-Marie?" I repeated, digging rapidly through my memory. Someone had mentioned Junie-Marie recently. It wasn't a name to forget but I couldn't immediately place it.

"You know her?"

"She was . . . Emmett's girlfriend before Gigi," I said. It was the Best Man. He'd definitely favored Junie-Marie to Gigi.

"You do know the family." He gave me a more studied examination.

"I've never actually met Junie-Marie."

"She's great. Check with her." His eye traveled to a young couple who'd just squealed into the lot in an oversized SUV. They stepped out, both wearing business clothes, as if they'd just come from the office, and there was something about their apparel that screamed *money*.

He was gone in a flash.

The reception desk counter was a large semicircle of blond wood, chest height, lit by a plethora of overhead can lights. As I neared it, I could see a woman's brunette bob come into view. Her hair was short, clipped just below her ears. What struck me first was how much she looked like Gigi. Second, I saw that the resemblance actually wasn't much past the short, dark hair, large brown eyes and sculpted cheekbones. Junie-Marie was prettier but radiated an overwhelmed tension that surrounded her like a force field. She smiled at me. "May I help you?"

Tiny diamonds, or maybe zircons, sparkled at her earlobes. Her lipstick was light pink where Gigi's was brick red. I put both women around the same age, but Junie seemed younger.

I started lying as soon as I opened my mouth. Sometimes it's clear in the first few moments how to respond to a potential interviewee. Besides, I like to lie. "I thought Emmett Popparockskill worked here, but I was told that he's gone now?" I tried to project perplexed disappointment.

Her smile dimmed a couple of watts. "I'm sorry. He's no longer with us. But all our salesmen are really knowledgeable." She reached a hand toward the intercom.

"I'm sure they are, but this is a personal matter."

"Oh?" She pretended merely a polite interest, but her body was practically bristling.

Leaning an elbow on the counter, I sighed hugely. "This is totally embarrassing, but I met Emmett at the clubhouse. We, well . . . we hit it off. But then I found out he was getting married! I was just devastated, you know. God, life's full of lousy tricks, isn't it?"

She didn't verbally agree with me, but it was in her face. She forgot the intercom, dropping her hand to her desk, fiddling with a notepad and pen within reach.

"So I was really, really bummed, to say the least. I *just* found out that he never got married. I haven't seen him around the club, though, so I thought maybe I could catch up with him here."

"Unfortunately . . . no . . ."

"Do you know how I can get in touch with him?" I asked hopefully. "Can you tell me where he's working now?"

She fingered an earring. "I'm not sure he's taken another job."

"Wow. Really? Like he's living a life of leisure? Gosh, maybe he's gone to a new country club."

"I think he's still at Willamette Crest."

"Well, he's been like a ghost, then," I said. "I've been there nearly every day." I tried on a pensive look. "Do you know what happened? I mean, why he didn't get married. *She* didn't call it off, did she?"

"No, oh no. Not by choice." Junie-Marie was struggling. Boy, did she want to dish with me! I was counting on her not considering me any real threat for Emmett's affections as I was more like a groupie, a little desperate, definitely not a real contender. Junie-Marie didn't want to seem unprofessional, but there had to be some deep resentment somewhere over the whole Emmett thing. I mean, what was she doing working here? In this nest of Popparockskills and Millers, all related to Emmett.

"Maybe you read about it?" she said carefully, shooting a look around the showroom. We were the only people for miles. Everyone else was outside in the overcast skies, looking at vehicles, or at the far end of the showroom, practically a football field away. "Emmett's fiancée, Gigi Hatchmere? Her father was killed the day of the wedding. By his *ex-wife*."

"What?" I repeated, aghast.

"So the wedding never happened. All that planning . . . all that money . . . and then boom! It's over."

"What do you mean? They broke up?"

"Not even," she said, hugging herself tightly. "They're living together . . . at the house where it happened."

"What happened? The *murder*?" I breathed, scandalized.

Her head bobbed tightly.

I blinked and shook my head, wondering if it would be too much if I stepped back, hand to my heart, and staggered around a little. I kinda thought Junie-Marie might buy it, though.

"Emmett up and quit a couple weeks ago," she said, pressing her lips together, as if there were more to say but she was scared to let it out. I pretended to be poleaxed. Just couldn't take it all in.

"Poor Emmett," I said. "That's awful."

"It *was* awful."

"Is he doing all right? I mean . . . really?"

"No," she stated flatly. "No, he's not. Emmett and his mom had a real loud fight about his decision. Goldy blamed it on Gigi. She's never liked her much. You know why they were getting married, don't you? She told him she was pregnant. All a big, big lie. Goldy tried to talk him out of it, but Emmett was going to do the right thing by Gigi. Wouldn't listen to anyone."

"He thought she was pregnant and he said he'd marry her." I tried to keep the skepticism out of my voice. There hadn't been a hint of this anywhere, and since it was obvious Gigi was not pregnant, why was Emmett still hanging around if that was the supposed "trap"? Plus, I'd witnessed Gigi's reaction to learning Emmett had quit his job. That sure wasn't her idea. To Junie-Marie, I murmured, "Sounds just like him," keeping up the hero worship.

"Doesn't it?" She fought a last thought toward discretion, looked down for a moment, then shot me an upward glance. There was a neediness in her eyes that made me feel a little guilty. "I probably shouldn't say this . . . since you really like Emmett and all . . . but I was with him before Gigi. We were seriously together, and if it weren't for all her tricks, we'd still be together."

"You and Emmett?" I gazed at her in astonishment.

"Oh, don't worry about it. You couldn't know. I was kind of hoping when the wedding didn't come off that he'd . . . figure it out. You know . . . that he'd get over her." She gave a half laugh. "Goldy didn't think I was good enough, but Gigi, well, she takes the cake. Goldy just hates her. All of a sudden I didn't look like such a bad choice, you know?"

"I didn't know," I murmured.

"Gigi's smart, though. I'll give her that. She saw how to get Emmett for herself, and just went for it."

"You said Emmett was fighting with his mom. Does she work here, too?"

"Goldy's just here a lot." She seemed to realize she'd said far more than she should have. "Still want him?" She half laughed. "You can have him."

She didn't mean a word of it. I pretended to be having trouble absorbing everything. "I can't believe you stayed on after everything," I said in a tone of admiration. "That must be really hard."

"Mike Miller, Emmett's uncle, hired me. That's how I met Emmett in the first place. It's not like I'd lose my job just because Emmett and I broke up."

"But the . . . memories. That's gotta be hard."

"Not really." More lies.

"It would devastate me."

Junie-Marie's mouth twisted. She looked outside, at the rows of colorful cars, but she was tuned into her inner vision. "Gigi came in to buy a convertible. She'd totaled her car and she wanted a Mercedes. Emmett helped her. After that, she came in again, and again. I could tell something was up, but what're you gonna do? You can't fight true love," she said with an edge.

"I'd want to kill her," I said. "And him, too."

"Yeah . . . well . . . she does have money. . . ."

That was it, I thought. Junie-Marie might lie to herself about Gigi trying to trap Emmett, but the truth was he went for the cash and she knew it, whether she wanted to still believe in her prince or not.

"I couldn't compete with that," she admitted. "But I stayed on. I needed a job and this is a good one. I'm sure it bothers her," she added a bit meanly.

Well, until Emmett quit, maybe.

My sales buddy came back inside and saw me standing at Junie-Marie's desk. He stopped short, unsure if I still needed help or not. I rapped my knuckles on the counter and said, "Thanks so much," then scooted toward the back hallway. Junie-Marie looked at me in surprise. "Looking for the loo," I said and hurried away.

I found David Popparockskill's office on my first try. Right past the water fountain. D. POPPAROCKSKILL was etched in a gold nameplate that was held tightly in a slot on the open door. I peered inside. My luck was holding, as he was seated at the desk: a gray-haired man in a gray suit and a gray-and-blue-striped tie. He seemed somewhat shrunken, like the chair was too big for him, and his gaze was out a small back window toward the parking lot beyond, though I suspected he, too, was seeing something in his inner vision.

He looked startled when I rapped on the doorjamb.

"David Popparockskill?"

"Yes, ma'am."

I strode across to him, hand extended. "Jane Kelly. I'm the private investigator who called you. I'm looking into Roland Hatchmere's death."

My direct approach caused him to rear back slightly in his chair. I shook his hand, which was dry and limp, and seated myself in one of the two dark blue club chairs in front of his desk, crossing my legs. I should have worn a skirt, I thought. I might have gotten further as his gaze was on my legs, which were tucked demurely away inside my black pants.

"I thought I made it clear in my message that we have nothing to say to you," he said huffily.

"I understand. I'm just following up. This shouldn't take long."

"I don't see how we can help you."

"Can you give me a timeline? When you and your wife arrived at the wedding? When guests started leaving? That kind of thing?"

"Give me one good reason why I should tell you anything, Ms. Kelly."

"For Gigi's sake. And your son's. Everyone's looking for some kind of closure so they can move on."

It sounded good, even to my own ears. I just couldn't bear to have one more person point out that I was helping Violet, and Violet was the enemy, blah, blah, blah.

He was momentarily stumped on how to get rid of me. But assistance came in the shape of one tall, very wide woman in a loose red dress that showed off way more decolletage than I wanted to see. Her breasts were huge, twin beach balls thrust my way, and there was something about her demeanor that made me realize she was proud of their size. I wondered if I should point out that they were losing both to gravity and in the race with her waistline to finish first.

"Goldy, this is Jane Kelly," David said quickly, scuttling around his desk. She might be in a dress, but it was clear who wore the pants in the family. "She's the private detective looking into Roland's death. The one who called us?"

Goldy gave me an assessing look, her mouth turning up slightly, forming a funny, little U. Her hair was a rather well-cut pageboy, her nails manicured a matching bloodred to her dress. The blue of her eyes was glacial.

"Are you good at interpreting clues, Ms. Kelly?" she asked, still smiling.

"Well . . ." I said cautiously, wondering where this was going. "I try my best."

"Maybe your best isn't good enough." Her chiding tone

said I was missing something big. I waited, figuring she was dying to make her point and this windup was just foreplay to the main event. She came through with flying colors. "We told you we didn't have anything to say to you, but you didn't pay any attention. Perhaps you would do better in some other profession." She practically *tsk, tsk, tsked* with her tongue.

We stared each other down. I had a sudden blast of insight on why Emmett might have quit his job. Good old Uncle Mike, and David and Goliath, and Junie-Marie . . . Emmett might have chosen Gigi for her family money, but there might be other reasons as well, like that he saw her as a means to leave the familial minefield of Miller-Kennedy Mercedes. Even Goldy, who didn't have a job here, appeared to haunt the dealership like a nagging ghost.

"You know, Dave and I were just talking," I said chattily, throwing "Dave" a conspiratorial wink. "He already told me you had *nothing* to offer. So I guess we're good."

Goldy's head turned as if it were on a ratchet. She fixed her husband with a blank look that I guessed would become a laser beam of evil intent as soon as I was out of range. Okay, it was kind of mean of me to throw David to the wolves like that. I had a feeling she'd be making his life a living hell for a very long time. But they just kind of pissed me off, y'know?

After that neither of them had anything to say to me, which I guess I kind of asked for. Maybe Roland didn't like them for the reason that they were, well, unlikable. The funny thing was, David was probably right: they had nothing to tell me. I would be much better off interviewing Emmett again, if I wanted to know anything further about the Popparockskills.

I nearly ran over Junie-Marie on my way out as she was coming down the hall toward David's office while I was zooming in her direction. She looked stricken that I'd been talking to dearest Emmett's parents. "Our secret," I mouthed to her on the way out.

She gazed after me in consternation.

I got to meet Uncle Mike on my way out. We did one of those little dances in the doorway where both of us moved one way, then the other. He took the opportunity to thrust out his hand and introduce himself as Mike Miller in a booming voice. "You looking for a car, you came to the right place!"

I murmured something to escape by. I could see the shape of Emmett's head in his, and the eyes were the same. Mike had a few extra pounds on him, but he looked more like his nephew than David did. I saw that if Goldy shed some weight, Emmett would resemble her more closely, too. He took after the Millers, which might be a good thing.

My cell phone rang on my way to the car. "Jane Kelly," I said, feeling oddly empowered. It had been a day of fighting snotty power trippers.

"Is now a good time to talk?" Deenie asked in a martyred tone.

"Now's a perfect time," I told her, looking forward to crossing her name off my list. "I'm putting together a time-line. If you could give me what events you attended, when you arrived, when you left . . . just any information about the wedding and the wedding week . . . I'll add it to what everyone else said. Maybe something will come to light."

"Shit," Deenie breathed. "He's beeping in. I'm going to have to call you back." And she was gone.

CHAPTER SIXTEEN

I called Gigi on the way home, realizing I didn't have a number for Emmett. She answered reluctantly. Whereas I'd lied my ass off with Junie-Marie, I hit Gigi with the point of my call before she could think of a reason to hang up on me. "I spoke with Dr. Daniel Wu, who said Roland was angry that you'd cleaned out one of your accounts to invest in some investment opportunity that Emmett suggested."

She inhaled sharply. "Daddy was way over that! He knew it was a good investment!"

"What was the investment?"

"It's none of your business." When I didn't bite, she said, "Fine. It's a golf shop. You know, that sells golf stuff? Clubs and clothes and things. That's why Emmett quit his job. He's going to work there. It's just kind of getting off the ground, so it's going to be a while, but Daddy knew it was a great deal."

I thought of the failure rate of most small businesses and wondered. But at least it sounded like the truth. "Where is this golf shop?"

"On the other side of the river. Near Willamette Crest. Emmett's a member there," she said with a touch of pride.

"Okay."

"Okay? That's all you've got to say?"

"Okay, Gigi."

"You know, it really hurts my feelings that Daniel could talk about me that way. He's like an uncle to me. My daddy's gone and that's what he tells you? He's *lucky* Daddy allowed him into a partnership at all!"

Since Roland needed a licensed plastic surgeon to get his clinics off the ground, I felt this was a serious stretching of the truth. I didn't say it, though. My good angel seemed to have control of my tongue for the moment.

I called Dwayne next and filled him in on everything that had transpired since I'd spoken to him in the morning. Neither of us brought up Keegan Lendenhal again. I think he was hoping I'd forgotten about going after him myself, and I didn't feel like having the argument. Beyond that, our conversation was a little awkward. I swear, the more I try to keep things on a friendship level between us, the more screwed up everything feels.

One of these days maybe I'll just give in. Why fight it? It's not doing me any good.

We said good-bye and I amused myself by trying out a couple of seduction scenarios in my mind, just for fun. I saw myself entering Dwayne's cabana and demanding he strip off his clothes and lie down on a bearskin rug. Wait. No. He doesn't have one of those. Besides, they're too furry.

Scenario two: I enter Dwayne's cabana and *I* strip off *my* clothes and lie down on . . . not the sofa. That's my workstation.

I blanked. There is nowhere to lie down in Dwayne's cabana unless I wanted to stretch out on the hardwood floor.

Scenario three: we're at my cottage and we go to the bedroom except . . . that . . . it's not going to *be my cottage much longer.*

"Shit," I muttered. What does it say about me that I can't even project a quality fantasy?

I put a call in to the Crock and asked for Megan Adair. After I was put on hold for an eternity, I hung up in disgust. I tried Sean's cell a couple more times and finally gave up and drove to the nightclub around ten. Sean's band was listed on a chalkboard propped against the building, so in that I guess I was lucky. I hoped he was there early.

The same bouncer checked my ID and made me fork over five dollars even though I had a two-hour wait till the band got going. He didn't intimidate me as much as last time, but then I didn't mess with him, either. There's only so much energy allotted for dealing with difficult people in any one day and I was feeling way past tired and cranky. It seemed grossly unfair that Sean was keeping me from my bed.

I went from being irked to worrying he wasn't around as I entered the urban, metallic scene and settled for a table against the wall. None of the seats near the stage were in use. The stage was dark, in fact. Not the faintest stirring of activity or glint of lighting. So, where was this band?

I looked around for Megan Adair. She wasn't immediately visible, so I settled for a barmaid whose hair was clipped in a short, mannish cut. She had huge eyes she'd ringed in black and a nose ring large enough to draw my eye and not let go.

"Is the band here?" I asked.

"They don't come on till midnight," she said tonelessly.

"I'm actually meeting one of the members. Sean Hatchmere."

"Don't know him. You want a drink?"

"How about a mercury?"

She left to fill the order and I was glad to be away from her mesmerizing jewelry. Sheesh. I can think of all kinds of nasty things a body produces inside the nasal cavity that could crust on that ring. I had to stop myself from an all-over body shiver.

I sat around for nearly an hour, nursing my drink, and was about to go ask more questions when Sean himself shuffled across the stage. The guy with the gray ponytail was hot on his heels and started barking orders at him. It was like a play in itself.

"Sean!" I yelled as he disappeared toward the back, but he didn't seem to hear. After a moment, I called on my last reserves of energy and hopped onto the stage, sauntering after him as if I owned the place. No one stopped me.

I nearly smacked into him when Sean suddenly turned back around one of the black, cardboardy walls in my direction. "Sorry," he mumbled, trying to scoot around me.

"Sean, it's me. Jane Kelly. I was here a couple of weeks ago, talking to you about your dad."

"God," Sean said, focusing on me with an effort. "You and the police."

"The police?"

"Why don't you all just leave us alone? I didn't want him dead. Gigi's right. Violet killed him. We didn't do it!"

He turned on his heel and headed toward the greenroom. I chased after him. His shoulder bumped into a tall stepladder, but he glanced off it as if he didn't feel pain. I steadied the ladder with my hand, looking up to be sure somebody wasn't going to fall off and squash me where I stood. When I was convinced it was safe, I followed Sean into the greenroom where he was slopped onto a stool. Like I'd done to the ladder, I put a hand on his shoulder to steady him. I wasn't convinced he wouldn't slide to the floor in a pool. "You okay?"

"We didn't do it. We didn't fucking kill him," he mumbled.

"The police talked to you about your father's death?"

He pulled himself together with an effort and looked accusingly at my hand. I drew it back. "You sent that detective here. I talked to Gigi. We know what you're doing."

"You mean Detective Larrabee?"

"Friend of yours?" Sean sneered.

It had been a long day and I'd had all I wanted to take of Sean's and Gigi's continued selfishness. "Your father didn't have time to disinherit both of you, but he was planning on it. Pretty good motive for murder, if you ask me."

"You told the police *that*?"

"They obviously figured it out on their own. That's what they do."

"What are you so pissed about?"

"I don't know. You and Gigi. Neither of you gave a damn about your father. He wanted you to stay clean and you're obviously on something right now."

"Just dope."

"Whatever. You get nearly half your father's estate and you're still using. Somebody killed your father and it wasn't Violet."

"How do you know? It must've been."

"The police don't think so."

"You really think I would kill my father?" Sean said, looking up at me with a hopeless expression.

"I don't know. I don't think you'd go out of your way to save him."

"Man, that's cold," he said with a doleful shake of his head.

I left him on the stool, his shoulders hunched forward, his feet planted in a way to keep him from turning into a puddle. Mr. Ponytail appeared and gazed at him in annoyance. Honestly, I didn't believe Sean had the stomach and conviction to physically hurt anyone, let alone kill them. He was just pathetic. A do-nothing. A disappointment to his father.

Fight or no fight, I didn't believe Sean had plotted his father's death over fear of losing his inheritance.

Saturday morning the sun actually made an appearance. I opened an eye to see it outlining the edges of my closed blinds. I climbed from bed and flipped the blinds open, earning bright stripes of light across my bed. Binkster opened her eyes, but that was the extent of her morning greeting.

"You can't sleep with me every night," I told her.

I checked my cereal supply, though I don't know why. I hadn't purchased any from the store during my last trip, and it hadn't magically appeared. There was a rolled-up silvery pack of some cereal-like stuff, opened eons earlier, and now sporting a large chip-clip to keep it "fresh." I took off the clip and poured some into my palm. Oats, bran, indiscriminate grain-type stuff and raisins.

I thought about Dwayne. It felt imperative, for some reason, that I decide what to do about him. Maybe I should have a wild affair with Vince Larrabee. That would end things with Dwayne once and for all, I was pretty sure. Of course, it also meant compliance on Larrabee's part, and I wasn't convinced the man was all that enamored with me as a possible love interest.

I also wasn't interested in completely tearing apart my relationship with Dwayne.

"Ah, the vagaries of love," I said, tossing back my handful of granolish.

Sawdust never tasted so good.

A noise sounded from outside the cottage. A kind of thud. Binkster, who'd roused herself upon hearing I was digging through the cupboards, suddenly went on alert, growling and yipping, the hair standing on the back of her neck.

"What's bark-worthy?" I asked her as I walked across the

living room and peered out my front blinds. I made out the pile of "treasures" being placed on my driveway, all around my car. Ogilvy was hard at work at his garage sale.

"Hey!" I yelled as I unlatched the front door. Before I tore out, I turned to Binkster, who was trying to squeeze past me. "You stay," I told her sternly. She'd been injured running out the front door and into an approaching car. Now, she sat down on her rump, but it was difficult for her. Her muscles were rippling and her gaze darted past me, the growling intensifying.

I shut the door on her and marched across to Ogilvy's pile of garage sales items. "You can't set up here. I rent this place. I have rights."

"You don't rent the garage," he responded, looking at me as if I were just trying to be difficult.

"My car's been parked in this driveway for years. I'd guess I'm renting that, too."

"You gonna stop me?"

"I'm sure as hell gonna give it the old college try."

He thought that over. "You buy this place, you're gonna want the garage emptied."

I slid my jaw to one side, holding on to my temper. "You haven't accepted the other offer?"

"Nope."

I gazed toward the garage. Why was I fighting him? What possible good would it do? I wasn't going to buy the place, but somebody would. A battle with Ogilvy wasn't going to change the inevitable.

"I need to move my car," I muttered, slamming back into the house for my keys. Binkster tagged after me, trying to assess my mood, which was dark, dark, dark. The sun had come out this morning and that was the only good thing about it.

I pulled the Volvo onto the shoulder of West Bay Road, near the end of my driveway, and hoped someone wouldn't come burning around the corner and rear-end me. Maybe no one would come to Ogilvy's sale and I would be spared.

No. Such. Luck.

By 10:00 a.m. the place was swarming with bargain hunters. I sat in my living room and watched women, men and families purchase items of all shapes, sizes and worthlessness. Ogilvy kept filling in with more treasures while people kept heading into the garage and appearing with yet more items, thrilled with their purchases. I watched the Fisher-Price people go by in the clutched fists of a three-year-old girl and her toddling younger brother.

Dwayne called. "Just talked to Larrabee. He got that member list from the Columbia Millionaires' Club."

"Yeah?"

"You might recognize one of the names. Michael Miller."

That dragged my attention from the wandering crowds outside. "You mean, Mike Miller of Miller-Kennedy Mercedes? As in, Emmett's uncle? That Michael Miller?"

"One and the same."

"I'd sure like to talk to Emmett alone, without Gigi around. Daniel Wu said Roland didn't think much of the whole family. Maybe that included the uncle?"

"You've got a perfect opportunity," Dwayne drawled.

"Why's that?"

"It's Saturday morning. If I were looking for Emmett, I'd try Willamette Crest Country Club."

"I'm on my way."

I dressed in my black slacks and leather jacket again and drove toward Willamette Crest Country Club, taking the Sellwood Bridge across the Willamette River. The private golf course meandered along the river and was reputed to be one of the nicest in the state. I turned at the sign, wondering how old the oak trees were that lined the winding drive. There were quite a few cars in the parking lot. Expensive cars. The slightest hint of better weather and the golfers came out in droves.

I smiled at the employees who were about the business office and large foyer. They smiled back. They didn't know me, but I was dressed the part, so I sailed right in.

I walked directly to the dining room and traded more smiles with a young woman at a podium. "Emmett Popparockskill?" I said, on a question.

She glanced down at her reservations. "Mr. Popparockskill canceled his reservation," she said in a worried voice, darting me a look.

I looked stricken. "Oh . . . I wonder if he left a message on my phone. . . ." I pulled out my cell phone and stared at the lighted screen.

"I'm sorry. Cell phones aren't allowed inside the club."

I shot her a look of despair. I was *really* going to have to work on those tears. I could tell she felt terrible for me. "We had a golf date," I pressed. "I couldn't make it and he knew that, but . . . I guess we got our wires crossed."

"He might be at the remodel," she offered hopefully.

"The golf shop," I said, as if I'd been hit with a bong. "Maybe he thought lunch was off, too. It's just down the street . . . ?" I waved a hand vaguely to indicate "somewhere else."

"Down the drive and take a left. You can't miss it. It's in that cute, new little center with the bell tower."

"Of course. I'll catch him there. Thanks."

I'd seen the bell tower strip center when I'd driven past. Now I found it without difficulty and, as there was only one business in the throes of a remodel, I assumed it was the golf shop. I parked the Volvo and walked toward the open door. Inside I could see sheet-rocked walls which were being changed from a vanilla shade to forest green. Cans of paint sat on a dropcloth that was splattered with a rainbow of colors. Emmett was surveying the area as I approached. The whole place was a narrow rectangle. Plans were laid out on the floor and I could see where a counter would be built and a store room across the back.

Emmett glanced at me and frowned. "What are you doing here?" Then, "I talked to my mother," he said, almost like a warning.

"She's a pleasant person," I responded.

"And Gigi told me you saw Daniel Wu," he swept on. "Sounds like you're just trying to stir up trouble."

"Until I'm off the case, I'll keep looking into Roland's death."

"I know Wu told you Gigi and her dad weren't getting along because of this investment. Well, that's an out-and-out lie. Did you ask him about the clinics? He got a huge chunk of Roland's business. I don't know why he's bad-mouthing Gigi and Sean."

"Dr. Wu is the clinics' main plastic surgeon," I pointed out. It seemed to me the Hatchmere clan kept conveniently forgetting that rather salient point.

"He always acted like he liked Gigi and Sean. I guess true colors show when there's money involved."

"How did you get along with Roland?"

Emmett gave me a hard look. "Did Wu say something about me, too?"

"He said Roland didn't get along with your family."

"Well, that's just not true. Roland and I were good friends. We knew each other before I even met Gigi." He started to say something else, then changed to, "He might have thought my parents were . . . not at his economic level."

"Roland had won and lost a couple of fortunes. Are you saying he was a snob?"

"God, no. He was just pathological about being 'taken'. Uncle Mike said something negative about my father that Roland never forgot, even though it wasn't true, strictly speaking."

Strictly speaking . . . "What was it?"

"Just a throwaway comment. Something about Dad living off him. Uncle Mike didn't mean it, but I don't think Roland ever saw it that way. I always kind of felt like I had to make excuses for my parents."

"Roland knew your uncle?"

"They met a couple of times." Emmett turned away from me, bending down to check a pallet of tile that seemed to suddenly need serious attention.

"At CMC? The Columbia Millionaires' Club?"

Emmett jerked as if he'd touched a hot wire. He didn't immediately answer. I got the impression lightning thoughts were sizzling across his brain. He opened his mouth and shut it. I waited, but he opted for silence.

I said, "Someone called Roland from CMC's business office the day of the wedding. Afterward, Roland was upset and that's when he and Violet got in a fight. I thought maybe your uncle called him."

"No."

"You sound pretty sure."

"What the hell do you want?" he suddenly snapped, his face darkening to a brick red. "Why are you asking about Uncle Mike? He's got nothing to do with this!"

"Maybe it was someone else from the club," I allowed. "But what makes you so certain it wasn't your uncle? Is there some specific reason?"

"No."

"So if I talk to him, he'll confirm that?"

"Yes."

"Okay." I glanced at my watch. "Then, I guess I'll head on back down to Miller-Kennedy and ask him myself."

I made as if to leave and Emmett practically raced me to the door. His hand thrust out, blocking my way. I gave him a sidelong look.

"My uncle's a family man. He loves his wife. Would never cheat on her."

"That's kind of what the club's all about, isn't it? Meeting other women?"

"He doesn't belong to it."

"According to the club's records, he does."

"My uncle's not the member. I am." Emmett's expression grew serious. "I used my uncle's name and credit report to join. I wasn't a millionaire, but he was. I told the members I went by my middle name, Emmett."

"When was this?" I asked, trying to fit this into the puzzle.

"A few years ago. I was involved with my ex-girlfriend, and it wasn't working."

"Junie-Marie."

"Oh, you met her," he said, nodding. "She got the job at the dealership and just took over my life. I joined the club and told her I was at meetings. I went to some of the parties, just to get away, y'know? I met Roland through the club."

"But you met Gigi through work?"

"Roland told me his daughter was going to buy a car. He sent her to the dealership."

"So, you're Michael Miller at CMC? Your uncle must know."

"I had the club paperwork sent to my home address. It wasn't that big of a deception."

"So, he doesn't know."

"He found out a couple of weeks ago," Emmett admitted after a moment.

I thought about it. "And that's why you quit . . ."

"More or less," Emmett said with a grimace. "Anyway, I didn't call Roland from the club that day and neither did my uncle."

I absorbed this news. "Do you know anyone else from the club who was a friend of Roland's?"

"Neither one of us has really been around the club much lately."

"Did you meet Roland before he was married to Melinda? She said he basically quit the club when they got married." I thought about Daniel Wu's cryptic comment about Violet being "one of them", meaning women Roland was seeing, and asked on sudden inspiration, "Had Roland started going again?"

"I don't know. I'm really not in that loop."

"How did your uncle find out you were using his name?"

"I don't know that, either. He just called me into his office and asked me how come he was a member of a club he'd never joined."

It sounded to me like someone from CMC had figured out Emmett was impersonating his uncle and had made it a point to alert Mike Miller. "Was there anyone at the club that Roland didn't like?"

"Oh. Sure. Dante."

"Dante who?"

"Just Dante."

"What's Dante's story?"

"He's got a bunch of businesses and the women like him, but the men avoid him. I talked to him once, but he wasn't interested in anything I had to say. He just kept talking about the girl he was with. Wanted to know what I thought of her."

"What did you think of her?"

Emmett glanced out the window at an approaching beat-up blue truck with ladders strapped across the top. The painters were returning. "I was more interested in *not* being with Junie-Marie than being with someone else. She seemed okay. A little hard, maybe."

I couldn't think of anything more to ask him. He hadn't given me the answers I'd expected, but I sensed what he'd told me was the truth.

My upcoming trip to the Columbia Millionaires' Club was getting more interesting by the minute.

Violet was on her way with sandwiches from Dottie's. When I got back I found the garage sale was still in full swing. I kept a sharp eye on the customers as I waited for Violet to arrive. I couldn't escape the fear that hordes of wild-eyed bargain hunters would descend on my cottage and clean out my personal belongings like a swarm of locusts.

"What's going on?" Violet asked as she breezed through my door and dropped the sandwiches on the counter.

"Don't ask," I said wearily. I debated on whether to bring her up to speed about Emmett. She was paying Durbin Investigations to clear her name, but I felt no compunction to blab everything I learned to her whenever I learned it. Sometimes it's good to let things percolate. Until I had time to assess what I'd learned from Emmett, I decided to stay mum.

I pulled out a couple of plates and helped Violet serve up the food. Binkster danced and danced at this activity. She even propped herself against Violet's knee, but neither of us fell for her tricks. Well, apart from some crust-nibbles. And a small piece of cheese. Or two. It's probably a good thing I rarely have food around my house, or Binkster would spend most of her time in a food coma.

Violet dusted crumbs from her palms onto her plate. She looked great in a long, dark green corduroy skirt and a white top that hugged her curves just enough to make her seem young without trying for "too young." Her blond, shoulder-length hair curved in at her chin. Her makeup appeared light and fresh. She was damn near twenty years older than I was and yet I felt like the ugly stepsister.

She must have thought much the same thing because she gazed at me critically, her blue eyes scouring me from head to toe, and then she said, "Come on. We've got work to do."

"Now?"

"I'm going to put you together, then you can touch up tonight."

I trudged to my bathroom like a prisoner to the proverbial firing squad while Violet dragged in one of my kitchen chairs. She plopped me down, plugged in my hot curler and started digging through her extensive makeup kit. I viewed the hot curler with a jaundiced eye. Not so long ago the damn thing had left a mark on my neck that caused me no end of grief. Operator error. I'd touched the wand to my skin and in that brief moment cooked myself but good, leaving a burn that everyone seemed to think was a hickey. Like, oh, sure. My life's that interesting.

Binkster sat in the doorway, watching us, wondering if there was food involved somehow. I stayed quiet, letting Violet work on me, and she remarked on how surprised she was by my passivity. "I thought you'd fight and bellow and generally raise a ruckus," she said, wrapping a tress of my brown hair around the hot curler. I tensed up as the thing got close to my skin, but Violet was deft with all things cosmetic.

"Yeah . . . well . . ."

"I'm so glad to be doing something positive," she said. "Roland's only been gone a few weeks, barely over a month, and it feels like forever. I've had this weight hanging over me, and it's been no fun. I didn't kill him. I think, well, it seems anyway, that the police know that?"

"I'm not sure what they think." Violet seemed happy enough at the moment, and I'd already decided not to give her specifics unless she absolutely forced me to bring her up to date. Curiously, she seemed to like to keep her head in the sand.

"Anyway, it's past time I got out and did something."

"So, back to the escort and/or dating service arena."

"Try it. You'll like it."

"You, Roland and Melinda seem to live by it," I remarked. "And Renee."

"You know what I predict? I predict you meet a really great wealthy guy tonight who'll make you fish or cut bait with Dwayne."

"How many times do I have to say it? Dwayne and I are merely business part—Ouch!" I reached up to where she'd pulled on my hair, practically yanking it from my scalp.

"Sorry," Violet said with a smile.

Violet was given the address to the night's floating party by e-mail. The super, secret way they worked made it seem like we were meeting for a sex party, but as the evening progressed it became clear this was merely someone's idea of how to make it all more *fun*! and *exciting*!

Tonight's destination was a home on the east side, one of those large, rambling houses that seems to push right to the edge of its lot. Maple trees flanked the walkway and modern outdoor lighting left little pools of illumination marching toward the porch. We'd driven ourselves in Violet's Mercedes, but there were limos sliding along and waiting nearby.

I called Dwayne as we walked toward the front door. When he answered, I said in a low voice, "Operative Kellogg about to enter hostile environment."

"Be careful," he said.

Was it my imagination or had Dwayne started worrying about me a little more? I wasn't certain whether this was a positive development business-wise, but it made my romantic heart skip a proverbial beat.

"You missed some action with Tab A and Slot B last night," he informed me. "They bought a new saltwater fish tank. Lots of backlighting."

"Sorry I missed that." I took the plunge and asked, "Anything new at Do Not Enter?"

"All quiet last night. Our friend's probably waiting for your call."

"He's going to have to wait."

"Good."

There was a lot left unsaid. I sensed he would have liked to forbid me from going back to Do Not Enter, but there was no way to do that without redefining our relationship.

"Operative Kellogg would like to know if you have any particular advice on this mission," I said lightly, into the loaded moment.

"Get in. Get out. Come back alive."

"Roger."

"And don't take unnecessary risks," he added quickly, as if he couldn't help himself.

"Keep this up, and I might think you actually care about me."

"Stranger things have happened."

"What's Do Not Enter?" Violet asked curiously as I hung up. "And wipe that smile off your face. Can't be thinking about one man when you're meeting another."

"I'm not smiling."

She snorted.

The house had oriel windows bowing out on either side of a massive front door. As we entered I looked out one of them, toward the front yard. I could see the glow from the mushroom-shaped ground lights lining the walk. Inside, the place had been redone in tones of tan, brown and gold with touches of bright orange in the scattered silk pillows, candles and lampshades. A huge fireplace, flames licking and fluttering around a large chunk of oak, was the gathering point.

The interior was grander than I'd first thought, with a full floor above that hid the bedrooms. I was amazed at how crowded it was. Lots of people attended these parties apparently. The women were all lavishly dressed and draped in jewelry. The amethyst gown and pushup bra I'd strapped myself into helped me look like I belonged. I watched Violet get handed a discreet guest book from a serious-faced young man in a tuxedo. Most of the male members wore tuxes as well. It was not an event for "casual chic."

Violet signed us in and we squeezed through the throng, past a rather sweeping staircase with a carved mahogany rail to a larger room that ran along the back of the house. Who were the people who owned houses like this one? It had been opulent when it was built, it was restored to even greater opulence now. I examined the light fixtures and determined they were either the originals brought back to former luster, or amazing replicas. Probably originals.

"Come on," Violet said, squeezing my arm. She threaded her way to a group of older gentlemen who seemed more interested in talking with each other than actually meeting any eligible women.

But Violet was in her element. She caught the eye of one of the men who looked to be somewhere in his sixties. I marveled silently as they were drawn to each other like magnets.

"Who is she?" a guy closer to my age asked at my elbow. "George never stops talking about the stock market."

"George . . . ?"

"Tertian. The club's president. Hi, I'm Martin," he said, sticking out his hand. He was a geek's geek, his tie askew, his Adam's apple jumping up and down.

"Veronica Kellogg."

"Could I get you a drink, Ms. Kellogg?"

"That would be great. A glass of Chardonnay?"

"I'll be right back," he said eagerly, hurrying off to do my bidding.

Martin, at least, seemed harmless enough. I wondered how he'd made his million, or if he'd lied like Emmett. I had a belated moment of worry when I thought about how Keegan Lendenhal had doctored the beers, so I followed after

Martin into another room where a bartending staff was mixing up drinks. One bartender opened a bottle of white wine in my sight and poured a glass for Martin, who turned back my way. I scooted around to where we'd been standing, scolding myself for being paranoid. This was no teen party presided over by an egomaniac demigod.

Martin brought me my drink and I learned he was twenty-nine and into computers. I flat out asked him if that was how he'd made his million. "Millions," he corrected, flushing. "No, actually, I inherited from my father and grandfather."

"Ah, the old fashioned way."

"You're funny," he said admiringly.

"Yeah . . ."

We had next to nothing to talk about, so I pretended a fascination with computers and let him ramble on for a while. I hated to be one of "those people", the ones who talk to you but keep their eyes on the door, but I confess that's exactly what I was doing. Martin didn't seem to mind.

I broke in once to ask him how long he'd been a member and he shocked me by answering, "Four years."

"Did you ever meet Roland Hatchmere?" I asked curiously.

"You know Roland?"

"I know his daughter Gigi and I know Emmett."

"Emmett Miller," he said, nodding. "That was sure a story about Roland, though, wasn't it? The murder. On his daughter's wedding day."

He didn't seem to know that Emmett was the groom and I didn't confuse the issue with facts. "It sure was," I agreed. "I heard someone called Roland from the club's business office right before he was killed. How's that for weird?"

Martin frowned. "Who?"

I shrugged. "Don't know. I just heard about it."

"Well, maybe," Martin said skeptically. "But he'd just started coming to some parties again. He quit after he got married. Nobody saw him till last summer. He came once or twice. I think he was at the pool party. Maybe not."

"Last summer . . . was he with anybody?" I asked casually.

"How come you want to know so much about Roland?"

He sounded more curious than suspicious, so I said, "I know his wife, Melinda. She thinks he was killed by one of his ex-wives. I was just wondering if maybe he brought her here."

"The only woman I saw him with was Tamara."

"Who?"

Martin glanced around. "She's here somewhere. She was working on Roland pretty hard, but I think he wasn't over his wife. You can tell Melinda that. It might make her feel better."

"You know Melinda?"

"Only from Roland's conversation."

The conversation stalled after that. I mentioned Dante's name and Martin's face filled with consternation. Clearly he didn't think much of the man, either, though he was too polite to say so.

Martin moved in closer to me, taking up more personal space than I cared to give. I sensed if I didn't ditch him soon he would be stuck to me like a burr for the rest of the evening. Glancing around, I saw Violet and George Tertian yucking it up. He was laughing and laughing, his face bright red. I hoped he wasn't going to have a coronary.

Martin said, "Maybe I'm reading more into this than I should, but just so you know . . ." He hesitated, glancing toward the stairs, uncomfortable but hopeful. I hated to shoot him down but it looked like that's where this was heading. "We could move to a private room? I could order champagne, or more Chardonnay?"

"Well, you know, that sounds . . . interesting. But right now I need the ladies' room."

"We don't have to," he said quickly, sensing he was losing me.

I extricated myself with an effort, heading up the stairs. The nearest bathroom had been temporarily designated: Women. I opened the door and was met with an attractive blonde in a shimmery gold dress who was applying lipstick in front of the mirror. I went into the stall and when I exited, she was still involved in application, rimming her lips in a frosty pink color, over and over. I watched her in the mirror as I washed my hands, wondering what the hell she was on.

Two women rushed in, talking and laughing, waiting for each other outside the stall. Then Violet stuck her head inside the door and waved at me to come her way. "Jane. Come here!"

I followed her back into the hall. "It's Ronnie, remember?"

"The man I'm with is George Tertian. He's the club president. He's practically offered me a hostess job, right here at the club!" Her eyes sparkled. "My God. I guess you can't fight fate. This is what I'm good at."

"Well, that's great. What does the hostess job entail?"

"Who cares. I can't tell you how freeing this is. George knew Roland well, so I had to come clean about who I am. It's okay, though."

"Are you sure?" I asked dubiously.

"Absolutely."

Violet tore back to George and I returned to the bathroom, digging through my beaded bag for my own tube of lipstick. The blonde woman was still at the mirror, but the other two were drying their hands and chatting. As soon as they were gone, my blonde friend stopped rimming her mouth but she seemed frozen and dull.

I couldn't find my lipstick. I cursed my failure at all things girl, met the eyes of the blonde in the mirror, had to settle for touching at my eye makeup with the end of my pinkie, examining the nonexistent results. "You okay?" I asked her.

"Yes . . ."

"You don't seem okay. You want me to let someone know you're in here?"

"No," she said abruptly, glancing past me to the door.

Her sudden panic made me look over my shoulder. "All right," I said, wondering what the hell was up with her.

She focused on me, as if for the first time. "Your name's Jane? You're new here."

Thank you, Violet. I could hardly pretend to be Veronica now. "This is my first time."

"Have you met anyone interesting?"

She was about as full of life as a bag of bricks, but she seemed keyed in on whatever my response would be. "Martin brought me a glass of wine."

"Oh . . . good." She seemed to relax. After a moment, she said, "I'm Tamara."

I tried not to react. "Doesn't sound like this is your first time," I said lightly.

"No."

I was in no hurry to join the festivities downstairs again, and apparently neither was she. I asked her how long she'd been coming to these parties and she smiled fleetingly. "Not that long," she said. "But way too long, too. It's not quite what it seems, is it?"

"Meaning?"

"Oh, you know . . ." She desultorily waved a hand. "I was that small-town girl hoping to meet the guy who had it all, looks, wealth, a nice car . . ."

"Where are you from?"

"Down I-5. Ever hear of Brewster Hill?"

I shook my head.

"It's not really a town. It's just a—place. My parents have

an honest-to-goodness farm there. Beaumont Farms. The best produce around. I mean it."

I was trying to figure out how to ask her about Roland. Should I just pop out with questions, kind of like I'd done with Martin?

"I thought I was dying there," Tamara said, turning back to her own reflection, as if she were practicing a monolog. "So, I went out to the big wide world. Then, I went home. Then I went out, and then I went home again."

She sounded totally disheartened and jaded. I started to think her apathy was due more to depression than drugs. "Maybe you just haven't found him yet," I said, since she made this sound like it stemmed from romantic disillusionment.

"Found him?" She flashed me a look, one of her only moments of animation. "The devil's always around, isn't he?"

I wasn't sure if she meant The Devil, as in Mr. Supreme Darkness, or if she were speaking off the cuff. Like the devil's in the details. Or idle hands are the devil's playground.

She went back to applying the lipstick as if she were going to be graded on staying in the lines.

"Are you still living in Brewster Hill?"

"As little as possible." She capped the lipstick with a tiny *snap* and headed toward the door. "Be careful what you wish for, Jane."

CHAPTER SEVENTEEN

I followed her out of the restroom. I hadn't found how to ask her about Roland yet, but she was my best bet for information. Maybe she'd been the one to call him from the club, or maybe she could lead me to who had.

She headed downstairs, her gold dress swirling around her knees. A dark-haired gentleman in his mid- to late-thirties stood at the bottom, but she brushed past him as if she didn't know him. He gave her a casual look, then turned his face toward me.

I had a very real feeling that this was Dante, the man whom women liked but men treated with caution, so I came down the stairs a bit self-consciously. I hoped to hell I didn't stumble in my shoes. This whole thing about looking good and walking with surety and grace requires way too much energy and skill.

Our eyes met. I had the tingling sensation he was viewing me with X-ray vision, sizing me up. Maybe I was making too much of it, but Dwayne had told me to trust my instincts and every instinct I possessed was sending warning signals down my nerves.

I lost Tamara to a good-looking middle-aged man. Her face was turned to his in a coquettish slant. Either she'd managed to throw off her depression or she was doing a whole lot of acting.

I spent another hour mingling. I could feel Martin's eyes on me, but I kept out of his range. I managed to insert Roland's name into a couple of conversations, but I didn't learn anything further, and mention of Dante's name earned me the cold shoulder.

I tried hanging by some of the women, but they seemed to collectively view me as a competitor and studiously ignored me. I was thinking about seeing if I could squeeze a few more drops of information from Martin when a male body came up behind me and grabbed each of my elbows with his hands.

He leaned over me and said, "Jane Kelly."

My heart leapt. I had a slamming image of Keegan Lendenhal. The voice. The attitude. The need for complete power. "Dante," I said, stepping forward out of his grip and turning to face him.

No surprise. It was the man from the bottom of the stairs.

"You know me?"

He hadn't expected that. I didn't like the guy's proximity. He was that kind of cool customer who moves in close and breathes on your hair. It was all I could do not to hold my position.

He regarded me in a penetrating way. I'm never sure what a guy—a stranger—expects when he gazes at you in that way, as if you're something to play with. Like this is fun? Like I was panting for him to toy with me?

"You've been asking about Roland Hatchmere."

Well, at least he cut to the chase. "Were you friends with him?"

"No."

"Did you call him from the club phone?"

"What are you looking for?"

"I'm not completely sure," I admitted honestly.

"You were talking with Tamara."

A shiver whispered over my skin. Although he and Tamara had ignored each other, acted like strangers, at a subliminal level I'd registered something between them. An energy. A scarcely leashed crackle in the air.

"You and Tamara are friends, then."

"We know each other."

I wondered if Dante might be the devil Tamara spoke of. "Did you introduce her to the club?"

"I've introduced a lot of women."

He was telegraphing something to me. Something he wanted me to know. I had a feeling it was Tamara, or one of the other women he'd introduced, whom he'd asked Emmett's opinion of. What was his game?

"Is it just Dante, or do you have a last name?" I asked lightly.

"Just Dante." He smiled faintly. "Like . . . Satan."

"Or Beelzebub."

"You've got a smart mouth."

"Yeah . . . well . . ." I murmured, my smart mouth getting dumber. I can't go with this kind of thing long without wanting to scream something. Like "You're a psychopath!" With an effort, I curbed that impulse, saying instead, "So, how does that happen? How do you get just one name?"

"How did you get an alias?"

I didn't have an answer for that one. He obviously knew about Veronica Kellogg. I wondered how he'd come up with Kelly. Violet had only called me Jane.

"There's a room at the end of the hall. Upstairs. The door's unlocked. For tonight, it's my room."

"Wow. Sounds like a proposition."

"You want to know who made that call? I made that call.

You want to know what was said? Come upstairs and I'll tell you."

I didn't believe him. It was a ruse. Had to be. "Why not tell me now?"

He ran a finger down my cheek. Actually ran a finger down my cheek. I stifled the desire to snap at it like a rabid dog.

"Because I think we could find a lot to talk about. Go on up. I'll meet you there in five minutes." He flicked a look past me. "I have something to take care of first."

I glanced over my shoulder. He could have looked at a number of people, but Tamara was in the midst of the group.

I watched him disappear into another room. After a few moments, Tamara followed. I debated with myself on which action to choose. Go after them, or go upstairs to the bedroom. Upstairs was danger, but I didn't think I would accomplish much by approaching them together.

I headed upstairs, my pulse laborious with dread. It was a bold, probably reckless move. I should have warned Violet. I should have warned someone where I'd be. My steps slowed as I walked down the long hall with doors on either side. The old house was almost like a hotel. I tried every knob as I walked along, but all the doors were locked. If Dante had a room, probably others did as well, and they probably had their keys to give to a willing participant.

I came to the door at the end of the hall. My heart was pounding. What was I doing? He'd followed me, learned what I was after, used the information to lure me upstairs.

Ridiculous.

I snatched my cell out of my purse and pushed Dwayne's number. Cell phone use was a no-no at this event, but to hell with that. Dwayne answered and I said, "I've met Dante. He says he's the one who called Roland. He could be lying, but I don't know. He told me to meet him in his room and so I am."

"Where's his room?"

"In the house. Upstairs. I'm going in now." As I spoke I twisted the knob and let myself inside. I got a glimpse of the cream-colored furnishings. Mostly I saw a large four-poster bed.

"I don't like it."

"I don't much, either," I admitted. "But it's not like he's going to do anything to me at the party."

"Not as long as he thinks you're Veronica Kellogg," Dwayne said.

That shut me up.

"Jane?"

"He knows my name and that I have an alias."

"Get out of there, Jane," he ordered.

Adrenaline shot through me. "But—"

"Get—the hell—out—*now*."

I had mere seconds to get out of the bedroom. Five minutes had already elapsed. There was no escape back the way I'd entered. I stood frozen, my hands useless appendages in front of me, my frantic heartbeats a roaring surf in my ears.

I heard treads in the hallway. Male footsteps.

Three strong strides and I was at the sliding glass door that led to the bedroom balcony. The door opened soundlessly to an itsy-bitsy, terra-cotta-tiled area wrapped by a wrought-iron rail. I looked down two floors. For a dizzying moment I considered jumping, but the patio below was cold, unforgiving stone.

I whirled back to stare across the room. Twelve feet of carpet led toward the bedroom door, the only other exit. From my peripheral vision I caught sight of the maple tree. I glanced over. Too far from the balcony, but just outside the bathroom window.

Quickly, I scurried into the bathroom and threw open the window. One branch was close enough to reach. For an instant I considered climbing down as I was: gowned, bejeweled, wearing the most expensive sandals I ever planned to purchase.

Kicking off the shoes, I threw them out the window. I ripped the zipper of the dress downward, yanked the slinky amethyst dress over my head, sent it flying after the sandals. I tossed my beaded bag after them, hoping my cell phone survived the drop. As I pulled myself through the window, cursing the space that was scarcely large enough for me to wriggle my shoulders through, I heard the suite's door open. A mewling sound entered my throat but I held it back. I reached for the branch, missed, reached again, arms shaking, fingers splayed.

Dwayne's urgency spurred me on: *Get—the hell—out— NOW!*

My fingers connected and I hauled myself out with adrenaline-laced strength. I swung my legs upward to catch the limb with my ankles and hung like a lemur. Then I shimmied toward the tree trunk and carefully eased myself down the bole. I lost swatches of skin. My pulse hammered in my ears. My face was wet with tears.

When my toe hit the ground I drew a breath and glanced upward. He was on the balcony looking down at me. In that strange, heightened moment between quarry and prey, I was very, very glad I stood where I was.

Maybe I was overreacting. I kind of didn't think so.

"Ms. Kellogg?"

Martin's voice came from somewhere to my right, near the front of the house. I stooped to pick up Violet's amethyst gown, shivering, glad she'd talked me into the padded, lacy bra, equally glad I'd held out for bikini underwear rather than a thong.

I smiled at him as he approached, hoping my lips didn't quiver. I could feel the gaze from the man on the balcony boring into the back of my head. I shook out the gown. Stepping into it, I said with forced nonchalance, "Would you mind helping me zip up?"

Twenty minutes later, pacing by Violet's car, frustrated by a cell phone that no longer worked, I started asking myself why I'd been so completely convinced Dwayne was right. Maybe we both suffered overheightened senses from Keegan. Maybe we were too in tune to each other to think clearly.

I wanted to call him and tell him to pick me up. Waiting for Violet could take hours and I was cold, uncomfortable and faintly embarrassed. But I was not going back inside. I was not going to have to explain myself.

Martin had been a little tricky to peel myself from. He had a lot of questions, the top one being about why I was in my underwear. In a moment of inspiration I told him a centipede fell down my neck from the tree. He recoiled as if I'd burned him. Whether he believed me or not, he definitely understood "bug horror." At least it had been enough to get me away from him.

There was nothing around this neighborhood but houses. No shops. No restaurants. No convenience stores. I wasn't sure how far I would have to walk to find a commercial establishment, and I didn't relish the thought of being alone at night anywhere, especially dressed as I was.

I kept checking my cell phone, willing it to turn on. These things should be made to be more indestructible.

I was just about to strike out on my own when Violet finally appeared. She was affectionately saying good-bye to George, who seemed to be walking her to her car. This was not okay. I didn't want to face any CMC member. I didn't know how tied in Dante was, and I didn't want any questions asked.

I walked half a block away while Violet and George canoodled, tucking myself around the bole of the next door neighbor's large fir. Finally, Violet and George came up for air and separated, gazing longingly after one another. Yes, it was pukey, but I hardly had the playbook on romance.

As soon as she was aiming her remote lock, chirping her alarm, I hurried to meet up with her. "There you are," she declared. "What the hell happened to you?"

"Can I use your cell phone? Mine's not working."

"No shit. I just turned mine on. Do you know how many messages Dwayne left? All about you?"

"He's worried about me."

"Why?"

"I'll tell you later." I practically grabbed the thing from her hand. Violet rolled her eyes and got behind the wheel.

Dwayne picked up with a sharp "Violet?"

"It's Jane. My phone broke."

"Jesus. How?"

"Gravity. Violet's driving me home. I'm fine. I took your advice and left when you thought I should."

"Is Violet right there?"

"Close enough. I'll call you when I'm back at my cottage."

I got in the passenger seat. I really wanted to go back to his place. Really, really wanted to. I clenched my teeth, fighting a wave of longing.

"What's wrong?" Violet asked.

"Nothing a lot of straight liquor couldn't cure."

I woke up the next day feeling the pain of every piece of sheared skin. I don't know. Sometimes this job is just really a lot of work.

In the afternoon I drove myself and The Binkster to Dwayne's. Binks ran onto the deck and had a bark-fest with the dog next door until I hauled her inside and the perturbed neighbor did the same with her dog. Across the way Lobo, the Pilarmos' dog, started baying in an eerie, mournful tone as if he were about to morph into an undead being.

"I thought they only turned to werewolves during a full moon," I said. "It's not even night."

Dwayne smiled. I had a diet A&W root beer and Dwayne had a beer as we sat down on the couch together, discussing all aspects of the case.

Dwayne said at length, "So, what do you think? Was Dante telling the truth about calling Roland?"

"I don't know. I left before I could ask."

"I still think it's a good thing you did."

I didn't argue with him. "Dante likes to play with people. He could have been lying, just to have power, to get me to do what he wanted."

"So, who's at the top of your list for the doer?" Dwayne asked.

"Neither Gigi nor Sean. They're both self-involved, but kind of passionless. Gigi may have angered Roland . . . she might even have pushed him into saying he would disinherit her . . . but she was all about that wedding. I'm sorry, she just wouldn't screw it up by having her father killed. And Sean's just too disinterested. Honestly, I think he used the fight he had with Roland as an excuse to skip the rehearsal dinner. No one's even mentioned him at the wedding. I'm sure he was there or Gigi would have had a fit about him being missing, too. Those two o'clock pictures could not be missed."

"I agree," Dwayne said.

"Emmett . . . maybe . . ." I thought it over. "He found the body around three-thirty? Is that too late for the time of death?"

"Violet hit him around noon. Three and a half hours later?" Dwayne was dubious. "I'll check with Larrabee, but I think that's too late. Doesn't mean Emmett couldn't have had him killed earlier," he said.

"He would hire someone rather than do it himself," I said positively. "But what's the motive? Gigi's inheritance?" I shrugged. "Maybe."

"The man had three ex-wives. Any reason any one of them would want him dead?"

"Violet's an ex-wife. The last I heard, you thought she was innocent," I pointed out. Dwayne gave me a smile. "What about Melinda? Violet was with her husband, and she wanted him back. She said if it weren't for Violet, she and Roland would have resolved their differences. And she really wants Violet to go down for this. But then she really wanted Roland. She would be more likely to kill Violet."

"What about Renee? She was disinvited to the wedding by Roland. Sounds like the rehearsal dinner was one big fight."

"Who's at the top of your list?" I posed back at him.

Dwayne stretched, lifting his arms over his head. "There was passion involved. No premeditation."

"The killer didn't bring a weapon," I agreed. "Just used the tray."

"Roland was upset and coming off a fight with Violet. Someone else came to the house, possibly fought with him as well. It escalated. The tray was there. *Bam.*"

"Roland received two phone calls," I said. "One from Sean. One from the Columbia Millionaires' Club."

"Apparently Larrabee went to see Sean." Dwayne's eyes narrowed. "That's the avenue he's pursuing. Not the club. At least not at the moment."

"If it wasn't Dante who called him, then who?"

"None of the women reacted to the mention of Roland's name?"

I shook my head.

"What did the men say? Anything?"

"Mostly what a shame it was to lose such a great guy."

"Did you bring up Emmett?"

"Some. They think his last name is Miller."

"Anything about him? Anything someone said?" Dwayne questioned.

I went back over it again in my mind. "Emmett mentioned that Dante had asked him about a particular woman. Emmett wasn't interested. It's almost like Dante's pushing these women on the men. Like . . ."

"A pimp?"

"Sort of. But then I don't know what the rules are." I'd already told Dwayne about Tamara, but now I added, "I think Tamara was referring to Dante when she said the devil's always there. Maybe she was the one he was pushing on Emmett?"

"Maybe she's worth talking to again."

"I know where her parents live. She acted like she's there some of the time. Either way, I could find her and ask her about Dante."

"It's worth a shot."

I got to my feet. "No time like the present. You mind keeping Binks?"

"You could leave her with me permanently."

"Fat chance," I said and headed for my car.

The town of Brewster Hill was about forty minutes south of Portland. The freeway exit offered nothing other than a truck stop and a faded homemade sign stuck in the ground at the end of the exit ramp that let me know I was ON THE RIGHT ROAD TO BEAUMONT FARMS. Beaumont Farms apparently sold various produce as there were pictures of apples, pears, corn, squash, tomatoes and the like. I followed the signs to a weather-worn white farmhouse, a gray, hulking barn, a number of shorter outbuildings and fields and orchards along a rolling landscape as far as the eye could see.

The sky was a bright, light gray as I pulled to a stop be-

side the farmhouse, and I had to shade my eyes as I got out.
I glanced at the sun, which was a fuzzy bright disc in a bowl
of overcast gray. A man of about fifty-five in mud-splattered
jeans, heavy work boots and a plaid shirt, a semicircle of
white undershirt showing at his throat, walked up to me, a
smile on his face.

"Hullo, there," he said. "We got some pumpkins left, but
winter's comin', ain't she?"

"Are you Mr. Beaumont?" I asked.

"Ron Ernsten," he said, wiping a hand along his pants and
examining it before holding it out to me.

"Jane Kelly." I shook his hand with care. Didn't want to
seem impolite when I was trying to make him my new best
friend, but I had a mental picture of cow pies and general
farm glop. "I met Tamara the other night," I told him. "She
gave me your address."

"Did she?" His face shuttered. "Beaumont's my wife's
family's name. Kept it 'cause it's so well known," he said, as
if I'd asked.

"Is Tamara here?" I asked.

"Oh, she'll be around, I s'pose." He headed toward the
back door and sat on a step, unlacing his boots. When I didn't
move, he gave me a look from the top of his eyes. "You plan-
nin' on waitin' for her?"

"Sure," I said, a little worried on how long that might entail.

"Come on in, then."

I followed him through the back door, wondering if I
should take off my shoes, too. We entered a walk-through
kitchen crowded with boxes of apples, pears and pumpkins.
The cupboards were painted white, worn around the edges
from age, not as some decorator's idea of current style, and
the laminate was chipped and broken out in a six-inch section near the refrigerator, which appeared to have been re-

placed at one time. The cabinets had been roughly re-
designed to make room for the bigger, newer version.

A middle-aged woman, her straight gray hair collected at
her nape with a bejeweled clip, was chopping celery with
abandon, not bothering with a cutting board. There were
thousands of slice marks in the laminate and I imagined a
host of germs congregating within.

She looked up when I entered, a large-bladed knife pausing in midair. "Hello," she said in surprise.

"Janet, this here's Jane Kelly. She's waitin' for Tammie."

"Oh." The knife swooshed down and she hacked away at
the remaining celery spears. She dropped the knife with a
clatter and scooped up the pieces, tossing them in a huge
pot. "You could be waiting awhile," she said dourly.

"That's okay. You're her parents?"

"That's right, honey." Janet pulled up a sack of potatoes
that had been sitting in the sink. "Might as well make yourself useful. Here." She rummaged through a door and found
me a paring knife. "Just leave the peels in the sink. We need
about eight of 'em in the stew. You can wash your hands with
this soap."

I was peeling potatoes before I could say, "I don't know
how to cook." I'm sure it wasn't necessary anyway, as I wasn't
the swiftest at my task. But it did give me something to do. I
concentrated hard, keeping a safe distance from Janet and
her flashing chef's knife.

Ron had gone off to clean up apparently, as he left the two
of us alone in the kitchen. A medium-sized tan spaniel mix
trotted into the kitchen and looked up at us followed by several gray and white cats, meowing and stroking our legs.

"Get lost, Fluffy," Janet said, shaking a cat from her
ankle. Fluffy seemed to take this as a challenge as she
pounced on Janet's foot. The spaniel started barking madly.
Fluffy hissed and got on her hind legs, claws extended. The

other cat sat back in a corner, its tail twitching, watching the ensuing drama.

Janet slammed down her knife and turned to the animals. They all looked at her expectantly and her fierceness evaporated. "They're like children. Well, like children should be. You got any kids?"

I shook my head.

"Tammie's got two. She tell you that? Lost 'em both to their daddies."

"That's a shame," I murmured.

Janet slid me a look. "How do you know her?"

"We met at a club," I said.

"Oh, really?" She sounded as if she were almost sneering. "That escort place? Tammie's been raving about it and raving about it. Like we'd believe anything she said. Is it really a place to meet a millionaire?"

"As I understand it."

She barked out a laugh. "You're as gullible as her!" She shook her head. "Nothing ever changes with our Tammie. It's all lies and cheap sex. You been to the truck stop?" There was a mean glitter in her eye that I couldn't quite fathom.

"On the freeway? I drove by it."

"Drove by it, huh?"

"On my way here."

She tilted her head and eyed me up and down. "You sure don't look like a hooker. This some new male fantasy, or something?" She gestured to my jeans and anorak. "You actually look like you're dressed for the weather."

"I am dressed for the weather."

"Huh." She gave that a long thought. "Tammie owe you money? 'Cause, babe, you came to the wrong place if you think you're gonna collect. My family has property, but we don't have ready cash. Y'hear me?"

"I'm just here as a friend," I said. I was getting an inkling to the roots of Tammie's depression.

"Tammie doesn't have friends," Janet said. "You sure she knows you're coming by?" When I didn't immediately answer, she said, "You'd have better luck at the truck stop. Go on over there and get yourself some apple pie. Those are our apples they use. It's good stuff."

Janet turned her shoulder to me, clearly dismissing me. I silently worked on my fourth potato before setting down my knife. I felt kind of sorry I couldn't finish the task. "If Tammie stops in, will you tell her I was here?"

Janet suddenly put down her own knife, leaned down and grabbed Fluffy, pulling the cat into her arms. Fluffy instantly tried to scratch at her hair clip, but Janet held her tight. Fluffy looked stricken, meowing piteously. Janet closed her eyes. Bitterly, she said to me, "Maybe you should remind her that *we're* here."

The truck stop was unremarkable—a rectangular box with a coffee shop on one end and a store of sorts on the other. I went through the coffee shop door and a little bell overhead announced my entrance. As it was my mission, I sat myself at the counter and ordered the deep-dish apple pie à la mode.

It came on a dinner plate, loaded with soft vanilla ice cream. I'd skipped lunch and my mouth watered at the monstrous portion.

"Wow," I said.

"I know," the young waitress responded, her hands stuffed into the pockets of her apron, her eyes smiling. "It's humongous." She was probably in her mid-twenties and looked ready to give birth yesterday. The apron stretched over her round belly. "My due date's Monday," she alerted me.

"Congratulations."

"It's my third."

"Wow," I said again. "I just learned for the first time that a friend of mine has two children."

"Oh yeah?"

"Tamara Ernsten," I said. "I came down to visit her."

"Oh, Tammie. How do you know Tammie?" Her demeanor grew remarkably cooler.

I pretended not to notice as I dug into the pie. "Oh my God, this is good," I said, feeling a sense of déjà vu. It took me a moment to place it. The Junior League Bake Sale. Jody's apple bars. Melinda's recipe.

"If you're looking for Tammie, you're at the wrong side of the building."

I glanced toward the little store, confused.

"Uh-uh," she said, resting her arms on her belly. She jerked her head in the direction behind her. "The trucks. That's where she'll be. Though, it's a little early for her to get going. Come about ten tonight, you'll see her. She's trying to be all fancy and snooty, but she's a ho."

"Ho?" I repeated, just to clarify.

The girl leaned forward, resting her arms on the counter. I worried for a sec she might try to take my apple pie back, but she was just getting closer because she'd lowered her voice. "You really didn't know she works at the truck stop?"

I shook my head.

"My husband tries to clear 'em off, but the truckers . . ." She waved a hand dismissively. "They aren't complaining. A lot of those cabs have nice sleeping quarters, you know? Somebody like Tammie'll bounce around a couple a night."

"Really?" I said.

"Stick around. See for yourself."

I decided to do just that and so I paid for my dessert, feeling guilty about leaving a pool of melted ice cream and about four uneaten bites, then headed back to the Volvo. It was about seven when I moved it from the front of the building to park around the side, angling the car so I could get a view of the back parking area. There were already some semis jockeyed into position, and as I watched more big rigs began rolling in for the night, rumbling, headlights scouring the asphalt as they turned into their spots. In their illumination, I watched the men climb from the cabs, hitch up their pants, head into the building.

I sank down in my seat, peering through my steering wheel. I waited about an hour, my butt nearly numb, till the truckers started returning to their rigs. It took about another hour, but then women seemed to materialize in the exhaust vapors, some of them under the men's arms as they headed toward the trucks.

A sudden rap on my window shot me up straight. I glanced up into a craggy, male chin. Tentatively, I hit the button to send my window down.

"What you want?" he asked, his face shadowed by a baseball cap.

"I'm a friend of Tammie's . . . ?"

"Tammie ain't here."

"Oh. She told me she would be."

He eyed me carefully. "You'd best go home now."

"She wanted me to meet someone," I said. "Her man, y'know?" I couldn't make myself say "pimp." It sounded so corny, like a caricature word from television.

"If you're meanin' Don, he ain't around, either. You want my advice, little girl? Go on home. You got a nice enough car. What're you doing here anyway? Now, go on."

"Is Don short for Dante?" I asked.

"You're askin' a lot of questions for a friend of Tammie's."

I didn't mistake the quiet threat in his tone. I put the car in gear. He stepped back as I circled around, but he stayed as a sentry, watching my every move.

There was nothing I could do but leave.

CHAPTER EIGHTEEN

"How do you get from truck stop prostitution to the Columbia Millionaires' Club?" Dwayne asked thoughtfully, as he had all week.

"Dante," I answered, as I had all week.

We looked at each other across his kitchen bar. Dwayne was in sweats, T-shirt and jacket. He'd taken to walking/limping around the bay, strengthening his leg; he was chafing to be at full speed.

My head was full of the Hatchmere case, which was fine with Dwayne, since as long as Violet was paying, we were still on the job. He was spending his time on the background check on Chuck's daughter's boyfriend, and he'd mentioned that some other jobs were stirring as well.

I'd driven back to the truck stop a couple of times, using Dwayne's surveillance car, parking in the front and staying out of sight of the truckers as much as possible. Dwayne had even come with me once, and we'd pretended to be a couple just stopping in for dinner. Dwayne had really stressed his limp, which attracted attention and was probably what any casual observer would remember if they wondered who we were. I wore my "disguise"—my glasses and baseball cap—and let my hair fall down the sides of my face. It turned out to be more an exercise in reconnaissance than a means to further our investigation, but I was glad Dwayne was engaged in the activity. I wanted him engaged in the business again, just as much as he did.

The week had passed without much incident. I'd had to go into my cell phone coverage provider and order up a new phone. My old one's trip to the ground had been fatal, apparently. Highway robbery on the part of the cell service company. Of course, they had a billion plans where I could get my new phone *free!!!* if I signed a contract for seventy-five years. A lot of the functions were the same as my old phone, but the few new ones I had to learn sent me into conniptions.

Yes, this is a flaw in my character.

It took me three times before I actually forced myself to wait to be helped, because each time I drove to the store the lines out the door of people needing help made me crazy. It was Thursday before I actually managed to bring myself to face the music, and then I began to seriously wonder if I had rage issues because I wanted to crack heads together over the customers' asinine questions and insane requests. By the time my guy asked how he could help me I'd had to put myself in a mind-zone to keep from going postal.

He showed me a variety of models—all X-tremely fancy, all X-tremely pricey. I finally picked one, pulling out my credit card with reluctance. I'm not one of those people who has to have the newest and the bestest. I just want the most reliable with the least amount of new things to learn.

I waited while he reprogrammed my new phone with my number. I watched him push buttons on the phone, add things into his computer, push some more buttons, go into the back, return and on and on and on. He was pleasant and fast, but it still took up more time than I wanted to spend. I was definitely going to have to be more careful about my phone because I couldn't go through this again *ever*.

My new phone beeped at me while I was driving home. Voice mail message. I wasn't exactly sure how to access it, so I left it for when I could use both hands. Then I forgot about it.

Now, Friday morning, talking to Dwayne, I suddenly remembered. I pulled out the phone and looked at it. "I've got six messages," I said. "Guess they've been stored up."

Dwayne took his coffee cup outside to the dock as I worked my way through the code to access my voicemail. I'd had my old phone set up to just push a button and it would automatically enter my password, but I hadn't waited for the customer service rep to program that feature. I could have been sitting in a corner, thrumming my finger to my lower lip, if I'd had to wait much longer as it was.

"Jane Kelly," Dante's mocking voice said on message one. A little breathier "Jane . . . Kelly . . ." was message two. Message three, four and five were about the same. In message six he told me he was going to see me soon.

I froze, my cell phone to my ear, processing a cold rush of fear that spread through my body. I tried to pick up the phone number, but it was unavailable, which is the way mine should read on someone else's phone. The logical answer was someone had given him my cell number. Someone who knew it.

I glanced outside to Dwayne, my mind racing. It was Friday and I had a date with destiny at Do Not Enter tonight. Dwayne didn't want me to go. I didn't want to go. I had distinct butterflies in my stomach. But Josh Newell and the Lake Chinook police were just a speed-dial away.

Dante . . . or Keegan Lendenhal. Of the two, Keegan was the better option. "Why did I get into this profession?" I asked out loud.

Note to self: learn origami. Consider its instruction as new career option.

"Did you say something?" Dwayne called from the dock. The binoculars were at his eyes again.

Dwayne added, as if we were in the middle of a conversation, "Don—probably Dante—has Tammie working both the truck stop and CMC. He's brought in other women to the parties, too. You didn't get a sense of any of them as being connected to him?"

"No," I said. Again. I walked outside and told Dwayne about Dante's messages.

He dropped the binoculars and looked at me. "You've scared him," he said.

I nodded.

"You're onto something."

"He doesn't want me to talk to Tammie, or ask about Roland, or anything connected to the case and so he's trying to get me to back off."

"I don't like it," Dwayne said.

"You don't like anything that involves danger and me," I pointed out.

"You got that right."

"That kinda defeats the purpose of me working for you."

He couldn't argue with that, so he stared through the binoculars some more. Now that I'd had a little while to think about it, I wasn't as scared as I thought I'd be. "Tomorrow, I'm going back to the truck stop and see if I can meet with Tammie."

"Why not tonight?"

"Do Not Enter calls."

Dwayne made a sound of frustration and yanked his cell phone from his pocket. "Forget that. I'll call your buddy Josh and get him to go after Keegan."

Quickly, I put a hand over his, stopping him. "Give me tonight."

"Jane . . ."

"Dwayne," I responded right back, warning him to quit while he was ahead.

I left before he could talk me out of my plans. I know myself and I was pretty sure a few well-placed words could break my resolve.

I got a burger at a fast food restaurant for dinner, then went home and changed into Glen's oversized Lake Chinook sweatshirt for hopefully the last time. I didn't know how many of Keegan's disciples were actual players, how many turned a blind eye, how many maybe honestly didn't know. I just wanted Keegan.

On my way to Do Not Enter, I called Dwayne to let him know, and he cut me off to warn, "If I don't hear from you by eleven-thirty, I'm calling the police."

"Midnight," I argued, glancing at my watch. "It's an away game. They've got to get there."

"I don't like it, Jane."

"This, I know."

"You don't have to do this."

"I know."

I hung up.

On Beachlake I passed by all the houses Dwayne had been watching: Tab A/Slot B, the Wilsons, the Pilarmos, Do Not Enter, Social Security. Boldly, I turned around in Social Security's driveway, though the house was tucked back and my headlights would probably be more a wash across the trees than expectation of an approaching vehicle.

No rain tonight, but I'd opted for the baseball cap anyway. Once again, I threaded my ponytail through the hole in the back. Once again, I filled my pockets with my cell phone and a rock. I ended up locking my purse in the car. I needed to be fleet of foot. It makes me nervous, all that identification inside a parked vehicle, just begging to be stolen. A phobia of mine. I have a recurring dream about losing my wallet, license, credit cards. It ranks right up there with standing naked in front of an auditorium of high school classmates.

Water still stood in mud puddles and it required some serious concentration on my part to keep my Nikes from getting soaked. My efforts to keep my feet dry helped me use my brain for something other than the awareness of paralyzing, escalating fear. I told myself that Keegan was, after all, barely an adult. He went to school. He lived at home with his parents. He was revered by his friends, his family, the community as a whole. Were both he and Dante truly the bogeymen, or was I being a tad hysterical?

As soon as this thought coalesced, I gave myself a mental shake. This was exactly the kind of second-guessing that predators count on. At the very least, Keegan was a rapist. Gut instinct said the guy was a monster in the making.

Do Not Enter was as quiet as a tomb. I hadn't gone to the game. I hadn't called Keegan once during the week, like he'd asked. I hadn't received a text message from Dawn. I'd simply expected everything to remain status quo.

A cold frost ran down my spine. I stopped short, at the bottom of the plank. The construction workers had started with some insulation. I could see rolls of it piled inside the entryway and into the living room.

A dark form materialized in the doorway, causing me to gasp in surprise. I saw the orange tip of a cigarette as he lifted it from his side to his lips. "Nobody's here," one of the disciples told me softly.

Something about his tone sent a buzz through my body, an electrical whizzing along my nerves. "Okay," I said, turning on my heel. Something was wrong. My urge to flee swelled like a balloon.

"Hey."

A wall of guys was approaching from the drive. I'd heard their footsteps, but distantly, through the filter of a growing fear. My cell phone was on vibrate, in my pocket. I wanted to whip it out like a pistol, but this was not a time to be rash.

"Keegan?" I asked, injecting an eager tone. Perhaps they didn't hear the faint tremor.

"He's not here yet. You Ronnie?" one of them asked. I recognized them as they approached as several of Keegan's most devoted acolytes.

"What's going on? Where is everybody?"

"You were supposed to call," another one of them accused. They stopped. Four of them, arms crossed, their faces obscured by darkness, their attitude watchful and faintly aggressive.

What the hell was this? Some kind of tribunal?

"I *did* call," I lied urgently. "Keegan never called back. I thought maybe . . . I don't know . . . that he was busy, or something . . . ? And I was having trouble with my cell phone. I had to get a new one. Honestly."

There was a potent hesitation. I looked around, back to the house with its door sentry. "Am I the only girl?"

"They'll be here," one of the guys said, breaking the silence. I realized it was Glen. He seemed less comfortable with this stand-off than the rest of them. I remembered him goofily flipping the bird at my Lakeshore sweatshirt, the one they'd lobbed into the tree.

"Do you want your sweatshirt back, Glen?" I asked, saying his name on purpose, identifying him, hoping to break the mob mentality.

"Hey, no. It's yours." He was embarrassed.

"Let's go inside," the tallest boy ordered.

We all single-filed our way up the plank. I found myself shivering though it wasn't really cold. It had to be eleven or later. "How was the game?" I asked.

"We lost."

"Oh."

Was that what all the grimness was about? I felt slightly

light-headed, wanting to laugh. This terror I was feeling was because they were upset that they'd *lost*?

My moment of hilarity faded when I considered what this might mean to Keegan's mood.

I heard more footsteps and shushing, feminine whispers. Thank God. Maybe these girls weren't exactly my friends, but they sure as hell felt like it tonight.

The mood continued to be glum. The scout had brought in the booze and other contraband and was handing out beers and passing around a fifth of whiskey. I watched all those mouths tipping the bottle and went into one of my germ "ick" modes. I suspected the bottle wasn't spiked with something nefarious, since everyone was taking a big pull, but I wouldn't put my lips to the rim unless forced. When it came to me, I politely passed and no one seemed to care.

I was the only girl not offered a beer. I could feel the question mark forming over my head, so I turned to the nearest guy I recognized. Judd. The horndog. "Can I get one of those?" I asked with a smile.

"Keegan'll take care of you." He sidled away.

I'll bet.

Judd tried to get close to Glory, but she was over him in a big way. She practically shivered with affront when he drew near. I realized she was staring at me, her chin thrust out belligerently. Another girl was giving me a cold look as well. Clarissa, I was pretty sure.

If Dawn were around, she probably would be expressing the same sentiment, but I didn't see her.

How did Keegan win all these girls' undying loyalty?

A few minutes later a murmur swept through the crowd. All hail the king. I tucked my hands inside my pockets. One around my cell, one around the rock. I honestly didn't know what I planned with either one, but it was comforting to have them at the ready.

Keegan stepped inside, his head thrust forward on his

neck, his face set and stony. Nope. Not a good night. Every-one remained silent, suspended, unsure of what to do until he suddenly barked that he wanted a beer; then there was a scramble to fulfill the order.

"Those fucking refs," one of the guys said, dolefully shaking his head. "They were, like, paid off."

"Had to be," someone else said.

"They missed that face mask on you," another murmured.

"Shut up," ordered Keegan, and everyone went silent.

I tried to blend into the background, but it wasn't to be. He caught sight of me and, if possible, his expression grew even stonier. I hadn't called. I hadn't done what I was sup-posed to. I was as big a spark to his anger as was the lost game.

"So . . . Ronnie . . ." he said in a deceptively soft voice.

"Hey," I responded.

He moved into my space, radiating heat. He grabbed my hand and silently led me downstairs. I was surprised by his bold move. No foreplay this time, such as it was.

Everyone else was still up and I stumbled a little on the steps. He didn't bother helping me and I scrabbled for a hold, ending up clinging to his arm. At the bottom he pulled me to a corner where there was a pile of blankets. This was the great romantic seduction room?

"Wait here," he told me.

"I'm not sure I can stay long," I said.

"Wait . . . here."

He went back upstairs. I knew he was getting our drinks. I was torn. Once again my urge to run was almost patholog-ical. Maybe I should just call Josh. Or Dwayne. What time was it? I couldn't tell in the dark.

His returning footsteps on the stairs sent little sparks of anxiety through my veins. I rubbed my hands together, then put them back in my pocket. Keegan returned, blocking out the light that filtered through the lakeside window-holes from the houses across the bay.

He held out an opened beer and I had to release my rock and reach for it, holding it with two fingers near its rim. "It's cold," I said.

"Drink up." He clinked his can to mine and we both hoisted our cans. I pretended to take a big swallow, even choking a little.

I've gotta say, his were the weakest, lamest seduction moves I've ever experienced. The guy didn't even *try*. But I guess that was the point of the exercise. Complete control. No choice. No objections.

"You got your cell phone with you?" he asked, catching me off guard.

"Um . . . yeah."

"Let me see it."

Reluctantly, I pulled it from my pocket. Keegan turned it over in his hands, giving me the heebie-jeebies anew.

"Keegan?" Dawn's voice sounded from above. "Are you down there?" Her footsteps sounded on the stairs.

"Get outta here," he snarled, whipping away from me and blocking the bottom of the stairs in a fluid movement that revealed his power and athleticism. I edged toward him, as he was in front of the doorway to this room. My free hand wrapped around the doorjamb, my other lightly held the beer can.

To my surprise, and Keegan's, Dawn ignored the order. She clattered to the bottom and said, "I saw her. Across the way." She pointed a telling finger at me first, then toward the back of the house, across the yard and bay, toward Dwayne's. "She was standing on the dock with this guy. He wears a cowboy hat and limps. He sure doesn't look like her dad, but isn't that who she's supposed to be staying with?"

How had she seen me? I couldn't credit it. Did she watch through binoculars like Dwayne?

"The Pilarmos' wolf was just howling," she said, as if she'd heard my question. "And these dogs across the bay were barking. I looked through our telescope and recognized one of them. A pug. *Her* dog. And then there she was! Standing on the dock, big as life. She's lying to us," Dawn said. "I don't know why. Why?" she asked me belligerently. "That's not where you said your dad lives. Who is that guy? Your *boyfriend*?"

"I don't know what you're talking about," I said. "I thought we were friends."

"I'm not friends with liars!"

The room I was in was framed in, but the space between the two-by-fours was wide enough for me to squeeze through if need be. I put one foot in the nearest space. The boards were sixteen inches on center. I could duck under the electrical wiring, edge through and get past both Dawn and Keegan. Maybe.

"You been lying to me, Ronnie?" Keegan asked, flipping on my cell phone. The lighted screen emitted a square of illumination. I hadn't had time to personalize the image on my new phone. An indiscriminate picture of nature, sky, clouds and trees flashed on.

"I thought you were all my friends," I pleaded, leaning hard, inching my shoulder through the space. "I can't believe this. You're as bad as the popular kids at my own high school!"

"Keegan, I need to talk to you," Dawn beseeched. "It's about Dionne. She's just out of control."

"What's this?" Keegan asked, showing me the screen of the phone. He'd scrolled through my address book and landed on LCPD. My acronym for Josh Newell's cell. "Lake Chinook Police Department?"

Dawn swept in a startled breath.

"You've got to be kidding," I said, but my voice was unsteady. "What time is it? If I'm not home on time, my dad probably will call the cops."

"I trusted you," Dawn said. "I talked to you. You asked so many questions."

Keegan pocketed my phone.

I squeezed through the open wall and ran pell mell for the rectangular light that signified Do Not Enter's back door.

It was the half beat of surprise that saved me. That and the fact that Dawn, in her outrage, unknowingly stepped in front of Keegan at the exact moment of my charge, impeding his chance to snatch the back of my sweatshirt. I banged my knee into the edge of the door and sucked in a breath at the pain but kept going, limping a little like Dwayne. I ran outside into the night. I was closer to the Pilarmos' yard and zigged that way. This fence was wood. I tossed the beer over and scrambled after it, my knee throbbing. There were shouts and running footsteps behind me. I landed on the other side. Slipped in the mud. Lost precious seconds searching for the can. Keegan was swearing up a storm behind me. A moan of fear tore from my throat. I sprinted for all I was worth toward the stone wall that divided the Wilsons from the Pilarmos. I hit something and stumbled. The can flew from my hand. I slammed into the ground, my cheek grazing something hard. A gnome.

Keegan was over the fence and heading my way with shocking speed. I had to leave the can. I grabbed the gnome and jumped onto the fence, scrabbling for a hold. Ropes of ivy hung down and I wound one hand around one.

His hands grabbed me from behind. He had me by the neck. I cried out as he yanked me from the wall.

From near the house came a low, canine growl. The kind of *ggrrrrr* that lifts the hairs on your nape.

Keegan ignored it. He was shouting, calling me names. All rage. No finesse. No concern for being caught.

He actually hit me, a haymaker to the side of my face that

semistunned me, although I didn't notice at the time. I was a whirling dervish, whipping around, trying to break his hold, intent on saving my life.

"You fucking bitch," he snarled, shaking me hard.

A black form leapt at him, catching his arm. Lobo's teeth flashed white.

I heard a yelp of pain and was released. I fell to my hands and knees. Something fell to the ground beside me: my cell! I snatched it up.

Keegan was screaming. The wolf-dog and the quarterback were duking it out in the mud. Lobo was ripping skin but Keegan had the dog by the throat. In a haze, I suddenly worried about the dog. I grabbed the gnome from where I'd dropped it and hurled it at Keegan, shrieking Lobo's name.

Keegan's grip slipped. Lobo backed off, growling, watching Keegan stagger to his knees and attempt to gain his footing.

The Pilarmos' lights flashed on, and a man yelled, "Lobo! Stop!"

In the illumination, a gleam of metal. The beer can. Keegan, breathing hard and frozen in the dog's glare, watched me gingerly pick it up. He moved but the dog feinted, his lips drawn back in a snarl.

I couldn't climb the wall. I had no strength. It took everything I had to make it to the edge of the dock and fight my way around the end of the stone wall to Tab A/Slot B's seawall on the other side. I had to search with my toe and then make a jump. One foot slipped into the bay but I made it. I crossed their property without incident. On the far side of their lawn, the neighboring property was divided by a tall wooden fence. I could scale it, but I didn't need to because concrete steps, shortening in length from elongated to normal step height, sloped upward along the eastern side of the property. I could get back to Beachlake.

I moved like an old woman, my head aching. In the distance I heard the welcome sounds of sirens. It was after midnight. Dwayne had called the cavalry.

I reached the step that was on level with the main floor of the house. An uncurtained window gave me a close-up view of the living room and Tab A vigorously inserting into Slot B, backlit by shimmery blue water, the home to indifferent redtails, angelfish and a shockingly scary eel with fat, protruding yellow whiskers.

Slot B looked up, saw me, threw back her head and screamed.

CHAPTER NINETEEN

I tried to sneak my bruised and battered body to my car, but the police showed up before I could. They had the nerve to throw some handcuffs on me and tuck me into a police car. I told them very specifically not to touch the beer can unless they wanted to screw up the fingerprints from the rapist who'd doctored the beer with a date rape drug. They looked at each other but were careful with the can.

At some point Josh Newell ducked his head inside and looked at me. I said, "I signed up for my Neighborhood Association board. Thanks for steering me the right way."

"Are you all right?" he asked.

"Peachy."

One of the other officers called to him and he ducked back out. They both looked in the direction of the road and I swiveled to see Dwayne approaching. You could barely discern the limp, he was so intent on getting where he was going. I would have waved at him, but it's tricky with your hands behind your back. The police used to be a lot more lenient about these things, but a couple of arrests gone wrong, and handcuffs behind the back were now basic operating procedure.

Josh and Dwayne talked a long, long time. I think I heard Larrabee's name invoked at some point. Maybe even my brother's. Josh did not want to let me go. That was clear. I think his nose was out of joint that I hadn't told him I was working as a private investigator.

The Wilsons showed up, yelling, which created its own disturbance. Dionne was with them though they tried to shoo her back home. They were all trying their damnedest to get Dawn released, but she'd been scooped up with the rest of the kids from Do Not Enter, Keegan included.

In the end, Dwayne won my release. I was uncuffed and allowed to leave with him. He and I walked to his surveillance car. "We'll pick up the Volvo tomorrow," he said.

"My purse is in there."

"You're lucky you're not at the Clackamas County jail," Dwayne warned quietly.

"What did I do?" Now that I was safe I was starting to feel really put upon.

"Trespassing. You scared the shit out of Maggie DeLuca."

"Slot B?"

"She called the police right after I did. Complained about a Peeping Tom."

I realized then that Dwayne's shoulders were actually shaking with suppressed laughter. It kind of torqued me at first. I mean, where was all the worry about my health *now*?

Then I had a remembered image of Slot B screaming for all she was worth. "Okay, it's funny. But the rest of it isn't."

"I had to do some fast talking to explain what you were doing. You're lucky you're friends with Officer Newell because he's 'by the book' in a big way."

"I heard you mention Larrabee."

Dwayne sighed. "Yeah. Had to use his name to increase

our credibility. They called him. He vouched for you—and me. We're gonna owe him. So, what happened tonight?"

I told him about Dawn's ratting me out, and my panicked bid for freedom, which wouldn't have happened if not for Lobo. Dwayne listened, then admitted he hadn't waited till midnight. He placed the call to Josh Newell as soon as he heard Lobo's snarling and growling and all the yelling.

We returned to his place. Binkster staggered off the couch and snuffled me, wagging her tail. I was covered in mud. Dwayne invited me to spend the night and I showered and washed my hair, changed into one of his T-shirts and crawled into his bed without a qualm. I woke once in the middle of the night and realized I was alone. He'd taken the couch and The Binkster.

This left me lying there in the dark on my back, reviewing my feelings for him. From personal experience, I knew he generally slept in the nude.

Don't ask. And no, we didn't engage in sexual relations. But now I was kept awake wondering what I would see if I dared step into the other room. I found myself faintly jealous of my dog.

I fell asleep right before daylight, then had to drag myself awake. I staggered into the other room, bracing myself, only to find Dwayne sprawled in his clothes on the couch, Binkster on the floor beside him. I had to hand it to Dwayne. He'd managed to roust her from sleeping next to him, something I can't seem to manage.

He came wide awake and looked at me. I was going to make some comment about sleeping alone and taking his bed, but he stopped me with, "You've got a helluva shiner."

This wasn't really a surprise as my right eye was practically swollen shut. I turned to the bathroom to take a look. Purple and black and fat. The blood was seeping into the flesh all around my eye socket.

"How does it feel?" he asked.

"Like it looks. And the rest of my body, too."

Dwayne thrust his hands in his jeans and leaned against the bathroom doorjamb. "Violet called and said to send her our last bill. We're off the Hatchmere case."

I gazed at him in dismay. "That's it?"

"At least Keegan Lendenhal's going to see his day in court. They've got his fingerprints on the can, and the Wilsons are going to press charges."

"Dawn? I don't believe it. You learned that last night?"

He nodded. "Dionne's the one who'll testify. She said Lendenhal did the same thing to her. I don't know what proof they have, but the secret's out."

"Good." I was undoubtedly going to be part of this legal circus as well, since the beer with the date rape drug had been intended for me. I had this picture of myself on the witness stand, some bright defense attorney pointing out that I had misrepresented myself as a minor.

"Why's Violet ditching the investigation?"

"She's convinced the police know she's innocent."

"That's not true," I protested. "Larrabee hasn't given up. It's an ongoing investigation."

He lifted his palms.

"I'm not giving up. Are you giving up? I'm not giving up. I'm going right back to the truck stop. I want to talk to Tammie. I want to know who Dante is, and I think she can tell me."

I could hear the belligerent tone in my voice, but I didn't care. I was mad at Violet. She drags me to the CMC party and then blithely says it's over? Talk about your unfinished business.

My cell phone rang. I examined caller ID and said, "It's Melinda," in some surprise as I said hello.

"Hi, Jane, it's Melinda. I suppose you forgot, but today's the pre-Thanksgiving bake sale at the Village."

"Oh." She hadn't been all that warm and fuzzy the last

time we'd spoken. "Right. I'll stop by. What time will you be there?"

"About three."

"See you then." Dwayne looked at me askance as I hung up. "Bake sale," I reminded him.

"Can you get more of those fruit bars?" he asked instantly.

"And I'm working on a rum cake, too. Oh God. Is next Thursday Thanksgiving?" I asked, knowing the answer in advance. I'd warned Dwayne about Cynthia's invitation though he didn't apparently regard it with the same horror I did.

I changed back into my muddy clothes and Dwayne drove me and Binkster to my car. I was thrilled to see my purse was still there, untouched, and all my credit cards and identification were right where they should be. Sketching Dwayne a good-bye, I headed back to my cottage, my gaze darting around in search of possible garage-salers.

Since last weekend, things had been pretty quiet, but I feared Ogilvy might be planning another event. I was happy to see there were no signs, no items on display and no cars. I noticed the garage was no longer locked and, snoop that I am, took a peek inside after I put Binkster in the house.

There was a pile of unwanted junk in the center of the floor, but the rest of the place was surprisingly cleared out. Almost clean enough to actually park a car inside.

I spent the rest of Saturday morning finishing my final report and billing for Violet. I gave her a quick call as I was getting ready to go to the latest bake sale, and when Violet answered we suffered through one of those conversations that's filled with a lot of hemming and hawing, and which I'm completely no good at. Finally, I said, "What gives? You don't want to know who killed Roland?"

"Hon, it's time to stop wasting money, don't you think? I appreciate the work you and Dwayne have put in. It's really helped. I think it even helped convince Dwayne's detective buddy that I'm innocent. But I'm ready to just put it behind me. More than ready. I'd love to know who killed him," she added, as if she heard how much she'd abandoned her cause. "I just don't think it's a priority anymore."

She deftly switched the subject to George Tertian and the Columbia Millionaires' Club, her voice growing animated. Her focus had completely changed. Why, why was it so hard for me to give it up?

"If you have a chance, can you ask George about Dante?" I finally cut in.

"The guy who sent you out the window?"

Violet found my aversion to the man slightly humorous. I said, "If all the men are millionaires, I'd like to know what his business is."

"Sure, I'll ask him," Violet said.

"Thanks."

The bake sale was at an empty storefront in Lake Chinook Village, a fairly new development where all the stores are designed to appear as separate buildings even though they're joined together. A small art gallery had failed and moved location, and its abandoned storefront was now rented conditionally by various groups.

The Junior League ladies were helping out the neighborhood association with another bake sale. They'd decorated with fall leaves and cornstalks and cornucopias. Inside they'd lined their tables with paper Thanksgiving-themed tablecloths, and the baked goods were displayed in all their luscious, mouthwatering glory. Leigh and Bitchy Anne were manning one table; Jody and Melinda another. I'd cleaned myself up again and wore a long black sweater that covered my hips and my best jeans. I'd combed my hair down straight and I'd worked pretty darned hard on my makeup. Couldn't do much about the black eye, though, and as I approached they gazed upon me with varying degrees of horror.

"Walked into a door," I explained.

I could see the "oh, sure" looks pass over their faces as they threw each other sideways glances. I wondered if they would believe me more if I told them star quarterback Keegan Lendenhal had clocked me on purpose.

Melinda regarded me with real concern. She was wearing peach-colored slacks and a cream blouse today. Her own hair was perfectly coiffed and her skin looked luminous. I wondered if she'd been to The Face. "What really happened?" she asked, pulling me away from the tables. I kept my eye on the goodies. I was pretty sure I saw some of Jody's peach bars. No rum cakes visible.

"This wasn't related to Roland's case," I assured her.

"Really?" Melinda couldn't tear her gaze from my injury.

"Really."

"Have you learned anything more about Roland?"

"Actually, I'm off the case. The police have turned their attention from Violet, and she decided to terminate our investigation."

A series of emotions crossed Melinda's face, relief being chief among them. "I'm glad you're going to quit harassing Gigi, Sean and Emmett. It was a waste of time anyway, since Violet killed Roland."

"I'm still going to investigate on my own."

"Why?" she asked.

"I want to know who killed him."

"Why is it so hard for you to realize Violet's guilty? She's not even paying you anymore. Why don't you investigate *her*? You've wasted your time on Roland's kids. And those Wedding Bandits, I guess. And Emmett! And probably me! The one person you haven't looked at is Violet."

A cell phone began ringing. Leigh said, "Melinda, it's yours."

Melinda didn't want to give up her tirade, but she tippy-tapped her way to her purse and dug out her phone. I watched as her expression darkened and she clicked it off like she had the last time I'd been with her. She clearly wasn't a slave to taking a call, but then I knew that from personal experience.

I purchased some peach bars, then wangled a rum cake out of Jody, who said I would have to come back the next day as she'd presold all of today's. I was thrilled she was going to make the extra effort for me.

"Treat it right, and it'll still be fresh for Thursday," Jody said. "I'll tell you how."

"Thursday? Oh. Thanksgiving." I had no intention of waiting that long. As soon as I got my cake I was going to have an orgy of calories all by myself. Okay. I might invite Dwayne.

Melinda offered to carry the peach bars to my car. I told her not to bother, but she had things on her mind. "What do you plan to do?" she asked me.

"About the investigation? I don't know. Follow some leads."

"What kind of leads?"

"The kind that lead to answers."

"You have stopped harassing us, haven't you? We can count on that, right?"

"I'm going in a different direction," I assured her, gently placing the peach bars on the seat.

"I'm glad to hear it," she said, but she didn't look glad about much of anything as I drove away.

In the evening, I headed down I-5 to the truck stop again, having squirreled away the peach bars untouched. It was like a strange hoarding need on my part, my cache of nuts for the winter. I figured I could have a piece of pie à la mode at the truck stop and get today's quota of sugar and calories and still have tons more at home. Yes, my diet leaves something to be desired, but I don't much care.

I tucked my hair into my baseball cap and put on my fake glasses one more time. It went a long way to taking the focus off my shiner, though anybody who took a good look at me couldn't miss it. I was beginning to recognize a few of the regulars, but hopefully they did not feel the same about me. I lived in a bit of anxiety that the trucker who'd shooed me away would burst through the doors and point an accusing finger at me. But, as I'd come to expect, no one paid me any attention as I settled onto a counter stool. The video poker machines at the far end were a lot more interesting.

My pregnant friend wasn't on duty tonight, probably at the hospital giving birth. I was served instead by a dour-faced, gum-cracking thirty-something whose gaze narrowed on my black eye like a target. I ordered the pie—which they were out of, more's the pity—and after reconsulting the menu ended up asking for a hamburger. Okay, I probably deserved more than the granulated sugar food group anyway.

She hustled up the burger and slipped it in front of me. I noticed there was no check, though she'd certainly dropped off the bill to every other customer. I looked up at her questioningly. "On the house," she said.

"Why?" I asked cautiously.

She gestured toward my face and turned back to her task with a surge of energy, an I'm-so-busy cover-up that left me mystified.

I ate slowly, thinking. I wasn't exactly sure how to proceed to learn more about Tammie. Should I question this waitress? Did she know what was going on? Or maybe I should just hide outside by the trash bins and wait for the truckers to come and go, hoping Tammie would be on duty tonight. A sane little voice inside my head had started questioning everything I was doing. What *was* I doing? This was dumb. Because Dante had possibly called Roland, and was possibly a pimp for Tammie, and was definitely intent on scaring me, here I was skulking around this truck stop, just for the fun of it.

My waitress came back my way but didn't make eye contact. "Don't know if I'd be here tonight, lookin' like you do," she said, flicking her towel across the counter at nonexistent crumbs. She leaned in close and dug her thumbnail at the counter. Since she wouldn't meet my eye, I dragged my gaze from her as well. For some reason she didn't want to appear as if she were talking with me.

She also seemed to think I knew something I didn't.

Around a last bite of burger, I said to my plate, "I don't care who sees me."

"Girl, you are askin' to get smacked again."

A guy at the end of the counter stood up and reached in his pockets for change. My waitress hurried over and picked up the money, exchanging a few friendly words. He took off his hat, smoothed his gray hair, then pushed through the door, heading toward the side of the building and, I assumed, his truck.

It took a few minutes, but she came back my way. I pretended to be chastened. "Maybe you're right."

"You got about ten minutes before he gets back." She shot me a look. "One of these days you girls'll smarten up."

"Like Tammie?"

Her expression darkened. "She tell you that? She's the dumbest of the lot of you."

"I think she just wants to get her kids back," I said, shooting in the dark.

"She's got a funny way of goin' about it. Now go." She grabbed my plate with a clatter and huffed away.

I hung around awhile, but she wouldn't engage me again. Finally, I ducked out the door and headed toward my car, but then walked right on by it. I did exactly what I'd planned to earlier: I hid by the Dumpster and watched the goings-on.

It got later. And later. And later. Apart from a few men climbing from their rigs and going in to eat or play video poker, the back of the building was quiet.

I'd put my phone in my pocket and it suddenly vibrated,

giving me an unexpected goose. I glanced around. There were a couple of truckers smoking outside their cabs and talking. They would hear me if I answered the phone. I didn't want to give away my position, so I let it go to voice mail.

I had a lot of time on my hands. I got to thinking about what Melinda had said about Violet. I got to thinking about my own feelings about Violet. I got to thinking about a lot of things.

I shifted position. I'd been squatting. Now I was sitting, my butt cold, numb and slightly damp from its perch on a wet curb.

I thought about Dwayne. I thought about myself. I thought about Larrabee, though that sent me back to thinking about Dwayne.

I returned to Violet.

I pictured her with Roland. I pictured that morning. I could almost see her electric-blue eyes, anxious, filled with concern after the uncertain night she'd just spent with the man she supposedly loved. I thought about Roland, thought about his change of mood after talking to Sean or whoever had called him from the club, be it Dante or someone else. I could practically feel the escalation of Violet's anxiety as Roland brushed her off. No, she wasn't invited to the wedding. No, she wasn't a part of his family anymore.

My mind's eye witnessed their fight. It ended with Roland grabbing her shoulders, pushing her to the wall, yelling furiously, blasting her with the news that he didn't want her. Violet didn't crumble. She wouldn't. She picked up the tray and whacked him hard.

He went down, holding his head, swearing. Maybe she backed away. Maybe there was a break. Maybe time went by. Or . . . maybe it didn't.

But Roland was getting ready to leave. To make it to the pictures. And there was no room for Violet in his life.

Maybe he was cruel. Maybe he laughed, or grabbed her again.

Hurt her.

From the freeway I heard a car backfire several times. The truckers lifted their heads and so did I. In a moment they went back to talking and I went back to my thoughts. I pictured Violet slamming the tray against Roland's head. *Bang.* She hit him once. But maybe . . . maybe Melinda was right . . . maybe she did hit him a second time. *Bang!* She hit him a lot harder, consumed with all the pent-up rage and emotion of rejection. I could see it as if it had truly happened. As if a movie had just played out in my head.

Everyone said she killed him. Everyone but Dwayne.

And Larrabee . . . sort of . . .

The cab door of one of the trucks suddenly swung open, sending a blast of country music into the night air. A woman's bare leg stepped out as she carefully pulled herself to the ground. She wore a short dress and a furry jacket and she kept reaching a hand back inside the cab, slapping playfully.

Tammie.

Her trucker friend climbed out after her. There were a few smooches. He grabbed her ass possessively. She eased away. He tried to talk her into going into the restaurant with him, but she gave him a toodle-loo with her fingers and blew him a big kiss. He seemed reluctant, but Tammie said something about being unable to go inside and that he knew that.

He finally headed off alone and after a minute she walked with surprising grace on her high heels toward a minivan parked at the back. She unlocked it and climbed inside.

I ran over to her and yanked open the door. She looked up, startled, in the act of reapplying lipstick. Big surprise. "You," she declared. Then her eyes widened. "Oh God, he hit you," she breathed.

I went with it. "Yeah, he hit me. And it hurt."

"He hardly ever does that. Honestly. I should have warned you. I heard you were looking for me. I should never have talked to you. I can't believe you're here!"

"I got a free meal out of it," I improvised.

"My God, do you know the trouble you've caused?"

"I've caused?" I repeated in disbelief.

"What do you want?"

"Some answers."

"Get in the car, for God's sake. Don't let anyone see." She motioned me in and I climbed into the passenger seat and slammed the door. "Christ. Damn Reina's good heart. She feels compelled to hand out a free meal whenever any of us gets bruised up. Oh, Jesus." She was gazing into the parking lot. I followed her gaze, expecting to see *him,* and I wasn't disappointed, although he sure wasn't Dante and he looked like every other trucker who showed up.

He was standing in the center of the lot, backlit, and instead of a baseball cap, which seemed to be the head adornment most of us preferred around these parts, he wore a cowboy hat. He had at least fifty pounds on Dante and he wasn't quite as tall.

"I've gotta go," she said. "You should disappear, if you know what's good for you. I'm sorry I talked to you. I don't know what got into me."

"How did you get from here to CMC?" I asked.

"You know. Dante. He doesn't always use his fists. Honestly."

"How do you know Dante?"

"Are you kidding?"

"Can't you get away from him?"

"I don't want to. Don't you get it? He's helping me. I want my kids back, and to do that I need a respectable life, a respectable husband."

"Maybe just a different job," I pointed out.

"It's not that easy." She uttered a squeak of frustration or fear, I couldn't tell which. "Get down," she ordered, "so I can get out without him seeing you."

"Dante?"

"*No.* My date."

Her fear was infectious and I didn't want to get her in worse trouble. I slid down to the floor and she let herself out of the car. I heard her footsteps round the front of the hood and move away. Cautiously, I peered out.

She'd hooked a hand through the crook of the john's arm and deftly turned him away. They walked toward another truck and he helped her into the cab, then followed her inside.

I climbed out of her car and headed for my own, locking myself inside and pulling my cell phone from my pocket. I needed to call Dwayne.

My phone said I had a message.

Oh, right. I looked at the number. From Violet, of all people.

"Okay, I can't believe I'm doing this," her voice said in my ear, sounding slightly bemused. "But George says Dante's a millionaire many times over. And apparently it's all legit and documented and all that, so don't go seeing all kinds of bad stuff. Apparently he owns a string of restaurants, but here's the funny part, they're all this kind of podunk diners across the state. One of them's even a truck stop. If you need anything more, just call. But I'm not paying!" She laughed happily and hung up.

I sat silently in my car, the phone in my hand.

Dante owned the truck stop restaurant.

Dante was Tammie's pimp.

Dante had called Roland and told him something that got him upset.

Good-hearted Reina had given me a free meal because she thought Dante had given me the black eye. What had she said?

Don't know if I'd be here tonight lookin' like you do . . . you got about ten minutes before he gets back . . .

Dante was coming to the truck stop.

I got back out of my car and looked around the parking lot. It had been hours ago, but maybe he was still here, checking on his investments.

I stuck my hands in my pockets against the cold and circled the lot. At the far end, parked at the front of the building yet angled into a spot to discourage anyone from taking the spots on either side, was a black Mercedes. It was parked away from the lights; purposely so, it seemed. There was scarcely a mud spot on it. I figured it must have gone through a wash very recently.

I'd bet my savings this was Dante's car. I almost believed I'd seen it the other night at the party. Maybe, maybe not. Every car there seemed to be slick, black and expensive.

But I was sure this was Dante's. So sure, in fact, that I practiced my lines as I approached.

Excuse me, Satan, mind if I kick your ass?

I had no weapon apart from my purse. No gnome to hurl at him.

But there were plenty of rocks.

I picked one up and weighed it in my palm. I was coldly angry and glad to be there. It would have helped to feel this way last night when I was facing Keegan Lendenhal.

I thought about tapping on the window, but surprise was all I had.

I yanked open the driver's door. "Excuse me, Satan" was as far as I got.

Dante rolled forward, slumping half out of the car. His eyes stared toward the heavens, dark orbs in a white face. The color was leached from the scene. Black blood seeped through the front of his shirt in two distinct spots. I smelled the burned scent of cordite.

I backed off, repelled, one hand digging at my pocket for my cell phone.

"Hey!" somebody yelled.

I pulled out my cell phone. Thoughts were slow in coming.

I dialed Detective Vince Larrabee.

CHAPTER TWENTY

I didn't get home till four in the morning.

Larrabee answered my call and in turn phoned the sheriff's department. I'd barely hung up from him when one of the truckers saw Dante's body, my reaction to it, and mistakenly believing I was responsible, hauled my ass back inside the restaurant, having to mostly carry me as my legs weren't working as they should. He pushed me, rather roughly, I might add, into one of the booths where I sat like a limp rag.

Several deputies interviewed me, and the sheriff himself appeared to ask me a lot of the same questions. Not that I had any answers for them. I went to the car, thinking the guy was someone I knew. I jerked open the door and this strange, dead guy rolled out. I was a friend of Detective Vince Larrabee of the Portland Police and had called him immediately.

It was a little like being drunk. Time telescoped. I told my story with minor variations. Sometimes I yanked open the door, instead of jerking it open. Sometimes the strange, dead guy sort of flopped out of the car instead of rolling out.

They really didn't know what to do with me, so they waited.

There appeared to be an endless cup of coffee on the table in front of me, which I sipped at. It wasn't half as good as the Coffee Nook's.

Somewhere in the dead of night Larrabee sat down across from me. He reached over and grabbed my hand, which sort of woke me up. "You okay?" he asked.

"Yep."

"You sure?"

"Yep."

"I'm going to talk to the sheriff and give them some background."

"I told them I didn't know the guy. I didn't mention Dante's name."

"I'm not going to blab anything I don't have to, Jane." He gave me a faint smile and left.

Dwayne took his place. By this time I'd propped my head against the window on the inside of the booth. Dwayne looked across at me, pulled a flask from inside his jacket, passed it over to me. I was really, really glad to see him and told him so. I unscrewed the top of the flask, wiped the rim with my sleeve, took a pull. I tried to be careful, but it burned like a son of a gun and I started coughing.

Through tears I gazed into Dwayne's blue eyes. He didn't look as concerned for my health as I thought he should. "Larrabee . . . called you?" I choked out.

"He did."

"They wouldn't let me make another phone call," I said, belatedly annoyed. "I was hustled in here and told to sit still until the sheriff came."

"I would say some of the patrons were concerned about getting Tammie and company out of the way before the calvary arrived and didn't want you phoning the police before they did. They didn't know you'd already called Larrabee."

"Has that—operation—been uncovered?"

"If it hasn't been, I'm not tellin'," Dwayne said.

"Not part of your quid pro quo with Larrabee?"

"Nope."

The sheriff's department didn't want to let me go. There was talk of taking me to the county corrections' facility. They didn't much like Larrabee and would have liked to tell him to get the hell out of their jurisdiction, but Larrabee had called them and brought them up to speed on who I was, thereby saving them a lot of time.

Dwayne was right: we were going to be in debt to Larrabee, big time.

In the end, once again I was told I could go home, but that I needed to be available for further questioning. I assured them I wasn't going anywhere but to bed. Dwayne wanted to drive me, but I didn't want to leave my Volvo at the truck stop, so I followed him back up the freeway.

I didn't sleep well. I had to put Binkster in her bed because she was just one more impediment to sleep. She stayed there for about ten minutes, then jumped in with me again, snoring for all she was worth. I cuddled up to her and she kicked me in my sore eye.

I woke up groggy and vaguely disoriented. There were voices outside. Throwing off the covers, I padded barefoot to the front window and was horrified to see Ogilvy wave an encompassing arm toward my cottage to a young couple with a child in a stroller.

If they came to the front door, I wasn't sure what I would do. I had things to take care of. Things to figure out. I had a life, for God's sake, and it didn't include being harassed by would-be home buyers.

I stalked to my bedroom and snatched up my jeans. I was pulling a clean shirt over my head when there was a knock on my front door. I was outraged. It was Sunday morning. I glanced at the clock. Okay, afternoon.

I threw open the door. Binkster tried to jump outside to

greet her new "friends," but I blocked her with my foot. "What?"

Ogilvy looked affronted by my tone. "This is Mr. and Mrs. Radcliff. They're interested in seeing the cottage and wondered—"

"*No.*" I slammed the door.

"Well," I heard Mrs. Radcliff sniff.

They wandered away and I stalked into the kitchen to feed Binkster breakfast. She turned an eye up at me, clearly cautious about my mood, but it didn't stop her from wolfing her meal down in seconds flat.

"You're not the only bitch in the room," I told her.

Dwayne called. And then Larrabee called. They'd obviously talked to each other, and what I gathered from their combined notes was that neither of them wanted me to do any more investigating on the Hatchmere case. I sensed a lot of testosterone and some one-upmanship going on and I thought *What the hell?* I was tired of fighting anyway. Keegan was found out, Dante was dead, Violet was no longer our client.

"I don't care who did it," I said to Binks. She gazed at me dolefully.

It was almost four o'clock when I remembered the rum cake.

In the midst of everything I almost forgot one of the most important missions of my day. I raced around in a flurry and charged to the bake sale, bursting into the store as if I were about to announce the winner of a race.

Everyone looked up at me. The usual suspects were all there: Leigh, Melinda, Bitchy Anne and Kathleen, along with other members I hadn't yet had the pleasure to meet. "Rum cake," I informed them.

"Jody's not here yet," Leigh informed me. "That woman is always late." There was a murmur of agreement amongst the envious, other would-be pastry chefs. They all looked in silent horror at my black eye.

I decided to spend my time waiting by sidling up to Melinda, who was distracted and short. She was not happy to see me today. Yesterday, fine. Today, I was dirt. I could get a complex, the way she treated me.

Jody blew through the doors, her hair practically standing on end, her eyes a little wild. I had a mental picture of her whipping up batter with one hand, an eye on the clock, her other hand lightly greasing a pan and dusting it with flour, all working so fast that it was a blur.

Melinda suddenly started gathering her things together as if she were about to leave. The other women were taken aback and Bitchy Anne said snarkily, "Somebody must have a hot date."

"I've got an appointment," Melinda said, heading toward the back room. She appeared a few moments later in her white coat, tucking the collar close to her neck.

Jody had wrapped my cake and handed it to me in a bag, holding it gingerly. "Keep it upright," she warned. "It's still warm and it's fragile."

"It would have been nice if you'd told us you weren't going to be here the whole time," Leigh said to Melinda. "What are we supposed to do with your extra pans and things?"

"There's nothing here. I took care of it all earlier."

"You've got half a dozen pans back there," Leigh argued.

"Fine. I'll get them later."

Melinda made a beeline for the door and I followed after her, wondering what this was all about. She damn near let the door fall back on my cake. "Whoa," I said, catching the swinging door with my shoulder.

"Could you leave me alone?" she snapped.

Now, what was that all about? It had been all I could do to pry her out of the library bake sale. She was hightailing from this one for all she was worth. "You invited me to this thing," I reminded her. She struck off at a fast walk in the direction of her condos. "You don't have a car?" I called after her.

"Brought everything earlier and drove back. Thought the exercise would be great."

"Good idea." I hurried up and fell in step beside her.

She stopped short, eyeing my cake. "You'd better be careful with that."

"Did I do something to piss you off?"

"You won't put Violet in jail. You harass everybody. You act like you're some big-shot detective and all you do is . . . get in the way!" With that she took off again.

Now she was pissing *me* off. "I don't have the authority to put Violet in jail, but you'll be happy to know, I think she's at the center of this."

"What do you mean?"

It was simply something Larrabee had said. Yes, I'd had my soul-searching moments about Violet the night before, but no, I did not believe she was guilty of killing Roland. My vacillations were over. But Melinda didn't have to know that.

"Maybe I should have listened to you sooner."

"Of course you should have."

I'd hoped to get her to slow down, but she seemed determined to keep on marching. We were getting farther and farther away from my car. I was worried about my rum cake.

"What finally changed your mind?" she asked. Her hands were in her pockets and her shoulders were hunched.

"She hit him with the tray. Maybe no one else did."

"That's not exactly news."

"She and Roland got in a huge fight. I think it was over you."

"What do you mean?" She threw me a sideways look.

I carefully shifted my rum cake from one arm to the other. We'd gone about four blocks and turned west. A couple more and we would be near her condo, away from the center of

Lake Chinook and deep into the residential district of First Addition. I wasn't sure what I was doing, why it felt so imperative to keep with her. There was something driving me I couldn't put my finger on.

"Roland took a cell phone call right before Violet hit him with the tray. The call was about you."

Her steps faltered. "Did Violet tell you that?"

"Yes."

"Why are you turning this on me? Didn't you just say you finally believed me about her? It's Violet. She killed him!" She picked up her pace again.

"You know Dante? From the club?" She didn't answer, just kept walking. "He was killed last night. Someone shot him at a truck stop diner down I-5 past Salem. Apparently he owned the place."

"Why are you following me? I don't have anything to do with CMC anymore."

"Don't you want to know how he was killed?"

"I don't know Dante," she said. "I don't care what you heard, he was not my introduction to the club."

"I didn't say he was."

"Well, that's what Violet thought."

Was it? Abruptly she turned into a small park that was surrounded by a tall laurel hedge. I followed after her. There was no one about. The scattered benches were empty, the water fountain filling with dirt and twigs. There was a play structure in the center that looked as if it had plopped down by Martians, its bright primary colors and twisting red, blue and parrot-green pipes jarring in the natural setting of trees, shrubbery and grass.

Melinda stopped short and faced me. "Stop following me. I don't know what your game is, but it's over, as far as I'm concerned. I'm going home now. Take your rum cake and shove it up your ass."

"What is it that I said? Melinda, come on!"

"You don't believe it was Violet. You just said that so you could grill me again."

"I did think it was Violet. Last night. I came to that conclusion."

"But now you've changed your mind."

My cell phone rang. Melinda threw a glance at my purse, made a sound of pure annoyance and turned her back on me. "I'm going home. If you keep following me, I'll call the police." She headed off again.

I stayed where I was, staring after her. I was harassing her and to what end? I was hanging on to Melinda for reasons I couldn't explain. So she'd known Dante. So she'd been a member of CMC. So Roland and Dante were both dead.

Feeling a little foolish, I juggled the cake and pulled my phone from my purse one-handed. It was a familiar number, but there was no name. I turned back the way I'd come. "Jane Kelly."

"Well, there. We finally connect," Deenie said, huffing out a sigh as if it were a big relief. "I promise my boyfriend won't cut in this time. He and I are through anyway. I don't know why I put up with his shit so long in the first place. I must be a glutton for punishment. Okay, now . . . I can't remember . . . what did you want? Something about the wedding."

I wanted to clap my hand to my forehead and I would have, too, if I'd had one free.

Before I could answer, she said, "Oh, it was a timeline. That's right. You wanted to know where I was and when. Who I was with, right? Let's see . . . I was with Gigi at Castellina. Melinda brought us mimosas and then she left. Then Gigi and I went in the limo to Cahill Winery. Nobody was there when we first got there. Except Melinda. She must have driven right over. Then the wedding party started coming and we were having champagne. The groomsmen were knocking it back, y'know? Gigi was a little concerned, so I asked

Melinda if she'd maybe step in, as someone older, y'know? Kind of let them know it was not okay? But she got that phone call and left, so I had to go up to them. Emmett wasn't there yet, or maybe he coulda done it. But the best man wasn't paying attention, so it was up to the maid of honor. Which, y'know, I was thinking, I didn't sign up for this. I just wanted—"

"Melinda left?"

"Hauled ass right outta there," Deenie confirmed. "I don't think anybody noticed but me. She was back before pictures, so it hardly matters. Anyway, I just wanted everybody to behave and not let it be my problem."

"Deenie, I've gotta go. I'll call you later."

"Well, goddamm it. How—"

I snapped off my phone. Melinda was nearing the far end of the park. "Hey!" I yelled. I set my cake down and ran through the mud to catch up with her.

She half turned, saw me coming, looked as if she were about to run for it, then seemed to make a decision. She turned around and marched right toward me. We stopped short of each other by the red and blue plastic play structure.

"See what I'm doing?" she said, holding up her cell phone, then punching the buttons with force. "I'm calling the police!"

"I don't know who you're calling but it's not the police. You don't want them anywhere near you."

"Yeah? Wait and see." She placed the phone next to her ear and glared at me.

I called her bluff. Just stood there and waited.

The phone rang and rang and we faced each other like a high noon standoff. It gave me time to think. Where I'd been running on pure instinct before, now I saw it for what it was.

"You're one of Dante's women," I said. "He did introduce you to the club."

"No, that's what Violet thought."

"Violet would have said so. You just made that up because you slipped by saying he hadn't introduced you."

"You—are—harassing me."

"Dante's a blackmailer, too. He brings you to the club, then when one of you actually meets someone who's interested, who might actually offer marriage, he steps right in. The bite's on you. He can blackmail you to his heart's content. And if things go wrong, he can call up the new husband. Maybe new hubby'll pay the blackmail."

Melinda dropped her arm, the phone loose in her hand.

"That's what happened. You stopped paying and Dante called Roland and told him you were a truck stop prostitute. And then he called you and told you what he'd done. He loved to make people squirm. Especially women."

"You've . . . you . . . are so wrong!"

But her face was the color of wet cement. She looked ready to pass out.

"You left the wedding and drove to Roland's, expecting to reason with him. But he was in a rage. At Violet, too, for hitting him, but mainly at you. He said he was divorcing you, and he was going to marry Violet."

"Violet *hit* him."

"But you killed him. And last night . . . you killed Dante."

She shivered hard. The phone slipped from her fingers and plopped in the mud. She tucked her hands in her pockets and hunched her shoulders, quaking with emotion. And then she looked at me, some of her color returning.

She pulled a handgun from her pocket and aimed it at me. Just like that.

Blood rushed to my head. All sounds in the park receded. In my peripheral vision I could see little birds darting in and out of the bushes, but it was as if someone had put the sound on mute. My own breathing and heartbeat filled my ears to bursting. My vision zeroed in on the end of the gun, its deadly little hole pointing at me like a finger.

Melinda was breathing hard, too. Beneath her white coat, I could see the rapid rise and fall of her chest. She didn't want this any more than I did. But she had a steely determination and a desperate secret to hide.

My mouth was dry and my brain was empty. I should have seen this coming. But in the park? *Here?* I hadn't expected her to be so reckless.

I tried to speak. Stopped. Cleared my throat. Tried again. "You don't want to do that," I whispered, gaze fixed on the handgun. If I were Dwayne I would know what type it was. If I were Dwayne, I wouldn't be in this position.

"I couldn't stop Dante from telling Roland," she said.

She'd stopped him pretty good from what I could tell.

"You tried to . . . reason with him . . ." It was all I could get out. My life had zeroed down to this moment, this gun, this woman . . . this breath.

"We were supposed to go to the wedding together. Roland and me. He'd said we would. But then he didn't want to go early, but I had the orange juice and champagne. He told me to go on without him and he'd come later. I didn't know he was with Violet. If I'd known . . ." She shook her head as if to clear it. Her body buzzed like a vibrator, emotion thrumming through her, a living thing.

I kept quiet, afraid to say anything.

"Everybody was getting ready for pictures. No one was looking at me, so I left. I went straight to the house and he was holding his head. Violet had hit him with the tray. But he didn't care! He only cared that Dante had called and told him I was . . . not what he thought. Roland called me a whore. I said he had it wrong and he laughed. He laughed." Her tone was full of disbelief, her face ravaged. "Then he walked away from me. To the sunroom, staring out at the garden. The tray was on the banquette. I was—pleading with him, begging him. We were supposed to be getting back together!" she insisted.

The gun wavered in my vision. My heart pounded so hard it hurt my chest. I was afraid she would shoot me by mistake, just in the telling of the story.

"He said he was divorcing me. Cutting me off. Those were his words. 'I'm cutting you off, you dirty, fucking whore.' And then he said he was marrying Violet. He loved her. She was passionate. She'd hit him with the tray, but he seemed to see it as some kind of . . . expression of *love!* Men are so stupid, don't you think?" she said, her tone shifting abruptly. "So stupid."

I didn't respond.

"Then he said he was going to expose me. Tell my secret to the world. He'd been angry when he first heard. Furious. He and Violet had got in a fight because he was so angry. He'd taken it out on her, but he saw it all so clearly now. I was dirty and cheap and worthless.

"I tried to talk to him. That was my past. Long ago. Like another person, not even *me!* He walked away from me and I grabbed his arm. I shook it. Shook it as hard as I could. He told me I was pathetic. Pulled my fingers back. I thought he was going to break them off." Her breath came in gasps at the memory. "I was crying and he didn't care. Violet was all he cared about. Violet."

At some level I was measuring the distance between us. Could I run? Zigzag? Escape? How good a shot was she? Would she hunt me down or let me go? She'd killed Dante and taken his gun. She was made of steel and purpose and rampaging emotions.

"The tray was just there," she went on. "His ear was bleeding. Violet caught him on the side of the head, but she didn't put any strength to it. She didn't *mean* it. But I reached for the tray. I had my gloves on. My wedding gloves. And I meant it."

She looked at me. She meant it now.

My first instinct is always to flee. Always.

But I stood rooted to the spot.

Melinda lifted the gun, sighting. A moment passed. And another. I understood instinctively that she would have trouble shooting me in cold blood without a jump, a dodge, a trigger.

In a distance I heard a dog woof. Someone coming to the park. Someone walking their dog. I thought of The Binkster. Of what would happen to my dog if I should die.

And I did the unthinkable. I leapt at her.

She jerked the gun in surprise. I made contact, grabbing for the weapon, my hands slipping. We fought, standing, slipping in the mud, my hands on her wrists, fumbling, flailing.

Blam!

The sound blasted through the air. My ears rang. The acrid and now familiar smell of cordite filled my nose. There was a numbness in my abdomen. I thought, *I'm hit, but I'm okay. I'm okay. I'm okay.*

I wasn't sure I believed it.

There were voices behind me. Alarmed voices. A sense of urgent scurrying.

Melinda stumbled back from me. The gun dropped with a thud into the muck beneath our feet, companion to her cell phone.

She said, "You shot me."

I blinked. Stared blankly. Didn't say that she was wrong.

She pressed her hand to her stomach, holding her white coat close.

I backed away from her, dimly aware that I felt no pain. None. I wasn't hurt.

She lifted her hand, looked at the palm. A smear of red showed. It lay in streaks on her white coat. Not a lot of blood. Yet.

She turned. The back of her coat showed dark red around a

small tear. An exit wound. The bullet was somewhere in the park.

She took two steps and collapsed.

I bent over her. There was a rushing in my head. A sense of my world shrinking, a loss of peripheral vision. My old buddy shock was trying to take over. I drew several deep, cleansing breaths and my head cleared.

Melinda lay on her side, her eyes open, her white coat soaking up dirty water. She made some sound, garbled words, that I couldn't understand.

Then with a sigh, her body relaxed and she fell into sudden, limp death.

EPILOGUE

I forgot about Thanksgiving.

And damned if some thief didn't pick up my rum cake and run off with it while I was trying to sort things out with the Lake Chinook police. Talk about low. Between the harrowing events of the weekend and the loss of my precious cake, I spent the next week disoriented, tired and needing time to recover. Maybe that was an excuse. Maybe battling with Keegan, discovering Dante's body and having Melinda die in front of me created its own form of illness and I just needed to shut down.

Once again I'd been taken into custody by the Lake Chinook police. Once again I found myself explaining what had happened. Once again Dwayne and Vince Larrabee came to my rescue, relating all the pieces of the story in my defense.

I sure was going to owe a lot of quid pro quo to Larrabee.

Violet greeted the news of Melinda's death with shock and horror, emotions almost immediately superseded by glee and relief as she was finally cleared. She celebrated by becoming CMC's new hostess, and George Tertian's girlfriend. Knowing Violet, I suspect she might be planning to make that relationship something more personal and permanent. After Rol-Ex, maybe it was time for husband number four.

On Thursday morning I took my dog for a walk, lifting my arms to a surprisingly nice day. Cold, yes. A bit gray, okay. But the sun was trying hard to stay ahead of the clouds, and the sky seemed higher and lighter than it had in weeks.

About nine o'clock Cynthia called and reminded me of the holiday.

I responded with a total lack of enthusiasm. I told her I couldn't come. I was sorry, but I just . . . couldn't. She said it was okay. She understood I'd had a tough week. She didn't mind. She would bring some food by later in the afternoon. She hung up before I could argue with her. I called back, but she sounded remarkably cheery and determined that it was okay. Things had changed, she said, sounding slightly mysterious. She would tell me about it later when she stopped by.

I got in my car and drove directly to Dwayne's. I'd spoken to him several times while I'd cocooned myself and he'd talked about the cases beginning to percolate. I'd tried to keep my mind on them, but honestly, I was currently simply not interested.

To my consternation, he was loading up his surveillance car with an overnight bag when I arrived at his cabana. "What's this?" I asked.

"I'm heading to Seattle to see my sister. No, I don't want to go. Yes, I'm a masochist. Yes, my stepmama will be there and will find a way to eviscerate me." He slid me a look and a smile. "But I'm a little good at that, too."

His drawl was deep today. I had an insane desire to throw myself in his arms and demand he take me to his bedroom and make love until the damned holiday was over.

Instead, I said, "Drive carefully. There are idiots out there."

He said, "Tell Cynthia hello."

I said, "Cynthia's coming to my house and bringing food. Something's happened. She sounds . . . happy, though."

He said, "Must not have to do with family."

And then he turned to me and for a moment I held my breath. We shared a look. That kind of scary awareness that sometimes we act on, sometimes we don't. I thought he was going to touch my face, or my hair, or kiss me, or something. He settled for a good-bye hug. I wondered if I held on a little longer, would something shift between us? I suspected it would.

I let him go.

Forty minutes later I was through a cold shower, dressed in my traditional Thanksgiving sweats, wringing water from my hair, when my doorbell pealed.

Expecting Cynthia, I was surprised to find Booth on my doorstep. Booth with a row of four earrings on the edge of one ear. Booth with shaggy, unkempt hair and an equally unkempt beard. My twin looks a lot like me, same hazel eyes, same light brown hair. He's always been more driven, more serious, more intense than I, but now he looked downright guy-tough and scary, exhibiting that kind of gangish, urban, dangerous aura that's so popular these days, and which I don't quite get.

"Wow," I said.

"What happened to your eye?" he asked, to which I shrugged.

Binkster came over, wiggling and excited, but it was a bit tempered. Not as wildly effusive as she can be. I didn't blame her.

Booth bent to pet her and I took it as a good sign as he'd been less than thrilled to learn I had a dog when Binks first landed on my doorstep. The extra attention garnered him a quick doggie lick on the lips. "That's huge," I told him as I closed the door behind him. "She doesn't give out kisses to just anyone."

Booth wiped his mouth with the back of his hand. "She have all her shots?"

"Except rabies. I kind of took a stand on that one. Don't think it's necessary."

Booth actually smiled.

"What brings you here?" I asked.

"It's Thanksgiving."

"Like that's something we care about."

Booth sank onto my couch. He seemed tired, yet pent-up at the same time. I decided right then and there that working undercover for long periods of time is detrimental to one's health. "Cynthia said we were meeting at your place."

"Cynthia," I repeated. Not *your friend* Cynthia. Not *that friend of yours who owns the art gallery* Cynthia. Just Cynthia. "I didn't know you knew her that well."

He didn't answer.

"I've never known her to play the 'let's get the family together' card before," I said, watching him. "Is Sharona coming by, too?"

"Sharona and I broke up," he said.

My shoulders sagged. "Over your undercover assignment?"

"I really don't want to talk about it, Jane." He narrowed his gaze on me. "I talked to Vince Larrabee about you."

"If you're going to start in with all the 'you can't do the job' bullshit, save it."

"What do I know?" Booth said with a shrug of his shoulders.

This was so unlike him that I stared. I asked him a few questions about what he'd been up to, but he said it involved drugs, gangs and a seamy underbelly of life that he didn't really want to go into.

Cynthia showed up about an hour later and Booth and I helped her carry sacks and trays of food inside. She pulled out a couple of bottles of wine, chattering in a way I found faintly disturbing. She wasn't acting like herself at all. Her friend/chef had prepared everything in advance. The turkey was ready to pop into the oven, which she did with a flourish, shutting the oven door with her hip. In a gray skirt and sweater, and silver chunky jewelry, she made me feel pretty damn low-class in my sweats.

"Did you lose the memo on the dress code?" I groused.

She laughed merrily. Now I really stared. "Cynthia" and "merrily" don't go together. And then I saw the way she looked at Booth from under her lashes, and I read the faint smile on his lips.

It was like a *zing* of energy shot across the room.

I was horrified. "Oh no. You're not—"

Booth said, "I walked into the Black Swan one afternoon."

Cynthia sat down on the couch beside him, her eyes all over him. "It was lust at first sight."

"What about Sharona?"

"She broke it off, Jane," Booth replied. "I didn't."

"But . . . I'm sorry . . . you were . . . so in love." They were freaking me out. Nobody could change that fast. Nobody.

"Her ex came back into her life," Booth said with a trace of bitterness. "Criminal defense attorney. Just like her. Being undercover, that's just been an excuse."

"Are you sure?" I asked. I hadn't realized until this moment that I'd depended on Booth and Sharona's relationship. Believed it was the bedrock of true love.

Cynthia and Booth both looked at me. I couldn't come up with an appropriate response. I don't know how other people feel about their friends getting together with members of their family, but yikes. It looked bad to me.

"Maybe I need a drink," I said and turned toward the kitchen.

My cell phone buzzed. I snatched it up like a lifesaver. Something to rescue me from the terrible complications of life.

Please, please, let it be Dwayne, saying he's turned around.

"Hey, Jane!" Chuck's voice boomed. "I bought your cottage! Signed the agreement last night. I'm gonna be your landlord. Woohoo! What do you think about that!"

ONE BY ONE, THEY'LL DIE . . .

Years ago, wild child Jessie Brentwood vanished from
St. Elizabeth's High School. Most in Jessie's tight circle of
friends believed she simply ran away. Few suspected that
Jessie was hiding a shocking secret—one that brought her
into the crosshairs of a vicious killer . . .

UNTIL THERE'S NO ONE LEFT . . .

Two decades pass before a body is unearthed on school
grounds and Jessie's old friends reunite to talk. Most are
sure that the body is Jessie's, that the mystery of what
happened to her has finally been solved. But soon, Jessie's
friends each begin to die in horrible, freak accidents that
defy explanation . . .

BUT *HER* . . .

Becca Sutcliff has been haunted for years by unsettling
visions of Jessie, certain her friend met with a grisly end.
Now the latest deaths have her rattled. Becca can sense that
an evil force is shadowing her too, waiting for just the right
moment to strike. She feels like she is going crazy. Is it all a
coincidence—or has Jessie's killer finally returned to finish
what was started all those years ago?

**Please turn the page for an exciting sneak peek at
WICKED GAME,
by
Lisa Jackson and Nancy Bush**

Coming in February 2009!

St. Elizabeth's campus, February, 1999, midnight . . .

The girl rushed headlong through the maze, stumbling, grazed across the face by a poking branch. She cried out softly in surprise, clapped a hand to her cheek. Blood welled against her fingers.

This was wrong. Impossibly wrong.

It shouldn't be this way! Couldn't!

Glancing behind her, she listened hard, deafened by her own heartbeats. She wasn't lost. She knew where she was. She knew the twists and turns that would take her to the maze's center and out again.

But she felt fear—true fear—for the first time in her life, because he *knew* about her. How could he? *How could he?* When she'd spent so many years—her entire life, it seemed!—learning the truth about herself.

And now he was here, following her, brought to the maze by her own invitation.

But things weren't going right. Not like she'd planned. Somehow the hunter had become the hunted.

He couldn't know . . . unless . . . he was *one of them*.

She heard something. A noise . . . a sibilant hiss . . .

What *was* that?

She froze, hands up, as if to ward off danger, her body quivering, poised on the balls of her feet, panting. *He was here!* He'd entered the maze. She could hear him now, easily, as he was making no effort to disguise his approach. Was he alone? She thought he was alone. He *should* be alone. She'd set this up so he *would* be alone, but now she didn't know. Didn't know . . .

And that's where the fear came in, because she *always* knew. That was her gift. She always knew. That's why they hadn't been able to keep the truth from her. That's why she'd found out who they were and who she was, even though they'd tried hard to keep her from learning.

For her own safety, they'd said.

And now . . . now she was beginning to understand what they'd meant.

She strained to listen, her heart pounding, her fear mounting. He was walking through the maze. Unhurried. Undeterred. Making all the right turns. Were there more than one set of footsteps? Someone else? She couldn't be sure.

And she couldn't stay where she was.

As stealthily as possible, she edged onward, toward the center of the maze, toward the statue. She'd always been slightly leery of the ghostly Madonna, but now she wanted with all her heart to reach it. Her need to find it was like a hunger, something she could almost cry out for if she dared on this dark night. Sanctuary. Safety.

Or so she hoped.

Fear filled her veins with ice. Paralyzing. Cold. Freezing her so thoroughly it felt as if her blood might solidify is she ceased moving.

She rounded a final corner and the statue of Mary suddenly appeared, arms uplifted, greeting her in pale white, accompanied by the shiver of the branches and the musty smell of dead leaves and mud. The girl stumbled and a tiny stick snapped beneath her shoe. She glanced backward, crouched, poised like a hunted animal. Behind her, in the maze, he came onward, steadily. She knelt at the statue and mouthed, "Mother Mary, save my soul . . ."

She hadn't been good.

But she wasn't all bad, either.

Behind her, she heard him move ever forward. No rush, no rush at all.

He *knew* he had her.

She kept silently, desperately praying.

Mother Mary save my soul.

She can't help you. You have no soul to save, he said.

Or, did he? Was that the voice inside her head?

Desperately she thought, *I am sixteen years old and I am going to die.*

Head pounding, heart beating wildly, her ears filled with the roar of the ocean, the battering of the sea against distant cliffs . . . though she was nowhere near the ocean. But it had always been this way. She had always heard these oddly familiar sounds, always sensed a remote place.

How stupid she was to have goaded him—teased him. *Dared* him.

What had she been thinking?

That was the problem with her. Not only could she see the future, she sometimes tried to change it.

And now he was going to kill her. But because that could not be—simply could *not be*—she dug her teeth into her bottom lip and surreptitiously dragged a small knife from her pocket.

She'd been foolish to lure him here, to let him follow her, to tease him into this meeting. He was a danger to her, and he was relentless. There would be no satisfactory ending. No loving reconciliation.

With all her strength she prayed for her life, her soul. Above her pulsing heart she heard the hunter's footsteps. Nearer. Relentlessly closer. Slowly she rose to her feet and turned to meet him. She knew she was in for the fight of her life. She must be strong. She couldn't hesitate.

Then suddenly his dark figure appeared, hovering near the wet and waving laurel branches. Words trembled on her lips. Questions he could answer but wouldn't. She knew that.

"I will kill you," she warned him harshly, and was answered by the glimmer of his deadly, self-satisfied smile in the darkness.

He knows he has me. The creep's enjoying this.

No way!

Lunging forward, she drove her knife toward him with all her strength.

But it wasn't enough.

Her gaze clashed with his . . . and strong fingers bent her wrist back. Pain burned through her muscles. Fear congealed in her heart. His breath a hiss through his teeth, he snapped her wrist back and tore the knife from her nerveless fingers. Before she could scream, he thrust the blade deftly between her ribs. "No more." he rasped.

She cried out. The night swirled around her, a kaleidoscope of pain and regret. She crumpled to the ground at the feet of the statue, aware that her attacker was staring down at her, his breath excited gasps.

She lay still as death at the feet of the Madonna and thought: *I am a sacrifice.*

Then the darkness descended.

St. Elizabeth's campus, February, 2009, midnight . . .

Kyle Baskin held the flashlight under his chin, beaming its illumination upward, highlighting the planes and hollows of his face.

"Bloody Bones entered the house," he whispered in his deepest, most ghoulish voice. His eyes darted around the circle of boys seated on the ground at his feet, their scared faces turned up earnestly. "Bloody Bones crossed to the stairs. Bloody Bones looked up and could see the children through the *walls.*"

"Like X-ray vision?" Mikey Ferguson squeaked.

"Shut up," his older brother, James, whispered harshly.

The branches overhead shivered. There was a moon, but it wasn't visible over the height of the maze's hedge. Only the faintest trickle of light wavered through the leaves.

"I'm on the first step."

Kyle hesitated for maximum effect. He gazed across the beam of the flashlight at the kids he and James had brought to the center of the maze. They were supposed to be babysitting, but that was boring as hell. "I'm on the second step." He drew a shaking breath and said slowly, "I'm on . . . the . . . third step . . ."

Mikey shot a look of terror over his shoulder and edged closer to James, whose smirk was fully visible to Kyle.

Tyler, that little piss-ant, started to snivel.

"I'm on . . . the . . . *fourth* . . . step . . ."

"How many steps are there?" Mikey cried, clutching at James' arm.

"Shut the fuck up."

"I wanna go home!" Tyler wailed.

"I'm on . . . the *fifth* step!"

"I'm calling my dad." Preston, the overweight prick, clambered to his feet, his normally toneless voice quaking a bit.

"The phone's in the car, moron."

"I'm on the *sixth step. I'm on the seventh step, I'm on the eighth step!*" Kyle declared in a rush.

The boys leapt to their feet as if yanked by strings, crying, heads jerking around, searching vainly for escape, but the hedges loomed, branches sticking out like skeletal arms.

Kyle's voice dropped to a whisper. "I'm on the ninth step . . ."

James started to worry a little. They couldn't have these dumbasses charging off in all directions in the dark. "Siddown!"

"I'm on the tenth step . . . and now I'm walking down the hall . . . I'm outside your door . . . I'm pushing it open . . . *cree—eeaa—kkk!!!*"

It sounded sorta dumb, the way Kyle did it, but it sure as hell did the trick. The kids started running around like Keystone Kops, shying from the dirty old statue of that lady, screaming and blubbering. James and Kyle started laughing. They couldn't help themselves. That ratcheted the kids to near hysteria, and Mikey stumbled right into the statue—the idiot—and knocked the damn thing to one side. The bulldozers had been at the site. The school was being razed and they were taking down the maze as well. That's why Kyle had come up with the idea in the first place. One last spooky hurrah where they could scare the snot out of the little kids.

"Moron, you knocked over the old lady," James said in a long-suffering tone.

He went to pick up his younger brother while Kyle corralled Tyler and Preston, who were crying like the babies they were. Mikey had practically turned to a statue himself. He stood frozen, staring. He slowly lifted one hand as Kyle approached and pointed toward a mound of earth that had humped up when the statue tilted.

"Bloody Bones," he whispered, his finger quivering.

James looked in the direction he was pointing. From the

ground a skeletal human hand lay upturned, its bones both dirty and oddly white, its fingers reaching upward, as if for help.

James' eyes bugged out. He started shrieking like a banshee and couldn't quit. Little Mikey grabbed his older brother's hand and hauled them both out of the maze, the rest of the gang thundering behind them, the touch of Bloody Bones feathering their napes as they ran for their lives.

CHAPTER ONE

"*I feel it . . . that change in the atmosphere, subtle but strong, like the slight tremor of a gentle earthquake with its aftershocks. I know what it means.*

I'm being summoned to her.

I've stayed here, waiting, believing the time would come again. I've known since the last one that my mission was not done, would never be finished. But for a long while, I've waited.

But tonight the waiting is over.

I can't resist. I'm lured. Excited. My blood thrumming hot through my veins, the thought of the next kill, that exquisite moment of pure power when one life is extinguished causes my heart to race, my skin to sweat with anxious beads of eager anticipation.

I sit up and imagine the scent of her skin. Like a rain-washed beach.

Tantalizing . . .

I can almost smell her. Almost . . .

But I know where she is.

Slowly I roll from my bed. My self-imposed prison where I've waited for so long.

It's time to leave.
Time, once again, to right an age-old wrong.
Time, at long last, for another sacrifice.
And I'm ready.

A frisson slid down Becca Sutcliff's spine. She inhaled sharply and glanced behind her. The girl at the counter of Mutts & Stuff slid her a look from the corner of her eyes. "You okay?"

"Someone walking on my grave, I guess," Becca murmured.

The girl's brows lifted and Becca could practically read her mind: *Yeah. Right. Whatever.* She rang up Becca's purchases and stuffed them in a bag. Thanking her, Becca shifted the packages she was already carrying to accommodate them. Yes, she was filling a need, shopping like it was an Olympic sport, a result of the messy, lingering aftermath of unsettled feelings that still followed from her split with Ben. And now Ben was dead. Gone, Never to come back. And it all felt . . . well . . . weird.

She headed back into the mall, slightly depressed by the cheery red and pink hearts in every store window. Valentine's Day. The most miserable day of the year for the suddenly single.

Okay. She wasn't completely happy. She'd known for a long time that she and Ben weren't going to make it. They'd never been in love. Not in the way she'd wanted, hoped, planned to be. When she'd learned he was seeing someone else, she was angry. At herself, mostly. She couldn't really even recall what had triggered their marriage in the first place. What had she wanted? What had Ben wanted? Had it just been timing? A sense that, if not Ben, then who?

Then she learned he'd died in the arms of his new love. Heart attack. Gone, gone . . . gone.

She was still processing. Still getting used to the fact that he'd left her for another woman. Left her . . . when she still believed that maybe, just maybe, there would be that chance for them. That chance to start a family. Have a child. A child of their own. A child of *her* own . . .

The window of Pink, Blue and You, a combined baby and maternity store, materialized in front of her. She'd stopped into it earlier and picked out a gift for a friend who'd just had a baby. It was a fine torture to be inside. She wanted a baby. She'd always wanted a baby. She'd lost a baby a long time ago.

Tears hovered behind her eyes. With an effort she held them back, turning her face away from the display of pastel pinks and blues and lemony yellows. Was that why she'd married Ben? To have a baby? To replace the one who'd been taken from her?

Becca gritted her teeth against emotion. She'd asked herself the same question countless times, had toiled and fretted over the answer. But it was all moot now. He was gone. And he'd left his twenty-two-year-old new lover pregnant, something he'd never wanted with Becca.

"I don't want children," he said. "You knew it when you married me."

Had she? She didn't remember that.

"It's just you and me, Beck. You and me."

Bastard.

Maybe she *had* married him to have a child. Correction. To *replace* a child. Maybe she'd made up the "I love you" parts. Maybe she just wanted the whole thing to be so much prettier than it was.

A lump filled her throat. She turned away from the window. No need to torture herself further. No need at all.

A food court was on her left and she glanced over as she headed the other way. But as she tried to hurry on, her vision grew blurry. Becca stopped short, her pulse suddenly rocketing. Damn. She was going to faint. She'd been this route before, more times than she'd like to admit. But it wasn't really fainting. No. More like . . . falling into a spell. A wide awake dream. But it hadn't happened in years. Not for *years!*

Why now? she asked herself a half-second before white-hot pain screamed through her brain. She staggered and fell to her knees, packages tumbling from her arms. Becca bent her head, instinctively hiding her face from curious onlookers, one last moment of clarity before the vision overcame her.

In a transformation that was both familiar and feared, Becca was no longer at the mall, no longer feeling the wrench of the loss of her baby. No longer in the real world but in a watery, unsubstantial one, a world that had plagued her youth yet had been curiously missing and distant for most of her adult life . . . until now.

In front of her, a short distance away, a teenaged girl stood on a headland above a gray and frothy sea, her long, dark brown hair teased by a stiff breeze, her shirt and jeans pressed to her skin from its force, her gaze focused across churning waves toward a small island, blurred with rain. Becca followed the girl's gaze, staring past her to the island as well, a forlorn, rocky tor that looked as inhospitable as an alien planet. The girl shivered, and so did Becca. The cold burrowed beneath her skin, and gooseflesh rose on her arms.

The girl was familiar. So familiar. . . .

Becca stared at her hard, putting a physical effort into it. *Is she someone I know?*

Becca struggled to remember. Who was she? Where was she? Why was she pulling Becca into her world?

Distantly, she felt the lightheadedness, the clammy warning that she was about to pass out. No, no, no! Caught between the two worlds, her body falling in one, her mind desperately searching for answers in the other, Becca focused on the girl.

"Who are you?" she called but the rising wind threw the words back into her throat.

The phantom girl took a step forward, the tips of her boots balanced over the edge of the cliff. Becca reached out an arm. Her mouth opened in protest.

"Stop! *Stop!*"

Was she going to throw herself to her death?

Becca lunged forward just as the girl turned to face her. Instead of a profile shot, Becca caught a full-on view of her face. "Jessie?" she whispered in shock, her head reeling.

Jessie just stared at Becca and Becca, powerless, stared back. The wind danced through Jessie's hair and around her small, serious face. Becca's heart pounded painfully.

Jessie Brentwood? Her missing friend? Gone for twenty years . . .

Except now, in Becca's vision.

"Be careful!" Becca warned. "You're too close."

The phantom girl lifted a finger to her lips, then mouthed something at Becca.

"What?" Becca tried to clear her mind. "*What?*"

In the gathering mist the girl's image began to fade. Becca pushed forward but it felt as if her feet were mired to the ground.

"Jessie!" she cried.

The girl melded with the rain and the watery world dimmed into endless gray.

Becca sensed tears on her lashes and a dull throb in her head. Somewhere a male voice said, "Hey, lady. You okay?"

With difficulty, Becca opened her eyes. She was in the mall. Sprawled on the tile floor. Packages tossed asunder. No more ocean. No more wind. No more Jessie.

Tucking her legs beneath her, Becca swallowed hard. It was difficult to come back to reality. It always was after one of her visions. The damn things. She'd thought they were behnd her. A symptom of her childhood. She hadn't had one since high school and she was now thirty-four years old.

But she never forgot. Not completely.

"I'm fine," she said in a voice she didn't recognize as her own. Clearing her throat, she fought the blinding stabs of pain that flashed through her head. Another unwelcome part of the visions. "I tripped."

"Yeah?"

The young man bending over her wasn't buying it. A small crowd of tweenagers had gathered, small enough that Becca figured she hadn't been out that long, maybe mere seconds. One of the girls was looking at her with huge, round eyes, and Becca could still hear the reverberations of the girl's scream as she watched Becca go down. She was holding a soda from the nearby food court. Vaguely Becca remembered glancing their way just before she was overtaken by her vision.

"You were, like, having an attack," a different girl said. This one wore a hat that smashed her bangs to her forehead and she peeked out between the strands of blond hair. They all looked ready to jump and run. Briefly, Becca thought about yelling, "Boo!" and sending them stumbling over themselves, away from the crazy lady.

Flash. Flash. Flash.

Becca heard the snap of a cell phone being shut. One of the guys had clicked off a series of pictures of her fainting spell. That did it. Becca climbed unsteadily to her feet and gave the kid the evil eye. He looked torn between bravado and fear. Becca was about to give him a piece of her mind, but was saved the effort when a heavy-set woman in a dusty blue uniform steamed toward them.

"Back off," she bit out at the boy who attempted to swagger toward his friends, even though he was boiling to escape. They all half-ran, half-loped toward the food court and an exit door.

"You all right, ma'am?" the security woman asked.

Flushing with embarrassment, Becca nodded, collecting her packages. She was definitely not all right.

"You look kinda pale. Maybe you should sit down."

"This happens to me. Not enough air getting in. Vagus nerve, you know. Shuts down the whole system sometimes."

It was clearly mumbo-jumbo to the security guard, and it was a flat out lie to boot. Doctors had once rubbed their jaws, speculating what caused Becca to faint and have visions. They ignored the visions, concentrating on the cause of her fainting. They had postulated and supposed and theorized to Becca's parents, Barbara and Jim Ryan, but there had never been any satisfactory explanations.

"I'm fine," she reassured the guard one more time, hanging on to the shreds of her dignity with an effort. Before she could be questioned further, Becca headed toward the mall exit and her car, a blue Volkswagen Jetta. She tossed the packages onto the passenger seat, feeling a twinge in one shoulder from the fall. Her body was still tingling, too, as if her muscles had been asleep. Sliding behind the wheel, she dropped her forehead to the steering wheel and took several deep breaths. This vision had been different. Almost touchable.

She'd actually *reached* for the girl. That had never happened before.

Was it Jessie? *Was it?*

Becca swallowed and lifted her head, gazing blankly through the windshield at the mall's cream stucco walls. Not since that last year of high school. Not once. She'd managed to convince herself over the years that she wasn't odd. Some kind of freak. That she wasn't losing her mind.

But this vision of Jessie had been stronger than anything she'd experienced before. And a helluva lot more frightening.

What did it mean?

Shaken, Becca drove from the parking lot, aware that the sky had darkened, night dropping quickly. One of her packages dumped over and the baby gift she'd purchased spilled onto the seat. It was a bright, whimsical mermaid puppet sewn in silver lamé and pink and green sequins.

Sadness filled her again. Pulling her eyes away from the puppet with an effort, she headed purposely for the little condo she'd once shared with Ben but which was now all hers.

It had been a hell of a day already, and she wasn't going to dwell on "what could have been" any more.

By the time she pulled in to her designated slot, Becca had pushed the vision and her own sadness aside . . . at least for the moment. Rain spattered in shivery waves as she headed for the front door, fumbling for her key. The evening paper was in a plastic sleeve on the stoop and she reached down and grabbed it, juggling it with her packages. Becca practically spilled herself inside, dumping everything on the dropleaf table that stood by the door. She shrugged out of her dampened coat and hung it in the closet as the ticky-tick of Ringo's nails across her oak floors heralded her dog's arrival.

"Hey, bud," she said as the curly-haired black and white mutt furiously waved his tail, gazing at her expectantly. "Look what I got you."

She held up the blue collar with its little white dog bone motif, but Ringo kept his eyes on hers. If it wasn't food, he simply wasn't interested.

"Okay," Becca relented, pulling out a jar of small, dog-shaped treats. Ringo barked twice, happily, as Becca unscrewed the lid and fished out a couple, tossing them to the dog, who leaped up and caught them in his jaws, one by one, then raced back to his bed and snuffled and chewed them.

"We'll go for a walk in a minute," she said, adding some of his regular dog food to his bowl. Ringo quickly finished his treat and hurried to the bowl, munching on his meal with the same enthusiasm as his treats. He was not a picky dog.

She gazed out the kitchen window, which faced the back of another condo across an expanse of grass. She could see right inside to the other kitchen, which was festooned with red and pink foil hearts. A young girl was seated at the table, licking the icing off a cupcake which was decorated with candy hearts.

She recalled last year's Valentine's Day. She'd been waiting for Ben. Though she'd sensed—known, really—that their marriage was in its death throes, she'd spontaneously bought a cake and a bottle of champagne. The cake had been heart shaped with white icing and in red gel script, it read: BE MINE.

Ben never came home that night. Becca opened the champagne alone, drank half a glass, and poured the rest out. Later that week, Ben broke the news that he was in love with someone else, and that that someone else was pregnant. Becca had tried not to be shocked, hurt and upset, but she'd failed on all counts.

"You told me you never wanted kids," Becca reminded him, trying to keep from yelling.

"I guess I changed my mind," he responded, turning away from her accusing face.

"You guess?"

"Look, I'm sorry. I didn't mean for it to happen."

"If you didn't mean for it to happen, you should have used a condom."

"Who says I didn't?"

"Did you?" Becca demanded.

He almost lied to her. She could see him thinking whether he could make her believe him. But he knew her almost as well as she knew him. "It wasn't supposed to be this way," he mumbled, heading for the bedroom and his suitcase.

She followed him, too betrayed to let him just go. She

grabbed down another bag and stuffed it full of his clothes, cramming them inside. "Take everything. Everything. Don't come back. Ever."

"Becca your just upset. I've gotta come back and get—"

"Don't be reasonable, Ben. I swear to God. Don't be reasonable or I'll scream." She glared at him but all she saw was the baby. The one he was having . . . with someone else. "If you can't carry it now, it'll be on the front porch."

"Don't be ridiculous!"

"I'm ridiculous?" she demanded.

Ben, the coward, couldn't hold her gaze. In tense silence, he finished packing his bag and stormed out. She tossed the other suitcase after him, not caring whether he picked it up or not. It sat on the porch for two days while she stacked other items beside it, crowning the pile with his most prized golf trophy. She half-expected the homeowner's association to complain about the mess, but Ben managed to sweep everything up before that happened. He came when Becca was away, so there were no more angry words. In fact, there were no more words at all for several months. Becca had just determined to open the lines of communication again, preparing for the inevitable divorce, when she got a call from Kendra Wallace, who between sobs, shrieks and tears, explained that Ben had died in her arms. For a good ten minutes Becca heard nothing else. Nothing past the fact that Ben was dead. She finally understood that Kendra's wailing was along the "poor me, what am I going to do" line.

"The baby," Becca said, moving from shock back to reality.

"The baby is mine!" Kendra snapped sharply, as if aware of Becca's desire to have a child of her own.

"Do you have family?" *Someone to help you?*

"You'll be hearing from my lawyer," Kendra choked back and slammed down the phone.

Becca was left staring into space. She was aware Kendra

was going to come after her financially, but if the child was Ben's, so be it. When she received no call, she dialed Kendra on the number caller ID coughed up. She learned that it belonged to Kendra's mother, who told Becca that Kendra had moved to Los Angeles with her new boyfriend.

"What about the baby?" Becca asked.

She was told, in a chilly voice, that Kendra's boyfriend was adopting the little boy and it was none . . . of . . . her . . . concern.

Now, Becca fitted Ringo with his new collar and clipped on his leash. They walked into a night black with rain and cold and strolled around the condo's grounds. Ringo waved his tail at several other dogs, but he didn't bark. Apart from a woof or two when food was coming his way, he was pretty quiet. Rarely did he growl or make any noise.

So, it was with a sense of the hair rising on the back of her neck when, about a block away from her front door, Ringo suddenly stopped, planted his feet, and growled low in his throat, that Becca glanced around jerkily, half-expecting the bogeyman to pounce on her.

Ringo stared into a space about a hundred yards away, where a thick grove of firs, branches waving like beckoning arms, stood tall and dark in the slanting rain. Ringo was so planted that Becca couldn't drag him away. He stared and stared toward the trees.

"You're freaking me out, dog," Becca murmured, sliding the wet dog into her arms and hurrying toward her stairs. Ringo's head swiveled to keep sight of the trees. She could feel the low "grrrrrr" that rumbled through his body.

Inside, she grabbed a towel she kept in the front closet and tried to towel Ringo off but he shot to the nearest window, rising on his back legs, nosed pressed to the glass, lips pulled back in a silent snarl. A shiver that shot down Becca's neck.

"Stop that," she ordered as she headed to the kitchen and

filled a teakettle with water. No champagne this Valentine's Day. Tea would be just fine.

When she returned to the living room, Ringo was sitting on his haunches, but his eyes were still fixed on something outside the window.

Becca tried to woo him to sit on the couch beside her, but when she went to pick him up, he sidled away and paced in front of the glass. Unnerved by the dog, she picked up the paper and slid it from its plastic sleeve. Her eye fell on a picture of a statue. The Madonna inside the maze at St. Elizabeth's. The bold headline read: BOYS DISCOVER HUMAN SKELETON INSIDE MAZE.

She inhaled in shock.

The teakettle shrieked.

Becca bit back a scream, sending Ringo into frenzied barking. It took long moments before she could calm the dog and her own rocketing pulse enough to actually read the article.

When she was finished, she stared at the rivulets of rain running down her window but her thoughts were far from this miserable Valentine's Day, her deceased husband, and whatever had spooked Ringo. Her mind was in the past.

For she knew the skeletal remains belonged to Jessie Brentwood, the girl from her visions, the friend from high school who'd disappeared without a trace, the girlfriend of Hudson Walker, Becca's own secret crush and the father of Becca's unborn child, had he but known it.

Jezebel "Jessie" Brentwood. She'd come to Becca in a dream today. She'd said something. Something important. While the wind had tossed her hair and she'd eased her toes over the edge of the cliff. It meant something. Something Becca needed to understand.

"Jessie . . ." she said aloud.